The Case of Scotch

Volume Three of
The Case Books of Octavius Bear

Harry DeMaio

"Alternative Universe Mysteries for Adult Animal Lovers"

Paperback ISBN 978-1-78092-838-8
ePub ISBN 978-1-78092-839-5
PDF ISBN 978-1-78092-840-1

Published in the UK by MX Publishing
335 Princess Park Manor, Royal Drive,
London, N11 3GX
www.mxpublishing.co.uk
Cover design compiled www.staunch.com

Dedicated to GTP

A Most Extraordinary Bear

Acknowledgements

These books have evolved over a long period of time and under a wide range of influences and circumstances. I am indebted to many people for helping to bring Octavius and his cohorts to the printed page. Thanks most especially to my wife, Virginia, for her insights and clever suggestions as well as her unfailing enthusiasm for the project and patience with its author. To my sons, Mark and Andrew and their spouses, Cindy and Lorraine, for helping make these tomes more readable and audience friendly. To Cathy Hartnett, cheerleader-extraordinaire for her eagerness to see this alternate universe take form. To Jack Magan, Dan Andriacco and Zohreh Zand for their assistance and support.

Thanks to the members of the Monday Morning Writers Group for their help and encouragement.

If, in spite of all this help, some errors or inconsistencies have crept through, the buck stops here. Needless to say, all of the characters, situations, and narratives are fictional.

The Development of Civilization Volume 3 Part 1
Our Origins
(From "An Introduction to Faunapology" by Octavius Bear Ph.D.)

*About 100,000 years ago, according to scientific experts, a colossal solar flare blasted out from our Sun, creating gigantic magnetic storms here on Earth. These highly charged electrical tempests caused startling physical and psychological imbalances in the then population of our world. The complete nervous systems of some species were totally destroyed. For example, "Homo Sapiens" lost all mental and motor capabilities and rapidly became extinct. Less developed species exposed to the radiation were affected differently. Four-footed and finned mammals, birds and reptiles suddenly found themselves capable of complex thought, enhanced emotions, self-awareness, social consciousness and the ability to communicate, sometimes orally, sometimes telepathically, often both. Both speech production and speech perception slowly progressed with the evolution of tongues, lips, vocal cords and enhanced ear to brain connections. Many species developed opposable digits, fingers or claws, further accelerating civilized progress. Some others (most fish and underground dwellers) were shielded from the radiation and remained only as sentient as they were before the blast. This event is referred to as **The Big Shock**. It remains under intensive study.*

The Players in Volume 3

Octavius Bear –Narcoleptic war hero; consulting detective; scientist; inventor; seeker of justice; mega-billionaire owner of Universal Ursine Industries; gourmet/gourmand; somewhat sedentary and grouchy just on general principles.

Mauritius (Maury) Meerkat – Part-time narrator; assistant to Octavius; African *émigré* with a French-Dutch background; clever with a shady history.

Inspector Bruce Wallaroo – Irrepressible but brilliant marsupial; an international law and order genius from Down Under; often calls on Octavius and Maury for support.

Bearoness Belinda Béarnaise Bruin Bear (nee Black) – Now wife of Octavius; very rich widow of Bearon Byron Bruin living in Bearmoral Castle in the Shetlands; Owner-pilot of the last flying Concorde SST; Gorgeous polar superstar, with the Aquashow, *Some Like It Cold.*

Otto the Magnificent – **AKA Hairy Otter** - An absolutely terrible illusionist magician, Otto the Magnificent escaped the claws of super villain Imperius Drake but not before he developed some amazing powers courtesy of Imperius genetic alterations.

Chita - Beautiful, fascinating, clever, sexy, immoral and highly independent feline who owns a North Sea oil rig. Chita reappears in each book as a principal character in her own right.

Cyd – Chita's probably fictitious twin sister.

Frau Schuylkill – Octavius' beautiful, Swiss she-wolf housekeeper/cook/pilot with many other mysterious and military talents. She rescued Octavius from his dive off the Breakurbach Falls while he was struggling with his nemesis, Imperius Drake.

Wyatt Where – Another wolf. Former military intelligence officer who had retired to a security post at the Bank of Lake Michigan in Chicago and then quit to join Octavius.

Howard Watt – A porcupine. High tech security authority who also left the bank with Wyatt to join Octavius. A laser and particle beam accelerator expert and overall scientific whiz kid.

Bearyl and Bearnice Blanc – Belinda's stunning twin polar sidekicks; Actress and singer, respectively; Co-pilot and flight engineer of Belinda's SST.

L. Condor - Andean Condor cyber-net genius with a 12 foot wingspan.

Bearon Byron Bear – Deceased husband of Bearoness Belinda.

Leperello – Himalayan Snow Leopard and singing partner of Bearnice Blanc.

Fetlock Holmes – The Great Horse Detective and sometime associate of Octavius Bear.

Hamish – A wild boar and retainer of Bearmoral Castle.

The Bruins – Belinda's rotten in-laws from the Bearents Sea polar community.
> **Lady Albearta Bruin** – Bearon Byron's Aunt.
> **Sir Ethelbeart Bruin** – Lady Albearta's husband.
> **Alistair and Ursula** – First cousins to Byron's father.
> **Roary and Bruinhilde** – Alistair and Ursula's son and daughter.

Dame Bearbara (Bearbi) da Savile-Row– Polar publisher and editor-in-chief of a number of female ursine magazines.

Clarence – Polar Bear - Bearbi's photographer.

Dougal – Shetland Sheep Dog - Gameskeeper of Bearmoral Castle.

Bearmoral Shetland Sheep
> **Dolly, Holly, Molly and Polly** – Housemaids and probable clones.
> **Mrs. McRadish** – Chief Cook.

Harold – Sea Otter in charge of the castle's beaches, pools and watercraft.

Doctor "Odd" Vark – Aardvark – Chief Geneticist at Universal Ursine Industries.

Doctor Chiti BingBang – Orangutan – Chief Physician at Universal Ursine Industries.

Superintendent Nigel Wardlaw of Shetland Yard – Bearded Collie-The Scottish Police.

Lion and Unicorn – Proprietors of the Baltasound pub of the same name.

Fergus – Spokescat for the **North Sea Oil Rig Wildcat Roughnecks.**

The Castle Pipers – A suspicious band of Skye and Dandy Dinmont Terriers.

Colonel McNeigh – Clydesdale, Royal Army, Commandant – Abeardeen Security Force.

Madame Honoria Heifer – Cow – Infuriating voice coach for Bearnice and Lepi.

North Sea Wildcat Oil Rig Owners:
Cathcart, Gordon, McRae, MacDowell, MacDonald, MacDuff and Pringle.

Wing Commander Stewart, Royal Air Force Retired – Red Fox.

The Prince of Whales – Just who you would think.

Marlin – Dolphin (sic) – the Prince's Chief Scientist, Magician and part time Jester.

Sir Flipsalot – Dolphin – The Prince's equerry.

Locations in Volume 3: Bearmoral Castle, Unst and Baltasound in the Shetlands, Edinbeargh, Glascow; Abeardeen;

Also from Harry DeMaio

The Open and Shut Case

The Case of The Spotted Band

Prologue
Abeardeen, Scotland

Can a platform with oil drilling gear
Simply drift off and then disappear?
Common sense would say NO!
But it seems to be so.
Yet the reason is not very clear!

"Are ya daft, cat? You can't just lose an entire oil rig."

"I didna say we lost it. I said it keeps disappearin' and reappearin'."

"Then somethin's awry with your radar, yer twit."

"It's nae just the radar. We've been losin' radio contact and when we sent a chopper out to look, it was nae at the GPS coordinates it was supposed to be at."

"Next you'll be tellin' me they've gone off to a different world or the Loch Ness monster ate them."

'Nae, I'm tellin'ya someone or somethin' is playin' fast and loose. When the rig reappeared on our screens, and we called the cats out there, they said they had no idea what we were talkin' about."

"And neither do I!"

"This is fourth time it's happened in the last two days, and not always on my watch, and not always the same rig."

"Why am I only hearin' about it now?"

"Because we knew your reaction would be exactly what it is. Ya think we're balmy or our equipment has gone south or both!"

"First thing you've said I agree with."

"I havena' got a superstitious bone in ma body, but I'm tellin' ya, somethin' weird is happenin'. And we've already spent a braw penny in overtime and techie specialists checkin' and re-checkin' our equipment. Nothin'! It's in grand fettle."

"Well, I'm nae gonna call for a general shut-down, if that's wha ya have in mind."

"I think we should have a wee bit of formal investigatin', that's wha I think. Get yer Inspector General to come over and give a guid look."

This "conversation" between the Director of the UK North Sea Oil Commission and the Officer in Charge of Inter-Platform Communications was pinging back and forth in Abeardeen, Scotland, the support center for the UK oil rigs. Abeardeen was soon to have a few more unusual and unfortunately, fatal distinctions. As was the whole Scottish North Sea petroleum industry, operated almost exclusively by Scottish wildcats. *(At the Norse, Dutch, Belgian and German platforms, dogs, wolves and bears held the majority positions.)*

The economic turnaround spurred by the oil fields had actually been the salvation of the Scottish wildcats, whose numbers had sharply declined in their native Highlands. More than once, they had been listed with the world's endangered species and were still flirting with extinction. Their talent for petroleum exploration and recovery had revived their place in the world. But there were rumors that North Sea oil and gas reserves were hitting a plateau, and worried frowns were appearing on the faces of many of the currently prosperous felines. The fields may have been reaching exhaustion well before predicted.

Then the "events" began. At first a breakdown here, a stoppage there – nothing too far out of the ordinary. And yet, the problems seemed to be strangely isolated to the Scottish platforms. *(The Scandinavian and Continental rigs, when they reported at all, seemed to be enjoying normal business as usual.)* There was no real pattern except increased frequency of problems and rising costs. Damaged drill bits required removal of thousands of feet of pipe for replacement; broken welds on support structures; electrical and electronic failures; helicopter and support boat breakdowns; a feeder pipeline needed repairs far too frequently; even an outbreak of feline flu among the roughnecks.

The wildcats were starting to put two and two together and they didn't like what came out of the summing. Not only was the output from the deep sea fields slowing down; there were too many costly stoppages and incidents even for a dangerous and unpredictable venture like oil recovery. Too many *strange* incidents. It was only the beginning.

Octavius

Chapter One
Somewhere Over the Atlantic

Off we go on the Concorde Express,
To the beautiful land of Loch Ness.
But before we are through,
If our luck still holds true,
We'll fly into another big mess.

"Ooops!"

"What?"

I said, "Ooops!"

This bit of sparkling repartee between Octavius Bear and me was the result of a small burst of air turbulence hitting The Aquabear – a plush Concorde SST, last of its breed aloft, and the aeronautical jewel in the tiara of Bearoness Belinda Béarnaise Bruin Bear *(nee Black).* I had just gotten out of my oversized seat *(Normally intended for a polar bear. I'm a Meerkat.)* and had started down the aisle towards the snack buffet. Instead I was now face-down on the floor pointing aft.

"While you're up, Maury, get me a mead!"

I decided not to point out that I was not *up* at the moment, since this bit of subtlety would have been tossed off by the Bear as mere quibbling. I rose as unobtrusively and with as much dignity as I could muster. Checking my balance and the stability of the floor, I continued my journey toward the self-serve galley in the tail. The Aquabear was fitted out with all the luxurious décor and amenities you might expect in an airplane once owned by the now deceased gillionaire playbear, Bearon Byron Bruin, the late husband of Bearoness Belinda. Crystal bowls for both the snacks and drinks. And sumptuous snacks and drinks they were, including my personal favorite, fermented coconut milk VSOP. Gold plating throughout the lavatories, including an on-board shower! *(No, I never tried it.)* Seats that converted into polar dens! At slightly over two feet tall plus tail, I was swamped by the adjustable, inflatable seat pads covered in blue and white satin. But I gritted my teeth and coped. I hadn't figured out yet how to manage the high definition, 8 channel surround sound entertainment and game center in each seat. I managed to eject myself into the aisle several times while trying to set up a three dimensional aerial dog fight.

As I mentioned, we were somewhere over the North Atlantic, flying at Mach 1.7 and 70,000 feet heading for Abeardeen's Airport in Dyce, Scotland. As I was to find out, the Scotch *(wrong!)* Scots are awash in fascinating place names. Our final destination was a place called Unst which was not far from Yell. *(Since we're normally based in Cincinnati, I guess I can hardly afford to talk.)*

I'm sure you've already concluded that my name is Maury *(Mauritius)* Meerkat - also known as Offscreen Narrator. When I am part of the action, I am the trusted associate and field captain of Octavius Bear. He is a huge Kodiak – over nine feet tall and 1400 pounds – and like many of his species is given to emotional outbursts. As you may also know, Octavius, among his many talents and accomplishments, is a brilliant, self-taught practitioner in the wide ranging fields of biology, physics, ursinology, voodoo, teleology, chemistry, apiculture and oenology. He is a self made gazillionaire and sole owner of UUI *(Universal Ursine Industries.)* He is also a first rate electrical, electronic, structural, marine, aeronautical, mechanical and chemical engineer. He has a few other interesting characteristics such as falling into brief, deep narcoleptic comas – side effects of his successful genetic experiments to eliminate the need for him to hibernate.

However, the talent and occupation that should interest you most is his avocation for criminology. The Bear works in close concert with Inspector Bruce Wallaroo from Australia, of whom more later, and with his own Cincinnati based team:

- Frau Ilse Schuylkill – Swiss she-wolf; housekeeper-cook; jet pilot and sharpshooter with other very strange and arcane abilities.
- Colonel Wyatt Where – another wolf; ex-military hero; security specialist and pilot; Frau Schuylkill's equally bizarre running mate.
- Doctor Howard Watt – porcupine; brilliant scientist and technologist; laser and weapons specialist.
- Your humble servant – African Meerkat; Octavius' indispensable assistant; operative; scribe; overall facilitator as well as a pretty clever detective, if I do say so myself.

When we are not out scouring the world for evildoers, in cooperation with local, national and international constabularies, we are headquartered in a rambling old mansion near Cincinnati which encompasses not only the Great Bear's opulent digs, but his massive laboratories and shops; his missile silo disguised as an Asian pagoda; and a large Roman temple that serves as a hangar for his three airplanes.

Anyway, it is in Unst in the Shetlands that the ancestors of Bearon Byron Bruin, late lamented *(?)* mate of Bearoness Belinda, had established their palatial estate which she had then inherited. Said estate is the locale where we will be spending two weeks *(sorry, a fortnit)* in rest and relaxation *(file that under Fat Chance)* as guests of the lovely Polar Bearoness and her friends, family and retainers.

None of these worthies were aware that the Bearoness and the Great Bear had recently become married. If they did, her in-laws would no doubt have already been on their way to the Scottish courts or the Parliament to start proceedings to strip Belinda of her bearonial title, estates, chattels and paraphernalia of office. There was little, if any, love lost between Bearon Byron's family and Belinda. On Byron's death in a skiing accident, they descended like furry locusts onto Bearmoral Castle, and stuck like the leeches they were. *(Actually, they were all polar bears!)*

Since the Bearon's demise, Belinda has pursued a more subdued but still active Merry Widow life, and sits in residence at the castle only six or seven months of the year. Even during this foreshortened schedule, the Bruins were unbearable. Now that she had re-married, she and Octavius were about to develop a two pronged strategy – one to keep them from knowing of the wedding, and the other to get them the hell out of the castle and away from the Scottish judiciary system. The Bearoness was convinced she would win out but as she said, "Who needs that kind of aggravation, especially from that lot?"

Octavius had consented to this junket only after Belinda had spent a similar period with him at his digs, the Bear's Lair, on the Ohio River. The two of them have a hard-to-describe relationship that dates back well prior to Belinda's first marriage and show-biz stardom. They had first met and parted in Churchill, Canada when Belinda Black was still a juvenile and Octavius was a post-doc researcher studying polar bear migration habits. Romance bloomed but then was squashed by Belinda's stage struck mother. Pulling every trick in the

Pushy Mom's Handbook for Promoting Your Star-Struck Offspring *(which I suspect she wrote)* she got Belinda a job in the chorus of the Aquabears, a world famous troupe of singing, dancing, swimming, posing Maritime Ursines. Bearon Byron, himself a polar, took one look at her and fell like the proverbial ton of fish. After a microsecond's hesitation, he bought the review and made Belinda his star attraction. No taking it away from her. She is beautiful and she is a great natural performer who has honed her skills to perfection. She is also one tough sow under that patina of elegance and style. In our previous adventures, she has mixed it up with the bad guys to their significant detriment. A true piece of work, as they say, but not to her face!

Not too long after they had married, Bearon Byron was killed in a skiing accident and left his grieving *(?)* spouse all of his considerable worldly possessions including the Aquabear Review, Bearmoral Castle, a huge pile of funds and, as we were about to find out, a dreadfully dysfunctional family of in-laws. A bit later, Bel and Tavi met again at a charity fete. He was by then a super-rich scientific entrepreneur and she was an extremely well-off widow.

The relationship picked up but by now both of these formidable animals had firmly established habits and lifestyles that seemed about to keep them from a final amalgamation. However, love won out and merge they did but they still hadn't settled on where or how they would live together. Octavius was reluctant to be away from his enterprises and mansion. Belinda could not move out of the castle without risking losing it. Hence, for the nonce at least, the shuttle visitations.

Before leaving Cincinnati, we had just completed a rather theatrical shoot-'em-up with two of Octavius' nearest and dearest enemies, Pontius Puma and Imperius Drake, both of whom saw fit to stage a simultaneous armed attack on UUI and the Bear's Lair and failed. The Puma is now in the custody of international law enforcement for illegally trafficking in defense information, among other things. We believe Imperius is dead, struck from the air over the Ohio River by a formidable condor we had all befriended. BUT, we thought Imperius was dead several times before along with his hench beast, Bigg Baboon. So while we are tempted to close their file, we have still left a bookmark there just in case.

The other star performer in our most recent drama has been appearing and disappearing in our lives for quite a while and driving Octavius nuts in the process. Chita – once Imperius Drake's top aide, then his mortal enemy after he attempted to kill her for betraying him. Clever, beautiful, amoral *(oh what the hell, immoral)* fascinating and short-tempered, she has one of the world's longest international rap sheets. Over time, she has also accumulated a significant amount of wealth both illegally *(fraud etc.)* and through singing, modeling, alliances and dalliances. After she had brained but not killed Imperius with a heavy lab retort in a previous adventure, she was rescued from the duck's vengeance for a second time - this time by a very unlikely hero *(to be introduced shortly.)*

She thereupon disappeared with a jaguar named Jake who plays a mean set of drums. Watch for copies of Variety International announcing a new smash feline musical act somewhere on the planet. Trust me. Chita will return!!! So after all this, Octavius and I were looking forward to a little R&R and I was also looking forward to spending some serious business time with the Bearoness. *(More of that later. We can't do everything in the first chapter.)*

We had left the Bear's Lair this morning and were rocketing across the Atlantic at supersonic plus speed for the Shetlands. Belinda, among her many talents, is an accomplished jet pilot and as usual, is at the controls of her sleek and costly toy. Her flight crew, Bearyl and Bearnice, like Belinda, are also gorgeous twin polar bears and are just about identical. Bearnice wears an ankle bracelet to tell them apart. When not in the cockpit, they share cameo roles in the Aquabear review, sing, act and are highly skilled in the arts of self-defense.

Two others make up the complement on board the SST today. Lepi, *(Leperello)* a very talented Himalayan Snow Leopard who writes operas, sings beautifully and plays the keyboard. He had been part of a rock quartet in Brazil called the Spotted Band *(see book of the same name)* that included Chita, the aforementioned Jake and a two-faced ocelot named Ozzie who was killed in an accident. Lepi and Bearnice, who is also a polaratura soprano, met in the course of our last adventure, discovered their complementary talents and are working on an operatic career together. Belinda has agreed to help promote their fortunes.

The final passenger is a remarkable river otter whose real name is Hairy Otter. An absolutely atrocious magician and illusionist, he fell under the perverse influence of Octavius' nemesis, Imperius Drake. Posing as a theatrical impresario, Imperius convinced the otter that he could enjoy international stardom if he placed himself under the Duck's tutelage and management. The otter agreed. After all, he was thinking seriously of killing himself after all his failures. What did he have to lose? Plenty, as it turned out.

Imperius then set upon performing a series of genetic experiments on Hairy and changed his name to Otto the Magnificent in the hope of turning him into the first of a series of super-beast slaves who would blindly do the duck's criminal bidding. Like many of Imperius' grand plans, this one didn't work out entirely as he wished. The new Otto does indeed possess super illusionist and telekinetic powers that he can invoke any time his adrenaline levels rise above a certain point.

However, he could not be brought under Imperius' control. In fact, by rescuing Chita from a murderous plot by the Duck, he was a major cause of Imperius' undoing. Otto is now accompanying our merry band to Scotland where Belinda is hoping to work up a variety act around his near-magical capabilities. He is also waiting for the final prognosis from the UUI physicians and geneticists, as to whether Imperius' serum that altered the otter's genetic structure will also turn him into a raving maniac like the duck. Thank goodness, early signs say No! I, in turn, have theatrical agent aspirations and would like to manage Otto's career while I still work with Octavius. Hence the planned discussions with Otto, the Bearoness and then with Octavius. Rest and relaxation for meerkats at Bearmoral may be a bit scarce. We shall see.

Bearyl's low pitched growl announced that we were reaching the western Scottish coast and would be slowing down to cross the mainland to Abeardeen in the east. Predicted arrival: fifteen minutes. I brought back Octavius' jug of mead and stopped off at Otto's seat where he had been trying unsuccessfully to teach Lepi a series of card tricks.

"Well, Otto," Lepi said, "I don't suppose you sing any better than I do card tricks."

"The best I can do is an off key squeak and even that's unreliable. How are you doing, Maury?"

"Fine, Otto, fine! All set for your big theatrical adventures?"

"Big theatrical flop, you mean. My on-stage track record hasn't been exactly stellar. Besides, I feel a little creepy taking advantage of the enhancements the loony duck inflicted on me. I'm scared stiff of the side effects and somehow it doesn't seem fair to use them for my own profit."

"Well," I thought, "so much for his ethics and sensitivities being warped by the duck's genetic juggling."

"Look, Otto," I said aloud, "I could see your point if you were entering the Olympics or competing for prizes against other performers somewhere else. Disappearing with the Stars! But if these routines that Belinda and the Aquabears want to work out with you turn out well, then you'll be entertaining thousands and thousands of animals, making a living and having fun. You won't be costing anyone else a job or a livelihood. In fact, you'll be providing quite a few. Sounds like win-win to me."

"I guess you're right. When I actually get into it, I'll probably feel better. I'm having opening night jitters without even having an opening night."

"And," I said, "You couldn't have a better coach, co-star or impresario than Belinda. She's a real pro and quite a lady to boot."

"Oh, don't I know it," said the otter. In a word, the Bearoness had Otto totally mesmerized. He was literally open mouthed and flatfooted the first time he saw her and he hasn't changed since.

This time it was her voice over the cabin speakers, advising us to take our seats, fasten our belts, raise tray tables and seat backs. Bearyl came swiftly through the cabin picking up loose materials and checking things out before returning to her flight engineer's duties.

Looking off to the side I could see an airport that looked like it had been attacked by a plague of giant locusts. Abeardeen, the world's busiest HELICOPTER airport! This grand distinction is the result of all the traffic to and from the North Sea oil rigs.

Belinda had made a major contribution to the Abeardeen Airport Authority to get them to lengthen a runway to accommodate the high speed Aquabear. I for one was delighted to hear this bit of news. My life has been full of aerial escapades ranging from acrobatic helicopters under the control *(?)* of Inspector Bruce Wallaroo and the Bearoness to almost vertical take-offs from São Paolo and a stealth arrival at Las Vegas. I have been thinking seriously of having a barf bag holder permanently attached to my tail. Meerkats were not meant to fly but somehow I persist in repeatedly soaring through the atmosphere, sometimes courtesy of explosions. This time might be different. A runway of rational length might actually induce a landing of the rational sort.

No such luck! As usual, we landed hot – a Béarnaise specialty, ever the showbear – and swallowed up every last centimeter of concrete before howling to a stop. We turned onto a taxiway rolling past a phalanx of helicopters in all shapes and sizes and headed for a white and ice blue hangar upon which the Bruin coat of arms showed forth boldly: *(Three polar bears rampant sejant on a field of porridge inside a roundel of spoons revertent.)* A white corporate helicopter *(complete with Bruin heraldry)* sat off to the side. As we taxied into the hangar, several animals came over with jetstairs to meet us.

The local immigration and customs officers – two very trim and officious Border Collies – waited while the baggage bay was opened and then, after asking to see our passports, took some rather cursory sniffs at our luggage. Then they waited as Belinda and her two crew bears exited the flight deck and trundled down the stairs.

With only the slightest of official tail wags, they welcomed the Bearoness and her crew, spoke briefly about our flight origin and other immigration administrivia, and then signaled to one of the ground crew that it was OK to load us and our stuff onto the helicopters. Given his size, Octavius and I got an oversize oil rig chopper to ourselves while the rest of the group went into the estate's executive craft. It was another 45 minute flight to Unst and Bearmoral Castle. Actually, it took Octavius and me over an hour because our chopper was built for lifting, not speeding.

"Did our airport reception seem a bit reserved?" he asked as we arranged ourselves in the cargo bay of the helicopter.

"Well, I'm sure they don't see a nine foot, 1400 pound North American bear every day, and you always help things out by standing erect when you submit your papers. I'm not sure I'd be giggling all over myself either, if I was a customs dog on the receiving end."

"Hmmm," said the Great Bear. A comment, no doubt, full of deep and portentous meaning, all of which escaped me completely.

We rose with some effort from the tarmac, and I looked at the expression on Octavius' oversized face. I have never been able to determine just how he feels about choppers. As an aeronautical engineer, he is well aware that unlike winged airplanes, helicopters don't want to fly. They are lifted and propelled by their rotors but their structural aerodynamics is suited mostly to sitting on the ground. Add to this the extra effort brought on by his 1400 pound weight, and the fact that he has always been somewhat dubious about these chattering, metal stage coaches of the air.

As we throbbed along toward our destination, the landscape below looked like it came straight from a scenic designer's handbook. Windswept moors, regal cliffs, sun bleached sand, cerulean sea, ancient ruins and……ersatz castle. All it needed to complete the drama was some grappling love-crazed couple; each trying to stop the other from deliberately hurtling onto the rocks below. Every time I see one of those scenes, I can never tell who is the *hurtler* and who is the *hurtlee.* Anyway, they usually both go flailing over the side. Or was that Fetlock Holmes and the nutty Professor?

As we came closer to our target done up in its nouveau antiquity, I looked over at Octavius. "I thought this was the Bearon's ancestral home. This place looks like a theme park."

"It started out that way. You have to remember the Bearon's Scottish ancestors only go back three generations. Polar Bears are not indigenous to the Shetlands although the climate suits them just fine. Like Belinda, most of the Bruin family is from Canada although to hear Bel tell it, they act as if you've fallen off the earth if you travel west of Unst. The first Bearon *(the titles are bought, by the way)* was a canny showman like his grandson and decided Northern Europe could be a great playground for ursines of all types, especially the polars from the Bearents Sea. He chose Scotland's northernmost land mass for his entrepreneurial endeavor."

"The castle began life as a hundred room hotel, spa and open sea swim resort. It did well but the original Bearon's other investments did even better and by the time he died, his arrogant son and daughter decided that the castle should be converted into a sumptuous residence suitable for bears of their breeding, stature, history *(fake)* and wealth *(real.)*"

"Down came the cutesy neon signs of cuddly polar cubs and up went the heraldic banners along with a mass importation of phony clan symbols, tartans, weapons and other status conscious folderol. Belinda thinks the whole thing is a big hoot and just enjoys the place for what it is. Her in-laws on the other hand, swallowed the fantasy as if it was a school of salmon *(which are excellent up here)* and have now taken on all the obnoxious airs of petty nobility. Most of the locals who know Bel are fond of her and admire her but in general the Bruin "clan" is not very much liked. If it wasn't for Belinda's generosity and social conscience, all of the Bearmoral Castle riches would still be locked underneath the moat."

"Moat???"

"What did you expect? It was a tourist attraction. They even have a drawbridge that they pull up at night."

"How do you know all this, Octavius? Isn't this your first visit?"

"I have been thoroughly briefed in minute detail by the Bearoness."

"They sound like a fun bunch. This may be a very long fortnit. It has also occurred to me that I am seriously disadvantaged here. Forgetting about my diminutive size for a moment, I am the only animal in this group who is not naturally conditioned to cold weather. Our party is composed of bears, a St. Lawrence River otter, even a Himalayan snow leopard. And in the midst of this well insulated crowd, sits warm blooded, short furred, teeth chattering me. I want to relax but I don't want to chill out. First thing on the ground, I'm going to get myself a bunch of heavy Scottish woolens. I wonder what the Meerkat tartan looks like."

"Solid ice blue!!"

"Very funny!"

We were touching down on the estate's helipad not far from the executive chopper that had already brought in the rest of our group. The Bearoness had piloted that aircraft. Bearyl had been jockeying ours. As the rotors of our craft wound down, Belinda padded over to us, accompanied by a wild boar meticulously dressed in the uniform of a butler, retainer, field marshal, whatever!

Belinda gave Octavius a short hug and me a squeeze and then said, "Octavius, Maury, this is Hamish. He is in charge of the workings and maintenance of the castle. The staff report to him and he should be your contact for any of your needs."

The wild boar smiled, his spotless tusks brilliant in the afternoon sunshine and said, "Welcome to Bearmoral, gentlebeasts. I hope yer stay will be a bonnie one." *(At least that's what I think he said. If they all sound like him, I shall have to call upon my impressive linguistic skills in order to cope. Technology won't help. Auto language converters like the UUI Pea-Pod are useless in this kind of situation. I'll try to translate, transliterate and/or paraphrase the Scottish burr into mid-western North American so you can stay with the story and not get bogged down in dialect dialectics. It's a no charge service of the Offscreen Narrator. Don't thank me. Tell your friends to buy this book.)*

A couple of Golden Retrievers grabbed our luggage and as we moved toward the golf carts *(Octavius got a small utility truck)* to take us to the "house," Belinda called out, "See you in bit. Tea's at two, Tours at three!!!"

"Hmmmm!" said Octavius.

Bearoness Belinda
Béarnaise Bruin
(nee Black)

Chapter Two
Bearmoral Castle

You can pick your own friends, so they say.
But when in-laws come planning to stay,
You cannot be polite!
You'd be perfectly right
If you sent all those pests on their way.

It's time for tea overlooking the cliffs of Unst. A solid bank of grey clouds blocked what sun there was supposed to be. The temperature was a chilly -2°C. *(28°F.)* and a brisk sea wind blew in over the courtyard. Perhaps warm enough for the furries but the Meerkat Wind Chill factor said it was more than a bit too cold for us fuzzies. I was raised in the African desert, not on an ice floe. Even Otto came from the St. Lawrence River and Lepi from the Himalayas. I looked for a corner to stand in where I might still be sociable but not get blown around the landscape.

The three Aquabears had already arrived *(probably in sync)* and there were several other polars I didn't recognize. The family, no doubt! Lepi and Otto came in right behind us. Otto was trying to fit in by wearing a tweed jacket that was too long for his arms - probably provided by one of the household staff. On a good day, Otto looks a bit goofy. Today was a very good day. Lepi just let his beautifully spotted pelt speak for itself.

Octavius simply relied on his ample fur as well. I had wrapped myself in a long scarf with an ersatz tartan from the clan Bruin. (Blues and Whites) It wasn't helping much.

Hamish was supervising the setting out of the elaborate tea service. I wanted to see Octavius handle one of those china cups in his basketball sized paws. Actually, he was quite deft at using his claws as hooks and grapples. The problem resolved itself when I noticed that the tea set had been heavily modified, probably at great cost, to suit the dimensions and dexterity of ursines - albeit bears who were smaller than Octavius.

This was an estate clearly built with bears in mind and in that regard

Octavius should have felt right at home. I think I've mentioned that the Bear's Lair in subearban Cincinnati is sized to his dimensions, a fact that causes me a great deal of additional effort and agita since at two feet high plus tail, I am the smallest member of the Great Bear's domestic unit. I could see that navigating and maneuvering in this replica noble manse was not going to be easy. The sacrifices I make are neither recognized nor appreciated. I think I'll have another scone to cheer me up.

Bel padded over with an entourage in tow – no doubt the inmates of the great castle plus friends, other relatives and/or hangers on. "Octavius, Maury, I'd like to present you to the current residents of Bearmoral Castle. Ladies and gentlebears, these two animals from the United States are longtime friends and associates of mine. I'm sure you've heard of Doctor Octavius Bear. He is the sole owner and chief executive of UUI, United Ursine Industries. He is a noted scientist and engineer as well as a world renowned private detective. He is also about to become my partner in a new genetic science enterprise that we agreed to set up while I was visiting him in the States." *(Several looks of disdain aimed at Belinda, no doubt for engaging in 'commerce.')*

She went on without even batting one of her extraordinary eyelashes "Mauritius Meerkat is his indispensable right paw animal and an entrepreneur in his own right." *(Was she guessing about my hankering, to be a theatrical agent?? Octavius looked a bit taken aback by her last remark as well. To quote the bear, "Hmmmm!')*

She waved and called over, "Lepi, Otto dear. Come and be introduced. These two animals are topflight entertainers *(more looks of disdain that Belinda once again chose to ignore.)* Leperello is a Himalayan Snow Leopard who is also an outstanding operatic singer. He and our lovely Bearnice will soon be treading the boards of the Edinbeargh Opera House performing their first joint recital."

This was news to both Lepi and Bearnice who looked simultaneously delighted and thunderstruck. Belinda was Chairbear of the Opera Board of Trustees and a major contributor. With the mention of opera, several of the raised eyebrows among the pretentious polars lowered an inch or two.

"Otto here, is a true phenomenon. A life-saving hero and a showbeast extraordinaire!" *(Quivering whiskers and blushes from the otter.)* "You will all be invited shortly to see rehearsals for our new multi-species act for the next

Aquabear Review so I won't spoil things by telling you any more about Otto's significant gifts." *(The words 'multi-species' caused an outburst of coughing by one of the senior citizens whom I had observed spiking his tea with a slim silver flask — medicinal, no doubt.)*

Then with all the theatrical smoothness that came so naturally to her, she turned and with a flourish, said "And now let me return the favor and introduce our Bearmoral Bestiary."

Winces from the family, stifled giggles from Bearnice and Bearyl and the slightest tremor of the tusks by Hamish who was ensuring that everyone was well fed and liquidated *(sorry!)* while the introductions wore on.

"I shall take you through the Bruin family tree when we tour the castle. For the moment, may I present Lady Albearta Bruin and her husband Sir Ethelbeart. Lady Albearta is my dear departed Byron's aunt. She and Uncle Ethelbeart have lived here at Bearmoral since its reconstruction."

Aunt Albearta was seated *(as you might expect)* and raised her head to peruse Octavius. She ignored the rest of us completely. "Belinda tells me you are an American. I am only familiar with one breed of brown American bear — ursus arctos horribilis — the grizzlies - interesting name. Are you a member of that group?"

"No, madame, I am not. The grizzly is also indigenous to Europe as I'm sure you know. I am a Kodiak or ursus arctos middendorffi. I am from Alaska." *(Middendorff was one of the first bears to settle in the Pacific Northwest. He created the first salmon fishery.)*

Albearta sniffed and said, "Alaska, the primitive wilds of North America."

"No more primitive than Canada, madam. And parts of it may also be more civilized than this island."

Touché! Well, the virtual claws were out and no doubt would stay out for the duration. Sir Ethelbeart mumbled something by way of greeting that sounded like a transmission stripping gears. *(I can honestly say that during the entire period we were there, between his bearly audible growl and Scots burr, I did not understand one word he said. He was the keeper of the little silver flask, a fact which no doubt, further enhanced his lack of intelligibility.)*

The next polar bear turned out not to be a member of the family at all. Definitely a female, she was one of the most "striking" looking 800 pound creatures I had ever seen. She was wearing long purple gloves with holes for her claws, ditto stockings on her hind legs, bits of scarves and drapery and enough jewelry to stock a cable TV channel. Her diminutive ears peeped out through holes in a wide brimmed, feathered chapeau. Her eyes, not a bear's most striking feature, bore false lashes, mascara and purple shading.

"This is my dear friend, Dame Bearbara da Savile-Row. Bearbara is the publisher and editor-in-chief of a number of female ursine magazines. She traveled up here from Edinbeargh just to meet all of you."

"My, Dohctor Beahhhr, aren't you the most delicious specimen! Belinda has told me about you but she didn't come anywhere near doing you justice! You are gorgeous!! I don't suppose you model, do you. Our flagship publication-'*Sow*'- has a hunky male pictorial feature each month including a centerfold that you would absolutely blow away. Think about it." *(If he could, Octavius would have hidden under the nearest covered surface. As it was, he just stood there and fidgeted.)*

"Mr. Meerkat, it's such a pleasure! You fellows are some of the cutest animals in the entire world. And this is Otto the Magnificent. What an appropriate name. I'm so looking forward to seeing your performances with the Aquabears. And Mr. Leperello, a baritone no doubt, and from the mysterious Himalayas. I simply must do a feature story on you and Ms. Bearnice for our Culture Corner."

"By the way, Belinda dear, da Savile-Row publications is no longer restricted to the ursine community. We are launching a new offering for felines called '*Purr.*' I have hired the most fascinating cat as my editor. Just closed the deal this morning. I've known her for ages. She has been all over the world and has been a model, performer, singer and adventuress. She is terribly exotic and opinionated. But she simply reeks class and inscrutability. She only has one name, Chita. Isn't that to die for?'

I'm not sure whose mouth was hanging open the widest but collectively we could have swallowed a whale. As to her last question, several of us have already come too damn close to dying because of Chita, thank you very much. Miraculously, except for exchanging a few furtive glances, no one acknowledged our prior relationship with the *Purr* editor-in-chief-to-be. Even Belinda quickly glossed over it.

"That's very interesting, Bearbara. Perhaps some day I'll get to meet her.'

"Oh, I've invited her to join us this weekend. I was sure you wouldn't mind. This castle is just dripping in unused rooms and I thought she might be especially interested in meeting your new feline protégé, Mr. Leperello. Oh, may I call you Lepi?"

Once again, everyone held on. Was he going to acknowledge he knew Chita? Instead Lepi just nodded his head. "Please do. Dame Bearbara. By the way, I'm a pardine, not a feline. I don't care much either way but my Asian family is rather touchy about it. Forgive me for not being more talkative. The Bearoness' news about our recital has left me speechless."

"But not voiceless I hope. I have heard Bearnice sing and she has an angelic voice from an exquisite chirp down to a shattering roar. I'm so eager to hear you alone, Lepi and the two of you as a duet. You may be the stars of our new musical season."

Sounds of clearing throats, which from polars resemble a category 5 earthquake.

Belinda hurried to conclude the introductions. "These are my cousins, Alistair and Ursula. A perfect North Sea match. He is a member of the Bruin family, first cousin to Byron's father and Ursula is from a noted Bearents Sea community - the von Bruin's. This gentlebear is their son, Roary and this is their daughter Bruinhilde."

Nods all around. I judged Roary to have reached maturity several years ago and Bruinhilde also seemed to be on the verge of abandoning adolescence. She was trying very hard to exude sophistication without too much success while Roary was exuding boredom very, very successfully. Their parents were an interesting pair. Ursula looked like she might have taken a few turns as a prison matron while Alistair had all the appearances of an inept wheeler-dealer. Oh, Belinda, you poor girl. But then again, if anyone could handle a group like this, La Bel could.

She continued, "We may have several more animals up for the weekend and I'll tell you later about some members of the family who couldn't make it. Meanwhile, why don't we forego the tour until the morning, *(Sighs of relief!)* I'm a bit tired and I'm sure that even with the SST, you've developed some jet lag. Perhaps you'd all like to rest before dinner. When will dinner be served, Hamish?"

"I checked with Cook, Milady, and she says any time after seven would be ideal."

"Fine, seven it is. Please finish your tea and if you wish to do anything besides going to your room just speak with Hamish."

Without making any attempt at individual conversation, the Bruin contingent padded off en masse, snouts at an elevated angle. Dame Bearbara cornered Octavius. He looked in my direction for salvation. I pretended not to see him. I will hear about that. I skittered over to Hamish. Lepi and Otto joined us.

"Hamish, is there any way we can get a tour of the island tomorrow? Some of the scenery and little villages looked very interesting as we flew in on the choppers."

"Certainly, Mr.Meerkat. I'll summon Dougal."

Hamish returned with a robust looking Shetland sheepdog, a handsome Sheltie, wearing a cap, a ring of keys around his neck and short boots on his back paws.

"This is Dougal, our gameskeeper. He will see to your needs. Good afternoon, sirs." Off went Hamish.

"Guid efternin, sirs! Coud a gie yese a paw wi sompin?"

"Hi, Dougal,' I said, "you're the gameskeeper here? I'm surprised at the Bearoness keeping game."

Oh, aye sair, we have all sorts of games: billiards, chess, croquet, archery, a golf course (only a nine hole, mind) curling; shuftleboaird, pinball, fruit machines. 'Twas a hotel here ance, ye knaw. Yer a wee bit too sma, Mr. Meerkcat but if yer friend the bear, would care to thraw the caber, we can get one for him." *(Only in Scotland do they throw telephone poles for sport.)*

"OK," thought I, "I can see I have some cultural adjusting to do here."

"Ah, I see!! I thought gamekeeper meant raising animals for hunting."

"Och, we wuid nae do that, sirs. 'Tis unbeastly."

"Well," said Otto, "we would love to tour the island some time tomorrow, if we could. We're all small animals, relatively speaking, and we doubt if any of the baroness' family or friends would want to come with us. Is there a small car or vehicle we can handle safely that could get us around? I guess you folks drive on the other side of the road from us."

(To keep you from running for your Scots-English dictionary, I'll

translate Dougal from here on in but don't blame me if some of it comes out sounding a bit strange.)

"Ah, that's the first time I've heard an American who didn't say the "wrong" side of the road. We think the right side is the wrong side. I'd be proud to take you tourin' m'self sirs. Life is a bit dull right now at the castle with only the family here. They're not much in the way of frolicking, if you get my meaning."

"We get it, loud and clear, Dougal," said Lepi and then to us. "I'll have to check with Bearnice. If we're going to practice tomorrow, I may have to take a rain check. I'm still floored by the idea of a concert in Edinbeargh. That Bearoness is unbelievable."

"Believe it," I said. 'Nothing she does surprises me."

"Aye, she's a fine lady, is the Bearoness." said Dougal. "Very considerate and not at all stuffed up like them others. And 'tis a totally different place when all the Aquabears are here. Laughin' and singin' and swimmin' the day and night long and the tricks they play. They're like five year old bairns. Them's the guid times."

"What's a "guid" time for us to go out on our tour?"

"'Tis a sma island, sir. 'Twill not take much time to cover it. Why not after ye have yer luncheon! A'll drap in on ye at the back of one o'clock and we can go about and then maybe make a stop at the Lion and Unicorn to cock the wee finger. *(Have a drink, but you figured that out, right?)*

"Sounds good to me! Otto? *(nod)* Lepi? if you can make it at all? *(nod)* Dougal, you're on!!"

It gets dark early this time of year in the Shetlands although like Scandinavia and Russia, they do have white nights in the summer. Dinner was still a few hours away but the mention of cocking a wee finger appealed to me. "Dougal, where can a dry Meerkat get a drink around here?"

There's a bar near the library, sir. Please help yerself."

We said goodbye to our Sheltie friend and headed indoors. As advertised, a rather well equipped bar was situated discreetly below the huge winding staircase right by the library door. We entered and discovered to our delight that the Bearoness had again thought of everything. Kelp juice and vodka for Otto, single malt scotch for Lepi and, ambrosia - fermented coconut milk VSOP for me.

"Could there possibly be two Chitas in the world that fit Dame Bearbara's description?" asked Lepi.

"Otto, you've spent time in Reno. What're the odds?"

"A million to one against!"

"Do you think the cheetah you rescued last week at the mansion was Chita's sister, Cyd? Does Cyd even exist?"

Lepi chimed in. "I've been singing and playing with that cat for months. That was Chita at the mansion. Never knew about a Cyd."

"So who's this one we're going to meet on the weekend? Could she have recovered and regrouped so quickly."

"What are the odds on that, Otto?'

"A million to one in favor. What Chita wants, Chita gets."

"Octavius is going to be in some mood at dinner tonight. Belinda is going to have to work some real magic on him to get him to come around."

And as we were talking, the British Airport Authority was announcing that Abeardeen Airport had sustained a major power outage of both their primary and backup electrical systems. All flights in and out were diverted or cancelled until further notice. No heliport activity could take place as long as appropriate lighting and instrumentation were unavailable. But, of course, we didn't know any of this at the time and if we did, we wouldn't have sensed its significance.

The Development of Civilization Volume 3 Part 2
Clothing and Adornment
(From "An Introduction to Faunapology" by Octavius Bear Ph.D.)

One of the more puzzling aspects of the advance of animals in this world is the selective adoption of clothing. We have evidence that before their extinction, most members of the species Homo Sapiens wore some form of body coverings (often skins of animals they had killed) primarily to ward off the effects of climate – rain, snow, cold, sunlight and even heat. Clothing also protected their relatively fur-less hides from damage from sharp plants, rocks and other natural hazards and helped in their defense when engaged in fighting or hunting. A third purpose seems to have been pure decoration. Unlike many of the other animal species on earth at the time, H. Saps were not endowed with much in the way of distinctive bodily decoration except perhaps, for the hair that grew from their heads.

As we all know, many species of animals are blessed with attractive, complex, vibrant or subtle skin, fur and feather coloration. They may also have spectacular plumage, distinctive tails, manes and head crests to add to the effect. Important as these characteristics were for mating, camouflage, distinguishing each member of a pack and providing some forms of warning to hostile species, there seemed little need for enhancing them.

From whatever facts we can glean from faunapological research, the use of clothing seems to have been exclusive to H. Sapiens and several offshoot species that also inhabited the earth at that time. After the Big Shock, some 100,000 years or so in the past as certain mammals, reptiles, birds, a few insects and some fish began to progress up the "sentient" ladder they also began to adopt many of the admittedly primitive customs and habits of the by now extinct H.Saps. We don't know exactly why.

However, it does seem apparent that the use of external covering. as well as decoration, became increasingly popular even when there seemed no practical need for it. As some animals ventured further and further into unfamiliar climates and environments, the need for protective covering may have been deemed convenient and even necessary. And as societal structure began to emerge, certain forms of identification of rank and status became common, sometimes in skin decoration, sometimes in clothing and sometimes, various forms of adornments and jewelry. Many species also saw such embellishment as a means of enhancing personal beauty and attractiveness. Conversely, a few species have sought to cover so-called "private parts" out of a peculiar sense of shame. These are very much in the minority, however. In many cases, just the opposite seemed called for.

Today we have the unusual circumstance of the selective use of clothing and adornment among and within most species. Certainly where protective covering is required, it is employed. At times of ceremony, artistic performance or play, all forms of ornamentation are called into service. But, by and large, clothes are an option left to the individual or in more structured and stringently organized cultures, imposed by peer pressure. There have been periodic efforts to establish global rules for the wearing of clothes and decorations. All have failed.

Chapter Three
Bearmoral Castle

Fashion experts all forcefully stress.
It's essential to know how to dress.
Be it dinner or drinks,
Every arbiter thinks
How you look is your key to success.

We reached the dining room by descending a faux-Tudor staircase under the baleful eyes of the original Bearon's purchased ancestors. Each portrait seemed designed to confirm that polar bears were indeed a very fierce and humorless class and that these particular examples had summa cum laude graduate degrees in supercilious snobbery. Just the right touch!!

Passing into the dining room under the oh-so-solicitous guidance of Hamish in his perfectly tasteful maitre d' garb, I unconsciously looked for the auto-tour guide I should have had attached to my ear and belt. A carefully structured and completely manufactured museum of ancient Highland banquetry. I looked for an audio-animatronic laird or thane to start reciting the history of the castle.

The dining room furniture was a mix of badly matched antique *(?)* pieces, heavy in appearance as well as size and weight; this in order to support the ponderous rear ends of the assembled ursi maritimi. Two chairs of near-throne dimensions dominated both ends of the twenty foot long table which in turn was suitably adorned with heavy weight candelabras, silver plate and crystal drinking bowls. It would be interesting to see who occupied those two seats when we settled down for dinner. Another huge table covered with chafing dishes and other serving paraphernalia stood to the side and ran the length of one wall. The walls were the standard distressed oak paneling adorned with by-the-numbers oil paintings of polar bears engaged in a variety of predatory activities. Being a very small animal myself, I was not the least bit comforted either by the décor or the prospect of sitting in one of those grotesque chairs without benefit of a booster seat.

The first thing that went completely wrong was the dress code or the total lack thereof. The local polar contingent showed up in full formal Scots regalia - you haven't lived till you've seen male polar bears - Alistair and Sir Ethelbeart - in kilts, sporrans and sashes.

Roary wore a dinner jacket and black tie and looked like the suave and debonair star of a 1930's Broadway musical or gangster movie. I'm surprised he wasn't wearing a fake mustache. Wait, he was! The ladies were bejeweled and adorned with tartan sashes. Dame Bearbara da Savile-Row was dressed even more outlandishly than this afternoon. Her colors of choice being a swirl of purples, reds and black. Her jewelry made "bling-bling" a major understatement and hung from or surrounded every one of her appendages including her nose.

We "colonials" on the other hand wore what we usually wore at dinner back at the Bear's Lair - anything that suited our fancy or in the case of Lepi, nothing at all. Belinda came over to us during the requisite pre-dinner drinks and apologized profusely for having forgotten to clue us in. Octavius had brought a dinner jacket and tie but had left them in his room. He hates the things. In an effort to acquire the image of the theatrical agent and impress the Bearoness, I was dressed all in black. I suspect I looked more like a "hit-beast" or a two foot tall Dracula. Otto was still in his oversize Harris Tweed jacket. I just hoped he wouldn't pull out a briar pipe.

Bruinhilde seemed taken with Lepi and was trying, without much skill or knowledge to look worldly and sound au courant in the world of music. Deliberately or not, she growled with a lisp. "Oh, Mithter Leporello, I jutht adore opera. Mamáh took me when I was jutht a cub to thee Thalomé. It was tho thenthuous." Eyelashes batting like runaway windshield wipers. Truly, a bimbo bear!

Lepi looked helplessly over at Bearnice who winked at him but then joined Bearyl in chatting with Otto. Sir Ethelbeart was sitting in a large leather chair, balancing a jumbo sized Scotch on his forepaws and looking like he was communicating with the spirits of his mail-order Scottish ancestors – all two generations of them. Ursula and Alistair came over to us and starting pumping Octavius about the length, breadth, depth and value of his vast empire. Unlike Aunt Albearta, neither of them seemed to be put off by talk of filthy lucre, commerce or in Alistair's case, a quick way to make a quid. There was something strange about these two. They were obvious in their shallowness but they also struck me as a pair not to be trusted for other reasons. *(Dramatic organ chord in the background! I'm paranoid. What can I tell you?)*

Alistair was as phony as a three euro note but oddly enough, it was Ursula who bothered me more. As I said, she reminded me of a prison camp matron. She was unusually blocky for a polar bear but perhaps that's what the Bearents Sea variety looked like. I was used to the white-furred sylphs who made up the Aquabears. While Alistair was regaling us with his latest and greatest investments, *(Arctic seal futures)* she was pumping both Octavius and me about UUI's technical capabilities.

If this was wartime, I would have sworn she was the Teutonic spy trying to wheedle defense secrets from the unsuspecting Yank. *(Ve haff vays to make you talk!!!)* However, she left a lot to be desired in the seduction department. Octavius seemed very wary of her as well. We both managed to avoid sitting next to them at the dinner table although Belinda had asked that we mix the seating between the "colonists" and the "Scots."

As the quite delicious meal progressed, Aunt Albearta sustained a lengthy monologue addressed to no one in particular on the erosion of quality in society. All those nouveau riche and upstart ursines! *(No doubt a shot at both Belinda and Octavius and maybe Dame Bearbara for good measure.)* This in turn inspired a self-pitying declamation on how one can no longer expect well-made goods, proper respect, superior service, civilized behavior, appropriate dress and last but not least, decent usage of the language. Since I was having difficulty with every third word she growled, I had no idea what the dear aunt's concept of decent usage of the language was. Ethelbeart nodded his head periodically like a truly uxorious *(and sotted)* ursine while the rest of the table seemed to be ignoring her except for an occasional "Oh, indeed," whenever she asked *(seldom)* for agreement. She was also, no doubt, discomfited by Belinda's occupation of the head table "throne" while Ethelbeart was semi comatose at the foot. I imagine the Bearoness was tempted to seat Octavius there but that would have blown the cover on the marriage and set the bears among the pigeons or some such thing.

At one side of the table, Roary was trying to put a move on Bearyl and was meeting with what polar bears do best – the cold shoulder. He didn't seem to get it.

At one point, Belinda asked the cook, Mrs. McRadish, to come in to be introduced and congratulated on the delectable meal. It was clear that the Bearmoral inmates thought this was unnecessarily democratic behavior on the Bearoness' part. *(Domestics should know their place!)* Mrs. McRadish was a Shetland sheep and had been with the castle for at least two generations. We were soon to find out that most of the domestic staff at the castle were locals – sheep, dogs, a badger or two, ponies, a couple of magnificent Clydesdale horses and in charge of the pool and beach, a sea otter named Harold. Of course, Hamish, the wild boar supervised the staff. The upstairs and downstairs maids were identical quadruplet sheep, Dolly, Holly, Molly and Polly. There may have been an interesting story about the origins of these ladies but it was only hinted at, never explicitly stated. Although, Octavius, the genetic genius, did allow himself another "Hmmmmm" when they were introduced.

Earlier, Otto had made a date to see Harold, the sea otter, in the morning and get the lowdown on lutrine affairs in the Shetlands. He was also due for an aquatic workout with Belinda, Bearyl and Bearnice. Clearly, Otto was here to work, if you call cavorting in water with three beautiful bears, work.

Dinner slowly wound down and we were treated to a "wee dram" to round out the evening. The food had been excellent. I couldn't help thinking about Frau Schuylkill, Octavius' chef-housekeeper-pilot-defender-airport manager-mysterious she-wolf back at the Lair and how she and Mrs. McRadish might get along. A she-wolf and a ewe in the same kitchen?? Not likely! While I don't think Frau Schuylkill would go so far as to try to make Mrs. McRadish a main course, *(oddly, mutton was not one of her favorites)* there might have been some significant howling and baahing going on. Better the Frau stays where she is – guarding the Cincinnati homestead with Colonel Where and Howard Watt, our new friend, L. Condor and Juno and Agrippa, the Great Bear's mother and half brother. More about all of these anon.

Eventually our Trans-Atlantic contingent got a few moments alone away from the pseudo-Scots to discuss the shock of the day – Chita. The consensus was that Dame Bearbara's description was too accurate for it to be anyone else. But how did the cat pull it off? It hadn't been a week since, after nearly being drowned; she took off in the middle of the night from the Lair where she was "recuperating." She left with *(or at about the same time as)* Jake, the jaguar drummer who was also a member of their rock group, The

Spotted Band. The only conclusion we could draw was that while she was wheeling and dealing with us and damned near getting herself killed a second time by Imperius Drake and Bigg Baboon, she was also negotiating with Bearbara. They obviously knew each other rather well. They both had spent time on the continent and Chita was enough of a fashion plate to appear in the same circles as the Dame. Talk about the fast lane! And now she was coming up here to brazen out the fact that she was a cat wanted by the police just about everywhere.

Octavius was convinced that her visit had more ulterior motives than to thank Otto once again for her rescue and perhaps to give the Great Bear the claw.

"She was anxious to get away from us back in Ohio." He said, "Why are we suddenly an attraction now? I wonder if she took up residence in Edinbeargh or if she's commuting from London. London is more her speed. I also wonder if she and Jake are together. If they're going to put together another version of the Spotted Band, London would be the place. There aren't many singing felines *(or pardines, Lepi!)* in Scotland."

"In fact," added Belinda, "they were almost eradicated about a hundred years ago in an attempt by other species to rid the area of wildcats. It's interesting that wildcats have made such a comeback in the off-shore oil business. They just about dominate the UK side of the industry. Poetic justice! My in-laws think the cats have gotten above themselves. Talk about pots calling kettles black. Their attitude would be ridiculous if it wasn't so pernicious."

This seemed to get Octavius into another one of his 'deep thinks.' He said, "It will be interesting to see Chita again. *(Excuse me!?)* For a loner, she certainly develops affinities for other cats."

Deep, very deep! The atmosphere was redolent with pungent import. Damned if I knew what. When Octavius gets into one of his pensive moods, it is a certainty that his great mind is operating on a plane far above those of mere mortals. It is truly inspiring to be present at such an event. It makes me thankful that I have had the opportunity to be his companion for so long. It also makes me want to give him a swift kick in the backside.

Lepi was working out a rehearsal schedule with Bearnice who was also on call to work out with Bearyl, Belinda and Otto. It looked like we could take our little island jaunt with Dougal at about one o'clock. Octavius, who couldn't

39

quite get the hang of relaxing said he had a number of e-mails to send and a teleconference tomorrow afternoon when the UK and US working time slots aligned. He and Bel went off to take a walk around the castle or perhaps a moonlight swim.

Otto came over to me and said, "How about a nightcap, Maury?"

Since the understairs bar was well stocked with fermented coconut milk VSOP, I saw no reason to deprive myself. Goodness knows I make enough sacrifices in the line of duty. Off we went.

As he mixed his kelp juice and vodka, Otto looked at me and said, "I'd like to ask you a favor."

Funny, I was about to say the same thing. "Sure, Otto, name it."

"Well, that adventure with the loony duck may or may not turn out to be the crisis point in my career but it sure proved one thing to me. I'm too naïve to handle myself in show business. I'm sure that unlike that lousy Imperius, the Bearoness has my best interests at heart but she's a busy world figure. She's got all sorts of things on her plate including this new venture with Octavius. I'm looking for help from a personal agent of my own whom I can trust and work with and I think you may be him."

In addition to his teleportation and telekinetics talents, it seems Otto can also read minds or at least Meerkat Minds. I looked at him and said, "Otto, I don't know if it's power of suggestion from my all-black outfit, a sharp perception that underneath this innocent expression I am a wheeler-dealer or maybe I talk in my sleep but you have just raised the issue I was going to propose to you."

"I have to be honest with you, Otto. *(Well, I didn't really have to, but it seemed appropriate under the circumstance.)* I have no experience as a theatrical agent. However, it is something I would very much like to do and I believe I'm smart enough and know enough people to be able to get us set up. Obviously, Belinda and Octavius would both have to sign off. I have no intention of getting in the Bearoness' way and I'm certainly not going to leave the Great Bear's employ. On the other hand, I believe an agent with only one client can certainly hold down another job. The answer is a tentative 'yes' with further discussions to be held with the other principals. I might also suggest we find you a lawyer and an accountant. But the first thing we have to do is find you an act."

During my speech, the otter was nodding his head enthusiastically. "I have some pretty good ideas for an act, Maury. My last round as a stand up magician was a disaster. So I thought I might use the fact that I'm an obvious klutz to build a comedy act around foul-ups and then pull off a couple of real eye-poppers when the audience isn't ready. Funny and amazing both! What do you think?"

"Otto, you're a natural clown and you should exploit it. It will make your real razzle-dazzle all the more difficult to believe. We need to talk with Belinda and the other bears. They have the stage experience. You'd be great comic relief for all the opulent extravaganza stuff that the Aquabears carry off. In fact, if they buy it, you can wander in and out of their acts doing silly stuff and then when you have the stage, they can help you distract the audience. Of course, there are a number of divas and prima donnas among the Aquabears, but I'm sure if Belinda likes the idea she can persuade the rest of them. Let's talk to her first before we talk to Octavius. If she buys our proposal, she can persuade the Great Bear rather easily"... *(I hope!)*

As we moved off toward our luxurious rooms, I thought I saw Alistair ahead of us padding stealthily down the corridor. I watched as he turned a corner and headed toward the family wing. What brought him over to the guest side of the manse? None of us had returned to our rooms yet so he wasn't visiting. Do we have a snoop on our paws? As I skittered past, I tested Octavius' door. Locked! I asked Otto to check his room when he got in there. My room adjoined Octavius and my door was locked as well. But from force of habit, I always do the old hair in the door jamb routine. The hair was gone. Could have been a maid, of course. When I opened the door, my bed had been turned down. Maury, you're getting paranoid again. Getting? I always was. Still! A knock on the door. Otto telling me his bed had been turned down but nothing else seemed amiss or missing. We bade each other another round of goodnights.

About half an hour later, I heard Octavius wander into his room. I knocked on the passageway door between the two rooms and after much jiggling and thumping, he opened the door.

"What?" he said, not in the best of moods. He and the Bearoness must have had words about something. I told him about Alistair and asked him to check his room. He uses more intrusion detection than I do. I guess I get my paranoia from him. His bed had been turned down as well but he checked around under the bed, in the drawers and closets and discovered *(voila!)* that someone had attempted to open his luggage. The numbers on the combination locks had been disturbed. I found it hard to believe that one of the *(D,H,M,P)*olly girls was prying but I've been wrong about animals before. Octavius came through like the champ that he is. "Hmmmmmmmm!!"

"I think our friend Alistair could use some looking into," I said.

"I agree, but I'm even more concerned about his wife, if she is his wife. There is something about her that is very familiar."

"Sure, she appears in every one of those horror movies as the housekeeper or the jailer in charge of all the sweet, young, innocent girl bear prisoners, complete with whip and super long claws."

"No, I'm serious."

"So am I!"

"Let's not mention this to Bel or the others."

I told him I had already alerted Otto and that he didn't notice anything wrong. But I'm not too sure how observant he is when it comes to intruders. Ironic! The guy can move around unseen but.......wait a second. There's an idea. I told Octavius that I thought we could bring some of Otto's talents to bear in our counterspy efforts. And, once again *(it must be the Scottish air)* he said, "Hmmmm" but this time it was accompanied by an affirmative nod. "Let's talk with Otto in the morning," he said.

Meanwhile, out in the North Sea, fire alarm klaxons had just gone off on two wildcat rigs about 50 kilometers away from each other. Emergency rescue choppers and fire boats were dispatched, as well as the rigs' own safety craft. One event turned out to be a kitchen fire but the other was more serious. A pumping unit inexplicably blew up and created a major conflagration. Several cats were killed and many more injured. Once again, as we were pondering our own potential intruder*(s)*, little did we know how deep we would be getting into the boiling oil and water off the coasts of bonnie Scotland.

Chapter Four
Still Bearmoral

Through the water they caper and leap
And a soft seaweed bed's where they sleep.
Otters eat on their back,
Giving shellfish a crack
With some rocks they bring up from the deep.

I woke with a start. Weird sounds in and through the walls. Wails and Screeches! Some animal being unmercifully tortured? Banshees? Close!! Bag pipes!! Well, I suppose it was better than a chorus of roosters singing "***Scots wha' hae'***." I looked at my travel alarm. Friday, 7 AM UK time. Good morning Shetlands!

I discovered later there's a quaint auld Bearmoral custom dating back at least seven years to pipe the sun and flag up every morning and down every evening. No twenty three gun salutes, thank goodness! I bet the tourists loved it. I guess I missed last night's concert because I had isolated myself in the bar where the only audible sounds were the clinking of ice and the pouring of fluid.

I washed, brushed my fuzz, stiffened my whiskers and smoothed my tail before donning once again, my talent agent's garb. I decided to forego the sunglasses. I didn't want to come on too strong *(or too ridiculous.)* Besides, I already have sexy black patches around my eyes. But those dark glasses do make a statement.

Down for breakfast. There was a sideboard full of all sorts of Scottish breakfast delicacies. I didn't have the heart to tell Mrs. McRadish that my diet is primarily insects so I picked and chose among the things she had left out and in general, had a good feed.

I set out in search of Otto, stopping first at Hamish's faux-vintage office to ask if there was a map of the premises I could use for navigating on my own. The walls were covered with small portraits of polars; no doubt the lairds and their offspring - all three generations of them. A photo of a charming wild boar sow took pride of position on his substantial oak desk along with the clerical instruments of his trade. Papers stacked neatly and squared away against the corners. When he heard my request, he was very deferential but not all that helpful or forthcoming. He gave me a museum-like "exhibit plot" of the overall building that illustrated less than a third of the place. I decided to try my luck later with one of the staff, maybe one of the (D,H,M,P)ollies. The map did show the pool, an indoor-outdoor, all-weather affair. No doubt the Aquabears and the otter would be there if they were up yet. There was also a solarium next to it where I could bare my beastly chest and absorb much needed warmth.

The pool! Splashes and laughter and wonder of wonders, Octavius was there as well. Actually he was physically there. Snoring none too gently, he had fallen off into another one of his narcoleptic dozes which he vehemently denies ever happen. He'd be around shortly. The siestas usually last less than a half hour but there's no point trying to wake him while he's out. Most of his associates are aware of his, um, "occasional outages" and act as if nothing has happened. Every once in a while he conks out at a very unfortunate time. For that reason, he doesn't drive *(to say nothing of the fact that he can't fit in most driver's seats)* or pilot a plane and he is very careful about machinery. Overflowing bathtubs happen once in a while. Given his size, it takes a lot of water to fill his tub and an overflow could be a dangerous event. We've had one or two near misses. We keep trying to get him to take showers but as usual, no cooperation.

Otto and the three polar bears were having a skull session at the edge of the pool. Belinda was showing them diagrams of potential moves and Otto was making suggestions for making mischief. I think his ideas of occasionally disrupting the precise formations of the Aquabears were good ones provided they didn't get out of hand and the super-serious artistes were not offended. Judging from the laughter, the three bears seemed to think there was something there.

I think I mentioned that, thanks to some genetic tinkering by Imperius Drake, when his adrenaline rises above a certain point, Otto can not only teleport himself but also move other things telekinetically. That makes him a pretty impressive entry and escape artist. Predicaments where he is locked up and bound ala the Great Whodunit turn out to be pup's play for him. Even more important to our planned program of reconnoitering the castle, he can get into and out of sealed environments, without disturbing any of the protective measures or devices. We don't know how he does it. Actually, neither does he.

He says that he thinks or wishes himself into or out of the situation. "Wishing will make it so…"

As soon as he wakes up, Octavius and I will brief Otto on using his talents to conduct a little scouting mission for us on the family side of the castle.

I skittered over to the merry foursome and sat at the perimeter of their tête-à-tête. They all ignored me. Suddenly, I found myself splashing around in the pool with the four of them laughing hilariously. Octavius came out of his dream state just in time to catch a view of my soggy self and joined his basso chortle to the chorus.

"Hey Otto, cut that out! *(splutter, splat)* Very funny, very funny! I hope this suit is washable. Just because I'm little, everyone thinks I'm the perfect patsy. You're not so big yourself, you dopey lutrine."

As I scrambled out of the pool, Bearyl suddenly did an involuntary back flip into the water courtesy of Otto. So much for picking on the little guy. The other two bears made a grab for him but he had disappeared. He blinked back into sight at the top of the diving board and executed a triple somersault into the water.

"We're going to have to curb his enthusiasm," said the Bearoness. "Although you do look funny, Maury! Soggy somehow suits you!" She started to giggle, "Oh, I'm sorry!" and then she laughed out loud, along with Bearnice and Octavius. Laughing bears are an experience not to be forgotten. It sounded like an avalanche was going to engulf the house. Bearyl swam her way up to the side of the pool and joined in the jollity at my expense. Revenge was called for.

It was obvious that as long as Otto was on his adrenaline high, any attempts to catch the elusive little guy were going to be fruitless. So….the objective was to get him down to normal *(!?)* life levels again and then dunk him when he wasn't looking. I could probably calm him down by getting him, Octavius and Belinda together with me to discuss our agency proposal. I really didn't care if the other two bears were within earshot or not.

I approached Bel and Bear and said, "Can I have word with you two. It involves Otto."

Quizzical look on Octavius' face, slight smile on Belinda's. I swear that sow has a master's degree in mind reading. Octavius looked over and said, "Otto, we need to talk with you."

When he saw it was the Great Bear doing the calling, Otto let down his defenses. He knew he was due for a dunking *(which for a river otter was no big deal)* but he couldn't imagine Octavius involved in such a juvenile prank. Matter of fact, neither could I. Octavius' sense of humor tends toward the cerebral – lousy puns and hundred year old jokes. I've been the frequent victim of his public speeches and they are truly awful, but no one yet has convinced him of it. He is badly in need of a remedial speechmaking course. Octavius at Toastmasters – now there's a thought.

Otto approached somewhat warily and seemed relieved that Bearyl and Bearnice had toweled off and were heading into the main house. I was still soaking wet, but I had other things on my mind. When the otter joined us, he and I launched off into a brief exposition of our idea for him to have agency representation – to wit, me. Belinda seemed to buy the idea. At least her body language seemed favorable. She actually said nothing.

Octavius surprised me by taking to the idea enthusiastically. It was only later that it occurred to my none too subtle brain that he saw it as an opportunity to keep a wide open channel to Otto and his talents for use by the Great Bear whenever and wherever he needed him. As I said, Octavius thinks outside the box, the wrapping paper, bow and gift card.

We all agreed in principle to the arrangement, understanding that the details still needed to be worked out, probably with the services of an accountant and a lawyer. Also since we were both citizens of the US, all contracts should be worked out back there.

Octavius then looked at Belinda and asked, "Let me change the subject. Bel, how well do you really know your in-laws?"

"Among the four of us, Tavi, not that well at all. On the other hand, I know several of them better than I'd really like to. I don't spend that much time here, as you know. On average, maybe six or seven months in the year. I'm still a show-biz wanderer. Why do you ask?"

"I'm not sure but I think I have run into Alistair and Ursula before and it was not a pleasant occasion. Actually, it's Ursula I remember. Quite a few years ago in Turkey. She was with the office of the cultural attaché in the then Soviet embassy. Inspector Wallaroo and I were searching for stolen Turkish art works that we believed had taken a trip behind the Iron Curtain. Bruce was still with the International Fine Arts and Jewelry Protection Squad at the time. To put it mildly, Comrade Ursula, if that was her name, was no help. In fact, I suspected she was in 'aid and abet' status with the thieves who purloined the statues we were searching for."

"I'm surprised she hasn't recognized you." I said.

"She may have and is hoping I didn't recognize her. Or maybe she just doesn't care. She was certainly trying to pump me for information last night."

"Odds are she's still working for a government," I said. "Which one, I wonder after the Soviet breakup?"

"I don't know what she does." said Bel. "She and Alistair just slip in and out of here after loading up on my food and liquor. He's always going off somewhere on some big deal and she's just cryptic. In fact, the only way I know they're related to me at all is through Aunt Albearta. They first appeared after Byron's death."

"Hmmm," said the Great Bear, "Maury and Otto spotted Alistair wandering around the halls near our rooms last night and some of the security measures I'd used on my briefcase and luggage were compromised. I may be jumping to conclusions, but we'd like to do a little reconnoitering in Alistair and Ursula's digs, and we'd like Otto to do it for us, if you don't object, Bel."

"I guess not, but they are still my guests, and as far as I can tell, family by marriage. But, to be honest, I don't like either one of them. *(I wondered if she liked any of them.)* I wouldn't put it past them to be up to no good but its sheer emotion on my part. I've seen Otto at work and I guess I don't have any problem with him doing a bit of lookie-loo. What do you think, Otto?"

"It'd be fun and I can test my 'mind-confounding skills.' When do we start?"

"Tonight during cocktails, assuming they come down for drinks. You can do your quick reconnaissance, and arrive a bit late, just in time for dinner. Don't worry. Maury will make sure you have a kelp juice and vodka waiting for you. If they don't come down or are late to dinner themselves, then perhaps you can excuse yourself early from the table as we are eating - *it's been a strenuous day* – and we'll keep them occupied during after dinner drinks. Just do a fast survey."

"What am I looking for?"

"That's the damndest part. I don't really know. I should really go myself but a nine foot bear sticks out a bit more than an elusive otter. I'll give you the same instructions they use in all the mystery movies. 'Look for something unusual.'"

"Got it! We can meet later in your room, Maury. Are you sure you're OK with this, Bearoness?"

"Actually, Otto, I'm looking forward to it. I'd love to have a reason to toss them and their brats out, and give the Bronx cheer to Aunt Albearta in the process."

Well, that certainly set things straight. It was almost time for lunch and then our island tour. Bearnice had gone straight from the pool to the music room, and I could hear her and Lepi singing a duet from Bearlioz' "Romeo et Juliette."

Bel went off to speak to Mrs. McRadish about lunch. Otto, Octavius and I stood by the poolside. Now there's a picture. A nine foot Kodiak flanked by a two foot Meerkat and a slightly taller otter. Where is National Geographic when you want them?

Suddenly, he reached down and tossed Otto into the water. The otter surfaced and stared at the Bear, who was convulsed in laughter. Otto was Shocked, Shocked!! Did Octavius actually have a comical side? Strange but true! Gee, maybe he could convince Octavius to be part of his Aquabear routine. The big, bumbling bear and the precocious otter. Once again, Otto's imagination was running in overdrive. This time right over a cliff.

As I leaned down to give Otto a hand out of the water, reality dawned a split second too late. Tug from the otter. Push from the bear. Marinated Maury! Clambering out, spitting water and trying to clear my nose, I looked past the treacherous ursine and behold! An apparition! Actually, Dame Bearbara in her version of morning sport clothes. Imagine a polar bear in jodhpurs, boots, a leather vest and a petite black derby atop her massive head. A riding crop in her right front paw completed the ensemble. The first question that rattled through my brain was what kind of horse did she plan on riding? Scottish Clydesdales are heavy duty equines but c'mon!

"Good morning, Dame Da Savile-Row," rumbled Octavius, trying to keep a straight face. "You look very fetching in your riding costume." *(Liar, liar! Tail on fire!)*

A cross between a blushing giggle, snort and what sounded like a hiccup ushered in her reply. "Oh, please, Dohctah Beaah, call me Bearbi. Everyone does and may I call you Octavius?"

"Please do, er, Bearbi! You're up and about early this morning.'

"Oh, the demands of journalism know no lates or earlys, Octavius." She lilted the "Tav" in Octavius. Otto stared at her goggle eyed and I was tying my tail into a tight and painful knot to keep from laughing. "We're doing a photo shoot on the horses of Scotland this morning. From those darling Shetland ponies to those hunky Clydesdales. I don't suppose you have an American steed in your entourage?"

"I'm afraid not but some of my best friends are equine." *(Fetlock Holmes??)*

"What a shame! I still intend to pursue you about our centerfold spread in *Sow*, you gorgeous beah. However, I just dropped by to tell you that my new editor, Chita, is coming up today. She'll be here in time for dinner. I'm sure you'll love her."

File that under "Not Bloody Likely." Although most of his team, including Wallaroo, likes or has a grudging admiration for Chita, Octavius takes the position that she is a one cat crime wave and should be doing time somewhere, preferably well away from him. However, knowing the boss the way I do, I suspect there's a small part of his complex psyche that enjoys her super-feline personality. He'll never admit it, though. Me, I get a big kick out of her but then I'm a *(semi)* reformed pickpocket and lookout.

We all continued to pretend to Madame Equestrienne that we didn't know Chita. Bearbi was in for a surprise. Or perhaps Chita would play dumb, too. With an insouciant "Ta, ta!" and a flick of her riding crop, the Dame trundled off, to immortalize the manes and shanks of Scotland's mighty horses. A true piece of work!

An early lunch was beckoning, and I went off first to change and dry off, and then to double check with Dougal on our sightseeing trip. I also touched base with Otto and Lepi to make sure I wasn't going to be a solo tourist. As I suspected, Octavius wasn't interested in squeezing himself into a Land Rover. He usually sat in the bed of a specially equipped truck at home. Anyway, off to the cliffs and the moors! *(after an appropriate meal to ensure stamina, of course.)*

Chapter Five
Bearmoral Castle and UUI

The lone Aardvark has claws that are strong.
And his tongue stretches ever so long.
Thus he gobbles up bugs,
Loads of insects and slugs.
But I still think his face is all wrong.

Octavius headed back up to his room and powered up his oversize laptop computer *(It matched his oversized lap and paws. Strangely, his claws are quite agile and precise for their size.)* He set up a video conference link with Cincinnati bringing in Howard Watt, L. Condor and Frau Schuylkill at the Bear's Lair mansion and Drs. Vark and Bingbang at the UUI labs in Kentucky. Colonel Where was elsewhere! Subject: Project Multiverse.

(For those readers unfamiliar with Project Multiverse, a short summary is in order. In Book Two – <u>The Spotted Band</u> – a troubling set of reports set the Great Bear and his security science team off on an extensive investigation. To wit: Colonel Where, Juno and Agrippa [Octavius' mother and half brother] as well as Otto all had experiences strongly suggesting the existence of teleportation and one or more possible parallel universes. Further, the Colonel and Agrippa both described seeing and/or meeting beings who disturbingly matched faunapological descriptions of Homo Sapiens, believed to be extinct on Earth for over 100,000 years.

The Colonel had earlier been one of a few unwilling subjects in a series of teleportation experiments conducted by a clandestine semi-government agency called The Business, under the direction of the ominous [and probably crazy] horse, General Turmoil. The experiments did not pan out, and all of the experimental animals mysteriously disappeared, except for the Colonel who escaped. Unknown to the Business, the Colonel had actually succeeded in teleporting, and once free of them, had set about improving his abilities, to the point where he found himself in the abovementioned world that was populated by H.Saps or reasonable facsimiles thereof. Thus far, he has not established contact; just observed.

All of the "teleporters" achieve their transported state while asleep (hibernating in the case of the bears) except for Otto who seems to be able to exert telekinetic and teleportation powers when he is in a state of high excitement. Thus far, however, Otto has made no alternative world excursions that he is aware of. Complicated?? You bet! Hence the top secret Project Multiverse was initiated by Octavius to get to the bottom of these phenomena before others, especially the Business, can. There is also the very real probability that the H.Saps, if such they are, could find their way from their world[s]onto our earth.)

To the extent that Octavius could delegate anything for very long, he had appointed Howard Watt, our porcupine physics and cryptography wizard, as project leader. When the last participant signed on to the teleconference, the Bear asked Howard for a progress report.

"Well, Octavius, it's only been several days since you left but we have managed to come up with a few ideas that might help sort this mess out. Let's start with Otto. First off, Imperius Drake's lab notes were encoded but I've managed to use my crypto skills to get most of them in readable shape. It does present a problem, though. After we reviewed them, nobody was sure whether I missed with my decryption; or the duck was writing pseudo-scientific nonsense; or he was so far over our heads in genetics that we're not going to get anywhere fast."

"On the one hand he follows classic gene-splicing procedures:
1. Isolate the genes of interest.
2. Insert the genes into a transfer vector or agent. (the serum)
3. Transfer the vector to the organism to be modified. (Otto)
4. Transform the cells of the organism. (Otto)
5. Select the genetically modified organism (Otto) and test for desired results.
6. Go to the top and repeat as often as necessary."

"But, if our interviews with Otto and Chita were complete and accurate, Imperius didn't get all the way to his desired result. In fact, the process may have backfired. Rather than producing a super high IQ slave single-mindedly dedicated to doing his will, he didn't seem to affect Otto's intelligence at all. Otto's smart but he's not remarkable. Nor did he create a slave. If anything, Otto is feistier, more honest and independent than he was when he first met

Imperius. What the duck seems to have done is bring to the surface and immensely enhance the otter's basic skills in high speed movement, sleight of hand and incredible strength through leverage. His wacky sense of humor seems to be scaled up as well. I suppose these could all have been useful to Imperius, but this wasn't the model he thought he had designed."

"The UUI labs have been analyzing the serum that he was using on Otto. When Imperius first began his work, the serum needed to be tailored to each subject individually. Now it seems he did succeed in generalizing the vector serum, so it no longer needs to be customized to the recipient. Originally, it would be fatal to any beast other than the designated target. You'll remember, that's how he planned to kill Chita – by injecting her with his own serum. That's also the way his mate died - by ingesting a vast overdose, in fact, all of the Imperius-specific serum, to stop his experiments because she thought he was going mad. She was right, of course. But I've wandered too deeply into the territory of Dr. Vark and Dr. BingBang. I'll let them talk for themselves. Then we'll move on to the teleportation, alternate universe and *Homo Sapiens* issues."

"Good day, doctors. What can you add to Howard's report?"

He was addressing Chief Geneticist Dr. Helix Oryceteropus Vark and Dr. Chiti BingBang, UUI's Chief Physician. Both of these animals were exceptional in their respective fields. Dr. Vark *(a member of his own singular species and thus known to all by his nickname "Odd")* was a rather eccentric African Anteater who had made many of the great discoveries that had put UUI's Genetics division in the forefront of scientific and commercial success. *(He was also going to be one of the principals in the joint genetic venture Belinda and a somewhat reluctant Octavius planned to develop here in the Shetlands.)* Communicating with him by videophone was necessary because his speech was supplemented by rapid flipping of his elongated ears and wrinkling of his snout, each with meanings of their own.

Dr. BingBang was an orangutan from Borneo who had met Octavius in his travels through Malaysia, and sprang at the chance to head up UUI's Medical Unit. "Sprang" is the apposite term since he did most of his work hanging from ceiling fixtures or other appendages. A remarkable physician, it was he who had gotten Otto back into top physical shape after the otter had been blown across a room by an Imperius laid booby trap. *(See Book Two - The*

Spotted Band). Now he and Dr. Vark had set about determining whether the mad duck's genetic tinkering would have any long term toxic effects on the otter.

Bingbang swung upside down into the view screen of the camera and said, "We have gone about as far as we can without having our test subject back in our paws, Dr. Bear. So far things look very hopeful on two counts: He may well retain his remarkable abilities and do so without any long term personality impacts. Unlike Imperius Drake, who started out as a badly obsessed genius and turned into a badly obsessed <u>evil</u> genius, Otto doesn't seem to have an evil gene in his whole furry body. BUT, we need him back to complete our tests."

"You shall have him, Doctor, in another week or so. Right now, he is working up a spectacular act with Belinda and the polar twins that will be incorporated into the next Aquabear Revue. By the way, let's not forget his telekinetic abilities. He willed Chita into the Missouri River several times. He also rescued her remotely from the sinking paddle steamer. And he moved a one ton hydroplane about half a mile through the air by wishing, he says. We've observed that his unusual talents seem to kick in when he is on an adrenaline high."

"That would agree with our findings although we're not quite sure yet what the connection is. There is still much to learn about our lutrine friend. Bring him back soon."

"He and I will be flying back at the end of next week. Now let's get on to the other subjects. Howard, is there anything new on the teleportation front? And please don't tell me that my ne'er-do-well half brother has been mixing it up with more *Homo Sapiens.* All we need is some gun-toting aliens barging in, looking for a card sharp bear who made off with their money."

"Not that we know of, Octavius. Your mother has him firmly under her paw at the moment. Since both of them seemed to have experienced some form of alternate universe shift while they were hibernating, she won't let him out of her sight. She's trying to keep him permanently awake. If Agrippa even yawns, Juno is on his case. Maybe some of your anti-hibernation potion might help."

"I don't think so, Howard."*(Octavius had developed a "cure" for hibernation to improve his personal productivity. He restricted its use to himself. It has a troublesome side-effect – occasional narcoleptic seizures which he will never publicly admit to.)* "Am I correct that none of our other world travelers have been on any recent excursions?"

"As far as I know, Octavius! The colonel is off checking world-wide incident reports right now but he assures me he will let me know if and when he takes himself off for parts unknown. He doesn't seem to be in total control of it. I've already told you about the two bears. Frau Schuylkill is convinced she doesn't teleport. She just moves at speeds high enough to become momentarily invisible. And of course, you have Otto with you."

"Have you and the other science mavens come up with any theories?"

"Well, all of us are tilting very heavily toward the existence of other universes made accessible by stray quantum fluctuations. That in itself is enough to set off world wide chaos, and we need to very carefully plan how to let others in on our theories. We know so little. For example, why now? Has this been going on for a long period and we're just stumbling on it for the first time? It isn't clear why one has to be asleep to experience a transfer. What makes some creatures susceptible and others not? Polar bears don't hibernate and you're chemically immune. Drs. Vark, Bingbang and I are all wondering if we're going to join the "The Alternate Universe Tourist Club" anytime soon. We have been searching scientific, military, UFO and police reports internationally for reports of incidents that would match what our team has undergone."

"And…?"

"And so far we've accumulated several hundred likely events occurring over the past twelve months. We're applying sophisticated data mining techniques to seek out matches and correlations. There's something there, all right."

"Any insight into incoming traffic from these other worlds? "

"Nothing conclusive. If the animals in those other worlds look like us and come here, it'll be damned hard to sort them out. There have been no sightings of *Homo Sapiens* that we can confirm. Personal opinion: it's just a matter of time."

"I was afraid you were going to say that."

The Development of Civilization Volume 3 Part 3

Spirits and Other Forms of Liquid Refreshment
(From "An Introduction to Faunapology" by Octavius Bear PhD.)

There seems to be general agreement that the first examples of intoxicating liquids imbied on earth were probably the result of accidental fermentation of fruits or grains placed in storage or stumbled upon (literally) out in the elements. There are faunapological records of digs uncovering gourds, baskets and other containers with trace elements of wine and ale-like substances probably from early settlements of Homo Sapiens before the Big Shock. There is no reason to suppose that other species both pre and post Big Shock did not also have some access to inebriating spirits. There are recorded instances of entire herds of gnus and gazelles weaving drunkenly after consuming fallen fruits that had fermented.

After the Big Shock, an increasing number of animals slowly but resolutely turned toward the purposeful creation of alcoholic liquids, and the arts and sciences of grain distillation, wine-making and brewing began to mature along with their end products. Certain other forms of inebriating and hallucinogenic substances were also discovered or developed.

Early studies suggested that there were strong religious ceremonial ties to consumption of spirits. (Hence the name?) Communing with and / or being taken possession of, by whatever deities the tribes or herds or sects worshipped, was facilitated by ingesting sacred and no doubt narcotic substances. The enhancement of courage before battle; recovery from strain, wounds or trauma; enhancement of mating processes; rejoicing at good fortune! All these and more provided ample cause and opportunity for the use of such psychic boosters.

Today, of course, these traditions are still carried on but many years ago another element was added to the motivational mix: connoisseurship - perfection of the product and corresponding appreciation by experts. Raised in some animals' minds as a highly refined craft, if not a true art form, the development of high quality vintage alcoholic beverages has all the respectability of the creation of gems, fine instruments and other highly valued art objects.

I personally have aspired, over the years, to develop the very finest elixirs from that culinary obsession of all bears: honey. Little do the industrious bees realize how ambrosial their product becomes when it is transformed into that queen of all wines: Mead.

Mead is an alcoholic beverage, made from honey and water and fermented with yeast. Its alcoholic content may range from that of ale to that of a very strong wine. It can be still, carbonated, or sparkling; dry, semi-sweet, or sweet. I prefer still, semi-sweet. The brewer may combine it with spices, fruits, or grain mash. It has been known and enjoyed for centuries throughout Europe, Africa and Asia and more recently, thanks in part to my own efforts, North America.

In addition to devoting all of my few spare hours to the production of near perfect vintages of this fortified nectar, I have been engaged in an ongoing search throughout the world, to find the finest examples of the meadery's output. I have succeeded in finding many honorable entries to my personal Mead Hall of Fame, but the search is not complete. I persist. So much to do! So little time!

Maury Meerkat

Chapter Six
Unst and Baltasound

Meerkats often are stars on TV.
But they aren't "mere cats," don't you see.
They're mongooses. (mongeese?)
Make this silliness cease.
It is all too confusing for me.

We had just about circumnavigated the island, taking in the harsh but stunning scenery; the houses, huts, crofts and other shelters used by the local fauna; pausing to talk with some of the neighborhood worthies who seemed as curious about us 'mericans as we were about them. Now we were trundling along a virtually nonexistent road that showed every sign of unceremoniously leading us over a cliff and onto the rocks and livid sea below. I was propped up on a couple of rucksacks in the shotgun seat *(left side in Scotland)* and Lepi and Otto were riding along in back with their heads popping in and out of the open windows. Unfortunately, I was on the ocean side of the SUV, and had a clear view of the long plummet we could take at any moment. As you know, bravery is not my strong suit.

Dougal, our driver and guide, was chatting away unconcerned *(both about the road and whether we understood a word he was saying.)* Everything about Dougal from his cap and pipe to his noble Sheltie profile shouted, "If you want the genuine Scots character, go to the dogs." I had fully expected our Land Rover to have a canine face painted on its hood – pardon, bonnet. But I guess the Bruins would have thrown a fit.

Thinking of Scots spirit and trying not to look too often out the window, I said, "Dougal, I seem to remember you promised us a chance to bend an elbow and raise a dram at an authentic Scottish pub. I could use a little lubrication right about now." Agreement from the back seat.

"Oh, aye. 'Tis where we're headin' now, sair. The Lion and the Unicorn. A fine piece of Shetlands history and lore, it is. Over four hundred years old and nae a thing been changed durin' the whole time. 'Ceptin, of course, they've had to refill the vats and jugs a few times, heh, heh! But, I tell a lie. They put in the electric about twenty years ago and they may have a radio to listen to the rugby matches. Aw, 'tis a grand place. Ye'd travel a lang way and ye'd no fin the brither o't in many a lang day." *(Rough translation, this place was unique!)*

We came over the top of a roller coaster hill and were suddenly staring down at a small fishing village straight out of a brochure: 'Visit Bonnie Scotland – The Tour of Your Lifetime.' I crossed my claws as Dougal switched into the lowest gear and rode the brakes down the steep incline. As we descended, we met a group of sheep and goats picking their way down the slope on our right. They waved and bleated at Dougal as we passed.

"That's the Ladies' Bingo Club on their way to th' afternoon social in the village," he said. "It sometimes gets a wee raucous when the stakes git high enow. Quite a sight and sound."

Baltasound village was a bit more than a mile square; mostly waterfront with a few fishing boats and other small craft tied up. A ferry slip, currently unoccupied, dominated a short breakwater and pier. A wee kirk and scatterings of cottages, shops and homes made up the remainder of the community. A small airport rounded out the civic features. Not quite! There is also a bus stop, fitted out with a TV, seats, wall and window furnishings that change with the seasons. Called Bobby's Bus Shelter, it was the result of a six year old's complaint about a plan to remove the school bus stop. The letter hit home and the stop was restored and then glorified into the current opulent structure. Only in Unst.

A few off-road vehicles were distributed around the streets. At the "four corners" of the village sat the police station, post office and town hall all in one thatched roof building. A petrol station was opposite. A general store occupied third base and at home plate was our destination. Dougal had not exaggerated. A great stone pile two stories high with small windows and blue and white shutters. It was actually three connected buildings all under a layer of thatch. It looked liked the combined willpower of the occupants was the only thing keeping the roof from sagging to street level. An adjacent car park was fuller than I would have expected at this time in the afternoon.

We piled out of the lorry and strolled along the cobbled street leading to the pub. Movie producers around the world would kill to capture the unself-conscious authenticity of the little town. I had visions of Bearbi and her crew crawling all over the cottages, cemeteries, kirk, shoppes and of course, the watering hole. A large, ornate, three dimensional sign mounted on a free-standing pole proclaimed that indeed, we had reached The Lion and the Unicorn. The sign's heraldry was straight out of 'Tales of the Noble Highlanders' and the two sculpted animals, rearing erect, no doubt recently repainted, faced off against each other across an elaborate shield capped off with a crown. My vexillary skills are very limited but I think I was looking at a reproduction of the Great Seal of Scotland.

Suddenly, there was a roar from within the pub and the door slammed open, followed by two North Sea seals barreling out as fast as they could.

"And don't come back in here with that balancin' ball act again. Ye broke half ma glassware, ye twits." This, no doubt, from the bartender or proprietor who was gifted with a very impressive and stentorian voice. The two seals, rolling over and over hysterically, barking and guffawing, waddled down to the dock.

"Those two are the village clowns." said Dougal. Then looking at Otto. "We have a few sea otters who also supply some merriment."

"Add one more to the crowd," I mumbled, as we went through the door into a large, noisy and smoky room that stretched through two of the three connected buildings. The other section may have been a kitchen or a 'ladies lounge.' There were stairs going to the second floor – transient rooms possibly. The walls were festooned with Union Jacks, St. Andrew's Cross flags and a large number of regimental drums.

As far as I could tell, the room seemed to be filled entirely with males but with some species, it's hard to be sure at a distance *(or even close up)*. A few dogs, badgers and a ram or two were standing in an alcove playing darts. Seated or standing at a number of the tables were groups of wildcats, staring into their drinks, arguing and looking not at all happy. I nodded at Lepi. Something for him to investigate, but first...libation time. I turned to the bar which ran the length of the room and stopped dead in my tracks.

Standing behind the ale and beer taps below a full-size portrait of the Prince of Whales was a real live, honest to God unicorn *(or a horse doing a hell of a makeup job)* and a bit further down the bar, putting a stack of glassware back on the mirrored shelves, was a very regal and currently very annoyed lion.

We moved over to the bar and Dougal did the introductions. It seems the unicorn was called Unicorn and oddly enough the lion, who had come over to us while wiping his paws on a bar rag, was called Lion. They welcomed Dougal who was no doubt, a regular. They seemed to have no trouble recognizing Lepi as a new but passable type of cat and Otto, a river otter, was close enough to the local variety not to cause any concern. I, on the other hand, was a whole new experience, especially to Unicorn.

"Maury Mere-Cat, I see the mere for ye're a wee bit of a fella but I dinna ken the 'cat' part. Ye look like nae cat I've ever met. Not at all like them fellas sittin' an standin' over there *(gesturing to the wildcats.)* or yer frien' here."

"No, it's Meerkat – m-e-e-r-k-a-t – I think the name is Afrikaans. I'm American, but I'm originally from Africa by way of a few other places. Actually we have no relationship to cats at all. We're sort of like a mongoose."

"Now, Mr. Mere-Cat, you tryin' to tak a rise out o me? I know for sartain that no goose looks like you. Where are your wings? Never seen a goose like you."

"Well, I've never seen a unicorn before and I've traveled a good bit. Didn't even know you were real."

"Och, I am indeed, but there aren't many of us, ye ken. Why don't we just agree we both exist and have a wee dram to seal the bargain. What'll ye have??"

I figured, "What the hell! Let's go for broke." I asked, "You wouldn't have a drop of fermented coconut milk VSOP in the house?"

The lion roared in laughter. *(Scary!)* "Fermented coconut milk VSOP, is it? Well, Mr. Goose, it so happens when I left Africa during the Great War, my uncle gave me a case of different liquors to remember the auld sod by. The only bottle left is some fermented coconut milk. I'm not sure it's VSOP but ye're welcome to try it. I've been tempted to throw it away a hundred times. No one here will touch the stuff."

He trotted into a back room and after a small symphony of crashing boxes and tinkling glassware, he emerged, blowing the dust off a bottle and onto everything and everyone else within range. I haven't had much opportunity to smell lion breath up close but if his was a good example, I don't recommend it.

He had a little trouble uncorking the bottle and I was afraid he was simply going to smash the neck on the bar. The cork finally gave and he poured a healthy swig into a bowl for me. I lapped at it. It wasn't bad. Coconut milk doesn't age all that well but it was more than drinkable. Otto had no trouble getting a kelp juice and vodka since there was a fair size otter population among the inn's clientele. Lepi decided for a wee dram of single malt as did Dougal.

Otto was looking around goggle eyed and when he got his drink, he decided he would join a few of his ocean going brethren. Dougal padded over with him to do the introductions.

Lepi stayed with me for the moment. We needed a little more information on all those wildcats. "Business seems to be booming, Mr. Lion." he said.

"Och, just Lion, if yez please. We're a first name crew here."

"OK, I'm Lepi and Mr. Kat here (ha, ha) is Maury."

"Lepi and Maury it is" he said looking at the unicorn who nodded his head and almost stabbed me with his horn.

"Weeeel. Actually, this is the kind of business we'd prefer not to have. All them cats have just been laid off from the rigs. It's a strange tale. All sorts of happenins that are out of thoct out there. Fires! Explosions! They've had to shut down five rigs for repairs and other problems."

"What kind of other problems?"

"Crew gone missin'. Communications interrupted. GPS gone astray."

"What do you mean, GPS gone astray?"

"Weel, accordin' to the GPS boffins, the rigs ain't showin' up where they should be. Now, you and I ken ya nae can move a million tons of steel and concrete like a wee bairn's toy. Those 'lectronics are prob'ly getting spooked. But some of these wildcats are pretty sooperstishus and they don't want to ga back out there until this is cleared up.

(Yes, the thought of teleportation did cross my overly active imagination. Otto could move a fair sized hydroplane but a full sized, well anchored oil rig? It would probably take a small army of telekinetic otters to even try. But I'd love to see it. Didn't sound likely to me.)

"Sounds like large scale sabotage to me.' I said. I turned to Lepi. "Maybe we should get Octavius down here. Let's go talk to the cats. But before we do. What's business like when these cats are not congregating here?"

Unicorn chimed in, "We could do with a few more customers. When the castle was a hotel, we got all the tourists comin' in fer a dram or two and a bit of local color. Lion and I used to put on our famous fight fer them. Now that those Bruins changed the old pile into their "bearonial estate," we don't see anyone from up there. Bunch of hopped up stiffs! Not a real noble in the lot. The Bearoness and her girl friends come down when they're in town. They're a bonnie, fun group but that only happens once or twice a year."

"I'm sorry. I guess news of your famous fight never reached America or at least Cincinnati, where I live."

"Have ye never heard the old nursery rhyme? It's been around for hundreds of years."

"I'm afraid my tender years were misspent. My mom never read me nursery rhymes."

The two of them stood together and the rest of the room all pushed back their seats and shouted/sang out in a massive and somewhat boozy chorus:

"The Lion and the Unicorn
Were fighting for the crown.
The Lion beat the Unicorn
All about the town.
Some gave them white bread
And some gave them brown;
Some gave them plum cake
And drummed them out of town!"

Loud shouts, applause and cheers as the two principals bowed to their audience.

"Who won?" Lepi asked.

"I did," they both said.

"What does it mean?"

"Damned if we know. Some smart boots around here think it has to do with Scotland and England comin' together but we were nae part of that parade."

"So you re-enact the fight for the tourists?"

"Complete with everyone drummin.' On special occasions, like our birthdays and such. It always comes out in a tie and we provide ale and whiskey and mead along with the brown and white bread. We dinna hae any plum cake anymore. Too sticky."

Several ideas struck my fervid brain. Theatrical Agent Maury in action. "You did say 'mead' didn't you?"

"Aye, the finest in the kingdom – the world even."

"Well, I work for a Kodiak Bear named Octavius who is absolutely the world's greatest connoisseur of mead. He makes it himself back in the States. I'd like him to come down here to meet you gentlebeasts and to taste your wares. *(I also wanted him to get a first hand hearing of the wild stuff that seemed to be happening on the oil rigs. The wildcats were our next destination.)* And on top of that, we have another guest, Dame Bearbara Da Savile-Row. She's the editor of the female bear's magazine - *Sow*. She's a bit strange but if we play this right, we can get you and the Inn some great pub-licity. Right now, she's doing a photo shoot of the horses of Scotland. I'm sure she'd make you the feature star, Unicorn, if you're of a mind."

"Och, I'm nae a horse, ye ken. I got a horse's head and body but I've got the tail and mane of a lion. Look at the two of us. Almost the same. The horn's all mine except some fish called a narwhal has one like it and my hooves are like deer's. I'm a unique animal."

"All the more reason to get you in the magazine. Most beasts don't even think you exist. Imagine the crowds coming up here to see you both and to watch you stage the fight."

"And buy our ale, mead and whiskey!!" said Lion.

"Exactly and I'm not forgetting you, Lion. Dame Bearbara has a brand new magazine about cats, coming out and her editor is coming up here tonight. She's an old "friend." I imagine we could get you two coverage in both magazines. Who knows? Maybe even centerfolds."

"Well now, we dinna want to do nothing undignified." rumbled Lion.

"Of, course not, everything in the best of Highland taste," I said. 'Do you have a phone so I can call ahead to you after I talk with them."

The unicorn looked around stealthily and said, "We do but we keep it hidden. We nae want to give the appearance of being too modern, ya ken!"

"I understand. I'll give you the number up at the castle and you can call me tomorrow and we'll see if we can arrange a trip down here for my friends. You'll have all sorts of tourists coming up here again in no time if we can pull this off."

"And what do you get out of this, my little friend?" said Lion, a skeptical beast, no doubt.

"Nothing from you, except the rest of that flagon of coconut milk and some mead to take back to my friend, the Bear, but the two grateful magazine publishers will be helping me with another client of mine, that otter you see over there. He's a great showman and I'm his agent. They could make his career *(and mine!)* Now Lepi and I want to go talk to the wildcats. Would you mind introducing us?"

Otto and Dougal saw us heading over to the wildcats and decided to join us. Lion introduced us as coming over from America and being guests of the Bearoness. They were especially interested in Lepi. Most of them had never seen a Himalayan Snow Leopard before. If there was a leader of the group, it seemed to be an older and scarred wildcat named Fergus.

Pawshakes all around at the main table. Several other tables looked over in half interest and then went back to their drinks, dozing or arguing. I counted about thirty wildcats in all.

"Fergus, Lion was telling us about some of the things you guys are going through out at the rigs. We don't get much news up at the castle, unfortunately."

"Things we wuz goin' through, yer mean. We've all be laid off till they get the stations pumpin' agin. And that looks like a long time."

"Who's investigating it?"

" Och, there's all sorts of police, military and regulator johnnies runnin' around but they nae seem to be findin' much. Shetland Yard is leadin' the investigatin'. Too many happenins to be coincidinks, I say. There's a plot against the Scottish oil companies."

"All the rigs affected are Scottish?"

"Aye, it looks like someone is trying to wipe out the livelihoods of all us wildcats."

"I work with an international detective who has quite a few successful cases to his credit. He's here at the castle. His name is Octavius Bear – he's a largish Kodiak – from Alaska originally. He knows just about every important law enforcement animal in the business. He's probably on a first-name basis with whomever is running the investigation. I know he'd be very interested in helping any way he can. At no charge, of course. I plan on bringing him down here tomorrow anyway. He's nuts about mead and Lion here claims he stocks the best mead in the world."

"That he does, if you're likin' mead. Too sweet for me but if your friend likes mead, this the place. Aye, we'll be happy to talk wi' him. We're nae getting' anythin' done here, sittin and mopin."

I turned to Lion and said, "I'll talk with you tomorrow. Hopefully we'll have a chance to get you and your inn some real promotion, as well as sell some mead and whiskey and maybe even help these wildcats."

Unicorn nodded to us as we made our way back out to the Land Rover. Otto was telling us about the sea otters and how they planned to meet for some fun and games tomorrow in the ocean. They didn't know about his "extraordinary abilities" but if he could get his adrenaline up, he could test out some of his stunts on them. We'll have to make sure they don't pull any of them off inside the pub.

We finally arrived back at the castle. The return ride was even more fur-raising than the trip out. This time, I was facing away from the sea so I could keep my stomach under control. The fermented coconut milk wasn't helping..

Speaking of which, it was just getting on to cocktail time and we needed to "freshen up" a bit, but before we did, a little sociability seemed in order. Otto needed to get upstairs so he could get going on his snoop work. But neither Ursula nor Alistair were down yet. Nor were Albearta or Ethelbeart. Bearyl and Bearnice were chatting with Octavius and Bel. Hamish was serving Roary with what looked like his second or third martini and Bruinhilde was sitting at the piano trying to pick out a tune with her highly polished claws. She jumped up at the sight of Lepi and began to sidle over in his direction.

As we walked into the library to greet everyone, one of the (D,H,M,P)ollies came running up to Belinda breathless and bleating. "Please mu'um, come quickly. It's Mr. Alistair. He's afloat in the moat."

Bel snorted, "Why can't that idiot swim in the pool or the ocean like everyone else. That moat hasn't been cleaned in years. Is he drunk?"

"No mu'um, he's face down. I think he's dead."

Chapter Seven
Bearmoral Castle

They're a strange but quite winsome quartet
Just a wooly and bleating matched set.
Were they separately grown?
Or is each one a clone?
They're the same as you're likely to get.

A new world's speed record – zero to pandemonium in three seconds flat. Aunt Albearta had chosen that moment to make an entrance and hearing the maid, swooned at the library door – with a substantial thud. Bruinhilde ran to her grandmother, all the while sobbing and screaming herself. The other three (D,H,M,P)ollies came running into the room and joined their partner in bleating, wringing their hooves and running around in circles. Bearyl ran off for some smelling salts for the old sow, and the rest of us headed for the front door and over the drawbridge.

About thirty feet from the bridge, floating face down and spread-eagled, was what certainly looked like Alistair from the rear wrapped in the sharp checkered jacket. He was in about four feet of water. Otto jumped in, swam up to the body and went under it. He came back up and said, "No heartbeat, no breathing!"

"Don't move or touch him, Otto. We'll have to call the police." called Octavius. He nodded at Bearyl who had just emerged. She ran back inside to make the call.

Octavius looked up. The body was floating at the foot of the castle's sixty foot walls. Part of the coping on top of the wall had broken away and was probably at the bottom of the water.

"It looks like he fell," said the Bearoness. "No surprise. He was always half-drunk but what was he doing up there on the roof?"

"Sightseeing?" said Otto.

"He might have been meeting someone." said Lepi.

"And he might have been pushed," I said.

Belinda looked at me and frowned, "Let's not jump to any conclusions, shall we? It's going to take the village police a while to get here. Hamish, call Dougal and see what you can do about covering the body without disturbing it. Has anyone seen Ursula or Ethelbeart?"

"I saw Ethelbeart snoring away in an arm chair when we left the room. Even Aunt Albearta's attack of the vapors and Bruinhilde's screeching couldn't wake him up. I wish I could sleep like that." This from Guess-Who.

Choking back at least seven or eight zingers all aimed at Octavius, I turned to Otto and said, "Now, it's even more important that we get the lowdown on their rooms. As soon as Ursula makes an appearance, if she does, excuse yourself to go dry off. God knows what was in that moat, but you better get it off you quickly. Then go on your scouting mission."

Octavius agreed with me and nodded at Otto. Then I looked at him and said, "I'm going up on that roof." Since a 1400 pound, nine foot Kodiak wandering around castle battlements didn't sound too practical, I had jumped into my aide-de-camp and field manager roles.

He said, "Good! Bel and I will restore order and wait for the constable."

Lots of luck! I could still hear Bruinhilde screeching through the open door. Bearyl came back out and announced that the constable and the doctor who was also the local medical examiner were on their way. They had also called down to Abeardeen to have an accident (or crime scene) investigation team fly up. Given it was Bearmoral Castle, they'd probably respond pretty quickly.

I was just about to go off on my architectural scouting trip when a Range Rover came screeching up to the front entrance. Dame Bearbara, along with two members of her crew was back from her day of shooting horses. Never one to leave a crowd unexplored, she trundled over. Somewhere along the way she had lost her derby and riding crop, but the rest of the equestrienne outfit was still pretty much intact.

"I say, Belinda, what's the excitement? Is there something there in the moat? OOOOOH!! Is that Alistair? Is he......? Clarence, bring over the cameras. Quickly!"

"No, Clarence, don't bring over the cameras!" roared Belinda. "Bearbi, I know you see everything in 30 point headlines, but this one is going to remain our own little secret, at least until the police have issued an official report. Then you can have your little scoop if there is one to be had. Now, I don't think I have to go through a litany as to whose property this is and who are the guests and who aren't. Do I make myself clear?"

Bearbi blinked and was obviously taken aback, but only for a few milliseconds. She crowded past us and watched Hamish and Dougal rig a tarp over the body.

"I say. That really is the pater, isn't it?" Roary had seen fit to amble out of the castle, glass still in paw and peered over the side of the moat. "I'm no expert, mind, but I'd venture a guess he's a goner."

So much for filial concern and stating the obvious. Too bad I was so small. I had a distinct urge to push him into the moat. I looked for Otto but he was on his way back into the castle. He could have certainly given Roary a flip into the flotsam with his telekinetics. Maybe later.

"Where's Ursula, Roary?" asked Belinda?

"Haven't the foggiest, dear lady."

"Well, how about you or Bruinhilde finding her, if you can get your sister to shut up for a few minutes."

Roary looked none too pleased at the 'take-charge' Bearoness but nodding his head flippantly, he padded back into the castle.

Belinda looked at Octavius and asked, "What do you think?"

"I think I'm suspicious. That's what I think. See what you can find, Maury."

Hamish was just climbing out of the moat. He was wearing waders and a fisherman's apron. I asked him how to get up to the roof and he turned to Dougal who was also emerging, soaking wet, and told him to accompany me up to the top. Dougal walked a few feet away to shake himself off and then padded back and signed for me to follow him.

"Just show me the way, Dougal. You look and smell like you could stand a quick bath."

"Aye, sair, 'twould be a grand thing. That moat is a foul place. Weel, ya just take the elevator to the top floor and go to the emergency stairs. One flight up and you're at the roof. Here, take this key. The door is always locked."

"So how do you suppose Alistair got up there?"

"Och, he may have had a key, sair. No tellin' what he might have had!" With that the dog headed off for his cottage at the end of the driveway.

Well, no love lost on Alistair in the gameskeeper department. I doubt if he was well liked by anyone but that wouldn't justify pushing him off the battlement. I know, I know! *If he was pushed.*

I made my upward pilgrimage and found the door to the roof was locked. No big surprise, the lock was set on automatic. The key worked and after scrabbling up a few stairs, I came out on the flat roof which was a landscape unto itself. Six towers or battlements – one on each corner and two larger ones set in the middle of the front and rear walls – each standing an additional twenty feet high. There were also little parapets spaced between them. In the center was a large utility area with a water tower, air conditioning compressors and electrical distribution racks. Each battlement and parapet had an access door. As I made my tour, I discovered they were all locked with electronic combination locks. As Octavius would say: "Hmmmmm!" Not something you'd expect on top of a pseudo-ancient castle. A flagpole stood in the center on a platform, no doubt for the piper and associates to perform their daily raising, lowering and wailing.

I walked over to the area where the wall had broken away. The fortification stood about three feet high at the point of breakage and was built of stones, mortared in place. They looked a bit weathered and worse for wear. Obviously polar bears are not much on building maintenance. I'm not all that strong but I could push one or two of them back and forth in their slots. Accidents waiting to happen or a great place for a deliberate defenestration. Sorry, when it comes to strange events, I always think the worst.

I looked over the side *(gingerly)* and waved at Octavius. He wasn't paying attention because the constable's lorry was just making its way into the parking lot. He and the Bearoness padded over as two figures got out. From six stories up, it was tough to make out features but one was a badger in a uniform, *(the constable)* and the other was a red deer *(the doctor??)* I wanted to be down there for the discussion so I took one more cursory scan of the scene. The dirt had been disturbed around the hole in the wall. Looked like Alistair had fallen down first and then went over the side – assisted or unassisted.

I got back down to the scene in time to join the conversation. Octavius introduced me and I told the constable, Sergeant Popper, what I'd seen up on the roof. I told the badger I hadn't disturbed anything, but he looked at me a wee bit askance. "Do any of ye ken why he woulda been on the roof, anyway?"

Belinda answered, "That's what we've been trying to figure out. Oh, at last!"

She had turned and spied Ursula coming out of the castle with Bruinhilde and Roary. Ursula, in full pre-dinner regalia, tottered over to the edge of the moat, stared at the body, turned around and growled, "Who did this to my Alistair? They will pay…dearly!"

Meanwhile Hamish and several of the gardeners were pulling Alistair's corpse out of the water and stretching him out next to the moat's retaining wall. The red deer, Dr. Livingstone, started examining him, especially around the neck and head.

The constable called over. "Anything tha signifies, Doctor?"

"Now, I canna be sure, mind, but I'm pretty sartain he was hit on the back of the head before he fell over the edge. He didn't drown as far as I can see. I think the impact broke his neck and few other things. Yer have a crime scene bunch comin' up from Abeardeen?"

"Aye, and a detective from Shetland Yard. They're comin' by helicopter."

"Well, I'd say we ought to wait until they arrive afore doin' anythin' else. Of course, you'll want an autopsy and a coroner's inquest. This doesna luik like any accident ta me."

Belinda called Hamish over and said "I guess we had better make dinner an optional event. Tell Mrs. McRadish to set out a buffet in some chafing dishes and we'll let everyone pick up food, if and when they want. She turned to the multitude by the moat and said, "I imagine some of you may not feel much like eating, but while we wait for the Abeardeen police to arrive, I'm having a buffet set out for you. It goes without saying that drinks are available for the asking. Doctor and Sergeant, please join us inside when you wish. We are at your disposal."

From the other side of the castle came the sound of helicopter rotors. Extraordinarily loud. We looked up as an official looking heavy weight chopper swung into view followed by another craft still a good distance off. Wow, talk about overkill. The first copter descended in the parking lot and a group of uniformed animals started piling out and opening hatches to pull out equipment. A bearded collie carrying a briefcase approached while the others were getting their act together.

71

The badger walked forward and saluted. "Sergeant Popper and Doctor Livingstone, sair. We arrived about half an hour ago. The body was face down in the moat. After examinin' the area, we pulled him out and he's lying by that wall over there. The victim is a member of the Bruin clan. Alistair Bruin. From the nature of the wounds and the circumstances, we suspect foul play although an accident is nae out of the question."

The collie detective said, "Thank you sergeant. *(British Midlands accent)* I'm Detective Superintendent Wardlaw. My crime scene team needs someplace to set up."

Belinda introduced herself and offered to set up the team in any of the available rooms in the castle. There were forty or fifty free, including a ballroom or two.

Wardlaw was about to respond when he suddenly looked aside and saw Octavius. His eyebrows, ears and tail rose as he looked at the imposing Kodiak and said, "Well, Doctor Bear, I hardly expected to meet you again, especially here in the Shetlands, much less at another crime scene."

Octavius nodded, "Good afternoon, Superintendent. I guess we should share some banalities about how small the world is."

Sergeant Popper's mouth gaped open. The Super said, "Aye sergeant, Doctor Bear and I know each other from way back. Friendly rivals, you might say. And I remember you too, Mr. Meerkat. Is Inspector Wallaroo here with you?"

(Readers of previous Octavius books know only too well who Inspector Bruce Wallaroo is. An Australian ace detective who has worked on and off with Octavius and me for the past several years. We've been around the world on a number of startling cases. To our knowledge, Bruce was currently taking some R and R back in Sydney after being with us as part of a strenuous "caper" in South America and the U.S. that only wound up a week ago.)

"No, I'm afraid my marsupial friend will be bounding around the Outback for the next several weeks. Taking a little vacation."

Belinda did the rest of the introductions. Ursula started to deliver a tirade about bringing the murderer to justice and Wardlaw said, "Now, Mrs. Bruin, we first must determine if it was murder."

"Vot else coot it be? Alistair hated heights. He vouldn't go up there unless he vas forced to." Her accent was getting heavier as she got more excited. I wondered if she was really distraught or was she making a bid for next year's Academy Award – best devastated wife in a grisly *(I know, I know!)* murder. Was she just getting dressed while all this was going on, or was she up taking the air on the roof while helping Alistair take the short way down to dinner? Didn't like that sow one bit.

While all this was going on, the second helicopter had settled down on the opposite side of the parking lot. This one had the Bruin Heraldry on it. I didn't realize anyone had gone off earlier. I looked closer. Bearnice was at the controls. The passenger door opened and Bearbi let out a shriek, "Daahhling! Do hurry. We're having ever so much excitement. Come, come, come, quickly, quickly!"

A beautifully dressed feline sidled out of the compartment and crossed under the still whirling rotor without mussing a hair or hem. A diamond collar glistened around her neck. She looked at Octavius, Belinda and me, winked and then said, "Hello Bearbi. Yes I know! Excitement just seems to follow me around."

Chita had arrived!

Chita

Chapter Eight
Bearmoral, Yet Again

Is there really a Cheetah called Cyd?
If there is, where has this sister hid?
She's a dancer, they say
With a distracting way.
Does she cover for things Chita did?

Hail, Hail, the gang's all here. The castle was well on its way back to becoming a hotel again. Arrivals by the hour! Bearbi, after gushing over Chita, did a round of introductions. We all played dumb.

"So nice to meet you. Did you have a good journey? Are you up from Edinbeargh or London? *(London!)* How long will you be staying? *(Four or five days!)* Yes, I'm afraid we had a bit of tragedy here. Alistair fell from the roof. We're not sure of the cause. The police are here. *(Chita didn't look too happy about that.)* I'm afraid dinner is going to be sort of a catch as catch can affair. If you're hungry we can have the cook set something out for you now *(Later, thanks. I'll just go to my room!)* Perhaps a drink after you settle in?"

We left the police and medical examiner to do their thing and went back into the castle. I felt a sudden urge for a fermented coconut milk VSOP. Chita, accompanied by Hamish, one of the *(D,H,M,P)*ollies and Dougal, all with her luggage in paw and hoof, strutted off to the elevator and her room. I looked around for Otto. No otter. I walked over to the Bear.

"I'd like you to come with me tomorrow to the local pub."

"I appreciate your desire to socialize, Maury, but with all the things going on here, especially with the police, pub hopping is not very high on my agenda."

"Actually, there are several reasons for you to change your priorities. First, I am told they serve the finest mead in the universe. *(This got his attention.)* Second, it's run by a real live honest-to-god unicorn and a very interesting lion. Third, there's a group of laid off oil wildcats who may be able to tell us what's going on out at those rigs. Finally, I have a funny feeling in my whiskers that this castle has something to do with all the problems they've been having, and that includes the late and possibly lamented Alistair."

"There are times, Meerkat, when you can very persuasive." *(The mead did it.)* "Let me speak with the Superintendent and Bel, and we'll see what time would be good for a jaunt. Are you sure the wildcats will be there?"

"Oh yeah! I told them about you and they're eager to talk with you."

"Sometimes you presume too much."

"I knew if nothing else got you, the mead would." I ducked a swooping paw that would have tossed me across the room.

A somewhat woozy Sir Ethelbeart made his tottering appearance. "I say! What's all the commotion. A fellow can't take a wee kip without some johnny rattling him all up. Where's Albearta? Where's Alistair? Where's Belinda? Who are those animals in uniform? I need a drink."

That, dear reader, was the longest continuous stream of verbiage I had heard from the noble knight since I met him. At that moment, Superintendent Wardlaw came out of the library where they had set up their crime scene unit and said, "Sir Ethelbeart, I'm Superintendent Wardlaw of Shetland Yard."

"Shetland Yard? Never did have much truck with you police johnnies. Belinda keeps inviting the oddest people. Yesterday there was this 20 foot tall bear. What brings you here?"

"I gather no one has informed you, sir. It's your son Alistair. He had a fall from the top of the castle into the moat.'

"The boy always was clumsy. Well, a good job he fell in the moat. If he hit the ground he might have been hurt. Told him to go easy on the drink! *(Nothing like a little paternal moral guidance from a sot!)* Where is he? I'll tell him myself."

"I'm afraid he's dead, sir. My deepest condolences."

Octavius and I both nodded agreement.

"Dead? Ridiculous. He had the constitution of a…a bear! Couldn't be dead! Where's Albearta?'

"She's up in her room resting. Your granddaughter is with her."

"Well, where's my no-good grandson? And why is Shetland Yard here? Can't the local constable handle an accident? What are my taxes goin' for?"

"I'm afraid all indications are that Alistair was struck and then pushed over the side. We believe it's a case of murder."

"Murder?? Never had a murder in our family. Well, there was the attempted assassination of the old duke but someone was always having that on. Old bastard deserved it. Died a natural death in the end. Pity!"

"I wonder if I might have a word, sir. I've spoken with your grandson and daughter-in-law and I'll need to speak with Lady Albearta and your granddaughter when they're up to it."

"You'd do better to question those American johnnies. Didn't like the looks of them from the moment they arrived. This bear here and that little fellow – African. Never trust an African."

"Doctor Bear and his colleague, Mr. Meerkat, are well known to us at the Yard. They have assisted us in several cases in the past."

"Hmph, well, what about that strange looking spotted cat, the one who sings? Never heard of a singing cat! A yowling cat, but never a singing cat!'

"We plan to interview everyone who was here at the time of the crime. We believe it took place while Mr. Leperello was off on a trip to the village with Mr. Meerkat and Mr. Otto, but we shall verify the time lines when the medical examiner determines the time of death. In the meantime, I'd like to speak with you about your son and his lifestyle, occupation, his habits and friends. Will you join me back in the library?"

Dog and polar bear trotted and waddled respectively, off to the library, Ethelbeart grumbling the whole while. I turned to Octavius and Belinda who had remained silent throughout Ethelbeart's soliloquy and asked, "Has anyone seen Otto? Ursula may be going back up to her room after her interview with the superintendent. It could get embarrassing."

Speak of the devil or at least the death matron. Ursula rumbled past on her way to the elevator without as much as a nod in our direction. Bel called to her. "Ursula, I am so sorry. Is there anything I can do to help?"

She paused and I thought she was going to unleash another tirade about revenge, but instead she said, "Perhaps you could get Bruinhilde and Albearta over their fits of hysterics. They set each other off. I cannot control either one. No self discipline. They should be ashamed. This is not a proper way for a polar bear to behave. I cannot stand to hear them."

Belinda grabbed the opportunity. "Why don't you stay down here, Ursula? Have a glass of schnapps and relax. I'll go see what I can do to calm them down." She looked over at me and mouthed "Where's Otto?" I shrugged back.

Like clockwork, down the stairs came our lutrine friend dressed in his tweed jacket. One of the maids must have shortened the sleeves for him. He didn't look bad.

"Hello, everyone! Boy, it feels good to be clean and dry again. No disrespect, Bearoness, but that moat could use a serious draining." He winked.

Belinda said she would go and see what she could do about the sobbing twosome, Leaving Ursula to her schnapps, Otto, Octavius and I headed off to one of the side reception rooms where we could be alone.

"Well?" we chorused.

"Well" said Otto, "Not much to report. No suspicious looking items in the rooms. No weapons. No files. No briefcases. Not even much in the way of clothes. It's as if they just use the rooms as stopovers. HOWEVER, one thing did get my attention. A closet in Alistair's room had a pull down staircase that led up to the roof. I figured I'd check with you, Maury, before I went up there. I wasn't sure how long I had before someone showed up."

I said, "That roof is very strange. Each one of the parapets and battlements has a complex electronic lock on its door. I don't know whether there's one coded combination for them all or if each one is different. I couldn't get any of them to open. Where's Howard when you need him? *(Howard Watt, our porcupine tech whiz had a major gift for code breaking. Unfortunately, he was thousands of miles away in the Bear's Lair.)* I suppose they could be storing the family valuables or something else up there. Maybe some holdover bits and pieces from the castle's hotel days! Or maybe a cache of more sinister stuff. Alistair could have been in one of those rooms for whatever reason before he took his belly flop. Do you think we should talk to Bel about it? It could be innocent or it could be…I don't know."

"We should definitely investigate the roof and the towers," said Octavius. "I'll talk to Bel. The odds are she doesn't know much or anything about it but as you say, it could be perfectly innocent."

The three of us looked at each other and said, "Naaah!"

"Now about tomorrow! Otto, I want to bring Octavius down to the Lion and Unicorn. You come, too. In the early afternoon, same time as we went today. I want to make sure the wildcats are there. Octavius should hear first hand some of the problems and weird happenings out on the platforms and shore points that they were telling us about. I'm not sure Lepi needs to come. He may have a rehearsal with Bearnice. But as part of a cover story, I'm going to invite Dame Bearbi and Chita down along with their camera crew. Bearbi will go bonkers over Unicorn and I'm pretty sure Lion will end up in Chita's first edition, if there is a first edition."

"My," said Octavius, "you're turning into the high energy media agent, aren't you, my little friend?"

"Well, yeah, but I also want to find out what's behind Chita's trip up here and I want to keep Bearbi occupied and away from the police. She'll have this whole thing plastered across her magazine cover – all her magazine covers. *'Renowned Peer Bear Dies in Mysterious Accident – or was it Foul Play? See page 3 for all the startling details'* "

"Do you think it's safe to bring her down to the pub? Suppose she overhears some of Octavius' discussion with the cats." This from Otto.

"That's my job, Otto. Agent Maury keeping the media informed, occupied, fascinated and out of the way. What do you think, Octavius?"

"You have obviously picked up some crumbs of crime-fighter learning while sitting at my paws, Maury. I concur. Now, while you sell the big magazine feature to Chita and Bearbi, I'll go track down Bel, assuming she has stopped the polar waterworks. I want her to know what we're doing. I don't think we need to ask her to come tomorrow. We might spook the cats with too large a contingent. Then I want to have a quiet sit-down with the superintendent. We probably shouldn't involve him in our little plan just yet. Let's see what unfolds. Otto, why don't you chase up Dougal and set up some transportation for tomorrow? I can't fit into any of those SUV's. I going to need a flat bed truck – sorry, lorry."

I set out in search of Bearbi and Chita. I found them on the terrace, each with a martini in paw, chatting away or at least Bearbi was chatting. Chita seemed preoccupied. No wonder with the police in the house and Octavius as an added attraction.

"Ladies," I said, "You both look quite lovely this evening. *(Charm school did wonders for me.)* I have a proposition for both of you."

Raised eyebrows. Ah, these worldly females!

"No, a business proposition." *(More raised eyebrows, such eyebrows as there were on a polar bear and cheetah.)* Suppose I told you I have an absolutely dynamite feature that you both can use simultaneously in each of your magazines. Dual coverage – An exceptional equine extravaganza and a fabulous feline foto-op."

Chita looked at me as only Chita can and said, "Maury, you certainly have a way with words."

"Anyway, Bearbi, how would you like to lead off your next issue's feature on horses with coverage of a real live unicorn – the unicorn of the Lion and Unicorn Pub right here on this island and Chita, the lion is real too. They do a dynamite reenactment of the old nursery rhyme. You know, "The Lion and the Unicorn were fighting for the Crown.""

Bearbi squealed with delight – a sound no animal should be forced to hear. Even Chita seemed interested.

"Yes, yes, yes!" gasped the polar. "Where, when, how?" *(Obviously Bearbi had gone to journalism school.)*

"In the village, tomorrow and I'll set it up. You bring your camera crew and I guarantee you'll have a set of features like you've never run before. How's that for a boffo cover for your opening issue, Chita? The Lion and the Unicorn fighting over a crown. I think we can get Belinda to lend us one or two from the castle's museum collection."

Chita managed to look interested but just barely. *(Something strange going on here. She always plays it cool but this was almost frigid.)* "Maury, I'll take you up on it on one condition. Stop immediately with the show-biz schlock! When did you go Hollywood?"

"In addition to my extensive workload supporting Octavius, I am now Otto the Magnificent's personal theatrical agent."

I'm not sure but I think she almost choked. Give her credit. She didn't break up in front of Dame Bearbara. She did give me a look that said very clearly, "Sonny boy, we need to talk, soon."

Bearbi went running off to get Clarence and the crew and I was left with the spotted scourge of six *(seven, five?)* continents.

"OK, Chita," I said, "Why are you really here? Don't give me any stuff about renewing old friendships. You took off from the Bear's Lair like the proverbial 'cat out of hell.' We didn't expect to see you again for a long, long time - which for your sake might have been just as well. Octavius isn't on his home turf here and I don't think he has any intention of tipping off the Shetland Yard Superintendent but you are once again living on the edge."

"Are you quite finished, little buddy? Actually, I knew this was Belinda's place but I didn't expect to see the Cincinnati contingent here. Yes, I am going to edit the magazine for Bearbi. It should be a hoot. I have all sorts of connections that will pay off big time in features and spreads. This was a chance for Bearbi and me to get together away from the editorial offices. But you're right, there is something else. I'm up here in the Shetlands to protect an investment."

"What investment?"

"Oil!!!'

"North Sea Oil?! Scottish Wildcat Oil!?"

"Yeah, one of my many admirers made me a present of an oil rig a while back and it was contributing very nicely to my life style and then in just the last few months, it supposedly ran dry. I don't believe it and I thought I'd come see for myself."

"Chita, have I got a deal for you! If I didn't think Octavius would kill me, I might almost ask for a commission. At this very same pub, there are a bunch of laid off wildcats who have some very strange stories about what's been happening to their livelihood. Octavius and I are going to make a trip tomorrow to interview them. You could kill two birds with one stone."

"I already tried to kill a bird several times and see what it got me. *(cf. The Case of the Spotted Band for the thrilling episode of Chita's unsuccessful attempt on Imperius Drake's life.)* By the way, do you think Imperius is dead this time?'

"After L.Condor hit him in midair, he saw him spin into the Ohio River. He didn't see anything float back up to the top."

"I thought cats were the ones with nine lives. That duck has more than his fair share. Don't count him out. I owe him big time now. If he's alive I personally will dismember him and send pieces to all my friends. You can have the tail feathers. So what's the story with this skydiving polar bear? What's his name? Sir Alistair?"

"Right! There's something very funny about that, too."

"Well, falling off a sixty foot parapet isn't my idea of fun. Did he fall or was he pushed?"

"Neither, we believe. The best guess is he was slugged from behind and then dumped over the side. The medical examiner and the police are still theorizing. Octavius has this idea the killing may be connected to the problems on the oil rigs."

"How did he arrive at that cockeyed conclusion?"

"Why don't you ask him?"

"You know. I just might. See ya, short stuff. Let us know what time tomorrow we're going pub crawling. A fabulous feline foto-op! Ick!"

Chapter Nine
Bearmoral Castle

Collies have a strict vow they must keep.
They are charged with protecting their sheep.
They must not let them stray.
They keep watch night and day.
Collies even count sheep in their sleep!

On his way to catch up with Belinda and the bereaved bears, Octavius got sidetracked by Superintendent Wardlaw. The bearded collie gave a subtle bark to get his attention while escorting Sir Ethelbeart from the library. "I say, Doctor Bear, may I have a word?"

"Certainly, Superintendent. Are you still on duty or would you care for a drink?'

"Much as I'd like to, with the rest of the team here, I'd better forgo it. I won't take much of your time."

"Take all you want. My alternative is going up to see the Bearoness and the two grief stricken polars. Lady Albearta and Bruinhilde. Odd how Ursula, the wife isn't sharing their emotional overload, although I did hear her calling for revenge."

"She is one of those frigid personalities from the Bearents Sea. She was not very forthcoming during our interview. We've placed the time of his death at somewhere between two and four this afternoon. She says she was reading in her room. They have separate living arrangements. From what I've heard of him so far and what I see of her, they were a strange couple."

"If you're wondering what I was doing, I too, was in my room but I was sending and receiving e-mails and making phone calls. I can show you my communications logs, if you wish. Sir Ethelbeart seems to think that Maury, Otto, Lepi and I are very suspicious characters."

"That won't be necessary in your case and I understand the other three were down at the village pub with the gameskeeper and a large number of witnesses. We haven't vetted the household staff yet. I'm sorry to say this but among the family members who don't have much of an alibi, there's Sir

Ethelbeart, Lady Albearta, Dame Ursula, Bruinhilde, Roary and….the Bearoness."

"In short, all of them…and Belinda? That's preposterous!"

"I'm sorry, Doctor Bear, but you, if anyone, should know we must carefully vet every suspect no matter how unlikely. After all, it would take a rather large animal to do what was done to Sir Alistair. So all the bears in the house are under suspicion, including those two crew members of hers."

"Bearyl and Bearnice? I doubt they even knew Alistair."

"Quite the contrary. They have been in the Bearoness' employ for quite some while now, and have had ample opportunity to meet, know and form an opinion of Sir Alistair. From what I have gathered so far, he was hardly popular."

"I thought he spent much of his time away from the castle on business jaunts."

"That seems to be the case, and I have several members of my team researching his business ventures now. From what we've discovered so far, some of them were just this side of honest. The bear, no doubt, had enemies, personal and business."

"But those enemies had to have the opportunity this afternoon."

"Or have employed someone or someone(s) who had the opportunity. We're not ruling out a conspiracy here. Absurd as it might seem to you, the wild boar butler and the four sheep maids could have ganged up on him. One to hit him and all of them to drag his body over the edge. After all, it was one of them, Dolly, Holly, Molly or Polly, who conveniently discovered the body in the moat. I can't tell them apart."

"Nobody can. They're clones. Forgive me, superintendent, but I think you are straining credibility with some of your suspicions. But of course, it's your investigation, not mine."

"Well, that's what I'd like to talk to you about. You're a guest of the Bearoness and have access to knowledge about the relationships and possible bad will between the family members.

"Superintendent, you should know that the Bearoness and I had a romance earlier in our lives before she married the late Bearon and we still feel warmly toward each other. *(You don't need to know we're married!)* I will

84

hardly be an unbiased participant as far as she's concerned. But I'll be as helpful as I can. So will my associates. Have you been up on the roof yet?"

"No, but my detective sergeant has. He didn't see anything very suspicious except of course, at the point where the bear went over the wall. Several of the stones were missing and from the marks in the dirt, it looked like he may have been dragged to the edge."

"But what was he doing on the roof in the first place? His wife said he disliked heights. Many polar bears do. My associate, Maury, went up there right after the body was discovered. He was careful not to disturb the scene but he chanced upon another item that drew my interest. Care to accompany me up there? Kodiaks have no fear of heights and I assume you don't either."

"No, you can't tool around in helicopters and chase felons around the cliffs if you have acrophobia. What did he observe?"

"As usual, something or nothing. All of the battlements and parapets have large fortified doors sealed with electronic locks."

"Not unusual. After all, this castle is rather new and was once a theme park hotel. They could have stored anything up there, including the remnants of its commercial days. Electric signs, decorations, even broken down thrill rides. I can understand why they'd have them sealed up. You'll have to excuse me. I have to get the body and my team back to Abeardeen before it gets too dark. The airport has been having instrument problems lately."

"So I've heard. Yes, well, I think I and my associates will go and take a closer look at the roof, if you don't mind. Perhaps Bearoness Belinda or Hamish can confirm your opinion. We'll let you know if we find anything. Should we call you directly or through the constable?"

"Directly. The constable and doctor have already left. Here's my card. Feel free to contact me any time and any way you wish. I'll be back up here on Monday when the autopsy is completed and we have sorted through what clues my team has assembled so far. I assume none of you are planning to leave the island."

"Not for a few days at least. We'll be in touch."

The Superintendent summoned Hamish and told him to ask the Bearoness to come down to the entrance hall for a few moments. He wanted to speak to her before leaving. So did Octavius.

Belinda came down in the elevator and walked over shaking her head. "I guess I can certainly sympathize with those two, losing an only son and a father, but they have been howling non-stop for the last several hours. I asked the doctor to give them each a sedative *(I probably should have asked for a stun gun.)* They should be calming down shortly."

"Well," said the detective, "I still have to talk with both of them. But it'll have to wait. I'm due back in Abeardeen and we're taking the body with us for further examination. We'll let you and Dame Ursula know when it can be released."

Ursula, who had been in the bar under the stairs, stoking up on schnapps, heard her name and trundled out. "You're taking his body away?? Vat will you do with it?"

"We're just going to examine it more closely, Madame. We're still not sure whether the cause of death was a blow to the head or the impact of the fall."

"What does it matter? He's dead. I want you to find his killer…soon. I will want the body returned intact."

"I'm not sure we can do that, Madame. Parts of our examinations are intrusive, I'm afraid. Do you have any plans for the body's disposal? Burial? Cremation?"

"Nein. I vill turn him over to a taxidermist. I want him stuffed and displayed prominently here in the hall." She glared defiantly at Belinda.

The Bearoness, the soul of discretion simply said, 'We'll discuss it when the time comes, Ursula dear."

Ursula who was weaving from an oversupply of liqueur, snorted and waddled off to the elevator. God help Bruinhilde and Albearta if she stops in to see them. We may have more than one polar bear corpse to dispose of.

"I'm afraid I have to hold you and the members of your family and staff under suspicion, Bearoness. The only ones who are free of doubt are the foursome that went down to the village pub. I also have no suspicions as far as Doctor Bear is concerned, although *(heh, heh)* one can never be sure, can one?"

"Well, that's something new, Superintendent! I've never been a suspect in a murder before, have I, Tavi?"

"I'm afraid you're not much of a suspect now, Bel," said the Great Bear, looking askance at the collie. "But the superintendent must follow procedure."

"Quite right, quite right! Well, I shall bid you farewell until Monday. Please notify me if anything new or untoward occurs in the meantime."

As he walked out of the front door and over the drawbridge, Octavius looked at Bel and said, "Is there someplace where Maury, Otto, you and I can meet without attracting attention?"

"Let's try one of the converted conference rooms. There are seven or eight of them. Sometimes I think I ought to change this place back to a hotel again. It was doing quite well when the old gentleman decided to withdraw from 'disgusting commerce' as Aunt Albearta would have it. I think we saved most of the hospitality and theme park trappings."

"Bearoness, there you go with your ESP again. Exactly what I want to talk to you about. Let's find Maury and Otto."

"You want to join me in another joint venture, Octavius. What'll we call it? Polar Paradise? Ursine Utopia? Chill Out Central?" she started to giggle.

"No, my dear, although Maury might think it's a great idea. I want to investigate those battlements and parapets and oh, here comes the great impresario now. Maury, we'd like you to join us. "

I had wandered back in to warn Octavius that Chita would be on his tail, but it looked like I was about to participate in a séance or something – perhaps to bring back the ghost of Alistair. *(Why we'd want to bring him back was an open question.)* I saw Otto through the open door, staring down at the moat and whistled at him. He skittered over as well.

Belinda said, "Follow me! *(Mysterious!)* We wandered through a labyrinth of halls and stairways and finally came to a series of doors marked with the names of ursine movie stars – Theda Beara, John Bearymore, Lauren Bearcall, Beary Manilow......we went into the Winnie the Pooh room.

"So, what's up, Doc?" said Otto and broke into gales of laughter. Octavius didn't see the joke.

"I'm interested in what is up there in those roof towers. Bel, do you know what's in those rooms and why they have such elaborate locks?"

"Honestly, Tavi, I've never stuck my nose in there. Do you think there's a connection with Alistair's death?"

"If Maury's correct and I have no reason to doubt him, there's nothing much else that could have attracted him up there. If he was just meeting someone, there are close to a hundred places they could have used inside the castle."

"Not if whoever he was meeting didn't belong here," I piped up.

"True enough, Maury. Bel, before it gets too dark, I'd like Maury and Otto to try and get inside at least one of those battlements. Feel up to a little teleporting, Otto?"

"Sure. You two stay here. Maury and I aren't very conspicuous. In fact, let's see if I can use that stairway in Alistair's room. Provided Ursula or someone else isn't hanging around inside."

"What's our excuse if we get caught in the room, oh great schemer?' I said.

"We were looking for Belinda! We thought she was with the grieving ladies."

"Weak, but what the hell."

We took the elevator up to the family wing. We could hear snores coming from Albearta's room. More than one. I guess she and Bruinhilde finally gave in to the sedatives. As we moved down the hallway, we passed Ursula's room. We heard her mumbling but couldn't make out what she was saying. Roary and Ethelbeart were nowhere to be seen so we slipped into Alistair's room which had been left unlocked by the police. Sloppy, sloppy! It didn't really matter. Otto could have gotten in there anyway. The otter scampered across the room and waved me into a large closet that was filled with....nothing. Strange! He jumped onto a shirt shelf and boosted himself up to the ceiling where a handle embedded flush with the surface was just visible. He grabbed, twisted and pulled and ended up suspended in midair.

"I don't weigh enough to pull it down," he said.

"Well, I'm not heavy enough to make any difference."

"Let's hope my adrenaline is high enough. I'm going to go through it and then I'll let it down for you." A blur, a thump and the stair case started to descend with Otto standing on it.

"That talent of yours has all kinds of uses."

"Let's hope it never gets me killed. I never know what's on the other side when I do that."

We made our way up the stairs without difficulty. The opening was big enough for a full size polar bear but certainly not Octavius. Out on the roof, we could see the sun starting to descend behind the cliffs. Not much time for snooping.

"Which one?" said Otto.

"I don't think it matters much. We just want to do a sample this evening. We'll come back and hit them all tomorrow morning."

He skittered over to the nearest parapet and….disappeared. A few seconds later the door opened. "The inside lock is just a conventional handle. Only the outside is electronic." he said. "It looks like a bunch of old signs and banners and a couple of stuffed bears. Maybe this is where Alistair will end up. I wonder if they're all like this."

"Let's try one of the battlements. They're much bigger. Might be something more interesting in there." I said.

"OK," he agreed and headed for the large industrial size door on one of the center battlements. He stood outside for a second, disappeared and then screamed, "Maureeeee!" The sound got weaker and weaker. I pounded on the door and then I noticed that this lock was different. Next to the keypad, there were arrows pointing up and down. Otto had teleported into an elevator shaft and it sounded like the car wasn't on this floor.

"Otto, Otto!!" No response. "Oh God!" My friend and first and only client was probably a lifeless bundle of fur six stories down.

Chapter Ten
Bearmoral with Chita

The Snow Leopard's also called "Ounce."
But his presence he'll never announce.
He's quite beautiful, too.
But don't let him near you.
Without warning, he'll suddenly pounce.

(From the unpublished *Memoirs of Mlle. Catherine Catt* - aka Chita)

I was just walking away from Maury when Dame Bearbara came bounding back.

"It's all arranged. The crew will be ready to go right after lunch tomorrow. Can you believe it, Chita? An actual live unicorn and a crusty old lion. I'm going to do some video of the battle. You never know what can come of something like this. I hate to admit it but I think that Meerkat has a bright idea. Joint features to kick off your new magazine, *Purr* and hype its relationship to *Sow* and da Savile-Row publications."

"Oh, I wouldn't sell that Meerkat short. He seemed pretty smart to me." Damn, I almost gave it away that I already knew Maury. I'm going to have to be careful about all of Octavius' bunch and Belinda. No slips in front of Bearbi and her crew or the other members of the household.

"Chita, isn't the death of Sir Alistair just delicious? I mean, I don't want to be insensitive or anything but what an unexpected plus for our visit. What ever do you think happened? I tried buttering up that detective superintendent but he's something of a cold fish. Are all bearded collies like that? That huge Kodiak, Doctor Bear, seems to know him. Maybe I could persuade him to get the police to loosen up on the story, but first I have to get Belinda to come around. This trip may turn out to be more than just an opportunity to get away. It could be the making of our circulation. Morbid stories just attract readers like honey or in your case, catnip."

You have already concluded, dear reader, that the polar and I are indeed a study in extremes. Hurricane Bearbi meets the Sphinx. Yet somehow, we're friends and work well together. Go figure.

Since there was no way I was going to get away from Bearbi without rousing her suspicions, I mentally postponed my search for Octavius and plunged into a bout of editorial planning with the bubbling bear. Of course, what I really wanted to do was get down to that pub tomorrow and find out from the wildcats what was going on. My rig, The Hot Spot, had been performing beautifully and then suddenly, nothing. As far as I know, the entire drill site was still intact, if not operational but this problem, whatever it was, seemed to involve more than just my unit. Something rotten was happening and it could have been coming from Denmark or any of a number of Northern European oil developers.

I kind of like the idea that I've been getting rich and helping the Scottish wildcats at the same time. Nothing like a little species nationalism but I definitely didn't like losing money or being done to. (*Editors Note: Readers of our previous books will know that Chita has quite a temper and was prone to fierce reactions. One minute she's the detached Ms. Catt; the next, a high speed weapon of dappled destruction. Of course, her recklessness had gotten her into several near death experiences, but what the hell, live fast [0-60mph in 7 seconds], die young, make a good looking rug.)*

I was half listening to Bearbi, throwing in the occasional "Of course, darling" or "uh-hum" and even disagreeing with her once or twice to keep up the show. I have my own ideas on what *Purr* should be and how it should be published but of course, it was Bearbi's money. At least most of it. I had kicked in a token amount for a minor partnership but essentially I'm an employee – a situation I seldom enjoy. After my days with Imperius Drake, where I had money coming in from modeling, singing, directing investors to the larcenous duck and from a healthy collection of swains and admirers. *(Actually some of them weren't that healthy and that's how I got the oil rig as an inheritance.)* Then there was the recent round in Brazil and the States. Pontius Puma/Paolo as well as the Spotted Band. Nah, let's not go there! Then, the Octavius incident! Imagine a clever, self-sufficient animal like me having to be rescued from a sinking paddle boat by an otter, of all creatures. And a dopey (but loveable) otter at that. I wonder where Otto is at the moment. I wanted to chat with him and say a more acceptable thanks than I did at the Bear's Lair.

Back to The Great Bear. Much as he proclaims his dislike for me, I'm convinced that something in our mutual chemistry works. Not that I'd ever say anything to him about it. He'd vehemently deny it and go about proving it by being even more of a pain in the ass than he normally is. But…but, but!

Just then, Bearnice and Lepi came along, holding what looked like bundles of sheet music.

"Hi, Bearbi! Hello, Chita! We're looking for someplace inconspicuous where we can practice our singing. I know its bad form with a death in the house but Belinda has us lined up for the Edinbeargh Opera in just four weeks and we need all the rehearsal time we can get. She's hired us a singing and acting coach who'll be coming up later."

"Hello, Bearnice. I'm sorry. Bearbi probably already knows all about it but I don't. What's this about the Edinbeargh Opera?"

"Lepi and I are going to perform together! Belinda arranged it. She's a trustee on the opera's board. Probably their major contributor. Not exactly fair, I suppose, to have a rich patron set you up that way."

Bearbi chimed in, "Sweetie, when opportunity knocks, answer the door! Most of your competitors would give their right canine for a chance like this, and they wouldn't think twice about it."

"In fact," I said, "we can give your careers a little more of a boost. Bearbi and I have been discussing my new magazine *Purr* aimed at felines. We're trying to develop a launch strategy. We're planning a joint issue with *Sow,* her magazine for bears and we've already come up with one combined feature. You two would be perfect for a second. A polar bear and snow leopard in their operatic debut. Oh, yes, absolutely."

Needless to say, Bearbi went ecstatic. *(Not something you want to watch every day.)* "Oh, of course! I was all set to put the feature in *Sow* but now that we're planning the joint issue, this would be perfect. I'm so excited. This will really sweep the newsstands."

Lepi said, "I'd love to be plastered all over your pages, ladies, but as a success, story, not a flop. Right now, in my humble opinion, and with all due respect to my lovely colleague, we are not quite ready for prime time or any time for that matter. That's why I'm looking forward to this coach Belinda has arranged. Meantime, we're just working along together."

"Well, would you mind awfully if we just listened in on your rehearsal for a few minutes. I'm sure you're being far too modest, Lepi. Belinda knows a good thing when she sees or hears it."

"Bearbi, I don't mind if it's OK with Lepi but we have to find someplace where we won't be disturbing anyone. I guess we can work without the piano but I don't want to be anywhere near the public parts of the castle."

"I know just the place. This castle used to be a full scale hotel and there are a number of conference rooms, named after movie star bears of all things. Bel took me in there for private discussions a few times. I think I can remember where they are." Coming Chita?"

I mumbled to myself. "Oh, what the hell! I wasn't doing anything important, anyway!"

We wandered around the hallways listening *(or perhaps not)* to Bearbi chattering away. She already had the whole photo shoot envisioned, stressing the inter-species thing and making a big deal out of the fact that Lepi was a Himalayan Snow Leopard, no less. "Aha, Theda Beara, I told you so. Let's go in here or would you prefer John Bearymore?"

"I'd love John Bearymore," giggled Bearnice. "Unfortunately he's dead."

"Yes, wasn't he scrumptious??"

I looked at Lepi who so far was playing his role of "new acquaintance" to perfection. What would Bearbi think if she knew that Lepi and I sang together for months in bistros in Rio and São Paolo? Bearnice was going along with the game too. I guess at some point we'll have to 'fess up but not right now, especially with the police hanging around. I arrived well after the crime and didn't even appear on the suspects list which is exactly the way I want it. I just want to stay well away from Shetland Yard and any other Yard for that matter. I winked at Lepi. He and Bearnice winked back as Bearbi went charging through the conference room door.

"Chita and I will just sit here in the back and be very quiet. *(Wanna Bet?)* Don't even think about us being here. Pay no attention! What are you going to sing??"

Lepi just laughed and said, "Well, in addition to opera and operetta plus a standard or two, we thought we might sing a few Scottish traditional songs. You know some of Sir Robert Bearns and some others like "Bonnie Annie Laurie."

"Oooooh, I just love Annie Laurie. Don't you, Chita. But you two go ahead. Don't mind us. Where did you learn to sing, Lepi?"

Convinced they weren't going to get much practice in, Lepi looked at Bearnice and shrugged. "I'm from the Himalayas, as you know. When I was very young, my family moved to China and my mother enrolled me in the People's Music School for Kits. I had some wonderful teachers, and I liked to write music as well as sing. I appeared in the Beijing Opera in several supporting roles. But then I wrote and staged an opera that the authorities thought was subversive. They shut us down and I fled before they could arrest me. I've been traveling around trying to get my career started. I was performing in a Rio de Janeiro bistro when I ran into Maury and some of his friends. One thing led to another and I came back with him and Octavius and the Bearoness to the States on her Concorde. That's how I met Bearnice. We were harmonizing on the plane, and when I discovered she was a polaratura from the Northern Lights Opera, well things just clicked."

I had been sitting with my claws crossed wondering how Lepi was going to tell the story of the two of us being members of the Spotted Band and the big blowup with Pontius Puma *(my former mate.)* He slid past it completely. Nicely done, Lepi, nicely done!

"We've disturbed you more than enough," I said, looking sideways at Bearbi who as usual was totally oblivious. "Please sing!"

"Maxwellton braes are bonnie; Where early fa's the dew; And 'twas there that Annie Laurie; Gave me her promise true. Gave me her promise true; Which ne'er forgot will be; And for bonnie Annie Laurie; I lay me doon and dee."

They went on through the snowdrifts, the swan, her fair face and blue eyes and when they hit the last refrain, I couldn't restrain myself any longer and harmonized:

"Her voice is low and sweet; And she's a' the world to me; And for bonnie Annie Laurie; I lay me doon and dee."

"Ms. Catt," said Bearnice, "You have a lovely voice. Have you ever sung professionally?"

(Stupid! Oh, well, Bearbi knows I was a singer!) "Yes, once or twice in my misspent youth.' I stared at Lepi.

"Yes, you do sing beautifully!" he said, "You should go back to it again!" He stared back.

"Oh, Chita, don't you dare. You're going to publish a magazine for me, remember?" This from Bearbi.

Before she could answer, the door to the conference room opened and two black noses appeared – one at eye level, the other up near the ceiling. Belinda and Octavius.

"Hello," said the Bearoness, "We were in the room across the hall and heard you singing and thought we'd peek in. I thought I heard three voices. You don't sing, do you Bearbi?"

"Only after several liters of champagne. That was Chita singing! We were just remarking what a nice voice she had. You worked in a few night clubs on the continent, didn't you, dear?"

I just shrugged.

Chapter Eleven
Still Bearmoral

An American needs verbal gifts
Just to bridge definitional rifts.
Have a care what you say
For throughout the UK,
"Elevators" all turn into "lifts"

(The Meerkat Narrator Returns)

That's when I interrupted the song fest. After Otto had gone through the door and down the battlement elevator shaft, I ran back across the roof to the stairway leading to Alistair's closet, skittered down and out. I couldn't replace the stairs unaided. Down to the interior elevator, down to the mezzanine floor, in and out of several hallways. I saw Belinda and Octavius standing half in and half out of the door to the Bearymore Room and breathless, I ran up and poked the Great Bear in his ample side.

"I need to talk to you two, now!!!"

Belinda looked back and saw the expression on my face. She apologized for disturbing the singers and backed out. Octavius kept telling me to catch my breath. He asked, "Now what happened?"

I squeaked, "I think Otto's dead. He teleported or translocated or whatever he does, through a door in one of the battlements and it was an elevator shaft. I think he fell all the way to the bottom."

"Let's go back into the conference room, and we can decide what to do. Did you actually see him fall?"

"No, but I heard him scream!"

"Oh, dear," said Bel. "Poor Otto. What elevator shaft, Maury? I didn't know there was an elevator in one of those towers. But then, I think I've been up there twice."

We opened the door and entered the room. Sitting on top of the conference table, dirty and disheveled but very much alive was the otter.

"Hey, where did you guys go? I came back looking for you."

The bears gaped. I yelped.

Otto looked at us and said, "What?"

"Whaddya mean 'what'? I heard you screaming as you went down that shaft. I thought you were dead."

"Well, it was a close thing as they say here in the isles. It is an elevator shaft and I think it runs all the way down below the castle. As I was hurtling down, I decided I'd prefer to be back here in the conference room and here I am. But all of you were gone. I figured you were still on the roof, Maury, but where were you two?" he asked looking at the bears.

"Across the hall, listening to Lepi, Bearnice and Chita singing while we waited for you both to come back."

"Chita's a singer?? Oh that's right. You told me you met her with the other Spotted Band members in Rio."

"Well, aside from a little grease and dirt, you look unharmed, Otto."

"I scraped my shin, Bearoness, but it's only a flesh wound. I'll survive."

(Oh brother!) "You think the elevator shaft goes below the castle?"

"Gee, Maury, I think so. I couldn't see bottom but exploring wasn't the first thing on my mind."

"Bel," said Octavius, "is there any kind of a cave or interior dock below the castle?"

"Tavi, there are all sorts of little caves and inlets all along the cliffs. When the tide's out you can see some of them but I never thought there was any kind of a dock or anything of that sort. I heard there was some kind of naval facility here during the war but I think that was torn down. The lifts inside the castle go down to the beach level and then to the parking garage."

"That elevator could be a perfect escape route for whoever hit and dumped Alistair. Bel, how much do you trust Hamish?"

"I have no reason to distrust him. He's always seemed a bit officious and smarmy to me. He seems to get along well with the rest of the family but they like his stiff formality. Every servant in his place, mum, doncha know!"

"Should we bring him in on our little expedition? We need someone who knows this place better than we do, even you, Bel."

"How about Dougal, the gameskeeper?" I said. "He seems a very honest and straightforward guy. And he's been here for dog's days. *(Sorry!)* I don't care for Hamish. When I asked him for a map of the house and grounds yesterday, I got the least amount of assistance he could spare without being totally uncooperative. I don't think he likes anybody, including you, Bearoness, poking around his castle."

"OK," said Octavius, "It's getting dark, and I for one could use a drink and a meal. Maury, you get hold of Dougal first thing in the morning. Tell him we want to speak to him before we take our little jaunt down to the pub. That mead better be everything you say it is. You *are* sure the wildcats will be there?"

"They don't seem to have any place else to go. By the way, I'm sorry but this is going to be a bit of a parade. Bearbi, her crew and Chita are going down there to film the Lion and The Unicorn, and to record their sham battle for the crown. I almost forgot. Bearoness, do you have any spare crowns they can use to stage the battle with?"

"There's a couple in the library. They're fakes, of course. Left over from the hotel days but if you don't look or shoot too closely, they should serve. I'll have one of the maids get them down and dust them off for you. Do you want me to come along?"

"With all due respect, Bel, I think if you came down there, your exalted position might put a small damper on the crowd, especially the wildcats. We'll give you a blow by blow when we return, and Bearbi will no doubt come back with enough footage to put on a mini-series. Actually, Maury, I'm glad the crew's going down there. We can go off with the wildcats without being disturbed. I want you to play theatrical agent with Bearbi, and also stick your head in on our discussions with the cats. Think you can swing that?"

"Fleet of foot, glib of speech, swift of mind, sire!"

"Yes, but can you do it?"

"C'mon Octavius!"

"What about me?" asked Otto.

"Oh, yes, Otto. To be sure. We're going to need you in every aspect of our investigations provided you don't go bungee jumping down any more elevator shafts without a bungee. Why don't you go clean up and join us for dinner. I guess we can get an informal meal, can't we, Bel?"

"Mrs. McRadish would be delighted. She's upset that murder or no murder, nobody's eating. She didn't care much for Alistair, anyway."

"You don't suppose she brained him with her frying pan, do you?"

"She would have done it long before this. Besides, I doubt she could have dragged him over the wall."

"The superintendent has one theory that the servants might have done him in jointly. Four cloned sheep and an old ewe with mayhem in their hearts."

"Tavi, does he know what he's doing? I'm not impressed."

I piped up. "You're just used to the stellar performance of the Bear's Brigade, Bearoness. Living with the elite has spoiled you."

"Actually, Bel, I believe he's quite competent. He just has this agonizingly slow approach to sifting everything and everyone. I'm just concerned that Alistair's death was the opening salvo rather than the end of the battle."

"What do you mean?"

"Frankly, I'm not sure what I mean. I just don't think Alistair was the victim of a grudge killing. He was somewhere or saw someone or something he shouldn't have. He had to be eliminated, and not too artistically, either. I still have that gnawing feeling that this is tied into the oil rig problems."

"Maybe that gnawing feeling is your empty stomach?"

"That too! Let's eat!"

Chita was sitting outside the door, no doubt waiting for us. "We need to talk, Octavius."

"Strange, Ms. Catt, but I feel no such necessity. What could we have to talk about?'

"No, I guess Maury didn't get a chance to tell you. I own one of the oil rigs out in the North Sea and it has suddenly stopped producing."

"That's seems to be an increasingly common problem but I repeat, what have we to talk about besides perhaps a few warrants for your arrest?"

"Or perhaps, you and the Bearoness receiving stolen property. *(cf. The Spotted Band)* How is your little genetic joint venture going, anyway? Can I make an investment in it? After all, I provided the intellectual property."

"I doubt anyone is going to defend Imperius Drake's property rights, and hopefully he's no longer around to pursue them. All right, you've made your point and no, we don't need another partner."

Belinda interrupted. "Perhaps we can talk about it, dear."

Octavius rolled his eyes and said, "Let's get back to my question. What have we to discuss besides that duck and this genetic foolishness?"

"I want to know why you think there's a connection between Alistair's death and the failures out on the rigs. I also plan to talk with the wildcats while we're down at the pub tomorrow. Some of them may actually work for me. It might help if we talked to them together. Let's get something straight! I have a stake in this oil rig mystery. You're just sticking your big black nose in another place it doesn't belong, Mr. Super Sleuth."

Octavius looked at me with his -You and I are going to have a discussion later about this - expression for which translate 'Maury, you're in trouble!' *(A meerkat's lot is not an easy one.)*

"I am assisting Shetland Yard in their investigations of Alistair's death. Perhaps you'd like to check on me yourself with Superintendent Wardlaw?"

Tie score: A bear-cheetah standoff and the game goes into overtime.

"I didn't think so." He continued. "If you must know, this castle strikes me as a perfect operations center for some of the weird things that are going on. While the police and military are combing the area around Abeardeen, this remote island could be the center of activity. This castle is huge and could hide all sorts of unwelcome guests, clandestine activities and equipment. I think Alistair was part of it or stumbled across it."

Belinda looked horrified. "Tavi, you don't think that I had something …"

"No, Bel. Of course I don't, but you're away so much they could be doing anything here and you'd never know."

"Have you said anything to your Yard buddy?" asked Chita.

"Not yet. I need more proof to get his attention."

Otto piped up. "Wow, maybe I should continue my scouting mission."

"Without a doubt, Otto, but we have to plan this out. I want to know where that elevator goes but without your dropping down the shaft again."

"What elevator?" asked Chita.

"An elevator shaft we found in one of the battlements on the roof.' I said. "Unfortunately, Otto discovered it the hard way and almost got killed after he teleported through the locked door. He zapped out of the shaft just in time."

"So that's why you're such a mess. Where does the elevator go?"

"We don't know" said the otter. "The shaft runs down the outside of the building and it certainly goes below the first floor. I can't be sure but I don't think it has any openings at the floors in between. I just held my breath and transferred. I wished myself back here. The shaft isn't readily apparent from inside or outside the building. I even missed the little up and down buttons on the door on the roof. It must be a big freight car. The shaft is huge. Very strange!"

"Bel, first thing in the morning, we need to go outside and see what's at the bottom of the castle at that point. We may even need for you or Otto to swim down and see if there's any kind of undersea entrance. I'm half tempted to seal that door on the roof but I think it's better if we keep watch and see if anyone uses it."

"Round the clock surveillance, chief! Just like the old days.'

"Except we were seldom looking for a murderer, Maury. Before we eat, one of us had better check on that staircase in Alistair's room. We don't want to leave it hanging down."

"I'll take care of that," said Belinda. "Nobody will question my wandering around the family wing. Then I'll meet you for dinner. Otto, go get washed!"

The otter, still under the mesmerizing spell of the beauteous bear, scrambled off as fast as his feet and tail would take him. We laughed.

"Chita said, "Well, you certainly have him in your thrall, Lady Belinda."

"Not only is he a sweetie, he's going to be a great performer, especially with Maury's and my help."

"Maury?"

"I'm Otto's theatrical agent, remember?"

"Oh, Riiight! You also plan magazine layouts in your spare time!"

"Well, who thought up tomorrow's Lion and Unicorn shoot?"

"True, short stuff, true! Be careful, Octavius. Maury is building a second career."

Another one of those - we're going to talk about this - looks from the Great Bear. I suggested we go eat.

Bearnice and Lepi (with interruptions, no doubt, by Dame Bearbara) were still singing their hearts out in the Bearymore Room as we bade farewell to Winnie the Pooh and his conference space.

Across the hall, behind the door to the Theda Beara Room, stood a shadowy figure taking in our whole discussion. As soon as we had passed into the adjoining corridor, the door opened and a large shape shambled down the hallway in the opposite direction, heading for the emergency staircase. The bad guys, whoever they might be, were on the move.

Chapter Twelve
Bearmoral

Dinner wasn't quite what I might wish.
Hostile in-laws are hardly my dish!
Roary sat with his smirk
And I stared at the jerk,
Strongly hoping he'd choke on a fish.

Over dinner, we figured out our stakeout schedule. Otto, Octavius, Belinda, Chita and I were all going to take turns. We would start whenever the piper and his cohorts had lowered the flag and continue until they came back at sunup. We probably should have had someone up there at that very moment. But we thought no one else would be moving around on the roof during the semi-daylight hours, this soon after Alistair took his swan dive. Who knows?

Hamish had come into the room to supervise the serving which turned out to be a cross between sit down and buffet.

At another table sat Ursula, Roary and Bruinhilde who seemed to have recovered from her hysterics. They all looked a little worse for wear. Ethelbeart and Albearta were nowhere to be seen but I heard Belinda and Hamish talking about sending something up to Albearta. Ethelbeart was probably working his way through another liter of cognac or scotch.

One of the (D,H,M,P)ollies toddled into the room, curtsied and handed a pair of ornate crowns to Belinda just as Bearnice, Lepi and the Mouth that Bored came in.

"Oooh, those will do wonderfully. I can just see one dangling from the unicorn's horn and the other propped on top of the lion's mane. They'll love it!!" Bearbi burbled. *(Why was I not so sure?)*

I suddenly realized I had not seen Bearyl all day and asked Belinda.

"She is down at Abeardeen supervising some maintenance on the Aquabear. She should be back shortly."

Dinner slowly ground to a conclusion and we started to get up from the table when Ethelbeart wobbled in, looking as if he had reached critical mass. "Didn't hear the dinner gong. Fellow's got to have ears all over this place to know what's going on." He sat at a separate table, ignoring his kin. "What's on offer, Hamish?"

"We have some splendid river salmon, sir"

"Good, tell the cook I want mine rare. I say, where are you five going? No manners at all. You there, spotted cat, have I met you?"

"Oh, Sir Ethelbeart," said Bearbi, "This is my associate, Ms. Chita Catt. She's a guest for the weekend."

"And who are you and why did you bring your family cat with you?"

Chita looked like she was trying to figure out the best way to attack the old bear's jugular. Belinda weighed in before any mayhem could transpire. "Uncle Beartie, you remember my good friend Dame Bearbara da Savile-Row."

Brief table-look up, a bleary squint and "Oh, yes, didn't recognize you in sensible clothes. *(Bearbi was wearing a tam, kilt, sash and tartan garter on her right front leg. Wonder of wonders, they all matched but none of us could place the clan. Better not to ask.)*

"Oh, that's all right, Sir Ethelbeart, there's been so much excitement, I don't expect you'd remember me.'

"Excitement? What excitement?"

"Well, er, Alistair, sir! The….accident!"

"Accident. Oh that, stupid twit. Told him to watch his step but he never does. Where is he? Tell him myself."

"I'm afraid he's dead, Uncle Beartie. Don't you remember talking to the police?"

"Oh, that Shetland Yard Johnny. Told him to watch out for that big American bear. They're a rough lot. Dead, eh? Well, I guess we'll still have that sour sow of a wife of his hanging about. Pity! Ah, here comes the soup."

Nobody dared look over at Ursula but she would have had to be deaf not to have heard the old ursine. There seemed to be a sudden urge on the part of everyone in the room to examine the ornamental fretwork that lined the ceiling.

Ah, me! More trouble in Paradise. Just wait till Aunt Albearta is back on stream. Then let the games begin in earnest! I was glad we'd be out of the house most of tomorrow. As for tonight, Octavius had the first shift on the roof, followed by me. Given his narcoleptic excursions, I tactfully volunteered to come along with him on the first stint to keep him company. *(Never mention his involuntary dozes!!)* He no doubt, would use the opportunity to chew me out at his leisure about Chita etc. but what the hell.

Before we could break up, Bearyl came in, still wearing her flying gear.

"Hi! Am I too late for dinner? Abeardeen Airport is not exactly famous for haute cuisine or cuisine of any sort, for that matter." She looked at Belinda. "The Concorde is up to spec, airworthy and ready for our next adventure. Wow, did I have a hard time getting in and out of Dyce. Their radar is down to one working unit. I understand the glide slope and ILS are acting up. Thank goodness I don't need them for the helicopter. Even their radios are on the fritz. They've had four blackouts in the last twenty four hours. Brief things – just enough to screw everything up – and management is tearing their fur out. The oil rig choppers are having a tough time getting in and out. Even the GPS seems to be off. Funny though, it's all concentrated at the airport. Abeardeen City is fine and so is the rest of Dyce. I hear the rigs and platforms are having their troubles, too. What's going on?? Oh, hi Chita!"

I thought the cat would turn into an albino. Bearyl had already left the castle when Chita arrived. The two would never have met before according to the stealth scenario. But Bearyl was acting as if they had been dorm mates at finishing school. Belinda interrupted, hoping nobody noticed who shouldn't have noticed.

"Why don't you grab a bite and then you can give us a blow by blow. We are very interested in what's happening."

"In fact, more interested every moment," said Octavius.

"Well," she said, chomping on a fish, "this has been going on for a month or so according to the operations crew at the airport. It's gotten more intense over the past few days. Our arrival on the Aquabear the other day came during a calm spell but they had been redirecting traffic on and off before and after our arrival. The gear just seems to fail at random. Nobody had put the problems out on the rigs together with airport troubles until it became obvious that disrupting the helicopter support traffic seemed to be the primary object. When a couple of utility boats also ran into a series of incidents – contaminated fuel, open sea cocks – somebody did some arithmetic and concluded there was some kind of organized sabotage program going on. Shetland Yard, airport security, the navy, the military and the industry safety groups are all on the alert and probably getting in each other's way. Strange! Anything new on Sir Alistair's death?"

We reviewed the bidding with her: The appearances of foul play; the head wound found by the doctor and the state of the investigation by Superintendent Wardlaw. We didn't say anything about the elevator and Otto's near miss. We didn't want that to be overheard by the resident polars or the household staff. Belinda nodded and said she wanted to speak further with Bearyl about the airplane when she had finished dinner. (That's when she'd be brought up to speed on what we suspected and what we were doing and oh yes, the Chita scam.) If we could ever get Lepi and Bearnice away from Bearbi, we'd brief them, too.

Bearbi had seated herself with the two singers and was showing all the finer qualities of a lamprey eel. Just as well, I suppose. We didn't want her sticking her omnipresent nose into our current activities. She was going to be a bit of a problem tomorrow if the photo shoot didn't occupy her every moment. She'd certainly notice us talking with the wildcats and for sure, she'd be on Chita's tail *(literally and figuratively.)* A lesser animal than I am might have contemplated involving her in a diverting accident. Nothing serious, mind you. Just enough to allow her sense of the sensational to turn the untoward event into the Slaughter of the Innocents. Idea regretfully rejected! Ah well, I am mellowing in my old age. Brought on, no doubt by Octavius' upright influence and a strong desire to stay out of jail.

Octavius, Otto, Belinda and I all sauntered casually out of the room. Chita, masochist that she is, walked over to Bearbi and began to distract her from Lepi and Bearnice. That probably scored a few points with Octavius.

The order of battle for roof duty was Octavius (with me); me alone; Otto; Chita and Belinda who would be there at dawn's early light just in time to greet the piper and the flag raisers. We did not intend to do this for more than one or two overnights. But that elevator had us all veeeery interested.

"Otto, could you get down to that elevator again without breaking your neck?"

"Gee, Octavius, I need an objective to aim at. I knew where the conference room was so that's how I got out of the elevator shaft. If I misjudged where the car is in the shaft, I could either free fall for a couple of floors before I reached it or end up buried underneath it somewhere."

"So that's how it works," I said, "Sort of like targeting a missile only you're the missile."

"I don't think that's very funny, Maury but yeah, I guess you're right."

"Well, then I guess we do it the old fashioned way – watch and wait."

Octavius and I rumbled off to the in-house freight elevator. He couldn't fit in the passenger elevator even though it was designed for polar bears. He stood several feet higher than most polars when he was fully erect and his massive weight was a bit much for the hoist mechanisms. When we arrived at the public stairway to the roof, the piper and his retinue were just descending. They saluted us and left the door open for the nosy tourists. We *(slowly)* made our way out on the roof.

"So this is what it looks like up here." He peeked over the side of one of the still intact walls. "Nice view. Plenty of storage space in those parapets and battlements, if that's all they're used for. I guess that structure housing the air conditioning is the only place we can stay out of sight." *(As if Octavius could stay out of sight under any condition. However, in the dark, he would just be another large shadow.)*

"We need to get inside each one of those storage areas. I can't believe there's more than one outside elevator shaft. Call Otto and ask him to come up here with a couple of flashlights. We can start poking around. We'll keep an eye on the elevator at the same time."

He went trundling off toward another of the four large battlements – there were also six parapets. Just as we passed the elevator battlement, a red light on the door started to flash. I grabbed Octavius' paw and tried to push him back toward the air conditioning housing. Too late! Whine, thump. The door opened but….there was no one inside. After a few seconds the door slid shut again. The little red light went off and we couldn't hear any movement. Someone had sent the elevator up to the roof. From where and why?

Otto had responded to my cell call and was on his way up. For openers, we could look inside the car. And then, maybe he could ride down and poke his head out. At the first sign of trouble he could zap back up to us on the roof. There was no question whether his adrenaline was at the right level. This was raising everyone's adrenaline, even Octavius.

Otto arrived and listened as we made our little proposal. I had been watching the lift's door the whole time we were waiting and the red light had not flashed again and there were no mechanical sounds. Odds were that the elevator car was still there. He agreed to go through the door and bounce right back out. The otter certainly was a gutsy little guy.

Zap-Zap! In and out!

"Well?"

"It's an oversize freight elevator. Looks like it could hold a small truck or even you, Octavius." He chortled and ducked the bear's swinging paw. "There are just four buttons – Up, Down, Door Open and Close. I didn't even see an emergency button. There was a little speaker but that's it."

"Want to try riding it down?" Octavius asked. "Make sure you have a good fix on the roof or your room or someplace safe so you can teleport out of there the minute anything looks fishy. Be careful! Maury is looking forward to his ten percent from your long show biz career."

Otto looked a little less daring this time but said, "OK, I guess, but watch out for a low flying otter if something goes wrong. I'll be coming back…fast."

He got into the car and then tried opening and closing the door several times from inside. It worked. With a jaunty 'thumbs up', he closed the door again and hit the Down button.

The car descended slowly. No indicators on the control panel to tell where he was but he sensed that this was going to be a long, leisurely ride. Suddenly the elevator bounced on its cable once or twice and jerked to a stop. The dome light in the ceiling went out leaving Otto in the very pitch dark. His first reaction was to split the scene pronto. So were his second and third reactions, but summoning up courage *(or stupidity)* from somewhere in his rattled psyche, he decided to wait a moment or two and see if the car started moving again. If it began a high speed plunge, he had his launch sequence all worked out. Back to the roof and his buddies ASAP. No movement, no sounds, no lights. Then a crackle and hiss from the wall. A high pitched voice over the speaker. A voice he didn't recognize. Male or female? The voice was obviously being disguised. Not sure how. Sounded hollow like in a barrel or …..an elevator shaft.

"Well, Mister Bear. *(He or she thought Octavius was in the car!)* You've stuck your big black nose in one place too many. I'm pleased to tell you that you have reached the final stop on your ride. You and your little

Meerkat friend are prisoners and you're going to stay there for a good long while. A little inconvenient for us, perhaps. We use this lift every now and then but we can wait until the two of you waste away from thirst or starvation. Not very artistic, I suppose, and certainly not up to your high standards of crime but it will have to do. You've gotten in the way and we don't tolerate anyone being in the way. Just ask Alistair. Oh wait, you can't, can you? He's dead and you will be soon. I doubt if anyone will find you in time. Besides, there's no access to this shaft other than at the roof and at the bottom. I don't know how you got in up there without knowing the codes but you're not getting out –at least not on your own power. And no one else is going to be able to get to you. If they try to force the doors, the cable brake will disconnect and you'll drop to the bottom very, very rapidly. I'm sorry, but we'll just have to keep you in suspense…..and suspension. Ya, ha, ha haa!"

Chapter Thirteen
Bearmoral

So who is this intimidator?
This maniac lift operator?
Who gets such a thrill
Out of trying to kill
In a huge runaway elevator?

"Maury, call Chita and Bel and tell them we're calling off the surveillance. If they want, they can join us in my suite. Are you sure you're OK, Otto?"

"Yeah, but I think I've had my quota of ups and downs for one evening, thanks."

"Let's go down and await the ladies. Meanwhile, rack your brain for as many little details as you can that might help us identify this crazed lift driver.'

Otto had held on in the pitch dark elevator until he was sure his vengeful nemesis had finished its spiel and then did a quick release tele-ejection back up to the roof where we were waiting.

"Well, one thing's clear," I said as we walked down the public stairs, "something's going on that's important enough to leave bodies strewn about, even conspicuous bodies like yours and Alistair's, boss. Although the intention seemed to be to keep us hidden in that lift until we died."

"Maybe! Or they could just be trying to scare us off. Keep us there for a while and then release us with another warning. It's either that, Maury, or we're dealing with a complete psychopath who enjoys dropping bears from heights."

"Or both," grumbled Otto. "I don't think he or she knew I was up here. The voice only referred to you and Maury. Remember I came up later."

"So someone spotted us on the way up or heard us talking."

"Or both," grumbled Otto again.

"The piper and his cohorts! They passed us on the stairs!"

"Right, we'll have to check with Bel and find out who they are. No matter what, they'll soon find out we don't scare easily, right?"

If you had taken a vote at the moment, you might have gotten a minority report from two very small animals. Anyway, I repeat, Otto's a gutsy little guy. Me? I'm just little.

We had reached the room and Belinda was waiting for us. I could see Chita ambling down the hall. Belinda looked very concerned. Chita looked like Chita. When we got inside and had made ourselves comfortable *(in Otto's case, with a good stiff drink)* we brought the ladies up to speed. Belinda ran the gamut from horrified to enraged. She was all for emptying the entire castle and closing it up.

Chita yawned and said, "Bearoness, that may be exactly what they have in mind. Get you and us out of here. To even come close to shutting this place down, you'd need round the clock armed guards *(if you could trust them)* and a massive amount of electronic security. And where would everyone go? You couldn't keep Shetland Yard out of the picture, either."

I looked over at Octavius. "Maybe we should call in some of our own heavy artillery. We may need it for those oil rigs too, if it gets to that."

"I was thinking the same thing. Bel, could a C-5A land at Abeardeen?'

"Bearly, but with Frau Schuylkill at the controls, the odds improve dramatically."

"Let's get Wyatt over here in the F-15 Strike Eagle and have the Frau follow up with Howard and L. Condor in the Ursa Major. I take very unkindly to someone trying to kill me off, especially in a thrill ride bear trap. I'm sure Otto does, too." *(I recall that the bad guys assumed I was also trapped in that thrill ride but that little incidental seemed to have eluded the Great Bear. It is easy to be overlooked when you are two feet tall – but very dashing.)*

(If this book is your first acquaintance with Octavius, I should tell you that he has his own small air force. The aforementioned Ursa Major, a super huge C-5A cargo jet; a F-15E Strike Eagle supersonic attack craft; a Twin Otter prop utility airplane and a small bevy of helicopters assigned to Universal Ursine Industries. All except the choppers were gifts from our grateful government to Octavius for services rendered from time to time in the national interest. The jets are used sparingly because of their immense operational and maintenance costs. All the aircraft are endowed with formidable weaponry. So too, are Frau Schuylkill and Colonel Wyatt Where, the two wolves who head up his security team and pilot the airplanes. Howard

Watt, our techie supreme and a redoubtable porcupine in his own right, rounds out the first line cadre. L. Condor, a temporary addition to the team is an Andean Condor and one of the most gifted telecommunications and network experts on the planet. He joined us during our last adventure and is staying with us in El Norte until things cool off for him down in Brazil. All told, the odds should be rapidly tilting in our favor with their arrivals.)

Since the Bearoness obviously bought into the idea and Chita kept her thoughts to herself *(not that they would have mattered to Octavius)*, I said "OK," and started placing an international hookup back to the Bear's Lair in Cincinnati.

Meanwhile the discussion went on fast and *(very)* furious.

"Someone has taken over part of this castle, Tavi. I'm sharing space with a bunch of criminals. But why? How did they get in here? What are they doing? What do they want? And why are you such a threat to them? Is it tied into the oil platform problems? What was Alistair's part in all of this? What do we do next?"

This cascade of questions bubbled out of Belinda who was doing an emotional minuet between outrage and concern. The lady wasn't given to fright. Quite the contrary. She was as feisty and aggressive as you can make them. She and her Aquabear flight crew had demonstrated over and over again that you don't mess with them without paying for it. But here she was. Mistress of the castle. Hostess to her friends and her newly minted but clandestine mate and someone was screwing around with her holiday plans. Not to be tolerated.

Before Octavius could even try to reply, I signaled that I had Frau Schuylkill on the horn. He took the phone from me and gave her a situation report and marching *(flying)* orders. He told her he'd have Bearyl or Bearnice contact her with the specifics about Abeardeen Airport and transfers to the castle.

"Everything seems quiet back at the mansion. She's going to call me back with their expected ETA's. The F-15 is ready right now. Getting the C-5A fueled and prepped is going to take a little more time. So Wyatt will be arriving first. The Ursa Major is a great deal slower but I want some of its weapons and electronic detection gear and I may want to use the ship for some patrolling. We need to check in with the authorities. They may not take kindly to a US based private attack bomber and flying warehouse showing up on the scene without their approval. Shetland Yard may not care much for our expanding their case for them, and who knows what the military will think. I guess Bel and I will have a fair amount of communicating and explaining to do in the next few hours."

"Speaking of the next few hours," said Otto, "what do you think is going to happen when our homicidal friend discovers you and Maury are very much alive and mobile?"

"I'm counting on him, her or them having to do a little regrouping. It was necessary for them to stop our snooping, and I guess we were getting pretty warm with our poking around on the roof. Once they see us at breakfast, they'll probably try to figure out how and why they failed. They'll almost certainly think we'll be calling on the police ASAP, so they may try to move some incriminating materials out of the castle and maybe even off the island. If my guess is correct, some of the problems out on the oil rigs are being caused by some complex electronic interference originating here. Even with miniaturization, that kind of gear has to be bulky. I suspect there are several boats moored underneath the castle at the entrance to the elevator. We need to locate that. And of course, I don't want to miss my date with the wildcats later on.'

"Or with the Lion and Unicorn's mead, either!"

"Shut up, Maury! Otto, are we all set for our jaunt to the pub in the afternoon?"

Otto nodded. Chita, who had been taking this all in said, "What makes you think they may not try to do the whole bunch of us in on the trip down to the pub or back. According to Lepi, that's a pretty treacherous run. You'd better check your truck or trucks out pretty damn carefully. Speaking of 'run' I may just do that instead of riding with you. No disrespect, but I think I'd like to return alive from this little junket. By the way, do you really want to involve Bearbi and her crew in this mess?"

I said, "If we try to stop her she'll escalate this into a frantic piece of tabloid investigation. *'Your editor in the jaws of death! Mystery attacks in ancient Scottish fortress!'* Besides, she'll have her own transportation. I'm not sure our lethal friends will want to attract that much attention by staging a major public accident but who knows? I couldn't have imagined them trying to kill off Octavius and me, either."

The ever pragmatic cat yawned and said, "Well, I need my beauty sleep. I'll see you in the morning. It'll be interesting to watch the faces when you two make an appearance at breakfast."

Belinda sat, obviously churning things over in her mind and Otto had a second drink.

"Hey, compadre, go easy on the joy juice." I said, "You're going to be a headliner in our band of top flight investigators tomorrow, and it wouldn't do for you to be hung over. Think what it might do to your adrenaline flow. Saggin' and draggin' when you should be zappin' and snappin'."

Octavius was on the phone to Superintendent Wardlaw. I'm sure he enjoyed being called after midnight but he did say "any time." I could tell from the sounds and expressions on Octavius' face that he was getting a fair amount of push back from the 'Shetland Yard Johnny.' I call anyone who won't allow a foreign national to fly in and activate two heavily armed, privately owned military aircraft and an A-team to go with them a spoilsport. To say nothing of Octavius taking matters into his own hands. But here I am trying to see both sides of the equation when my job is to be foolishly and unstintingly in the Great Bear's corner at all times.

They must have reached some kind of an agreement because he then got on the phone to the local military authorities responsible for Abeardeen. This one didn't seem to be going well. "Alright, we won't send the F-15 and you can quarantine the C-5A until we can clear up the details." He said.

Details!? "Excuse me, general, while I invade your country with heavy armament in the interest of tracking down some nasties who tried to smash me to bits. We'll clean up when we're finished." Oh, boy!

I know, I know. I was the one who came up with the idea in the first place. Meerkats are never consistent. Anyway, it looks like they have clearance to land in the Ursa Major but not much else. If I know the Great Bear, he'll create a multi-national task force before this thing is over. And who knows, it may be what is needed.

Back on the phone with Cincinnati. Updates on the airplane situation and arrival estimates. 18 to 24 hours. The Strike Eagle was a no-go. The C5-A will be armed "selectively" to reduce the angst with the UK authorities.

The hour grew later. Yawns all around. I half expected Octavius to do one of his narcoleptic numbers. So we all decided to go to bed for what was left of the night, checking out our rooms very carefully and locking up tight.

Needless to say, *(but I will)* I didn't sleep very well. Excitement, anger, curiosity and a certain amount of anxiety do not make for a restful night. I must have finally dropped off because the next thing I heard was those damn bagpipes. I jumped out of bed. We needed to identify that piper and his flag raising companions. Throwing on the nearest clothing and bounding out the door, I came face to face with Otto and Octavius. All of us seemed to have the same idea.

By the time we reached the stairway to the roof, the piping had stopped and I was afraid we had missed them. We emerged on a fascinating scene. Her Ladyship the Bearoness Belinda Béarnaise Bruin *(nee Black and now Bear)* was standing on all fours at rigid attention with her head inches away from the piper's nose. He was a Dandie Dinmont Terrier and his two cohorts were matching grey-blue Skyes. All three were bowing down on their forepaws, tails at half mast and looking anywhere but at Belinda. The bagpipes were unceremoniously dumped on the ground.

"I'll ask just one more time and if I don't get an answer I can believe, the three of you and the rest of the piping staff will be on a boat to Glascow and the animal rescue farms before lunch. Now, who was on flag duty last night? You dogs know the roster by memory so don't try that - I don't know - stuff."

The piper gave his head Terrier Tilt #12 and said, "Truly, milady! Jock, Trevor, Angus and auld Robbie were on duty last night but we've nae seen hide nor fur of any of them since. We dinna ken where they cuid be."

Octavius had rumbled over by then, further menacing the terrified terriers. "Now just where would four dogs go at night?"

One of the Skyes, obviously scared out of his wits got enough composure back to say, "Truly yer bearship, we dinna ken. They did go off together of an afternoon or two but we always thought they were goin' to the pub."

"Who do you all report to?" asked the Bear.

"Why Hamish, sair. Of course we all work for the Bearoness here.

"What do you know about Sir Alistair's plunge off the roof."

"Only what we were told by the police, sair. We were nowhere near the roof on that afternoon. Course, there have been rumors." This from the Dandie, named Angus, if you can believe it.

"What kind of rumors?" asked Belinda, maintaining her threatening stance.

"Weeell, Sir Alistair was reputed to be a bit of a tippler, ye ken, and at first we all thought the drink had done him in. But then, we asked ourselves 'what was he doin' on the roof in the first place?' That's when Malcolm here remembered that Sir Alistair and the younger bear, Mister Roary were given to wanderin' all over the property. They say that he had a complete set of keys. I ken he came into our quarters unannounced one day but backed out when he saw us all there. We thought you might have put him in charge of sompin', milady."

"No, I definitely would not put him in charge of anything unless I wanted it completely botched up. Tavi, do you remember? Did he have a large set of keys on him when you and Otto recovered his body?"

"No, but that might have been a damn good reason for him going over the side. Suppose someone wanted the keys and Alistair put up a fight. But why did he have them in the first place? And who gave them to him. I think it's time for an extended chat with Hamish. Wardlaw said he'd be up later today. I think we'll get together with your wild boar retainer right after breakfast. Right now, I'm hungry and I want to see if anyone gets upset when Maury and I put in an appearance."

Belinda looked at the three dogs and said, "If you guys want to keep your jobs and your heads, you'll stay in the castle until the police come back. I want them to talk further with you. Meantime, when and if the other four show up, I want to know immediately. Tell them not to leave the premises, either. Don't tell them what it's about."

"We dinna ken what's it all about, milady."

"Good, let's keep it that way. Now," she said, looking at Otto, Octavius and me, "let's go eat before I develop a taste for dogs roasted on the spit."

Chapter Fourteen
Bearmoral

They're a beautiful sight to behold,
With their shimmering coats of white gold.
Polars rule in the North.
Over ice they set forth.
But they never seem bothered by cold.

Breakfast at Bearmoral! The clink of glassware and the sounds of chafing dishes being opened and closed greeted us as we entered the dining room. Belinda, Otto, Octavius and your obedient servant! Hamish stood near the door supervising. Roary, Ursula and Bruinhilde were shuttling back and forth with piles of food. And, miracle of miracles, Aunt Albearta had condescended to join the merry throng and was bitching and moaning about some *(probably imagined)* fault with the food. Bruinhilde had drawn the duty for serving her great aunt. The (D,H,M,P)ollies were busy pouring coffee and/or tea and refilling the chafing dishes. Sir Ethelbeart was in Absentia. *(A little town on the other side of the island.)*

Give them credit! Not a raised eyebrow, not a choked swallow of coffee, nary an amazed stare at Octavius' and my arrival. If any or all of them were participants in yesterday's elevator escapade, they were controlling their reactions very well. Bearbi and her crew were sitting at their own table, no doubt working out the details of the day's shooting at the pub and Lepi, Bearyl and Bearnice had just entered from the opposite door. They waved at us. As we moved toward the sideboard to start our stuffing, Chita made a sweeping entrance into the room.

She had developed a serious case of Bearbi-itis in the clothing department. Her ever present diamond collar was set off against a black nylon catsuit *(really!)* and she had done something around her eyes to further darken her already exotic expression. Femme fatale on the prowl. Watch out wildcats! You're in for an interesting ride this afternoon. You never know what is going on in that unfathomable mind but you can be sure it is operating at hyperspeed. The only real emotion I've ever seen her demonstrate is irritation scaling up to raging fury. But wait, she had some kind of crush on her Brazilian mate, Paolo, until she discovered he was really the major gangland figure, Pontius Puma, rich and powerful as quite a few governments. She went into a frenzy when she found out he had been secretly cutting her out of some big time action. So much for sentiment! Anyway, he's behind bars now *(cf. The Case of the Spotted Band)* and she's skidding on a very thin oil slick, herself. Today should be interesting.

Belinda called Hamish over and asked him to step outside with us for a moment. She asked him whether Alistair, Roary or anyone else besides him and herself had a complete set of keys to the castle – or even a near complete set.

According to the boar, Alistair had insisted on having a set of keys while she was away. He felt that some member of the family should have access to the estate besides Hamish. Neither one of them ever bothered to inform Bel. She was furious at Hamish for keeping her in the dark. He tried to assure her that it was an oversight and certainly not a deliberate attempt to deceive but the Bearoness was having none of it. This morning was not a good time for members of the castle's domestic staff. An angry Belinda was not a pleasant experience.

"Where are those keys now, Hamish? They were not on Alistair's body nor in his room. Did you inform the police that he had keys to the entire property?"

"I don't know, milady and no, the subject never came up."

"Who else has a full set of keys?'

"No one, milady."

"Well, I hate like hell to have to change every lock in this place but I will if I have to."

"I hardly think that's necessary, milady."

"Why not? Someone killed Alistair and is roaming free with keys to the whole place and you don't think it's necessary. What does it require? Another attack by the Spanish Armada? Get a team of locksmiths up here immediately and have them change the locks on every door in the place. I don't care how long it takes or how much it costs. Then we'll talk about your continued employment. You'll be lucky if I don't take the cost of the locks out of your wages. Meanwhile, I'm getting the police up here *toute suite*. No one is going to steal my castle from me or cause any more deaths or injury. Understand?"

118

For the first time since I'd seen him, the famous Hamish shell was cracking. He was quivering. This was a side of Belinda I had never seen before and it was indeed formidable. I looked over at Octavius and I swear he was dumbstruck with admiration. If there was any trace of the original bimbo bear that Belinda once had been, it was buried very, very deep.

"Now, for the moment, I want you to give me your keys. I'll give you back only the ones you need to do your job and I'm sure the maids, cooks and other staff can lend you their keys if you need them. And then go find Dougal."

Hamish was not a happy camper but he reluctantly handed over the massive ring of keys he kept on his belt.

"These can't be all of them. I assume you keep others in your office?" she asked.

"Aye, milady, they're locked in a safe cabinet."

"Give me the key for that cabinet. Who else has one?"

"There was one on the ring Sir Alistair had but I'm not sure he knew which one it was. None of the keys are marked."

"That will just slow our opponents down. It won't stop them." said Octavius. "Please ask Dougal to meet us on the lower level at the pool in fifteen minutes."

Hamish walked away briskly, his jaws slackly open. We headed back to the table to finish breakfast.

"We have several hours to explore before our caravan takes off for the village." I said. "I assume you want to try to get to the bottom of the cliffs under that elevator shaft and look for that opening."

Otto piped up. "Maybe I should get a hold of my sea otter friend, Harold the beach manager. He could probably give us a small boat and even show us where the entrance is."

"Good one, Otto. Let's do it. That assumes of course, that he's not one of them."

"You could say the same for Dougal, Maury."

"I doubt it. He was with us when Alistair took his dive. But then again since there's probably more than one person in this murderous crew, who knows?"

At that point Ethelbeart made his entrance and spotting Albearta, he headed in the opposite direction. "Ethelbeart, where have you been? I have been suffering for days over poor Alistair's loss and you have not come near me. You are a thoughtless brute."

I would have guessed a *gutless* brute, myself but who am I to make judgments. I wondered if the doddering polar was really as ga-ga as he made out to be or was he simply posing to keep to himself and his endless supply of liquor.

"Now, now, m'dear! Thought you would want to commiserate with Ursula and Bruinhilde. No place for us rough hewn males, y'know."

Otto almost choked on his fish and said, "Excuse me. I'll go find Harold. We'll see you at the pool."

We finished up and took the house elevator down to the pool area. Bearnice and Bearyl followed us down to get in some early morning laps. Belinda called them over and brought them up to speed on the latest developments. They, in turn, decided that one of them or both would stay by Belinda's side during the waking hours. The Bearoness protested but Octavius joined in and agreed with the two crew members.

"Bel, remember you're not going with us down to the pub this afternoon. You'd be vulnerable without the two girls. We don't want someone trying to take away your keys and dumping you over the side. While I'm sure you'd be a much more difficult victim for them than Alistair was, I'm even more certain that very few beasts would want to take on two or three highly trained polar bears at the same time. It's just for a day or so, Bel."

She didn't like it but she agreed. "Just don't hang onto my tail, that's all."

The two bears laughed and promised they'd be discreet.

Dougal arrived, looking very puzzled and a bit wary of Belinda. No doubt, Hamish had given him some inkling that the Bearoness was not in the best of moods.

"How can I be of service, milady?"

"You can help us get down to the bottom of the cliffs, Dougal." said Octavius. "Harold will be here shortly. We're trying to find an opening in the cliff that leads to a dock area and an elevator up to the roof."

"Oh, aye, 'tis the old artillery lift they built durin' the war. Ye could unload heavy weapons and radar off boats and take them up to the roof to spy or fire on ships in the harbor and out at sea. It was faster and easier than trying to bring them in overland. I dinna think the lift works anymore. I'm not even sure who knows about it. It hasn't been used in years."

"That's where you're wrong my friend. It was in use last night."

"Oh, aye?? Then someone has been repairin' it on the sly. 'Twas shut down by the military when they gave the castle back to the first baron. He had na' opened his hotel for muir than a few months when the hostilities broke out. He turned the place over to the government for the duration. 'Twas only for a little less than a year and we were back in bizness but the lift and the sea platform were closed up."

"We believe they've been reopened but we don't know why or by whom. We tried going down the shaft but that didn't work out, so we want to come in by water."

"Weeel, the tide has to be right to do that, ya ken. Here comes Harold. He'll know when you can get there."

The two otters skittered up to us. Harold had obviously worked up a friendship with Otto because they were laughing and shoving as they approached. But then he was all deference and awe before Belinda.

"Otto tells me ya wanta go to the boat platform, milady. It's above water now, if ya want to come wi' me. We can take a wee boat"……Then he looked at Octavius and said, "Perhaps, sair, we'd better get something a bit sturdier for you."

"Dougal, Harold! Why was I never told of this lift and platform?"

"Och, milady. 'Twouldn't be our place but Hamish knew and I think perhaps Mr. Alistair knew about it."

Suspicious looks exchanged all around.

"Alright," said Octavius, "Let's go. We want to keep our appointment this afternoon down at the pub."

 Harold smiled, thinking here was a bear after his own heart. Let nothing get in the way of a fine dram or two. Dougal, on the other hand, had a pretty good idea what the trip to the inn was really going to be about.

The castle was built on the cliff but there was a semi-paved roadway on one side that led down to a narrow beach at the foot of the overhang. More rocks than sand, it was here that the former patrons of the hotel would come to cavort in the icy surf. For the less rugged, there were pedal-boats, several Zodiacs, a windsurfer or two and a whaler powered by a heavy duty outboard.

Octavius and I headed for the whale boat while the three polars and Dougal took a Zodiac. Otto said he wanted to swim around. Chita had joined us but being water averse, especially after her near-drowning in our last adventure, and afraid of ruining her catsuit, decided she might sit this one out. We tried to persuade her to come in the whaler but close proximity to Octavius in heaving surf wasn't her idea of an ideal situation. He might just get it into his head to toss her overboard. We pushed, pulled and tugged Octavius into the boat. Harold clambered aboard with us and took the controls of the high powered outboard. And off we went.

The cliff jutted out, surrounded on three sides by the ocean. The site of the elevator shaft was on the side nearest the beach. As we came around, we saw a tower that had been built onto the side of the castle and ended in one of the battlements on the roof. As it stood on the cliff, it just looked like part of the building. The lower part of the shaft below the building's foundation had probably been drilled out of the rock all the way down to water level below. Quite a piece of work but in war, no expense is spared. When we reached what looked like the probable spot for the sea entrance, there was nothing there. But Dougal, steering the Zodiac at high speed, headed straight for the sheer wall. We shouted at him and I'm not sure what his passengers were thinking but at the last minute, the Zodiac disappeared. First reaction: they'd hit the wall and capsized. Dougal was on a suicide mission to kill off the Bearoness and the two Aquabears.

But then Harold did the same thing with the whaler and my second reaction was: Ohmigosh, it's an optical illusion. The cliff face was actually two overlapping walls sheltering a small inlet. Dougal had steered between the walls. We followed. Otto was skidding along in our wake, jumping and diving as he went. The entrance was hidden from all views except an extreme angle close-up and parallel to the face. Talk about camouflage. I turned to Harold as we throttled back and drifted toward a large opening.

"Is this opening natural or was it constructed?"

"A little of both, Mr. Meerkat. The military expanded it when they put in the shaft but the inlet was always there. We don't tell many people about it. Never know what mischief they could get up to in there."

Octavius and I looked at each other. We already knew what they could get up to. Or at least we thought we did. The water was calm as we trolled along inside the "cave." Harold had turned on the spotlight at the bow of the whaler and Dougal had a hefty flashlight he was raking across the walls. Straight ahead stood an outsized concrete platform, surrounded by large bunker-like structures. Something about the looks of the walls and the bunkers bothered me. Suddenly it dawned. Less than a foot from the top of the structures was a continuous water mark. I turned to Harold and Octavius and said, "Am I seeing straight? Is that how high the water rises in here?"

"Oh, aye, sair. And it's pretty swift when it comes. All of those bunkers are watertight to keep whatever and whoever is in them dry until it recedes. It's not time for high tide for several hours though, so ya needn't worry yerself."

I noticed that the huge doors on the bunkers had pressure seals and large handwheels. Several had sliding doors. One of those was probably the elevator.

There was nothing on the platform except some seaweed and an unlucky fish or two. Whoever was using this place had to keep a very careful schedule of the tides and keep schlepping gear in and out of storage. Whatever equipment they used was, no doubt, stowed on the other side of the watertight openings. One especially large bunker probably stored a boat or two but all we had at the moment was guesswork.

We walked around testing the doors. None of them would budge. Each had some type of electronic lock that probably only responded to a remote key pad. I guess that was true of the lift as well. That's how it seemed to work on the roof. Well, now we knew the place was here and what it looked like but not much else.

Belinda was pacing around and shaking her head in frustration. "I wonder if Byron knew this was here. He never told me about it." *(Implicit in her statement was a worry that her dear departed husband might have been using this facility for some illegal activities, like smuggling. Byron was primarily a playbear, but he did seem to have an ample supply of replenishing funds, and not just from buying theatrical revues.)*

Dougal and Harold had returned to the boats. The rest of us had wandered around and started re-assembling in the center of the platform. Suddenly, Otto looked up and yelled at Harold. "The tides coming in....fast!"

The other otter looked around and said, "It can't be. It's nowhere near time. But it is…!"

Octavius shouted, "Bel, you and the girls get out of here! Otto, give Maury a hand. He's not much of a swimmer. Where's Dougal?"

The water had come in so fast that it slammed the Zodiac against the wall and Dougal with it. Harold had the motor running on the whaler and the three polars swam, scuttled and flailed their way onto it. The odds on them swimming out in the face of the onrushing tide were not particularly good. Same applied for Otto. Harold, Bel, Bearnice and Bearyl were all shouting for us to come aboard but it took all the power the boat had to ride out the incoming flow. Octavius grabbed Otto. Dougal had crawled out from under the Zodiac and grabbed my paw and the four of us ran for the far wall. The sea was crashing against the bunkers and we held onto the hand wheel on one of the doors for dear life, trying frantically to get it open.

Suddenly, there was a loud hiss and two hydraulic doors started opening on the adjacent bunker. It was the elevator. As the doors slid back, a haughty, striped and spotted face peered out and snarled, "Get in here quick. You know how I hate water."

Chapter Fifteen
Bearmoral

Spotted Chita's breathtakingly swift.
It's a really remarkable gift.
From zero to fifty
In no time! How nifty!
And what's more, not one gear must she shift!

Octavius picked up the three of us and tossed us into the lift and then trundled in himself. Chita already had the doors closing. About a foot of water sloshed on the floor but was flowing out of holes in the four corners. The car was obviously built with drainage in mind. The elevator started to rise before any of us could get our breath, or reclaim our presence of mind. I noticed Hamish standing in the back and I looked over at Chita. Otto, Octavius and I all blurted, "Chita, what, how did you….?"

As the car continued to rise, she shook herself, looked down at her outfit and said, "Ooh, there goes my catsuit. It'll never survive the salt water. Can't you Rover Boys stay out of trouble? The things I do for you, Octavius Bear. Otto, at least, I owe a rescue. And I suppose you too, Maury but you, you big boob. You're worse than a little kid playing detective."

Envision, if you will, a gigantic Kodiak bear, his matted fur soaking wet and dripping all over the floor, mouth agape, teeth bared, a rumble building deep in his chest, eyes locked on his target. Imagine a cheetah about one eighth his size staring right back at that open mouth as only a cheetah can stare. Visualize an otter, Sheltie and wild boar looking on in amazement. Picture a freight elevator about to become a venue for extreme ursine-feline conflict. Think of Bearbi missing out on pictures of the battle of the century. Most of all, imagine a meerkat wishing he was anywhere but where he was.

The elevator stopped and the doors opened. Saved by the roof.

Octavius turned and ran out to look over the wall. "Where are they? Maury, Otto, check the other walls. Can you see the whale boat? It looked like they were getting away but I can't see them anywhere."

Otto shouted from another corner, "I see the boat but it's overturned. Out there! I'm going down to the beach." He disappeared.

Those of us who required more conventional means of travel headed for the stairs and then the lifts. Octavius and I took off for the freight elevator while Dougal, Hamish and Chita went in the passenger lift. As usual, it took forever for the damn car to arrive, open its maw and swallow us up, before heading down to the beach road level. After an eon or two, we arrived. Dougal, Chita and Hamish were running off ahead of us. But then they stopped at the top of a rock pile, staring out to sea. We caught up with them just in time to see two otters cavorting and pushing each other around, and three water soaked Aquabears rising from the surf. Octavius' sigh of relief created a new pile of pebbles.

Dougal sat panting and wagging his tail. Hamish made a sincere effort to maintain his dignity. Octavius and the three polar bears had a hugging session that sprayed water in every direction. The beach resounded with thumps and squishes. I sauntered over to Chita, who was still looking mournfully at her salt caked catsuit and said, "Well, that would have made for an interesting conflict. You really like to live life on the edge."

She yawned yet again. This was becoming an affectation. "Oh, his self control would have kicked in, although I admit he could have bounced me off every wall and the ceiling for good measure. I'm sorry. I just enjoy twisting his tail – figuratively, of course."

"OK, how did you do it?"

"What?"

"Get that lethal lift to obey your commands."

"I didn't."

"You didn't? Chita, stop being cute!"

"I simply told that overbearing boar that he'd be nursing a large number of gashes if he didn't go with me and get that elevator working. He knows the electronic key sequence and now so do I. Oddly enough, he didn't even think to take me on. That would have been an interesting fight. I guess he's been domesticated for too long – a not-so-wild boar. Anyway, when you guys set off to sail through Scylla and Charybdis, I thought it might be worth staging a little dry land backup. Little did I know, I'd almost drown anyway."

126

Octavius trundled over, relief replacing his rage. He looked at the cat and said, "I suppose I should thank you."

Chita stared back and said, "Yes, I suppose you should."

"Thank you. How did you get that elevator going?"

Belinda, Bearnice and Bearyl came over still shaking themselves dry. The Bearoness had just heard the bearest outline of how we had been saved by the cat.

"Yes, Chita, how did you get it going?'

"As I told Maury, I didn't. Hamish did after some persuasion."

All eyes on Hamish, who coughed, stiffened and tried to regain his dignity, in spite of the fact that he too was soaking wet from the deluge in the elevator.

"I have known the codes for the lift ever since the Bearon started using it, milady."

"Lord Byron used the lift?" asked Belinda, "When, how, why?"

"I'd rather not speak ill of the dead and noble, milady."

"I'd rather you did, Hamish. I'm reaching the end of my rope with you."

"As you wish, milady. From time to time, the Bearon would engage in activities that were somewhat irregular, shall we say."

"Shall we say illegal?" said Octavius.

"Illegality is often in the eye of the beholder, sir. The late Bearon had a number of pastimes that were a bit out of the ordinary but certainly consistent with local mores."

"In other words, he was a smuggler."

"Not to put too fine a claw on it, sir. Aye."

"Was that all, Hamish?" asked Belinda.

"Well, milady, shall we say he occasionally entertained some unusual guests."

"Who no doubt arrived by way of the inlet and the lift."

"Aye, milady."

"Hamish, this discussion has all the finer elements of pulling teeth or in your case, tusks. We are all going to go inside and bathe and repair our sodden conditions, but then you and I are going to have a long history lesson. You, the teacher and I, the student. Understand?"

"Perfectly, milady!"

"And I want the codes to that lift changed immediately. Better yet, you will show me how and I will change them…alone."

"As you wish, milady."

("And then, Hamish," I thought, "I want you to take a good flying leap off the top of this castle and take all of Belinda's relatives with you.")

Octavius turned to me and said, "There are a few things that still need explaining like that rogue tide that suddenly showed up but let's get cleaned up first. I still want to get down to that pub, preferably before Bearbi gets there and turns it into a circus."

He turned to Chita and said, "See you at lunch!?" and then he shouted, "Hey Otto, cut the clowning with Harold, and let's get ready for this afternoon."

We headed up to the castle and our various rooms and forms of solace. It was a little early for fermented coconut milk VSOP, but the mini-bar in my room was well stocked, and I saw it as a remedial step for my extreme psychic trauma and several bruises.

This situation was getting more and more complex. We weren't even sure if it was one situation or several. Were the problems on the oil rigs connected to our mishaps, or were we creating a giant conspiracy theory where none existed? Why did Alistair take his dive, and who is the nut who tried to knock us off, maybe twice, if that gushing water in the inlet wasn't a freak of nature? I could use a good dose of Wyatt, Howard and the Frau. I hoped they were well on their way.

On the way back, Octavius had asked Otto to zap or swim around to the inlet and platform to check for any types of underwater sluice gates or pipes that could have unleashed that torrent of water on top of us. Before he could say, "Do it when we come back from the pub," Otto had disappeared. I'm going to have a nice long talk with my client about overdoing the teleportation act. We still haven't heard from the doctors at UUI about any permanent effects the Duck's serum may have had on Otto's brains and body beside the obvious one. He seems mentally and emotionally normal enough for an otter, and Harold didn't seem to notice anything different. But I doubt if he's seen Otto do his 'now you see me, now you don't' routine.

A quick shower, a fluff and buff of my fur and fuzz, on with the agent's outfit and I was ready for lunch albeit still a bit weak in the knees. I get that way when someone is trying to kill me off. Ursula, Roary and Bruinhilde were already in the dining room, chowing down. I wondered what the Bearoness' monthly food bills were like, to say nothing of the liquor. I know, we're consuming our fair share (and possibly then some) but Octavius had treated Belinda and her crew royally when they were at the Bear's Lair. These jerks were just A-List spongers. Ethelbeart probably consumes the total output of a mid-sized distillery every month. I'll have to ask about polar bear livers and their resistance to alcohol. Maybe he'll just keel over and die of cirrhosis. Speaking of whom, he made his entrance with the redoubtable Aunt Albearta who was lecturing him loudly on some world-shaking annoyance like the temperature in her bath. It was never cold enough.

Lepi was seated by himself in a corner, and after loading up my plate I went over and joined him. He had his luxuriant tail wrapped around the back of an adjacent chair. Himalayan Snow Leopards are strikingly handsome cats. He's going to be a major matinee idol with or without Bearnice.

"Hey Maury, que pasa? I saw you guys coming back into the castle. Bearnice looked like she had swum the Irish Sea."

"She almost did." I brought him up to date on the Perils of Polars, our adventures in the flashing flood and Chita's last microsecond rescue.

He shook his beautiful head and said, "Chita is an original. Only she would face down a Kodiak bear after calling him a boob to his face. I have to tell you. I have a crush on her but I can't imagine living with her. I was amazed that she latched up with that sleaze, Pontius Puma, *(I beg your pardon, Paolo)* down in Brazil."

"I guess power really is an aphrodisiac. We meerkats have little or no opportunity to explore that particular maxim. With us, it's more like a wuss is a wuss is a wuss."

"What's this latest thing of hers? The magazine?"

"***PURR – Feline Fashion, Foibles and Fun***. She's working with Dame Bearbara. You and Bearnice are going to get joint coverage of your operatic debut in her magazine and in Bearbi's *SOW*. Today we're heading back to the Lion and Unicorn for a shoot of the "famous" battle for the crown. It'll be in both magazines, too. I helped arrange it. Come with us. You can help keep Bearbi out of our hair while Octavius and Chita interview the wildcats about the dirty doings on the oil platforms."

"Bearnice looked beat and probably isn't up to rehearsing. I'll tell her I'm going. I wouldn't miss this circus for the world."

"We're going at 1:30. We have several utility vehicles and a flat bed truck (lorry) for Octavius. Bearbi and her crew are going separately. Chita said she wanted to run alongside. She thinks someone is going to sabotage the truck or the UV's."

"Grim thought but not entirely unlikely given what you just told me. We better give those sets of wheels a complete going over."

"Dougal is at it right now but we're going to double check him. I have a hard time suspecting him of anything, especially since he was almost drowned right along with us, but my paranoia is running high and heavy. You look pretty dangerous yourself, Lepi."

"We snow leopards all look dangerous. That's part of our charm. You don't evade the Chinese state police for three months without learning a few nasty tricks. Look who's here."

In yet another tweed jacket with leather elbow patches, Otto sauntered into the room trying for all the world to look like a bored aristocrat. He was failing. I waved at him and he walked over, pulled back the chair and said, "I'll be right back as soon as I get a plate of fish."

Here I am waiting to hear whether we were booby trapped down at the water platform and he has to get some fish. Oh, relax, Maury. He's doing all the work, so I guess he's entitled.

A cadence of thump-thump-thumps announced the arrival of Octavius. He paused at the door, surveyed the room, nodded at Lepi and me and moved over to the sideboard where he stood on his hind legs and filled two large plates. Octavius standing fully erect never fails to get the attention of everyone in his vicinity. It's like trying to ignore Mt. Everest. I watched the expressions on the faces of the polar bears, no small animals themselves but still no match for the Kolossal Kodiak. Ursula and Bruinhilde both seemed veeery interested. Roary was trying to pretend there was something equally interesting on his plate. I'm not sure whether Albearta or Ethelbeart could see well enough to distinguish the details and features of that huge mass of fur. But I'm sure their noses were good enough to pick up his distinct scent.

Another distinct scent suddenly filled the room. Bearbi swooshed in with her crew, wearing her idea of a safari suit. That would certainly go over well with the locals. She also reeked of a perfume that I later learned was called Ultra Ursine – five hundred euros an ounce. I had to join her on the trip to the village to do the introductions at the pub and smooth over what I was sure would be a case of cultural mismatch. I waved at her and by sign language told her I'd be with her in a few minutes.

However, first things first. Otto was returning to the table and so was Octavius. No Chita yet and I think Belinda, Bearnice and Bearyl had cornered Hamish in a different room where if he didn't give her the answers she wanted, he might end up being their lunch.

Otto dropped his plate on the table, sprang up on the chair and with a self-satisfied smirk looked at me, Lepi and the approaching Octavius. "Boy, were we taken for a flume ride. There are two large – maybe ten foot – diameter pipes aimed right at the platform about five feet under the surface. They have steel mesh on the outlets so I couldn't swim through, so I zapped in to investigate. There are a couple of super-sized pumps that can flush out or suck the sea back into a couple of huge tanks or reservoirs. Perfect for concealment and disposal of unwanted noseybodies like us. The water had receded by the time I swam in there. I shot right back out into the inlet in front of the platform so I don't think anyone saw me, but that whole setup is probably carefully watched and controlled from somewhere."

"This place has close to a hundred unused bedrooms, conference spaces, utility locations and God knows what else," said Octavius. "There could be a small army co-residing with us here and we'd never know it, unless we were specifically looking for them. They could eat, sleep and do whatever they do with little fear of discovery during most of the year. They could always evacuate unseen by boat when necessary. I don't think they counted on us showing up. Something serious must have happened to make them show their paw like that – first Alistair and now us. I need to talk with Bel now and the Superintendent when he arrives tonight. This place needs a thorough fumigation."

Lepi looked at the Great Bear and said, "Aren't you jumping to conclusions, Octavius? Everything that's happened so far could have been the work of one, maybe two or three perps. Some nut with a couple of assistants."

"I'd tend to agree with you, Lepi, if I could believe that all this violence and harassment on the oil platforms wasn't related. That takes more than one or

131

two hostiles. I know I'm out on a limb. Maybe our conversations with the wildcats this afternoon will clear things up a bit.'

"And if nothing else, you'll get to sample some of the world's finest mead," I added.

"That, too. Let's finish up here and get this circus on the road. You're going with Bearbi, right Maury? Otto and Lepi are coming with me and Chita's going on her own. Before we do anything, I want to check the truck and the utility vehicle out. There have been too many incidents to suit me and from what you've told me, the run down to the village is going to be a bit of a challenge under the best of circumstances."

He was right.

Chapter Sixteen
Bearmoral

"Sus scrofa" are often quite brusque.
That's the boar with the threatening tusk.
He can smell you, no doubt,
With his sensitive snout.
And his body's the color of dusk.

(From the Diary of Ms. Bearyl Blanc of the Sauvignon Blancs)

In a side room near the dining salon, the Bearoness, Bearnice and I sat with a healthy supply of food and drink. Hamish sat on the fourth side of the table but had passed on eating. (*Not proper, y'ken, for staff to eat with the family. It rankled him that Bearnice and I, whom he considered to be staff, were eating with her ladyship.*) Such niceties of class and caste were wasted on us two polars. We had shared candy bars and everything else with Belinda on long, supersonic flights.

"OK Hamish, time for Show and Tell," said Bel. "I want chapter and verse on that lift including its wartime uses. I want to hear all about Byron's escapades, both before and after I married him and most of all, I want to know what the hell is going on right now. And unless you can convince me that you are going to be part of the solution, I am going to treat you as if you are part of the problem, and that could be dangerous indeed."

The boar stiffened in his seat and said, "I have always been loyal to the Bruin clan, milady, even when such loyalty caused me great moral dilemmas. I assure you, I have had no hoof in any of the bizarre happenins of the past few days. I have held my silence about the Bearon because I felt it would only create unnecessary disturbances where none needed to be had. However, I will comply with your wishes and tell you what I know of the lift and its uses, as well as my thoughts on the untimely death of Sir Alistair. Of the events involvin' Doctor Bear and his friends and of course you, milady, I know nae more than what I have been told."

Shifting in seats, piercing stares, ominous music in the background *(just kidding!)* I surreptitiously shoved another fish in my mouth as Bearnice lapped at her wine. Bel just sat there.

"As I'm sure Dougal or Harold told you, milady, the military requested and received the rights to use this castle during the last Great War. Sittin' as it does on this promontory, it is indeed a strategic site. Actually, the castle had only been finished a few months and the auld Bearon had just about gotten it ready to open as a theme park-hotel – "Polar Paradise." There are large neon signs to this effect stored in one of the parapets on the roof. Weeel, the war broke out. Patriotic to the core and assurin' himself that he would be generously compensated at a time when tourism would be at a standstill, the auld Bearon, his family, including your late husband who was but a wee bairn, and his retainers includin' m'self, took up residence in a small enclave within the building. He turned the remainder over to the military, includin' the beach and adjoining properties."

"After conductin' a complete survey of the cliffs and surrounding water, the government decided to take advantage of the natural, hidden inlet that existed at the base of the promontory. At first they thought to build submarine pens, but the cost and time was too great for the value. Instead, they decided to make the castle a radar observation post and coastal artillery/missile site but they were perplexed by how to handle logistics. Then someone got the idea of supportin' the installation from the water and, if ya can credit it, proceeded to build in secret, a large lift attached to the side of the building. What was truly amazin' was the shaft they drilled all the way down the cliff without disturbin' the castle. Rather than break into the walls of the buildin', they built the lift to run straight to the top. They installed missile launchers, radars, communications and all manner of electronics up there. They also built a sort of booby trap – pumps and tanks that would flush tonnes of sea water onto the platform and surroundin' rooms if it was invaded. 'Twas a major feat of Scottish engineerin'."

"I know about the booby trap. I saw it in action." She ignored Hamish's quizzical look. "What happened when the war ended? Was the castle ever attacked? Did they just leave it like that?'"

"Nae, milady. They had only joost completed the work and the war ended. Never a shot fired in anger. No attacks on or from the castle. The canny auld Bearon convinced the admirals and generals to leave the lift and some other facilities in place in case there should be another breakout. They decommissioned and sealed the structure both on the roof and down below and left it. To ma knowledge, there was never any further use of it until the young Bearon, his grandson, your husband, discovered it. He opened up the seals, updated the mechanisms, put in electronic controls and strengthened the cables' and the car's liftin' capacity. And so it is today."

"Didn't they use it for anything at all when the place was restored as a hotel? It might have been an interesting thrill ride. The Mysterious Tower! The Lost Lift! Complete with stories of ghosts and unsolved deaths." Belinda caught herself. No matter what the situation, she couldn't help thinking show business angles. But she was getting too close to the events that had just happened. She didn't know how much detail Hamish knew about the incidents in the elevator with Otto, Octavius and Maury. I wondered what Chita had said to him to "convince" him to reveal the operating codes, other than she'd tear him apart if he didn't.

"You may not know this, milady but I managed the hotel and park for the auld baron. 'Twas only when Lord Byron's father decided to change it to a family home that I became chief retainer. When I was manager, the lift was definitely never opened, much less used."

"All right, let's talk about Byron, my late husband."

"Weel, it's not really my place, milady."

"Hamish, if you want to hold on to your place, you'll start talking.'

"Veery well, but I do so under protest, ya ken. The young Bearon was a hearty young lad who inherited his forebears' skill for makin' a shillin' or two. A good time and a full purse! That was his motto. As you can imagine, the hotel had all the fixtures, furnishins' and supplies of a first class establishment before the auld Bearon's son turned it into the family homestead."

Bearnice snorted to herself. "Some homestead! I suppose Buckingham palace is a cottage."

Belinda looked at us two and said, "Are you keeping track of the family as we go along? The trouble is: All three Bearons were called Byron. I guess it would have helped if they took numbers but they never did. Go figure! Just remember grandpolar built the place, papa bear converted it to a family enclave and sonny-bear, my husband, was running it that way before he was killed in an avalanche on a ski slope, filming a commercial for Pola-Cola."

"Correct, milady. Speakin' of Pola-Cola, the late Bearon's father unfortunately was a complete tee-totaler, so although the castle was converted into a true baronial manse, the immense stock of wines, brews and liquors that had been amassed for the hotel just sat locked in the cellars much to the general dismay of the rest of the family."

"And the staff, no doubt..."*(my contribution.)*

"Weel, they were rather dour times, Ms. Bearyl. We all had to take our little pleasures in whatever way we could manage. Young Bearon Byron knew better than to be caught drinkin' in front of his father. The old gentlebear wouldna sell off the cellars for he feared that the demon rum he sold would cause the downfall of many and it would be his fault. On the other hand, being a frugal bear, he couldna bring himself to destroy the stock either. So there it sat until yer husban' hit upon an idea of making a few quid *(this was before the euro, mind)* by selling it off to smugglers behind his father's back. He couldna use up the entire cellars, of course, in case the old bruin were to check but he made a mickle at it, natheless."

"I don't get it. I only met Bearon Byron once but he seemed to be rolling in money. Why did he have to resort to smuggling?" I asked.

Bel replied, "You met Byron after his parents died from eating contaminated fish. They were both very strict and on top of that kept very tight control of the purse strings, which frustrated him no end. The best way to get the young Bearon-to-be to do something was to tell him he shouldn't or couldn't do it. He was constantly looking for riskier and riskier stunts to pull off. After the passing of his dam and sire, he had control of the family fortune. He actually settled down a bit and seemed to be content with making and spending money in big business deals and the occasional flutter. When he first saw me, he bought the Aquabears Revue outright simply because it was easier than trying to get my stage-struck mother to let him near me. Of course, when Mom found out how rich he was, she almost shanghaied him into marrying me. Good old Mom, romance personified! But on balance, I guess we had a good marriage, short though it was. He could be lots of fun and I confess we did paint the world red or actually blue and white. And he made a business sow out of me."

She paused for a moment and then said, "Oh, well! Hamish, I want you to tell me what other uses he made of that lift and sea platform. I can't believe that the Byron I knew would confine himself to some petty smuggling."

"True, milady, true! I believe the young Bearon got himself tied up with a few vicious characters resultin' from his smugglin', do ya see? They were Kellas cats. Oh aye, they do exist and a nastier bunch ya couldna' ask for. And they had ideas about usin' the castle as a sort of crime headquarters. This was before he met you, incidentally. Weel, the Bearon was bit wild, ya see, but he was not about to get himself sent off to gaol for the rest of his young life. He played along and then one night, when the gang was returnin' from hijackin' a floatin' casino, he waited until they had all gotten off their attack boat and onto the platform and he released the water tanks, drownin' them all in the deluge. Then when he was sure there were no survivors, he sank their boat out in the bay. Not a trace was left of them."

Belinda was thunderstruck. Her carefree, bon vivant husband had been in fact a mass assassin instead of an upstanding ursine. She had no pity certainly for the criminal gang. They deserved to sink but it was becoming clear that he too had been a murderous criminal. A very uncomfortable thought crossed her mind. "Hamish, what do you know about Byron's skiing accident?"

"Simply that he was caught in a freak avalanche in the Alps while filming a commercial, milady."

"One would have thought that a professional film crew would have checked slope conditions very carefully before setting up for a day's shoot. I was in Japan on tour with the Aquabears when it happened and I got the story second hand from the police and the film producer. Two crew members were also killed. Was there ever any question raised about foul play?"

"Foul play, milady. What sort of foul play?"

"Perhaps the avalanche may have been induced," she said nonchalantly.

Bearnice and I gasped in unison – *(roughly equivalent to a broken steam pipe.)* Hamish just stared and then shook his head mournfully.

"The thought did occur to me, milady. I'm nae sure the Bearon really understood who he was playin' with.'

"Did you, Hamish?'

"I didna ken who they were but it seemed to me that there were more than just the Kellas cats who were usin' the castle. It seemed like a big time operashin' from all appearances."

"And from all appearances, they may still be operating and even trying to use this castle?"

"I canno' be sure but I wouldn't dismiss it."

"Do you think Alistair's swan dive is connected to all of this?'

"I have not a clue about Sir Alistair except he was constantly comin' and goin' and nobody could say for sure where or why. I dinna ken what he was doin' on the roof. He may have had business there, but I canna imagine what."

"Suppose he was killed somewhere else, brought in by sea, taken to the roof and pushed over."

I piped up. "Why not just dump the body in the water with some weights attached? Why go to all that trouble?"

Bel paused and looked at all of us. "Sounds to me like a message was being delivered. By whom and to whom isn't clear but the content certainly is. That, and the other stuff going on are all warnings. 'Don't put your snout where it doesn't belong.' Alistair probably found out a few things and subtle opportunist that he was, tried a little blackmail or wanted a piece of the action, whatever it is. "

She turned to the Bearnice and me and said, "See if Octavius has left for the pub yet. He may be in more danger than he thinks. We all may be in more danger than we think."

Chapter Seventeen
On the Way to Baltasound

The great Lion has a menacing stare,
And a mane of such glorious hair.
Yet his cavernous jaws
Should not cause you to pause.
When he eats, he just wants his fair share.

Maury: I'm Back!

Situation Report: A Land Rover and a flatbed lorry sat waiting in the driveway. Bearbi and her crew were piling into the SUV. Clarence was driving. Lepi and Otto were sitting in the cab of the truck with Dougal. I was going to ride in the back with Octavius. We had some of the photo crew's equipment loaded in with us. Uncomfortable.

Estimated Time of Departure: Shortly.

We had just completed a second inspection of the two vehicles – brakes and brake lines, tires, looking for strange stuff under the chassis, loose anythings, unnecessary or unfamiliar items in the engine compartments, under the seats etc. Dougal had gone through the whole routine half an hour earlier. He found nothing. We found nothing. Proves nothing!

There had been some discussion as to whether I should ride with Dame Bearbara, but there was no room in the Land Rover even for someone my size. I, of course, was going to act as intermediary between Bearbi and her band of paparazzi and the gentle folk at the pub. I was reasonably sure that Lion and Unicorn for all their bluster, would love the publicity, especially being able to reenact their famous fight on video and for magazine stills. I was less certain what the reaction of the offshore wildcats would be, and I wanted to keep the groups as far apart as possible. Octavius, Chita, Lepi, Otto and I wanted to glean as much information as they were willing to give us without interruption or getting them ticked off. We had decided that we would not mention our suspicions that the castle might be the focus of all these problems and attacks. We didn't want a vengeful mob trying to burn the place down. Shades of Frankenstag, the deranged doctor deer and his monster moose.

Chita had decided to come with us but since neither vehicle would be setting any speed records, she decided to lope along on the ground as we went. I wasn't sure whether she was just trying to keep her hide in one piece if anything should happen to the truck, or whether she planned to do a little scouting of the terrain as we went. Possibly both.

I had been trying to make some sense out of that cat for quite a while and then it occurred to me. She probably doesn't make sense to herself. A beautiful face, spectacular legs, ferocious teeth and a towering IQ brain all attached to an agile, high performance body, but under the control *(maybe)* of a hair trigger, whirlwind response nerve center. Tough, but touchy and often single-minded to the point of disaster. Easy to like but, oh boy, even easier to hate. Anyhow, there she sat, tail hypnotically swaying back and forth, back and forth, waiting for us to finish our inspections and get on the road.

Showtime!! Dougal and Clarence gunned their respective engines and the Great Unst Expedition was underway. Just as we were heading out of the parking lot, I caught sight of Bearyl or Bearnice waving at us. A nice touch! I waved back and over the hill we went.

The trip was only a few miles as the crow flies. *(Why is it always a crow? Some crows I've met couldn't fly a straight line on a bet, even assuming they were sober.)* But as the vehicle rolls, it was a good deal longer with tight little switchbacks and steep, winding paths created no doubt, by flocks of disoriented sheep. Speaking of whom, there weren't any neighborhood ewes and nannies this afternoon on their way down for Bingo. We had the road, such as it was, to ourselves.

Octavius' oversize cell phone chimed a chorus of 'The Teddy Bears' Picnic' and the Great Bear flipped it open with an officious, "Bear here!" It was Belinda and whatever she was saying captured his complete attention. Nods, grunts, uh-huhs, frowns and assorted other signs that set my whiskers twitching.

"Thanks, Bel, but I think we're past the point of no return." *(Didn't that sound consoling!!)* "We checked out the vehicles twice and we're being very careful on the road. She won't admit it but Chita is our point cat dashing back and forth in front and then in back of us. Whoa, she almost went over the side of the cliff that time. We'll be back for dinner and we can have a war conference then. You be careful, too. Make sure Bearyl and Bearnice are with you at all times. Yes, I know. You're a big bear. So was Alistair. No, I'm not comparing you to Alistair or any of those other creepy in-laws of yours. If anything happens, we'll call right away. You do the same."

(Assuming we can, thought I.) He hung up and fed me the two euro version of Bel's session with Hamish. I'm sure a lot was lost in the transmission but what I heard, I didn't like. He was right, though. It was too late *(and the road was too narrow)* to turn back and that might have been exactly what the bad guys wanted us to do. As we topped the next incline, we could just make out the main street intersection and the thatched roof of the pub below us. The village was sheltered in a light coat of haze, and it looked for all the world like Brigadoon with a bad case of jaundice.

Suddenly, Chita chirped and howled, scrambled up on the bonnet of the lorry *(hood of the truck)* and pounded on the windscreen. Dougal tromped on the brakes and Clarence came very close to making a sandwich out of Octavius and me before he stopped behind us. About ten yards ahead, on the cliff side of the road sat an unobtrusive arrangement of rocks and gravel. There were plenty of them all along the route. This one had the distinction, however, of being right at the beginning of a sharp curve and even more to the point, as we found out a few moments later, was salted with a small array of dynamite sticks.

We piled out of the trucks. Dougal and Clarence both had weapons, as did Octavius and I. Chita pointed to a metal wire stretched across the road that was practically invisible from the cab of the truck but at four-footed animal eye level, it was pretty easy to spot.

Now what!? Otto to the rescue!

He skittered out and under the trip wire and gingerly approached the pile of rocks. The wire looked like it was rigged to trigger the explosive rock pile and blow the road out just as we drove over it. The truck would have been a goner and I wouldn't have cared for the odds on the SUV behind us. "There's a detonator and a small stack of dynamite here. I think I can teleport the whole thing into the ocean without touching it. My adrenaline level is certainly high enough."

"Can you do it without blowing it up?" yelled Octavius as Otto padded back toward the truck.

"I'm not sure, but I think I can heave it pretty far out over the edge before it explodes. We don't want it sliding down the side. Not much point in it going off and disintegrating the bottom of the cliff, either. Top down or bottom up, we're still stuck if it starts a rockslide."

Chita was watching all this from her perch on the hood of the truck. Bearbi and her crew had come running up from the Land Rover, cameras at the ready. "Doctah Beah, Doctah Beah, whatever is going on? Ooooh"

Octavius had grabbed her just before she trundled into the outstretched wire. "Dame Bearbara, I think we have everything under control. As you can see, you almost walked into a booby trap that was designed to dump us all on the rocks below. Chita saw the wire and stopped us just in time."

"Chita, dahling! How terribly brave and clever! What a story! Oh, we must capture this all on film." Then it dawned on her that she was just inches away from having sent herself and everyone else to that great ice floe in the sky *(in very small pieces.)* If it was possible for a polar bear to turn white, she would have. Instead she just fainted, damn near hitting the trip wire as she fell.

Octavius picked her up and unceremoniously dumped her in the back of the lorry. Then he turned to Clarence and said, "I want you to back the Land Rover up as far as you can. Get your helpers to guide you. Then we're going to back up the truck out of range. Then we'll see if Otto can teleport this thing out over the water before it blows. If you plan on taking any pictures, may I suggest a very long telephoto lens."

I had scurried out to join Otto and in a moment of sheer stupidity had shimmied under the wire to see what the detonator rig looked like. My aunt would once again have written me off as a complete idiot. There was a trigger on the detonator being held back by a short wire that, in turn, was connected to the one across the road. Slacken either wire and the thing would go off.

The objective now was to keep from destroying the road. We were reasonably certain we could avoid personal injury by backing away and letting Otto do his thing but the castle could be permanently cut off from the village if we didn't do this right. Chita and Lepi were standing behind us. Octavius was supervising the "back-up procedure." Chita searched the surrounding area to make sure no one else was coming, going or standing around where they might get hurt. Then she strode down the road to stop anyone coming up. Clarence did the same on the up side.

Lepi looked over and said, "One of us who is strong enough has to hold the short wire in place while someone else detaches it from the trip wire across the road. Then if he lets go when Otto says OK, we may be able to keep it from exploding before it starts its ride into the water."

"And," thought I, "that same someone might find themselves hurtling into the water or being radically disassembled if they let go at exactly the wrong time."

We all looked at each other. Octavius was just too damn big to handle something this delicate and I was too small. With a major sigh of relief from me, Lepi volunteered to hold the short wire while Otto disconnected it from the roadway trip cable. Octavius gave the signal that the two vehicles and all extraneous passengers including me had been backed as far away as we could go. Lepi grabbed the wire in his claws and Otto went about the delicate maneuver of unhitching it from the booby trap. If either one of them slipped, the Edinbeargh Opera and the Aquabears would be missing two star attractions. *(I know, once a theatrical agent, always a theatrical agent.)*

"OK, Lepi. I'm gonna give you a count of three and an interrupted "Let-Go." said Otto. "I'll stand over here where I have a clear view of the detonator and you tell me when you're ready for me to start the count. At the word "go" drop it and run like hell."

I thought Chita was going to pace herself into the ground as she watched from the far side. Octavius rumbled that anyone who so much as peeped or clicked a shutter would go over the cliff edge without a second thought. He stared at the now conscious Bearbi who was peeking over the side panel of the lorry. She nodded her head nervously.

Lepi gave the feline equivalent of a thumbs-up and Otto started: "One, Two, Thuree, Let…GOOOOO!"

The blast echoed off the sides of the cliff and rattled up and down the valley. Lepi and Otto were both flat on their backs but they had gotten far enough away behind some rocks before the dynamite went off. Octavius, Dougal, Clarence and I had watched the trajectory of the package as it went "out to sea" before it blew. I was blown back against the lorry. Bearbi was cowering on the bed of the truck and Chita had been knocked over by the shock wave. The camera crew was doing what camera crews do…taking pictures.

Octavius shouted, "It blew in midair over the water. But the vibration might have still set off a few rock slides. We'll have to check. Great work, Otto and Lepi! Are you both OK?" He gave them each a bear hug. Lepi winced. He had hit something when he was flattened and a hug was NOT what he needed. Otto looked like he might have preferred being blown to bits. Paw shakes all around. Sighs of relief. Bearbi showed her nose over the panel and asked if the coast was clear. She had lost her safari hat and starting sniffing around for it.

Chita was checking Lepi out for broken bones and I was doing a similar check on my client. "Nice work, Otto. Any second now, Bearbi is going to come to her senses and realize what you did. Just give her a few 'Aw shucks, m'am' but don't explain your telekinetic powers, OK?"

"Got it. First thing I have to do is catch my breath."

Octavius trundled over. "Alright, let's all catch our collective breaths! (*Always there with just the right advice.*) And then, let's take a few moments to figure this out before we continue on to the village."

Bearbi looked as if she wasn't sure she wanted to continue on but she kept her mouth shut. Chita strolled over and said, "I don't suppose you noticed the road barrier pulled off to the side of the road back there. It was dragged under some overhanging bushes."

"No, we didn't. That might explain why we didn't see the Bingo brigade. Are you saying someone put it up earlier and then dragged it away when they saw us coming."

"Right, they didn't want the wrong bunch to knock out the road. That thing was not designed to just rearrange scenery. They wanted to kill US. If anyone else hit it, their whole plan would have been ruined."

"Which means someone may still be still hanging around watching what we're doing."

"Or," said Octavius, "they may have rigged a second trap further down the road just in case. Of course, they would have had to stop traffic coming up the hill too, to make sure we were the ones to set off the explosion. So they had to be active in the last half hour or so."

Dougal had come over at this last statement, "Och, three vee-hicles a day would be a traffic jam on this road. Nothin' much comes or goes that doesn't originate at the castle. Maybe a shopkeeper or two from the village. And of course, the Bingo ladies. but they always walk. Not a driver among them."

"Well, whoever's doing this is probably on foot at the moment or just hiding out. We can't turn around here, so we might as well finish our trip to the pub. When we finish talking with the cats and Bearbi's photo shoot is over, maybe we can call up to the castle for a lift back on the helicopters. Dougal and Clarence can bring the wheels back up. I can't believe either of them were the targets. Speaking of the castle, I'll better call Bel. She probably heard the explosion."

She had, and the conversation seemed alternately animated and soothing. She no doubt wanted to come down and pick us up right on the spot. Not the easiest place to land a couple of choppers. Octavius finally talked her out of it and arranged for us to be picked up in the village later on.

We started somewhat gingerly to get back in the vehicles. Chita once again was playing forward scout and two of Bearbi's crew were guarding the rear. Octavius picked up his phone again and this time called Superintendent Wardlaw. Yes, he'd be up in the evening. He was quite concerned when told about what had happened over the past forty-eight hours and quite put out that we hadn't called him earlier. Octavius tried to smooth things over but I doubt if it did much good. Oh, well, life in the fast lane or in this case, the only lane.

We edged our way down the rest of the road into the village looking like a group of fleeing refugees instead of smart, worldly-wise sophisticates about to solve a massive crime wave. Bearbi had recovered her vivaciousness *(God help us!)* and was babbling loudly enough from the SUV behind us to hear her in the truck ahead. She couldn't wait to get her hooks, mikes and cameras on everyone and everything and now especially on Otto – the Miracle Otter. Now she knew, or thought she knew, why he was going to be appearing with the Aquabears. *(You ain't seen nothing yet, Bearbi!)*

The parking lot at The Lion and The Unicorn was pretty full; meaning the wildcats were probably there in force but there was also a fairly large contingent of locals as well, standing around, eager to watch the battle and the photo shoots. Big doings in the village!

Lion came out to meet us with a crowd in tow. "We heard an explosion a wee while ago. Wuz ye involved?"

We told him we heard it too and thought there might have been some construction going on somewhere. Lion looked at us askance, knowing full well he was being conned. I winked at him and murmured, "We'll have a story for you in a little while and some questions, too after the multitude thins out."

He winked back and strode over to Dame Bearbara, who was immediately at full gush. "Oh, Mr. Lion, this is a great honor. Where is your horned associate? We are sooo eager to capture every minute of your thrilling battle and this pub just oozes with charm and local color."

Give Lion credit. He knew which side of his publicity bread the butter was on. He smiled at Bearbi, scaring her out of her wits with his teeth and invited her in for a wee dram before the festivities began. I fell in with them to act as intermediary and if necessary, referee. She went totally bananas or whatever the polar bear equivalent is *(fishes???)* over Unicorn. Turning to give her his full profile, the noble beast reared up on his hind legs and struck the pose in the Great Seal. Not to be outdone, Lion matched him. Unfortunately, Otto was standing between them with a foolish grin on his face looking not at all like the Scottish coat of arms. Clarence was quick on the draw with his SLR and I now have a collector's item photo that hangs in my office. My first clients!!!

While the preparations and negotiations were going on for the Great Shetland Photo Op, Octavius, Chita, Lepi and Dougal went over to the tables where the wildcats were nursing their brews and introduced themselves. Fergus, once again, acted as the rig crews' spokescat and invited them to be seated. Otto and I were shuttling back and forth between the two scenes, Otto trying *(unsuccessfully)* to avoid Dame Bearbi and I trying to keep the dame and her crew from causing another Highlands Uprising.

A sweet little Dandie Dinmont barmaid came over wagging her tail and asked, "Greetins, folks, what's yer pleasure?" Octavius called immediately for the finest mead in the house and ordered another round for all the cats. Dougal, Lepi and Chita all asked for the local single malt scotch. I managed to ask the capering canine if Lion had any more of his fermented coconut milk stashed away. She looked at me with a sly wink and said, "I'm sure we kin find yer a drap or two, Mr. Meerkat. Considerin' yer puttin' us on the map agin."

News travels fast. Bearbi was busy trying to convince Lion and Unicorn to try on the crowns she'd gotten from the castle. Unicorn had discovered he could twirl his on the end of his horn and proceeded to put on an impromptu juggling act with the hallowed hat. Lion would not allow Bearbi to fasten his with bearbi pins. "Tis neither regal nor comfortable. I'll hold it in my paw along with the rod and orb and put it on when ye need it."

We were just about to organize the first round of shooting and Octavius and Chita were already deep in conversation with the cats when my cell phone rang. It was Bearyl. Someone had just tried to set fire to both of the helicopters. Damage was minimal but she wasn't sure whether they were still airworthy. Don't let Dougal or Clarence leave. She'd call me back. This day was turning out to be quite annoying. All we needed now was…Bingo! Octavius was sound asleep over his mead.

The Development of Civilization Volume 3 Part 4
Empires, Nations, Governments and Politics - Society
(From "An Introduction to Faunapology" by Octavius Bear Ph.D.)

This discussion and Part 5-Languages are related. They briefly explore how and why over the past 100,000 years since the Big Shock, the enhanced surviving denizens of this earth have formed and re-formed into distinct groups, subdivisions and factions, adopting specialized behavior and customs and individual modes of communication.

You should remember that before the Big Shock most animals, while not sufficiently developed to be described as sentient, still had rudimentary social characteristics that helped them survive, co-exist and in some cases, at least, grow in numbers. To be sure, there were and still are some species that live alone and come together only briefly to mate and then retire to their seemingly preferred isolation.

After the magnetic blasts in which many species, notably Homo Sapiens, apparently became extinct due to neural decomposition, some of the surviving animals slowly developed heightened mental and emotional characteristics. These included self-awareness and the seeds of advanced communication. Those totally unaffected by the Big Shock, most fish for example, retained whatever "social" characteristics they already had such as travelling in schools but only evolved further within certain proscribed limits.

It would seem natural then, that the already established social "mores" of individual species should expand over time and become more subtle, sophisticated and effective. For example, the concept of the Alpha male and/or female advanced to the concept of royalty. The idea of fighting for the top positions seems to have hung on, regardless of how much progress was otherwise made. Advisers and assistants became more formalized members of the group with their own privileges. In contrast, many other members fell to a level of subservient or even disposable parts of the society. In this way, over thousands of years, herds, packs, flocks and other intra-species groups developed more intricate systems for establishing and conducting their "business" of living.

Other interesting results materialized as inter-species societies began to build. First predator, prey and, scavenger developed ever more complex symbiotic relationships (not always unfavorable for the prey.)What a shock it must have been to the first lionesses who discovered that instead of running away, large herds of antelope would all turn at a leader's command and run the cats down. Although one or two antelopes may have been sacrificed in the process, the idea of the greater good began to formulate itself and "society" as a working concept began to emerge. Soon thereafter the even more complex ideas of "preserving (defending) society" developed.

Powered by the movement toward societal preservation, organizations evolved. Some were populated by a single species but many consisted of multiple animal varieties, tied to each other by geographic, climatic, and eventually purely social bonds including religion.

Belief in supreme or superior powers often bound the groups together. Individuals who claimed access to the "gods" gained control over many of the decision making processes of the assemblages. Others gained ascendancy by providing defense; supply of necessities; control of anti-social behavior; maintenance of folklore and history; communication; education or diplomatic skills in dealing with other species external to the group.

Needless to say, conflicts arose and the world population or major segments of it came very close to self annihilation on several occasions. Witness the Great Inter-Species War. Nevertheless, today, our geopolitical structures persevere as direct consequences of these earlier societal formations. No doubt, far in the future, other generations will examine our societal progression with the same somewhat amused curiosity.

Frau Schuylkill

Chapter Eighteen
Dyce Airport Abeardeen

Yes, of course, unicorns do exist.
He's a beauty no one can resist.
With his spiral horn's flair
And his fine-looking hair,
It's no wonder by maidens he's kissed.

Dyce Airport at Abeardeen was momentarily operational and the Ursa Major lined up for a low, slow touchdown on the oversized runway that had originally been lengthened for the Bearoness' SST. Luft-Kapitan Frau Ilse Schuylkill looked over at Colonel Wyatt Where, co-pilot and security specialist, and yipped once. He nodded. Both wolves along with Howard Watt, a protection technology expert *(and a porcupine)* made up the core of the Great Bear's defensive and crime fighting organization. *(I hesitate to brag about my own status as Octavius' executive officer and field manager.)* Howard had brought along our recent *(and extremely capable)* guest, L. Condor, an Andean Condor who is one of the world's most skilled communications and computing specialists. It was he who ruined Pontius Puma's rackets in Brazil and may have sent Imperius Drake to the bottom of the Ohio River. A good bird to have along! The Bear's A-Plus Team was on final approach.

The C5-A, at the insistence of the Shetland authorities, had been stripped of its armaments before taking off from the US, although the occupants had managed to break down and stow a prime selection of weapons and com gear in various nooks and crannies in the flying warehouse. Not the least of these was the particle beam accelerator. When disassembled it looked like a nondescript tube attached to a few parts labeled "Auxiliary Weather Radar." This innocent looking but highly destructive contrivance had played a pivotal role in our previous adventures and there was no reason to think it couldn't supply an encore on demand.

Wyatt got on the intercom as the massive tires thumped on the runway and said, "This ship will no doubt be quarantined until customs, the police and military are convinced it's just an oversized ferry boat used by a big, eccentric tycoon bear and his friends. Please refrain from any mention of the aircraft's capabilities. In fact, say as little as possible. We have come to assist Octavius Bear and Shetland Yard *(who didn't ask for us!)* in their investigations up at the Bearoness' castle on Unst. We'll leave the weapons hidden on board for the moment till we clear all of their searches and investigations. As you might expect, they're all pretty touchy right now. These oil field and airport disruptions literally have them chasing their tails. Please let me do the talking."

In the opposite seat, Frau Ilse Schuylkill nodded her head and showed her formidable teeth – possibly a smile, possibly not. Down in the hold, Howard Watt and L. Condor who needed all the space he could get for his twelve foot wingspan, presented the rodent and avian equivalents of thumbs-up.

As it whined its way along the tarmac, the huge aircraft was drawing a minor crowd of onlookers. The painting on the Galaxy's nose of a large Kodiak Bear encircled by a constellation of stars over the name Ursa Major caught every beast's attention. "Who are these guys?"

Ground control vectored them off to an area of the airport that already housed The Flying Aquabear *(the Bearoness' SST)* and several bearonial helicopters that were used as shuttles between the castle and Dyce. Belinda had her own not insignificant air force. Thank goodness! The two choppers up at Bearmoral may or may not have been put out of commission by our little arsonist friends.

As the C5-A rolled up to its assigned parking spot, a "welcoming" committee was already forming. Frau Schuylkill revved the engines briefly to instill a bit of caution among the greeters. They got the message. The Frau was feeling a bit playful as she shut down the power.

She opened the cavernous aft loading bay doors as well as the jetstairs beneath the cockpit. Several airport police border collies went running up and down the length of the massive fuselage to cover each exit. "They need the exercise!" she muttered, "Swiss dogs wouldn't be that fat!" The two wolves exited down the jetstairs and after the rear loading doors were fully deployed, the porcupine and the condor, flexing his wings to full length, strolled down the length of the cargo bay and exited the ramp. All told, they made quite an entrance into Scotland's bonnie climes.

A brawny Clydesdale wearing a regimental blanket and headpiece that announced to the world that he was a colonel in the Highland Defense Force stood at attention with his head raised so he could stare haughtily down his equine nose at the visitors. "I am Colonel McNeigh, Royal Army, Commandant of the Greater Abeardeen Security Force. Since this is supposed to be a decommissioned military aircraft, it shall be quarantined until we have fully inspected it for weapons and other potential threats. Until that time, this ship will be under military guard and you will not be permitted to return to it without an escort. One of you may be present when we conduct our inspections."

"You may take your personal effects and baggage with you. These officers of the Customs and Immigration Department *(gesturing toward three uniformed border collies)* will inspect your immigration documents and your baggage. You may then transfer to one of these helicopters for your journey to Unst. Welcome to Scotland. Who is in charge of this group?"

"I am Colonel Wyatt Where, US Army Retired and this is Oberst Frau Ilse Schuylkill, Swiss Guard, Retired. She is the commander of the aircraft. I am nominally in charge of our group. This is Doctor Howard Watt, a highly respected security technology specialist and Senhor L. Condor, a computing and communications expert noted throughout the world. We are here to assist Doctor Octavius Bear and the authorities in any way we can in pursuit of the murderer of Sir Alistair Bruin. We can also be of service, if you wish, in helping to resolve the disturbances and anomalies that have been taking place here and on the North Sea."

A dignified bearded collie who had been standing behind the horse came forward and extended his paw. "Inspector Wardlaw of Shetland Yard. Doctor Bear and I are auld acquaintances and are working together on this case. Welcome to my patch. My team and I will be flying up to Bearmoral castle shortly. We have room for one mid-size animal in our craft. It would seem Senhor Condor will require substantial room to accommodate his wings so perhaps Doctor Watt would like to fly with me and the rest of you can take that large utility helo over there. Are either of you colonels rated to pilot a helicopter?"

Two wolfish heads nodded and two wolfish tails wagged in unison.

"Splendid. Well then, let's get the formalities over with, shall we, and we can be on our way. A number of recent developments have escalated the situation at the castle *(he didn't know the half of it!)* and we will leave as soon as you're ready. Colonel McNeigh, when do you plan to hold your inspection of the aircraft?"

"Not until tomorrow or the next day. We'll inform Colonel Where well in advance."

Perhaps to make up for the annoyance of the Ursa Major being quarantined, the foursome was passed through customs and immigration in "joost a wee moment."

Howard was prepared to cede his seat on the police chopper to Wyatt or Frau Ilse but they urged him to take it. "You are not military, Herr Doctor Howard. He may open up more to you. We will see you at the castle."

As the two choppers rose from the tarmac, it became instantly apparent to Howard that even with headsets, the rotor noise was going to make conversation with the policeman difficult, if not impossible. Over in the other craft, Wyatt, who had more hours in a chopper, had taken the controls and Frau Schuylkill went about reporting in to Octavius.

L. Condor was sorting through the comm gear that he had brought with him and had miraculously gotten through customs. He convinced them it was all required for his electronic voice box. Andean condors are voiceless but with the help of the UUI staff, he had developed a neural audio system that had turned him into quite a conversationalist. He could actually produce a wide range of very realistic voices. His version of Octavius had us rolling on the floor. The whole thing was micro-miniaturized and everything he needed he wore around his neck. The rest of the gear was unrelated cloak and dagger stuff. Customs didn't need to know that. They had never seen a condor before, let alone a techie condor. For all they knew, he could breathe fire or rise up from ashes.

Octavius didn't answer the Frau's call. He was off on his involuntary siesta. Next on her list was good old me.

"Herr Maury? This is Frau Schuylkill! Herr Bear is not answering...oh, I see! We have arrived at Abeardeen. We are coming north on a helicopter. Are you at the castle? A pub? A Lion and a Unicorn? Lions in Scotland? I didn't know unicorns really existed! I'm having trouble hearing you. You want us to come to the village below the castle? There are problems?!? We are two helicopters. The other one has the Shetland Yard Superintendent and his crew. Howard is with him. Ja, you think it better if the police don't arrive yet. All right! We're flying slower than they are. We'll just let them go ahead to the castle and we'll come down in the village. A battle scene? Herr Maury. This pub…have you been into the coconut milk again? Ja, we'll watch out for the film crew. In about thirty minutes. Nein, we had no problems. I tell you when I see you."

She turned to Wyatt and relayed the situation and instructions over the intercom. L. Condor looked up quizzically as she passed on what she had heard. Forget about condors in the Shetlands. You'd never find a unicorn in Brazil. Say what you like. His time with Octavius and his merry band has been…interesting. This next round sounded like it might have some minor fascinations as well. He heard the wolf mention Chita. Was she here? That's news.

The police copter pulled further and further away from the slower utility craft. It was still hazy from the earlier fog and it would take very little effort for the trio to simply drop behind and search for the village while still staying on a general vector to the castle. If the police had them on radar they'd just disappear below the hills at an appropriate time and place. It would take a while for the superintendent to catch on. They would simply say they were answering a request from Octavius to make a short detour.

Wyatt saw the village first and pointed over the port side of the chopper. Several fishing boats were in the small harbor and there seemed to be some kind of a parade going on at the village green. They spotted the pub from the description I'd given them. Wyatt looked around for somewhere to land that wouldn't start a riot. A helicopter itself wouldn't cause any problems. Old stuff in the Shetlands! However, a helicopter with two wolves and a condor might. The green was taken up with whatever that ceremony was all about. Next best place turned out to be a cemetery. No joy there, either. Finally, they spotted a soccer *(football, rugby, whatever)* field that stood behind a small school. No kids at the moment so down they went.

On the ground, I was watching three things at once – (1) the semi-organized chaos that was going to be the Lion and Unicorn Fight for the Crown – under the direction *(sic)* of Dame Bearbara Da Savile-Row; (2) the beginnings of discussions in the pub with the oil rig wildcats now that Octavius had awakened; and (3) the descent of the Bearmoral utility chopper. A meerkat's work is never done. Chita was bounding back and forth between the doings on the green, where she was trying to keep Bearbi from starting a replay of the War of the Daffodils and the pub where she really wanted to be. So did I. With the explosive events of this afternoon, we were all on edge and convinced that there was some connection between the activities at the castle and the problems on the rigs and at Abeardeen. Somebody didn't want us talking with the wildcats. Somebody didn't want us investigating Alistair's death. Somebody didn't want us nosing around Bearmoral. Somebody just didn't want us.

Suddenly, on the village green everything and everyone stopped. Jaws, muzzles and beaks all fell into a coordinated gape. From behind the schoolhouse emerged two wolves in flight suits and the biggest bird any of the locals had ever seen. Bearbi screamed at Clarence and suddenly the trio was surrounded by the Highland equivalent of paparazzi. L. Condor looked at the hyper-energized Bearbi and in a deep baritone said, "Take me to your leader!"

Both wolves broke out laughing. Unfortunately, a wolf laughing looks identical to a wolf about to chew your leg off. Dougal, Otto and I ran up to greet the world travelers before the good citizens of Unst decided to attack. I jumped up on Dougal's back and shouted something to the effect that these were our associates from the U.S., wonderful animals all *(although endowed with a warped sense of humor.)*

The village mayor *(a Cairn Terrier)* and the chief constable *(a Gordon Setter)* gave all of us a sharp dose of Scottish scrutiny as only they can do and then came forward to meet the trio. L. Condor was the new center of attraction and Bearbi was beside herself trying to manage the battle reenactment, get as many shots of the bird and wolves as she could and keep things under control. She was failing miserably. Lion and Unicorn were both a bit put out over losing their audience and the villagers who had been hired to drum and chase the combatants were getting restless. Otto performed a few magic tricks to keep their attention. At one point, he turned and said, "You know Maury! It just occurred to me. If the Colonel and the Frau ever got married she would be Ilse Where! Get it? Get it?

"Keep juggling, Otto!"

Agent Maury to the rescue. I got Clarence and his photo crew back on the village green, settled Bearbi down *(only two more miracles and I'm up for sainthood!)* got the wolves and the condor safely in front of bowls of ale in the pub and checked to see how Lepi and Octavius were doing with the wildcats. Chita, who had momentarily made herself scarce, joined their discussions.

I went over to Wyatt, the Frau and L. Condor and proceeded to bring them up to speed on our volatile adventures earlier in the day as well as the unsuccessful attempts back at the castle to destroy the choppers. I reported on Belinda's session with Hamish. They in turn, told me about the arrival of Superintendent Wardlaw who, no doubt, was meeting with the Bearoness as we spoke. They also filled me in on the situation with the Ursa Major. We turned to look out on the green.

Almost on cue, the drums reverberated, cheers went up and the antagonists started playing Keep Away with an ancient crown that looked like it wouldn't make it through the battle. Back and forth. In and out. Feint, drop back, circle around. Up on their hind legs. These two guys knew how to play to the cameras. Out of the blue, Unicorn speared the crown on his horn and ran around the perimeter of the green with Lion in close pursuit. Suddenly the mythical beast veered and headed full speed through the doors of the pub. The little bar maid shrieked, bowls smashed and splintered, everyone scattered as he thundered through the room with Lion at his cloven heels. Lion skidded to a stop under the portrait of the Prince of Whales and roared after him at the top of his fearsome lungs. "Yer twit. D'ya see what you've done. You've wrecked the place. What were ya thinkin'?"

A few moments later, Unicorn stuck his horn with the crown still perched on it back into the room, blushed and said, "I was in a hurry. I had to use the privy."

"Well, git back in here and help clean up the mess. There go our profits for this day. Ye're hopeless."

"But I still have the crown!"

"I ken ya have it and ye're welcome to it. I hope that gormless polar bear and her poncy crew got all the pitchers they wanted. I'll nae play any more today."

Bearbi had indeed gotten enough pictures and video for a full scale costume epic. Chita went through the motions of conferring with her while the rest of us righted chairs and tables, helped clean up shards of broken drink bowls and stood to one side as the bar maid and Lion wielded mops and rags.

Looking over at Octavius, I announced that the next round of drinks was on the Great Bear. Smiles, purrs and yips!

He, in turn, used the interruption to ask Unicorn for a keg of his finest mead. (*The day may yet be saved.*) Bearbi, Clarence and the photo crew piled back into the SUV and with the local constable riding in the front seat with his head and tongue sticking out the window they headed off slowly for the trip back to the castle. They'd probably be safe on the trip home. I doubted that they were a target. We knew who the bad guys were after and we were beginning to understand why. We were getting too close for their comfort.

Fergus called the wildcats back to order and Lepi, Octavius, Otto and I sat down with them. Octavius invited the wolves and condor over and introduced them as part of the team that would be helping clear up this mess on the rigs *(with Shetland Yard's and the military's permission.)* Chita sidled over and sat next to Fergus. Story time!

Chapter Nineteen
The Lion and Unicorn Pub

Scottish wildcats are hip-deep in oil
Off-shore platforms are where they all toil.
But unless we can find
The malign mastermind
They'll be driven back onto the soil.

Our meeting with the wildcats was taking on all the finer characteristics of a huge college keg party. After introducing them to the cats, Octavius excused himself and took the wolves and L. Condor aside. First, he briefed them about the attempted rock slide and why he wanted them to take us all back in the helicopter. Then he asked them to schmooze with Lion and Unicorn and see what, if anything they could learn from them. Even without those three, that still left quite a crowd of 'us colonials' conversing with 'them wildcats.' Each of us had a good reason. Chita, of course, owned The Hot Spot, one of the rigs. I'd made the initial contact with the cats. Lepi *was* a cat and no one had the heart to shoo Otto off after his heroism earlier today. And Octavius certainly wasn't used to fading into the background.

He faded back into the foreground and without going deeply into chapter and verse, gave the wildcats a brief rundown on what had been happening at the castle and then explained to them his theory that somehow that stately pile was connected with the problems they and the Abeardeen authorities had been battling. He mentioned that Shetland Yard and the Bearoness were both aware of and concerned about what was going on and that Superintendent Wardlaw was up at the castle as we spoke, sniffing about. He said that we were willing to assist in any way we could, looked over at Fergus and sat down. Chita interrupted to say that she owned a rig and knew that several of the wildcats here today were her employees. She wanted to meet with them later.

Fergus began: "The military and the poleece kin give you the history of the doings at Abeardeen airport. We've been outta work for twa weeks naw and our purses are gettin' empty. Lion and Unicorn, bless 'em, have been lettin' us run a tab but we'd rather be pumpin' oil than sluggin' down ale. (*On this last point, I expected a minority report from some of the cats but he just went on.)*'Twas a long fight fer us to establish our rights to pump in the North Sea. There's still a lot of prejoodice against wildcats in Scotland. And we're not goin' to give up on it now."

Yowls of support!

"The authorities have ordered us off the platforms. 'Tis a safety precaution, not only for ourselves but for the shipping lanes and ecology. Oil slicks and fires are not to their likin' – or ours. But we dinna see any progress in the offin.' If ya think ya kin help, we're willin' and able to work with ya. Isn't that right, fellas?"

More yowls of support!

To my amazement Octavius refrained from uttering one of his ponderous 'Hmmms.' "Now, can you tell me what sort of patterns these incidents have followed?"

"Tweren't incidents. 'Twere attacks and vandalism." This from a brawny wildcat whose tail had seen better days but could no doubt hold his own in a fight. In fact, that seemed to be the major source of frustration. These were tough, action loving felines, not pussy-cats and it ruffled their fur not to be able to claw a few hides in revenge.

Fergus, looking around the room at his co-workers, brought his tawny eyes back and stared at the Great Bear. "Corbett is in the right! These were all deliberate and planned out. Seven fires in four weeks. Mostly at night. Two support boats sunk. Communications and GPS smashed or jammed. Three helicopters put out of service. Two breaks in our off-shore pipelines. Two runaway drills. Electrical failures and even wholesale tamperin' with our food. If this was a war, we'd be fightin' back long afore this."

"Tis a war! 'Tis a war!" shouts from the group. "Someone's trying to cripple the Scottish oil industry and take our jobs with it."

I piped up. "Who? Who benefits if all of your wells stay off line?"

"We been askin' ourselves that." said Corbett, "Of course, the price of oil will go up but why joost the Scots rigs and facilities? Nothin's happenin to all those continental platforms."

Chita asked, "Nothing at all?"

"Not even a wee glitch! They're all drillin' and pumpin' away and laughin' at us, no doot."

Chita asked, "How many North Sea rigs are Scottish? Count in the pipelines and the storage tanks."

Fergus scrunched up his face and looked at the other cats. "Fifty?!" "No, there's only forty five! Some of the rigs are jointly owned."

"Well, how many Scots owners are there?"

"Three large companies and aboot half a dozen indies like yerself."

She turned to Octavius. "Those are the ones we need to meet with. Right away! This is some kind of power play against the wildcat oilers. Somebody wants them out of action."

"Or," I said, "Wants them to sell out at garage sale prices."

The room turned quiet. Everyone was staring at me. All I did was let my larcenous mind cut loose. I'm surprised Chita, extortionist extraordinaire, hadn't thought of it before this.

Octavius pounded his fur covered volleyball *(fist)* on the table, upset a few brews and *(Horrors!!)* came close to upsetting his flagon of mead. "Meerkat, you're right! Fergus, how serious has the damage been to your rigs?"

"Serious enough, but nothin' we couldn't fix in a couple of weeks. A few of the lads are still sick from the tainted food and we almost lost two of the crew on one of the support boats. The two boats are the only permanent loss. The choppers are all right. We might have to divert to one of the other pipelines while we fix ours. There's a sort of grid out there. The real loss has been in stopped produkshun. No income and a couple of the independent rigs were running verra close to the penny to begin with. "

"So, enough damage to hurt economically but not enough to make things unsalvageable after a takeover. If several of the current owners got pushed to the wall, they might sell in order to get out with half a pelt. That could start a panic run on all the rigs."

Chita looked at Fergus and then Octavius. "Give us the names of all the owners. As an owner myself, I think I can get them together at a meeting and we can compare notes. Let's see if somebody has opened the bidding yet."

"Meantime, we're going to offer our help to the authorities in tracking down what's going on out there and who's doing it. We're going to ask to go and inspect the damaged platforms, pipelines and support gear. We're also going to crawl all over the castle. Someone is trying to take it over from the Bearoness and that's something we're not going to allow. You cats be careful.

Knowing us and working with us may not be very advantageous to your health."

Looking at all those ferocious faces, I got the impression that health wasn't the topic on their minds. Octavius beckoned to the wolves and then turned to Fergus. "Would you be willing to come up with us to the castle and meet with Superintendent Wardlaw and the Bearoness? I can also promise you a good meal and some fine ale."

Fergus nodded and turned to Corbett. "I'll keep yez posted."

Octavius turned to Lion. "How much of this splendid mead are you willing to part with. I'll buy all you're willing to sell!"

Lion grinned widely, scaring both Otto and me with his massive teeth. "How much can ye carry?"

"What are you flying, Colonel?"

"A modified Chinook. Heavy duty!"

"Well, Lion, we'll empty your cellar for you."

"Och, for that kind of sale and because you're helping the cats here, I can give you a ten percent discount. *(Once a canny Scot, always a canny Scot.)*

Chita took her "employees" aside for a few minutes. I wasn't sure but I think some money passed paws to help them along. That cat has a unique set of values. I wonder if Robin Hood was really a cheetah instead of a bird.

Then, a small procession headed out to the Chinook cargo chopper. Chita, the wolves, L. Condor, Lepi, Otto, Fergus, Octavius and myself. Each one of us was towing a cask of mead under the watchful and nervous eye of the connoisseur bear. Otto dropped out of the line of march and said, "Someone should ride back with Dougal in the truck. I'll go. If there's another bomb on the road, I can take care of it. I didn't hear any explosions or crashes when Bearbi's SUV went back up but we can't count on it."

I decided to join him. My measly weight wouldn't make any difference on or off the heavily loaded copter but they could probably use a third set of paws in the truck if there were any problems. The lorry had at least one and possibly more guns on board.

Colonel Where started the twin rotors spinning while the members of the parade loaded mead into every available nook and cranny and then settled themselves in. I had volunteered to take some of the mead in the truck but

Octavius didn't want to be separated from it. "We'll go down together, if we go down at all!" he said.

I called up to the castle and reached Belinda. I told her briefly what had transpired at the pub and how we were coming back in two parties. She in turn told me about Wardlaw's arrival with Howard and then Bearbi's appearance. No incidents on the road. We'd all gather for drinks later and compare notes.

The big chopper had taken off, following a relatively straight course up over the cliffs and then I suppose, onto the castle grounds. We, on the other hand, had an uphill climb, twisting and turning and always looking down the side of the cliff to the icy, black, tempestuous, swirling, roaring, rock-filled, not-very-hospitable sea.

When we reached the spot where we had almost been blown up, we stopped and gave the place another inspection. The cables were still there and Otto, Dougal and I tugged and pulled them into the back of the lorry for later inspection. This job clearly had taken one or more very strong individuals, certainly bigger and stronger than any of us. We looked around for tire, foot, hoof or paw prints. Nothing distinct. Some broken shrubbery. We may have done that ourselves. In fact, in the process of trying to save our pelts we probably got the crime scene well and truly messed up. And Bearbi and her bunch *(plus God knows who else)* had been up and down the road since the blast.

We stopped further on at the barrier that Chita had first spotted. It was still off the side of the road, half hidden in the brush. Professional paint job: 'Road Closed.' Probably stolen. Maybe the local cops could help track down where it came from.

Finally, breathing again, we came over the crest and headed down to the castle parking lot where a couple of Land Rovers and the two helicopters sat. Several members of the castle staff were unloading flagons and kegs of mead under the watchful eye of Hamish and the Great Bear. Belinda and the Superintendent were standing next to him engaging in, if not heated, at least luke-warm conversation.

Bearbi, thank God, had disappeared with her minions, no doubt reviewing the day's shooting. Belinda, Bearbi and Chita - the mysterious trio! I referred to them as the Bearmuda Triangle. I made a mental note to find out a bit more about the flamboyant polar publisher. How did she ever meld in with the sophisticated cat and her lofty ladyship. Strange combination! I would have thought one or the other would have killed her by now but I have a very low annoyance threshold.

I wandered over to the spot where Octavius, Super Wardlaw and Belinda were thrashing out something. Polite but animated!!

"So you believe this string of violence here in the castle is all tied to the problems out on the oil rigs. I must confess, Doctor Bear, that I am having trouble supporting your conclusions. I honestly believe the death of Sir Alistair was the result of some sort of family squabble that went too far. Do you agree, Bearoness?"

"Superintendent, this morning I discovered that my late husband, Lord Byron, had another side to his personality. It seems he was mixed up with some pretty shady characters who thought nothing of piracy and full scale smuggling. They may even have done him in. I've always been suspicious of that convenient avalanche that killed him and two crew members. Now between us, I wouldn't mind hanging a murder charge on one or two of my in-laws but I tend to agree with Octavius. This is bigger than getting rid of an irritating relative. This castle is huge and I think you and your investigators should go over it stone by stone. Someone thinks we're getting too close for comfort and is trying to scare or kill us off."

Octavius saw me coming over and asked, 'Maury, any incidents on the way back?"

"No, but we brought back the cable and trip wire that was attached to the bomb. We also took a good look at that barrier that was used to keep the road closed until we came down. Looks like an official police traffic barrier. You might want to check with the local constable, superintendent, to see if any have been stolen."

"Bearoness," said Wardlaw, "I'm still not convinced but in the absence of any stronger clues to pursue, I'll have my team inspect all the accommodations in the castle. Do you or your retainers know of any hidden passages or rooms that we might otherwise miss? I also want to see that mysterious lift and boat dock first hand."

Belinda called over to Hamish who was supervising the unloading of Octavius' liquid cargo from the Chinook and Dougal who had just closed up the lorry and had dragged off the cables. "I have a top priority assignment for both of you. You are to assist Superintendent Wardlaw and his investigators in a complete search of the castle. Every room, every passage, every cellar, every closet and especially any secret doors or hidey-holes. That includes the family, guest and employees living quarters. Everything! I don't care how long it takes. Give your household assignments to the other members of the staff. You start when the police are ready."

Octavius waved Otto over. He had been helping Dougal with the cables. "Otto, I think you've met Superintendent Wardlaw. He's looking into the death of Sir Alistair and we're trying to convince him to connect his investigations to the oil field incidents and the attempt on our lives out on the road. Superintendent, Otto has several talents that I believe you may find very useful in your searches. Otto, please take the superintendent into one of the unused conference rooms and give him a demonstration. Humor me, please, Superintendent. The secrecy is necessary. We don't want everyone to know what out little friend here is capable of although after today's events on the road that will be tough to keep quiet."

Wardlaw cast a skeptical eye on the little otter and glanced over at Octavius with a raised eyebrow. Nevertheless, the two of them went off together.

"Now," said Octavius, "Let's find Chita and Fergus and go somewhere quiet where we can figure out our next steps in the oil mess. Then we'll gather our forces and lay out a plan of action, hopefully in cooperation with the authorities. I'll be with you in a moment."

He padded over to the helicopter where the last of the mead was being unloaded, picked up a small keg, sniffed long and hard and with a foolish grin on his furry face, tucked it under his arm and returned to Belinda and me.

"There may yet be some compensations for all this nonsense we're going through. Why don't you two get some champagne and coconut milk and join me. A little lubrication for the mental engines. Anyone see Chita?"

Chita was, in fact, sniffing at the cables we had brought back in the truck and looked over at us. "Chita, find Fergus and join us! We're having a war council. Get yourself a drink and meet us inside."

The cat waved and headed for the drawbridge. Suddenly she stopped. Coming out over the moat were Ursula, Roary and Bruinhilde, towing a large object wrapped in plastic. They stopped in the middle of the bridge and Ursula looked over at Belinda.

"Bearonin, I have just received my Alistair's body from the taxidermists. I wish to discuss with you the best place to put him on display."

The Development of Civilization Volume 3 Part 5
Languages
(From "An Introduction to Faunapology" by Octavius Bear Ph.D.)

The evolution of languages on our planet is influenced by a combination of many elements: physiology; geography; tradition; politics; education and the urge to create classes and castes. First and foremost, it had its origins in survival. No doubt some of the very first forms of verbal or telepathic communications were forms of warnings; sightings of potential food, water, fire or shelter, directions for cooking, planting, developing tools and the like - and of course, keeping babies and juveniles from getting into trouble.

How and why languages differ is a complex area of study and the obvious answer is not always the correct one. For example, one would assume that within given species, say sheep, horses or bears, their spoken language world-wide would be the same or sustain only minor variations. After all, the vocal and auditory equipment is essentially the same. The range of sounds that can be produced is governed by the physical structure of the "voice-box," lips and mouth, breathing apparatus, teeth, jaws and the like. Why then, today, do we find some horses speaking French, some speaking Chinese and some speaking a guttural African tongue? The answer seems to rest not on intra-species communication - horse to horse, sheep to sheep- the basic requirements of the herd, but rather on inter-species communication.

Once animals on our planet made the first movements toward cross-species socialization within a given area, a need for a common linguistic base became apparent. This base, no doubt, evolved over long periods and was certainly influenced by which species or even individual animal was dominant. "Talk like the leader(s) talk." There is one case where an entire kingdom talked with a lisp because their sovereign did.

Certain species believed (and still do believe) themselves to be superior to others. This has resulted in lingual classes and castes within the same civic group even though they all profess to be speaking the same language. Certain species speak a unique, arcane tongue in order to be unintelligible to outsiders and enemies. Young animals, in order to maintain cliques and to keep their elders guessing will continuously invent slang and argot on the spot. Similarly, professional animals salt their speech with terms that apply only within their working sphere.

Finally geography rears its head by isolating or canalizing certain groups to certain locales and affecting the breadth and variety (or lack thereof) of linguistic choices.

The advent of the written word was similarly affected by species differences. Hoofed animals, if they write at all, produce vastly different end products than species with opposable thumbs or talons. It is only in most recent years with the advent of voice to print translation, that all animals have attained a level of skill in producing the written word. Universal Ursine Industries is proud to have made a major contribution in voice synthesis, voice recognition, voice translation and voice to print and print to voice output. With the increase of availability in easily carried and utilized graphic displays, spontaneous communication between individuals or groups has become ever easier.

Of course, since the advent of broadcast technologies, motion pictures and the Internet to name just a few, the barriers to common shared speech have broken down even further. It is not unusual for animals to be conversationally multi-lingual and even more capable of reading the printed word in many tongues.

This has produced some nationalistic and academic resistance to the deliberate or passive movement toward a common denominator language. These opponents cite loss or perversion of long standing cultural characteristics or even linguistic colonialism by certain powers. The obvious question is which language or language family will emerge as the speech of choice for the planet. To avoid any national or species dominance, specially invented meta-languages have been attempted but so far have been nothing more than linguistic curiosities for academics and social experimenters.

Even telepathic transmission has suffered from language differences for, you see, we telepathically transmit and receive in the language in which we think. In some instances, telepaths have had to rely on the substitution of images for words in order to make themselves understood. As we have indicated earlier in our discussions, telepathy can have more problems than advantages.

Another linguistic breakthrough spearheaded by UUI has been the computer based conversational translator. Initially, these devices were large, clumsy and limited to translation dictionaries for only a few dominant languages. Today, of course we have the paw size Pea Pod equipped with miniature earphones and microphone. It is able to instantly recognize over 500 languages as they are being spoken. This provides the user with the ability to participate smoothly in multi-lingual meetings, phone calls and social events. New designs will provide even greater language choices; recording if required; more precise recognition and smaller form factors. Nor has the telepath been forgotten. Neural implants with the same linguistic capabilities are being test marketed by UUI and should be widely available within the next several years.

With an increasing proportion of the world's population becoming multi-lingual and the emerging dominance of certain languages worldwide, the future may present a more simplified and hopefully, a more optimistic prospect for mutual understanding. However, if, as some animals believe, our world is not alone in the universe or universes of sentient beings, we may have to struggle all over again to be able to have social, business and intellectual discourse with our yet undiscovered neighbors. We shall see.

Chapter Twenty
Bearmoral Castle

Condors fly through the Andean air.
In the States they're incredibly rare.
They can endlessly soar
On wings twelve feet or more,
Climbing up through the sky with no care.

As the Bear's war council was about to begin, another group was gathering in an upstairs room. Howard, Frau Schuylkill, Colonel Where and L.Condor had decided to have a geek session and see how they could apply their techie skills to the situation. *(Lepi had gone off in search of Bearnice. They hadn't rehearsed in over twenty four hours. Bearyl was with Belinda as part of the on-site committee for protecting the patrician polar pelt.)*

L.Condor opened up several of his bags that he had gotten past customs and started pulling out electronic goodies. "The first thing I want to test is how they are disrupting the GPS systems at Abeardeen and on the rigs. The only way I know it can be done without staging all out electronic warfare, is to subtly corrupt one of the reference signals that all the systems tune to and calibrate against. A couple of numbers off and everyone will be miles out of their way. Then after the damage has been done, the attackers return the system to the true reference points. But that signal isn't easy to intercept or distort. And there are several of them used in this area. We'll see. This unit here will monitor the signals and tell us if anything changes, assuming they try to mess up the GPS again."

"Next, we'll set up to monitor any radio traffic in and out of this location and then I want to take a good look at the controls of that lift. Interested, Howard?"

"According to Maury and Octavius, they use encrypted key locks on some of the doors and the elevator," said Howard. "If I can figure out the type and how they've been encoded, it might give us a lead on who installed them." The porcupine had many security specialties. Cryptography was high on the list.

"I'm going to rustle up a couple of high speed boats we can use to get around to the platforms," said the colonel. "There may have been insiders pulling off some of those hits but now that the rigs have been evacuated, we need to keep a watch on any incoming traffic, especially at night. I think we'll also need a fast chopper, Ilse."

Frau Schuylkill *(Ilse to her very good friends)* nodded. "I'll talk to Bearnice and Bearyl."

The colonel looked up. "Did anyone see where Otto and the Shetland Yard Super went? We should get together with them ASAP and pool resources, provided the police want to play."

"He has only three members on his team," said the bird. "I think our skills and equipment would be very valuable to him if he's not one of these 'only the police know what they're doing' types."

"All right! Howard, why don't you track down Otto and the Super before you join Condo at the elevator? Condo, figure out where and how you want to install your gear! Ilse, check on the chopper. I'll ask Dougal about the boats. When should we get together again?"

"When Burnham Wood doth come to Dunsinane," shouted Howard, rolling over in a fit of laughing. *(Which is tough if you're a porcupine.)*

Faced with a solid field of blank stares, he started to explain, "You see, there's this Scottish play, 'Macbearth' and…….aw, you hadda be there!"

"In an hour," said the Frau, raising her eyebrow at the spine-covered rodent. "Does that suit you, Herr Howard?"

"Fine, fine, fine!" *("Geeks, nerds! Exposure to a little literature would do you some good!" he mumbled.)*

The wolves and Howard trooped out of the room leaving the condor assembling and testing his equipment.

Meanwhile Octavius, Fergus, Chita and I had assembled in the conference room awaiting Belinda and hoping that Ursula would finally settle on some place to display the very dead and very stuffed Alistair. Roary and Bruinhilde were with their mother, pushing and pulling on the dolly that held Alistair's rejuvenated remains as they all played spin the body. I'm sure Belinda and Bearyl were very rapidly getting to the end of their combined patience over this bizarre body bickering. I'm willing to bet that once it's dark, Alistair will take a second trip from the roof, this time into the ocean.

As usual, Lord Ethelbeart was nowhere to be found. Probably wrapped around a wee bottle of the dew. Lady Albearta was also among the missing – a boon for all concerned.

Octavius, impatient even when he is in a state of repose *(!?)* was currently building to an irate crescendo. "Damn that stupid bear and her brats. Why don't they just shove him in a closet and bring him out on Halloween. Let's begin. I'll bring Bel up to date when she arrives. My tech team is getting the detection gear set up and the site visit logistics under way. Fergus, as Chita well knows, they are all outstanding professionals when it comes to crime fighting." *(That was a cheap shot and both the cat and the bear knew it. Besides, no one was supposed to know about all our previous relations with Chita. I'll have to have a brief chat with the boss later on.)*

"We still have a few items quarantined on the plane *(including the disguised particle beam accelerator)* but we have enough resources at hand to begin a well organized investigation. Now Fergus, how about giving us a more detailed description of what's been going on? Have all the rigs been hit equally? Are any one or two companies bearing the brunt of the attacks? Tell us about the sequence of events. Did they start with one type of incident and graduate to others? Have there been any communications from the perpetrators? Has anyone or anything suspicious been seen just before or after one of the fires or explosions? Have any of the wildcats suddenly disappeared?"

At this point I threw up my paws and said, 'Octavius, for Pete's sake. Give the cat a chance to answer one of your questions before hitting him with another and another. I counted eight queries just then and it sounds like you've got several hundred more. Give him and us a break!"

The Bear who had little patience with a world that couldn't keep up with his lightning fast synapses, frowned but then just nodded at Fergus and said, "You know what we're interested in. Tell it any way you want." He looked over at me with one of his "Are you satisfied?" looks that was supposed to make me fear for my life and future. Neither consideration bothered me much, especially since I could see bright prospects as a theatrical agent, maybe even a producer. *"Maestro Mauritius Meerkat presents: Unbridled Unst – Songs, Dance, Laughs Galore and Beastly Beauties!!!"* OK, it needs a little work!

Fergus had just started to repeat what he had told us at the pub when Bel entered the room with Bearyl in tow. She shook her head, sighed *(Think simultaneous blowout of all the tires on a 16 wheel rig)* and sprawled out on a couple of pillows. "In-laws! Sorry, Fergus, please go on."

The cat recited his turbulent tale pretty much as we had heard it before. No one rig seemed to be singled out, although the indies were getting more than their fair share of the abuse. That matched my theory of forcing the little guys to sell. The attacks seemed to be surreptitious. None of this "lob a rocket and run like hell" stuff. Destruction was usually delayed until the perps were off the scene. This, of course, assumed that not every job was conducted from the inside.

There was one strange series of events that didn't quite line up with the others. Although we had strong reason to believe and hopefully, L. Condor would prove, that there had been some interference with the local GPS systems, there were still some diehards who swore the rigs actually were disappearing and reappearing. Several aerial observers swore they saw a platform vanish as they were approaching it. And the radar signals also bore that out. Now you see it…now you don't. Shades of Imperius Drake.

I brought this up to Octavius, admitting that since we had started on this Multiverse Project I was beginning to see alternate worlds and teleportation everywhere I looked. Oddly enough, he took me very seriously and said, "You may have something. See if you can free up Harold, Otto and a boat tomorrow morning. There's a short sea voyage I want to make."

No further explanation but then that's Octavius at his most pain in the ass mysterious. I shook my head in agreement. I guessed he wanted to see one of the wildcat rigs up close – maybe Chita's.

As we were discussing this, Superintendent Wardlaw and Otto joined us. The collie had a bemused expression on his face and Otto looked even more impish than usual. Octavius pointed to a seat at the table and said, "Superintendent, please join us."

He looked at Octavius and said, "I know you Americans don't like to stand on formalities, so when I'm not in front of my staff or questioning suspects, please feel free to call me Nigel."

The Great Bear returned the compliment and we started first-naming like crazy. I thought sure Chita was going to insist on Mademoiselle Catt but she surprised me. The Bearoness was going to be Belinda. Weren't we all chummy?

"Your associate, Otto here, is a most remarkable creature. I gather there is still no certainty on whether his condition and characteristics are stabilized."

"Don't I wish," murmured the otter. "I don't suppose we've heard any more from Doctor Vark or the lab?"

I shook my head – negative. The otter just shrugged.

"Nigel, not to put too fine a point on it, we have a wide range of resources to put at your disposal if you'll allow us to participate freely. I'm not suggesting you're incapable of untangling this whole mess yourselves but with us on your team, I think we can get there faster and hopefully, keep any further damage and loss of life to zero."

"Octavius, you're still convinced the death here is connected to the North Sea incidents."

"I am, Nigel, and I think my compatriots, who I might add are quite capable of independent thinking, *(hard stare in my direction)* agree with me."

"Well, the military and MI5 don't seem to be getting anywhere and so far they have shown no interest in Unst or the castle. I'm sorry, Fergus. I interrupted your narrative. Please go ahead."

"Fergus," interrupted the Bear yet again. "Try to think of any strange similarities that made the fires and outages seem like more than just random accidents."

"Weel, ya ken, I wasn't at most of 'em. All of us wildcatters have been comparin' notes and that's how the picture's been gettin' painted. But we're all sure the "events" were nae random. Two dead. More injuries but so far none are life threatenin'. Most of the attacks occurred where or when we couldn't stop 'em. Middle o' the night. Open sea. Unmanned boats. A couple of near misses on choppers and of course, Abeardeen Airport. The damage wasn't that great. We can fix most of it but we got to stop this and get back to workin' the wells."

"Did anyone unusual show up on any of the rigs during those weeks?"

"Unusual? Like who??"

"I don't know! Contractors? Inspectors? Service personnel? Aliens from Mars?"

"Inspectors!!! Several of the rigs had safety inspections by the guv'mint. The rigs warn each other when they're out and about. But if anything, I wudda thought that would have reduced the chances of anything happening."

"If the inspectors were really inspectors," I piped up.

"Whaddya mean?"

"Who else would have had free access to anyplace on the rigs? How many crimes are committed each year by phony coppers or members of the military?"

"I was on the rig when they came up. Looked OK to me. Terriers, as usual. Uniforms. ID papers. Seemed to know what they were about! Boat with government markings."

"A boat? Not a helicopter?"

"Aye, that was wee bit unusual, but they had some test gear with them, checkin' the surroundin' water for leaks and pollution. Examining the fire suppression systems and the alarms. Not sure it would have all fit in a wee helicopter."

"Were you due for an inspection?"

"All inspections are surprises. As I say, the best we can do is warn the rest of the sites when they arrive at the first platform. Sometimes they only hit one and then wait a bit afore goin' on to the next ones. They're pretty clever."

"Can you check with your cohorts and see how many platforms have had inspections in the past, say, six weeks or so?"

"And," Nigel chimed in, "see how many of them that were inspected also had some kind of incident afterwards."

"Nigel," said Octavius, "how would you like to bet that there's a boat with government environmental protection markings stowed in one of the dock storage areas down below the castle? Let's go look, shall we? Bel, do you have the electronic key to the lift?"

The Bearoness nodded and uncurled herself from her pillows.

It was Chita's turn. "Fergus, I want to meet the rig owners ASAP. Probably at Abeardeen. Can you do that?"

"I can give you their names, Miz Catt, but I think you and the Bearoness and the Super here, would swing more weight than I would. Some of the owners think I'm a rabble rouser. Which I am! I'll make you a list. Then I'll check on those inspections. The more I think about them, the stranger they seem. I didn't recognize any of the inspection team. They're not always the same, mind, but usually you ken one or two. I'll check with the others and see if they recognized any of 'em."

175

"OK, do that. But give me the names right now and I'll start making calls. Bearoness, can I have a copter when I need one?"

"And a pilot. I'll ask Bearyl here to stand by. I think Bearnice and Lepi are catching up on their arias."

Octavius turned to Nigel and said, "If we can find the condor and Howard on the way to the lift, they may be able to help us undo the locks down below. Ready Bel?"

Belinda got to her feet and Chita and Fergus put their heads together and started planning out the calling campaign. The game was apaw! Once more into the breach, dear friends, and hurrah for good old St. George!

As we were bumping and thumping out the door, Colonel Where, the Frau and Howard were padding along the corridor.

"Hello, Bearoness, Superintendent, Octavius, Otto, Maury! *(I'm always last!)*

We said complementary greetings and then Bear looked at Howard. "Two things: First, I need you and L. Condor to join us. We're going to take another look at that lift, roof storage, and the ocean platform. Not all the locks have the same combination and Hamish only gave Bel the one to the lift. We may have to do some brute force electronic lock picking, and I don't know any two guys better able to do it."

 "Second, when we finish that, I want to get the Project Multiverse Team together for another session. I'm beginning to think teleportation may be playing some role in this whole affair."

Howard nodded and agreed to get the condor and meet us on the roof. Frau Ilse and the colonel went off on their transportation roundup. I told the colonel that Octavius also wanted a boat and Harold's services early tomorrow. He and the Frau weren't needed. It would be Harold, Otto, Octavius and I doing some damn thing or another out on the deep water. Oh swell! *(no pun intended)* The colonel looked at me and Octavius, raised a lupine eyebrow, shook his head in agreement, and trotted out after the Frau. He was learning not to ask too many questions.

Superintendent Wardlaw was shaking his head. "You have an entire Mission Impossible Team here, don't you? What is Project Multiverse?"

176

"A study we're carrying out on the possibilities of teleportation. Way out research into arcane subjects. Part of the UUI remit: Make the strange commonplace!"

"Or the commonplace strange," said the collie, with what may have been a grin.

"Nigel," said the Great Bear, "You know my motto – After eliminating the possibly improbable, whatever is left is probably impossible – and that's when I call in my team."

The dog cocked his head, started to speak and thought better of it. We had reached the roof stairs and started to labor our way up. No one was supposed to have access except us. The Bearoness had suspended the morning and evening piping, much to the chagrin of the family traditionalists. Aunt Albearta, who sounded like a bagpipe herself whenever she spoke, was especially truculent. But, "plus ça change, plus ça meme chose!" – an old Scottish proverb.

Belinda led the way up the stairs and turned off to her right, heading for the mysterious lift. She stopped, causing Octavius to halt and Nigel, Otto and I to slide backwards down the staircase.

"Bel, would you please keep moving. We can stop and chat when we're all clear of the doorway."

The Bearoness didn't answer immediately and then said, "Sorry! I think you all better get up here quickly. There's something you should see."

The 'something' turned out to be the sprawling hindquarters and midsection of a formally dressed wild boar. Hamish *(he was the only boar on board)* was stuck with his neck compressed between the steel doors of the lift. And he was very dead.

Chapter Twenty One
Still Bearmoral Castle

Carousels can be wonderful fun
As in circles they merrily run.
Now their parts are of use
To get Hamish sprung loose.
The amusements have only begun.

Nigel barked and stepped to the fore. "Please touch nothing! Otto, my friend, would you be so kind as to summon my sergeant and the Crime Scene team. I'm afraid we have another scene. You'd better call the locals, too – Sergeant Popper and Doctor Livingstone. We won't be able to get the coroner up from Abeardeen for a while. Meantime, I would like to know cause and time of death, if I can."

Otto took off. *(I'm not sure whether he ran or zapped. Coming on a dead body can usually get a rise out of your adrenalin.)* Anyway he was gone. Belinda was shaking her head and Octavius was down on all fours examining the body without touching it.

"It's difficult to tell," he said, "but I don't think the doors killed him. As you know, our phantom has a macabre sense of humor and he or she just loves to involve this lift in the mayhem. I'll bet Hamish's head, when we can get a look at it, will show wounds just like Alistair's."

Staring at the body, I felt a small twinge of conscience, considering I had silently wished he would jump off the roof several hours ago. So did Belinda, apparently. She looked at Nigel and Octavius. "Somebody thought he knew too much and could tell too much, I suppose. But about what?? We've got to get to the bottom of this and fast. I will not have my home turned into a Grand Guignol."

As she was saying this, Howard came out on the landing. I looked at him and said, "Where's L. Condor?'

"Look up, Maury!"

A large avian shadow blocked the sun for a moment and I could spot the condor, wings at full expanse, riding the thermals up the side of the cliff, the castle and then far above. He looked down at us, folded his wings momentarily and dived toward the roof, opening up at the last minute and making a graceful landing.

"Sorry for the aerobatics but I haven't had a chance to stretch my…" He stopped when he saw the boar's body wedged in the elevator entry. Howard noticed for the first time as well. "Hamish?? What happened?" asked the porcupine.

I replied, "Well, he's definitely dead and not from natural causes. The superintendent has the doctor coming along with his crime scene team. We're not sure how he died. Howard, you and L. Condor may have to hack the electronic lock if the Bearoness' combination has been changed again by animal or animals unknown."

Octavius looked over at Belinda. "From what I can see, the lift car is not on the other side of the door. Depending on how this was committed there may not be much of a head to examine. The descending car may have decapitated him. Do you want to stay here?"

"Tavi, I am not going to swoon. If you don't know me that well, we have some remedial familiarization to go through. Nigel, I have the combination that Hamish gave me. Do you want me to try it?"

"Not until my team and the doctor arrive, Bearoness. If the body still has a head, I wouldn't want to remove it by calling the car back up. We'll see if we can wedge the doors open with a little combined brute force." He glanced at Octavius, who at the moment, looked like he could take the whole structure down brick by brick.

Otto reappeared. This time I'm sure he zapped. "Your team's on their way. The doctor and the sergeant will be up from the village in about twenty minutes."

Octavius looked over at the otter and said, 'Otto, I don't want to waste time fooling around with all these locks. Can you get into each one of those parapets and open the doors from the inside? Maybe we can find something to use to jam open the elevator doors and slide his body out. I also want to get a better look at what's stored in those rooms."

In rapid fire order, each of the turret and parapet doors swung open and the otter hadn't even seemed to move. L. Condor, who had only briefly seen Otto in action, was dumbstruck and Nigel was even more impressed than he had been. We walked over to the nearest storeroom and peered in. A disassembled carousel took up most of the space. No doubt, the little polar cubs who had come with their parents to the resort hotel had a merry time spinning around on top of exotic plastic animals like tigers and lions and horsies. There were several steel support bars from the carousel that looked like they might be able to withstand the pressure of the doors if we *(not me)* could force them further open. Octavius and Bel between them lifted two bars out of the room and dragged them over to the lift.

Octavius looked around and said, "There don't appear to be too many of us strong enough to force the doors *(translation: him)* but if I can pull them open a bit more and if you, Bel, can jam a bar in the opening while the rest of you pull out the body, we may be able to bring this off."

And that is exactly what we did. Hamish still had his head, albeit battered and bruised, so we had another case of the assault being committed first and then the corpse being positioned theatrically. How the perpetrator got the door open when the car wasn't there was a bit of mystery. Maybe he or she was also hoping one of us would fall down the shaft while trying to extricate the body.

Howard and L. Condor got the faceplate off the elevator controls and set about trying to break the combination. We had tried Belinda's and it hadn't worked. Howard attached something that looked like a PDA to a couple of wires in the call mechanism and started it going. Electronic brute force, trying every possible combination at picosecond speed! Suddenly, the doors flew all the way open and the steel bar went hurtling down the shaft. Then they closed and we could hear the cables moving and the car ascending.

"Did you get the code?' shouted Octavius.

"We have it," replied Howard, "although I doubt it will work on anything else. We'll just have to do trial and error on all of them."

The car arrived, the doors shot open and out tumbled Alistair's freshly stuffed cadaver with a big sign hung around his neck.....BOOO!!!

Belinda growled *(loudly!)* "Oh, this is absolutely too much. Half an hour ago, my stuffed brother-in-law was standing in the library menacing the collected works of Robeart Bearns. Now, he's here. Someone has a very bizarre sense of humor, and no sense at all if they think they can scare me out of this castle. Nigel, Tavi, if you haven't organized that top-to-bottom search yet, do it now." *(The Bearoness had adopted the imperious command voice of the nobility. She would brook no refusal or resistance.)*

"My team is already at it, Bearoness,' replied the Superintendent. "We had expected Hamish here to assist us in getting the exact layout of the castle. I understand he managed the place when it was a hotel."

"That probably explains why he's lying here, dead" said Octavius. "Certain parts of the castle are not to be discovered, if our adversary has anything to say about it. Otto, you can be of great value in helping the Superintendent's team. Maury, you, Howard and I are going to take an elevator ride after we move Alistair's remains yet again. *(Joy supreme filled my quivering veins. He seemed to forget that this particular lift had a few lethal features.)* Senhor Condor, would you mind flying down to the inlet and the underground dock. We should be down shortly but I'd like to cut off anyone who might either be waiting for us or trying to get away. Bel, why don't you have your staff put Alistair back wherever he was? Then face down Ursula and her spawn about this latest caper. I doubt Ursula herself had anything to do with it, but the perpetually bored Roary and the simpering Bruinhilde may have discovered a jolly way to pull mama's and Aunt Belinda's respective tails."

"But how did they gain access to the lift?" I inquired.

"I don't know," he riposted.

"That would seem to be an impediment to their merriment," I declared.

"You may be right," he retorted.

"Perhaps the Bearoness should query them about it," I proposed.

"A worthy thought," he responded.

We all set about our tasks after getting Alistair out of the car and laying him down next to Hamish. A roof-top morgue! A new concept in forensic medicine.

The condor had already taken to the air and was spiraling downward as the three of us got into the elevator. Otto remained behind with Bel and the Superintendent. As the doors were closing, I could see the crime scene team along with Bearyl emerging from the stairwell.

"Not that I care all that much," I said, as we descended to and through the cliff. "But has anyone seen hide or fur of Albearta or Ethelbeart? Senile though they may appear, I wonder about them. Especially the old sot."

"All that exposure to my finely honed detection talents has sharpened your own perceptions, my little friend," said Octavius. "I was thinking the very thing, earlier. Especially since they come from the Bearents Sea community - possible beneficiaries of the collapse of the wildcats' North Sea holdings. A coincidence perhaps, but they may know something worth investigating if we can ever get her to shut up and him sober enough to respond."

The elevator door hissed open and we stepped out onto the platform. L. Condor was there. He said he had spotted a small boat moving rapidly along the coastline as he was descending, but he didn't follow because he wanted to prevent another possible mishap inside the "grotto" like a repeated super flood.

Since there didn't seem to be any "hostiles" on the platform, Octavius asked him to take a check down the shoreline for that boat he had spotted. The bird flew up and out over the concealed waterway and disappeared. Howard walked over to one of the larger storage structures and tried Belinda's combination. Then he tried the one they had hacked from the elevator call mechanism. It worked and a door creaked open on salt-encrusted hinges. We swung it fully open and stood face-to-face with one of His Majesty's Environmental Protection Ministry Patrol Boats. Forty feet long, it filled the entire storeroom. It was apparent from the hull that it had seen some use lately.

"Well, there's our oil rig connection," said the Bear. "Damn it, cell phones are useless inside this cavern. I should have brought Otto along. He can zap up and down that shaft at will."

Suddenly, we heard the sound of an outboard echoing against the walls of the inlet. Howard, Octavius and I did a rapid inventory of our available weapons and came up with a total of – zero – rounded to three decimal places. Stooooopid!

"Hallo, Herr Bear, Are you there?" A loud Switzerdeutsch growl echoed around the cavern. *(Sighs of relief from us!)* The Frau and the Colonel had rounded up some water transport and were out looking for us, no doubt to organize next steps.

Octavius roared back at the top of his lungs, "Heeeeeerrrre!" dislodging several large stones from the ceiling and causing ripples in the water. The boat with the two wolves aboard came puttering into sight, rounded the last mini-jetty and headed for us on the platform apron.

"So this is the hidden bunker," said the Colonel as they tied up a 20 foot Boston Whaler at the edge of the pier.

"Yes, Colonel," said Octavius "complete with a huge freight elevator, hydro power booby traps and who knows what else. This entire space can be deliberately flooded in less than a minute, as we found out. So, one of you stay with the boat! We may need it for a fast getaway if our playful adversaries have another flight of whimsy."

"As you can see, we just unearthed *(wrong word)* a bogus environmental inspection boat. I think this is the beginning of the trail to the attacks on the oil platforms. They wait till the tide rises or deliberately make it rise, open the storage room, float out the boat and with phony inspector's uniforms, credentials and gear, they head off to create another carefully planned disturbance. Enough to do some damage and interrupt drilling or pumping but not enough to completely destroy the rig."

"We haven't figured out yet what's causing the electronic disturbances, but I'll bet L. Condor gets something on his monitors. By the way, have you seen him? He was up scanning the coastline, looking for a small boat that left here a while ago."

Frau Schuylkill looked up, "So that's what he was doing. We were wondering why he was out joy-riding on the winds when there was so much work to be done. He can probably circle this island in twenty minutes."

"Octavius, I think we ought to do a little destruction ourselves," I said. "First, cripple those pumps so they can't flood this place again. Dougal and Harold know the natural tides down to the minute, and we can time our entries and exits around them. Let's not have any more surprises. Then, let's cripple this boat or jam the storeroom doors or both, so they can't take it out again."

Octavius turned to Howard and asked, "Can you set the door controls so only we can operate them, Doctor? I'm not sure I want to wreck the boat. We may need it. But Maury's right. We need to take command of those pumps so we can flood the place if we need to, but they can't. Is that too tall an order? What do you think, Colonel, Frau?"

Frau Schuylkill said, "I think we could use Herr Otto right now. He could swim in there and disconnect or rewire the controls or take out a critical part. Where is he?"

"He's with the police, scouring all the empty rooms in the castle." I said.

"I'll get him," she said and disappeared. I looked at Octavius.

"Transylvanian Meditation!" he said, shrugging his massive shoulders.

The Colonel got back in the whaler and started up the motors, keeping them idling for our possible rapid departure. Howard skittered over to the doors of the boat storage room and started to dismantle the electronic lock. Out came his hand-held "computer" and he went to work; blanking the memory of the opener; substituting a veeeery sophisticated encryption algorithm and key; and inserting them into the control circuits. A couple of tests –Open, Shut, Open, Shut! Ali Babar and the Forty Thieving Elephants came to mind.

"They should have a few problems with that one," said the porcupine. "Like several years worth."

Otto and the Frau popped into view on the edge of the pier. Otto promptly plunged into the water and zapped right back out. "I need a few tools," he said. Howard reached into his bag and handed him a portable kit and the Colonel started searching in the whaler's stowage for anything that might help. Otto disappeared again.

Suddenly the water started to boil up and we all ran for the boat. But the tide stopped as rapidly as it had started and a sheepish *(!?)* otter poked his sodden head out of the basin and said, "Ooops! Otto the Klutz scores again. Sorry about that! Crossed the wrong wires."

We decided to stay with the boat until he came out again. After a few minutes, he joined us, shook himself off, slapped his tail on the dock and said, "The controls get their signals two ways. Hard wire and infra-red. Radio won't work in here. There's an IR receiver at the entrance to the inlet and another above our heads right next to the elevator. Jump in the elevator, start the doors closing, flash the IR and while you're climbing skyward, your enemies are drowning. Pretty clever! I'm not sure where the hard wires go so I disconnected them. Howard, show me how to re-program the infra-red as well as this remote I have here, and we can lock them out."

As they set about that, we heard a flutter of wings and L. Condor came swooping into view. He has been having a ball, adjusting and readjusting his artificial voice box to imitate different individuals. This time, Octavius said to Octavius, "Well, I found them and I didn't!"

The Bear raised an eyebrow and the condor switched to a non-descript but breathy, lisping voice. He was imitating Bruinhilde. "They beached the boat on the other thide of the island and took off in a waiting helicopter. Thilver, no markings. Unfortunately, I couldn't keep up with it. They were heading thouth. Toward Abeardeen, I'd gueth. I examined the boat. I'd ethtimate there were four to six of them but I couldn't identify the thpecies. They didn't leave anything dithtinctive. The boat ith just a thmall fishing boat, rigged up for trawling."

"Well," said the Great Bear as we got into the whaler and started out into the channel, "I think we've done all we can here for the moment. Howard, are we the only ones who can use the lift?"

The porcupine nodded. "That combination will give them fits, too. Octavius, I'll give it to you and Maury. The rest of you wall zappers don't seem to need it. How about you, Condo?"

"I'll fly up and down, if it's all the same to you."

"We'll have to update Nigel and Bel, if she hasn't already murdered Ursula, Roary and Bruinhilde. Incidentally, Senhor Condor, please change that voice! Anyone seen Chita?" he asked as we emerged into the sunlight.

The sound of helicopter rotors whined and thumped overhead. A white polar face peered out of the bubble and across from her we could just make out a haughty feline visage. Chita was on her way to have it out with the "oil barons" – God help them.

185

Chapter Twenty Two
On the Way to Abeardeen

Cows don't just stand around and say "moo"
They give milk and have lots more to do.
And don't pity the bull
For his life is quite full
In a field full of Holsteins, Hoo, hoo!!

(From the unpublished Memoirs of Mlle. Catherine Catt
- aka Chita

I wonder if stupidity runs in my family. I never met my father (probably just as well) but Mom seemed pretty clever. In my relatively short life, I have been tied in with murderous ducks, idiot baboons, pompous pumas, bears, bears and more bears, to say nothing of meerkats, wolves, condors, porcupines and a miraculous otter. I doubt this is the way the life of a cheetah is supposed to play out.

On the other hand, I doubt if many of my kind have large flats in major cities, jewelry by the ton, scads of rich *(very)* and generous *(very)* admirers, and a large, diversified and quite profitable portfolio of stocks, bonds, businesses and properties. So I put up with it.

Speaking of which, I have to get this oil rig thing resolved. (*If it belongs to Chita, it has to produce...or else. Words to Live By!*) I came up here to Bearmoral purportedly to meet with my ditzy publisher friend, Bearbi da Savile Row, to discuss her latest and greatest media spectacular. (*"PURR, dahling!! Isn't that name delicious? We'll start with a magazine; then a website; then twitters and blogs; then a TV reality show starring you, dahling; world-wide distribution, and who knows, maybe even a theme park!!"*) Well, we might already have the makings of the theme park if Belinda wants a piece of the action, and wants to re-convert this castle to a resort. Although, it might be a tad cold for my feline physique and psyche. We'll see. I'll have to talk with the Bearoness as soon as she comes down from the ceiling or whatever she hit after Hamish got squashed. This place is beginning to give me the creeps...dead bodies, roadside bombs! But I have to admit the Lion and Unicorn were a hoot.

Back to business, Chita! One more phone call from the list Fergus gave me and we're good to go. Dinner tonight in Abeardeen. My treat, of course. *(I had reached all the indies and two of the three large companies had condescended to provide emissaries.)* The name "pp" kept coming up in the conversations. They had all been approached by "petropol," the Russian polar power consortium *(modest lower case title with a North Star-burst logo)* with offers to buy them out well below the going value of their properties, at least the value before the "unfortunate" accidents began. Yeah, sure!

Several of the independents have their backs up against the wall and are strongly considering selling. The three biggies might not. I had to convince them all to hold tight. Let's hope the Blustery Bear comes up with something. Or maybe that Shetland Yard collie. The military didn't seem to be able to find their way out of the harbor. I dialed.

"Hello, this is Catherine Catt, owner of the Hot Spot oil rig. I have some interesting facts and theories I'd like to put before you concerning the incidents we've all been suffering. I think I and my associates know *(claws crossed behind my back)* what's been going on and who is doing it. No, no! We want to meet in person. Every other owner is coming to dinner this evening at the Petro Club in Abeardeen. My treat! *(The frugal Scots all fell for that one.)* Seven o'clock. You'll be there? Good! By the way, have you had any contact recently from 'pp'? I thought you might. See you in Abeardeen. Catt! Catherine Catt! Owner of the Hot Spot well and pipeline."

OK, Chita. Showtime! Let's find Bearyl and head on down to the mainland. With any luck, I can avoid Bearbi. Where's Fergus? I'll tell him what's going on.

(The wildcat had just stepped out of the loo and was on his way back when I caught up with him.) "Hi Fergus, we're all set up for an owner's meeting this evening in Abeardeen. Are you sure you don't want to come? You'd be my guest."

"Thank ya, Miz Catt, but I think ye'd do a muckle more with me not bein' there. The owner's don't cotton to me, y' ken."

"OK, I'll keep you posted. I'm going to be making some of it up as I go along, but I just want to stop them from selling out before we get to the bottom of this. Wish me luck."

As I turned to go down to the main hall in search of Bearyl and my helicopter ride, I heard the one voice I didn't want to hear.

"Yoo hoo, Chita dahling. Whatever is going on, dear? I understand there's been another murder. I'm on my way up to the roof as soon as Clarence arrives with the cameras. Do you know anything about it? How deliciously horrible! This weekend is turning into the news event of the decade."

Needless to say, that was Bearbi. Dressed in a long flowing nightdress.

"Hello Bearbi. What are you all togged up as?"

"Why, Lady Macbearth, of course. With all the murders, I thought I'd dress the part. Of course, I'm hardly homicidal but one must hold up one's end in the drama, don't you think?"

I'm not sure what was holding up her end besides a pair of oversized legs, but after promising to get together later and avoiding all mention of my upcoming session in Abeardeen, I watched as she and Clarence, loaded down with photo equipment, headed for the elevator and the crime scene. I set off across the hall in search of Bearyl.

A rather large cow came tottering over the drawbridge and through the doorway. Dougal was trundling after her with a cart filled with oversized baggage.

"OOOOh," she lowed, "I do detest those helicopter things. All that vibration disturbs the inner harmonies and tonal textures. Thank you, my good dog. You may take my belongings to my room. Young lady, *(meaning me)* please direct me to your mistress, the Bearoness Belinda Bruin. I am Madame Honoria Heifer, vocal virtuoso and advisor to the stars of opera. I came here from the Edinbeargh Opera House, specifically at the Bearoness' request, to take Ms. Bearnice and Mr. Leperello under my toootelage."

"I'm afraid the Bearoness is a bit tied up at the moment, Madame. We have lost our chief retainer due to a tragic accident. However, I'll be happy to take you to your two charges. Please follow me."

"Isn't it a bit unusual for a feline to be a domestic in a family of ursines?"

(Sure, dopey, all domestics wear diamond collars!) "Unusual indeed, Madame, which is why I am not a domestic. I am a guest. Mlle. Catt."

"Oooooh. I am soooo embarrassed! Please forgive me," she mooed.

"Nothing to forgive." We entered the room where Bearnice and Lepi were rehearsing. Introductions all around. The heifer did not seem very impressed with their experience at The People's Opera of China or the Northern Lights Opera Company. Wonderful start! I left, wondering who would be teaching whom. Now where the hell was Bearyl?

She would probably be with Belinda but I had no desire to go up on that roof with the corpses and the minions of the law, to say nothing of Bearbi. No, Chita. We will stay down here. Maybe I can ask Dougal to fetch her for me. As I walked back into the hall, Dougal approached and asked. "S'cuse me, mum, but did you say Mister Hamish had an accident?"

"I doubt it was an accident, Dougal. I haven't been up on the roof myself but according to Otto, who was there, his body was found with his head caught between the doors of that giant lift."

The dog looked shocked but there was another expression crossing his face as well. Not sure what it was. A little bit of satisfaction, perhaps? Could there have been some bad blood between Hamish and Dougal? Enough bad blood for Dougal to do him in? Didn't seem likely, but what the hell *is* likely around this place?

"Dougal, you could see for yourself and do me a great favor at the same time. Would you go up onto the roof and tell Ms. Bearyl, if she's there, that I'm waiting for her here in the entry hall. I'd rather not go myself. I'm a bit squeamish about dead carcasses." *(Oh, Chita, you have got to be kidding. Even a Sheltie won't believe that.)*

I doubt he did. With a cocking of his head and a short stare, he licked his chops once and said, "Cert'ny, Miz Chita. Would you watch the ol' cow's bags for me. I don't know where the Bearoness is going to put her, although I have an idea or twa of m'own."

I laughed as he set off for the elevator. I could hear Lepi and Bearnice doing scale runs, interrupted by emphatic "mooos." Blasé though I may be about Bearbi's magazines, she's right. This recital will make a great cover piece in both books along with those two eccentric personalities down at the pub. Maybe we could get one of the local sea lions to pose with them and we'll call it the Great Seal of the Empire. I'd probably get deported. But we do have that one goofy picture of Otto grinning between the two rearing opponents. Lion and Unicorn Rampant on a Field of Otter. Who knows? Magazines may be fun…for a while. Or until Bearbi drives me over the edge.

The lift swooshed open and out came Bearyl followed by Dougal. The dog had a very self-satisfied look on his face and his tail was wagging at a respectful pace. Bearyl looked at him, turned to me, bowed and said, "Miz Catt, may I introduce the new Retainer of Bearmoral Castle, Mr. Dougal."

Aha, so that was it!! Did he want the job badly enough to knock off the boar and if he did, why now? Maybe to throw off the scent while all this other nonsense is going on. Much as it galls me, I'll have to confer with Octavius and Maury about this *(but stay away from that "Shetland Yard Johnny.")*

"Congratulations, Dougal. Long service well rewarded. It's a shame that your accession had to come about this way but fate *(or a dog?)* does strange things.'

"Aye, 'tis a sad event, mum, but I will be proud to wear the keys of the manor, so t' speak. The Bearoness is a wonderful mistress. 'Twill be a pleasure to serve her in m' new duties. I'm thinkin' of askin' Harold to be the new gameskeeper."

I wonder if Harold wanted to give up the water. I doubt it. None of my business! I turned to Bearyl.

"I have all my wildcats in a row. I have a dinner date with that oily bunch in Abeardeen at seven o'clock at the Petro Club. Can you fly me down there? I'd like you to join me at dinner. Sort of an informal envoy from the Bearoness." *(Even though she doesn't have a damn thing to do with the oil rigs, Belinda's a local legend and invoking local legends is always good psychology in Scotland.)*

"Sure! I'm getting a little antsy with all this mayhem going on. Thanks for the invite. What are you going to tell these guys?"

"It's more what I'm going to ask them. I'm convinced, even if the police and military haven't arrived there yet, that this is all a big power play by someone trying to take over the Scottish rigs. I want to pry out of the cats any offers they've had from foreign bidders. Now, as you know better than I, a Scotscat will not part with any kind of financial or business information, especially in front of his competitors without a damn good reason. I wish I had one. I'm going to build up a conspiracy theory in the fine old tradition of Elver Stone, and "prove" it by inference and innuendo, a thing I excel at. Having you there as some subtle muscle may also convince them to open up a bit. Let's go. But first!"

After spending a few minutes freshening up, *(I was half tempted to go as a leopard but decided not to)* we both headed out for the helipad.

"I called Belinda and told her where I was going," said Bearyl. "She's OK with it. The police are doing their crime scene and body examination things. They think Hamish was hit first and then wedged between the elevator doors. Octavius is wandering around somewhere in that cave under the cliff with his sidekicks and Otto. No one has seen "the family." And that's the latest from PBS, the Polar Broadcast System, all the news, all the time, all screwed up." She burst out laughing.

We got into the chopper. I wouldn't admit it to that operatic bovine bitch from Edinbeargh but I can't stand helicopters, either. If I'm hovering in mid-air, I want to be attached to a tree or something else that's firmly planted in the ground. Bearyl acted like she matured directly from cave to copter with no stops in between. We lifted and swung out over the parking lot, past the castle and out over the sea. The condor was swooping around just outside our airspace. There was a boat moving away from the entrance to the cave. I could make out Octavius. How could you miss him? Otto, the wolves and the porcupine seemed to be with him. They were heading for the beach. Bearyl banked over, buzzed them and waved. Suddenly our radio crackled. The bear was on the horn.

"Chita, we found something very interesting that you may want to use in your discussions with the wildcats. A fully equipped patrol boat with Environmental Protection Ministry markings inside a storage area in the caves. It's been to sea recently. Those inspectors are phonies. We haven't told Nigel yet. Right now, I assume he's tied up with the second murder. I think we have our link between the castle and the rigs. Now, we have to find out who the hell they are."

I thanked him. *(I didn't want to mention my musings about Dougal over the radio or in front of Bearyl.)* So, our theory about the incidents and the castle was right. Well, this dinner may turn out to be quite interesting, indeed. I hope they don't serve haggis.

Chapter Twenty Three
Meanwhile, Back on the Whaler

One concern has us tied in a knot.
Are there other worlds out there or not?
Is there some other being
First touching, then fleeing
Playing tag in a cosmic gavotte.

After he put down the radio, Octavius turned to me and said, "First, we have to catch up with Nigel and intensify the search for this gang. Deprived of their boat, they're not going to be able to get out of here so easily."

"Wait a second,' I said. 'What about the boat Condo followed and the chopper they took off in afterward."

"Do you have any idea how many people were in that boat, Senhor Condor?" asked the Bear.

"Four, six at the most. Maybe only three. Both the boat and the copter were small. No government, corporate or private markings."

"There's more to this group than three or four." The colonel had run the whaler up to a floating dock and we started piling off. "By the way, Colonel. Were you and Frau Schuylkill looking for us for a specific reason?"

"Geez, I almost forgot. The military and customs people want to give the Ursa Major a going over tomorrow morning. They want us present to witness the search *(and probably arrest us if they find anything.)* I talked them out of your being there but Ilse and I have to be on hand."

"Splendid, after the inspection, bring back the particle projector and any other piece of weaponry you can take off the ship. I have no doubt the plane will pass without a problem." *(Octavius was quite confident of our collective cleverness and quite cavalier about any of his staff ending up in the clink. The Colonel, Frau and I were not quite as sanguine.)* "Meanwhile Maury, Senhor Condor, Howard, Otto and I will continue with our room to room search tomorrow along with the Superintendent and his staff. We'll also have to wait and hear what Chita learns at her wildcat wingding. Now this seems as good a time as any to have an update on Project Multiverse. Howard?"

"Just before we took off for the Shetlands, the team reviewed the incident reports that the Colonel had assembled. I'll let Wyatt fill you in on what he's found so far."

"Ilse and I have been conducting major searches on the internet and other sources trying to develop some correlation of all the data points we've uncovered. First, there are not that many and there only seem to be one or two clusters of any significance. One of them is a colony of New Age enthusiasts who are constantly reporting alien appearances and government cover up conspiracies. That doesn't mean they may not have something but it sure makes it difficult to separate the wheat from the chaff. We have been using data mining techniques to come up with events that seem to match your mother's and your half brother's as well as my own experiences. We've been especially looking for mention of *H.Saps* or similar beings. Please bear in mind that we haven't the slightest idea how many experiences haven't been reported, so we may be out in left field statistically."

"And…" *(Octavius is not famous for being patient.)*

"And…we have a group of hits that we were about to pursue when we got called over here. Geographically, they're all over the map. There is a recurring pattern of induced or heavy sleep. We have one from several koala bears who spend about ninety percent of their lives sleeping."

"Another came from a pride of lions in Africa who as you know enjoy sleeping right up there with eating. They reported a safari of strange beings that appeared and disappeared in the savannas. Their description sounds like *H.Saps*. Several of the lionesses chased after them but the truck just vanished. The strange thing is most, if not all, of these events last only a few minutes. I seem to be one of the few who has had an extended period in alternate space. Agrippa stuck around for a few hours as well but most, like your mother, are transported for a very short time, maybe minutes. I don't want to jump to conclusions but it's almost like a mechanism that is short-circuiting periodically or is out of balance. Does the universe have the hiccups?"

(Here it comes!) "Hmmmm!" said Octavius. "So what do you recommend?"

"I believe we should go semi-public."

"And start a panic? Are you out of your mind?"

"We need to gather more data. To do that, we should identify the project openly as a harmless boondoggle by a couple of wild-eyed investigators with more time and money than they know what to do with. Then we can make inquiries of some of the subjects and scientists, while convincing them that we're out on the fringe and in danger of toppling over. There are hundreds of projects like that. Some are crackpot; some not so cracked!"

"We must try to stay out of the press or at least the serious press. The less seriously we are taken, the more profitable will be the results. We especially don't want to put General Turmoil and his bunch on the alert. By the way, I think if Howard is our face to the teleporters, we can move about relatively freely. We can switch back and forth between different team members so we leave a scattered trail."

"OK!" said the Bear, "I see your logic. I concur. Good work! Howard, have you come across anything in the way of research papers or symposia that might suggest the scientific community is becoming alert?"

"There is one astrophysicist in Genoa!"

"Oh no," I shouted. "Not Ferrucio Ferretti!! Has he switched to astrophysics?" *(Readers of our first book – The Open and Shut Case - will recall a sleazy ferret from Genoa who had managed, he thought, to convince Imperius Drake who was posing as a moneyed benefactor, to contribute a large sum of euros to his two bit genetics lab. It didn't work out well for Ferrucio, who was last seen being dragged off to jail for trying to skip town without paying his debts.)*

"No, Maury. It's not the ferret but it is an odd coincidence. This guy is a ground hog."

"He's probably the mastermind behind all of those crazy Italian Ponzi schemes."

"Maury," said the Bear, "control your chauvinism. Let's make sure we're following up on the science, Howard, even if it sounds off the wall. Anything else from any of the team members?"

Negative shakes of heads.

"All right, back to the problem at hand! Otto, would you please find the superintendent, and ask him to meet us in the room where Senhor Condor has set up his equipment. I want to see if we've gotten any results from the radio and GPS surveillance." Condo went off with Howard.

"What about the Bearoness?" asked Otto.

"By all means, if you can find her. She's probably still with the Superintendent and the bodies. For God's sake, don't say anything to that loud mouthed media sow or her photographer. I'd love to give her a first hand reality experience and push her down that elevator shaft. We'll probably have her all over us tonight at dinner."

"If there is a dinner. The staff may all be in turmoil." Otto spoke as he disappeared. *(!?)*

Octavius turned to me. "Otto may be right. Speak with Mrs. McRadish and one or two of the clones and see what kind of a state they're in. And while you're at it, check the whereabouts of the relatives. Let's see how they react to this death. After all, he was only one of the serving class."

I wondered. As the others headed for the house, I walked past the beach house and waved at Harold. He waved back and skittered over, tail slapping the rocky sand. "I s'ppose yer heard about Hamish, poor old sod. 'Tisn't safe for an honest workin' animal to be here in this place. Makes a body think. Ol' Hamish has been here since they first started luggin' in the stones to build this pile. Knew everythin' about it, he did. Wouldn't think anybody could put one over on that ol' boar. He was canny, was Hamish."

The thought had occurred to me more than once in the last few hours that Hamish might have been a little too canny for his own good. Did the oil rig raiders knock him off because he knew too much about their activities and their setup here? Perhaps the old boar saw a way to build an expanded retirement fund, if he hadn't already accumulated one, courtesy of the Bearonial Bruins. Even if he had a full trough somewhere, there's nothing like a hedge against inflation.

"Kept his own council, did Hamish," the otter continued. "Verra close mouthed but those piggy eyes of his saw everythin', everythin."

"How is the staff reacting, Harold?"

"Weeel, the (D,H,M,P)ollies go beserk any chance they kin. Not a brain in the bunch. Mrs. McRadish is takin' it in stride. She wasn't all that fond of Hamish. Thought he put on airs, which he did. And Dougal, bless 'im, is the new retainer. Quite pleased, he is. Wanted the job for quite a while. He asked me if I wanted ta be gameskeeper. I said I'd think on it."

So Dougal is the new Hamish. That didn't take long. I guess the Bearoness wants to keep the operation going without skipping a beat. Of course, that might have given Dougal a motive for clubbing Hamish, if he was letting his ambition get out of control. In the words of the Great Ursine – "Hmmmm!" I thanked Harold for the update, mentioned our sea-going voyage the next morning, and headed for the service entrance and the kitchen.

Mrs. McRadish and one of the clones were preparing what looked like a full multi-course dinner. The young sheep looked a bit upset but the old ewe was as solid *(stolid?)* as the vegetable she was named after.

"Good afternoon, ladies. Not letting the tragedy on the roof interfere with domestic progress, I see."

"Guid afternun, sair. Nae, Mr. Hamish would've been mortified if his death interrupted the meal schedule. 'Mrs. McRadish,' he would say, 'the sign of a quality home is stability and proper procedure.' So we're going to serve dinner on the spot of seven as usual."

"I suppose it's going to be a little difficult getting used to Hamish not being around."

"Weel, we'll see how Dougal works out. He's not polished like Hamish but he's an honest and hard working dog. And smart - verra, verra smart." She looked over at me and winked. Being winked at by a stoutish ewe with flour on her nose and hooves is a unique experience. "Now, if you'll scuse me, I have a meal to attend to."

That certainly was enlightening. Based on her testimony alone, I can now conclude…absolutely nothing. Where's Fetlock Holmes when you need him? I decided to join the others in Condo's equipment room. As I was coming out into the hall, the library door opened and Howard stuck his prickly nose out, peering up and down the passage. He saw me and starting waving frantically for me to join him. As I walked toward him, he grabbed me and pushed me into the room. Alistair was no longer on his shiny new platform with the bronze memorial plaque. Still up on the roof, no doubt, along with Hamish and, I guess, the police.

"C'mere, c'mere, c'mere! I've got something very interesting to show you." He skittered over to a tapestry that covered most of a large paneled wall and pulled on it. I expected it to come falling down on our heads but instead, it swung around on a pivot, leaving the wall clear. He reached over and pushed back one of the small walnut panels and revealed an electronic lock face. He pushed a few buttons on his handheld "wizard wand" and the lock glowed and with a slow rumble, the paneled wall slid behind its neighbor, and there sat the car from the mystery lift.

"The lift doesn't just go directly from the cavern to the roof, like we thought. So far, I've discovered one other door on a deck below the garage. I think it opens on a storage area these bozos have been using to store their nasty toys. I found it by playing around with the codes. There may be others."

"Well," I said, "That explains how Alistair made his trip to the roof. Not with whom, but how. Close it up and let's go meet with the others. A few things are starting to fall into place. What rooms are on the floors above this one?"

"I think it's the family wing. Hamish, bless his now deceased heart, would never come up with a house plan, so I'm guessing" said Howard.

"We'll have to do some surveying on our own but not right this minute. Let's get back to Octavius and Condo and see what they're coming up with. I think we finally have the makings of a campaign here." *(Gee, I love that swell adventure talk.)* "Let's close this panel and tapestry up. I don't want anyone else stumbling across it, although the way things have been going we may be the only ones who didn't know it existed. Let's hear it for the detectives."

We went out into the public hall and took the lift up to the conference room that L. Condor had commandeered for his monitoring activity. Otto, Bel and Nigel were there as well as Octavius, the wolves and the condor. Condo was looking at a display and scrolling back and forth.

In a voice that perfectly mimicked Colonel Where, he said, "These are the registration signals used by the GPS systems in this area. They're very solid over the past twenty four hours but if I go back to the point where I first started recording, you can see an occasional jump in the reference numbers that lasts about fifteen minutes and then goes back. That's enough to throw all the local systems off for a few hours. They only recalibrate several times a day. When they do, of course, they get back on normal settings. That's what's been driving the Inter-Platform Communications techies nuts. Everything scopes out normal whenever they test."

"Where's the interference coming from, Senhor?" asked Nigel.

"Right from this building, Superintendent, and there are also random radio jamming and spurious radar blips being sent out. That's still going on. I think it's on some kind of a programmed sequencer. I'm not connected to the Internet at this moment but I wouldn't be the least bit surprised if they also had some computer equipment sending out worms and viruses to knock off the local PCs. It's a general purpose harassment job."

"Well, my men and I have been interrupted from our search by the death of the retainer, but we'll start again as soon as the medical team takes the body. What should we do with Sir Alistair's carcass?"

"Cover it up and put it in one of the storage rooms that Otto opened," said the Bearoness. "We'll take it back to the library if and when I'm damn good and ready. Booo, indeed! Sometimes I think we're dealing with arch fiends and the next minute, it's like we're being overrun by an unruly kindergarten. If this turns out to be members of my own sweet family, they're all getting pushed off this island on a leaky raft. I'm well and truly sick of this."

"As you say, Bel, on the one hand we have this carefully engineered and executed destruction program. On the other, it's Trick or Treat on Halloween." This from Octavius.

"Before you go too far off in speculating,' I said, "Howard has some interesting information for you. By the way, Mrs. McRadish says that she will be serving a full dinner at seven. Twenty minutes from now. She says Hamish would have wanted it that way.'

I heard a stomach rumble, an ursine stomach. Howard told about the "local stops" on what we thought was the "express only" external lift. That explains a lot of comings and goings, especially if there were several more hidden stops on the family floors. Our primary target for tonight is that newly discovered deck below the garage. But first, dinner! Among other things, we wanted to see who was still in the castle and showed up for the evening meal. We had no idea who those animals were that took off in the boat and helicopter earlier in the day. Maybe by a process of elimination, we could come up with something.

Speaking of dinner, I wonder how Chita and Bearyl are doing in Abeardeen. I wouldn't mind being a little Meerkat hiding under the furniture listening to that session.

Chapter Twenty Four
Petro Club - Abeardeen

There's a wildcat and there's a wild cat
And the second type's where I am at.
I am playing it tough.
I am taking no guff
From a feline who's monstrously fat.

From the unpublished Memoirs of Chita
- aka Mlle. Catherine Catt

The Petro Club is a turn of the century pile reeking with the smell of wildcat and oil. Not reeking literally, I suppose, although some of the members seemed to have bathed in their product. But the place is awash in petroleum related furnishings, memorabilia, books, art, papers, magazines, even a stained glass window of an oil rig.

It sits on a hill in downtown Abeardeen daring any of the upstart local establishments to try to out "prestige" it. The funny thing is that while the building is well over a hundred years old, the Petroleum Club only dates back to 1969 when the first Scottish underwater fields were found off Abeardeen. The building started out life as a school for wealthy Shetland bairns and progressed through a series of transformations as an orphanage, a newspaper, a library and briefly, a house of ill repute before it was taken over by the oil rig owners. Some local cynics say there was little difference in its last two occupants. Anyway, at the moment, the club was feeling the pinch just like all of its members and was more than delighted to host Ms. Catt's dinner party. A euro is a euro!

As a result of being a platform owner, I had automatic *(but grudging)* membership in the place. I'd been here once or twice with my now deceased benefactor. All I got back then were admiring stares. I was still getting stares this evening but I don't think there was much admiration in them. Bearyl really got a going over. I'm not sure a bear had ever set foot inside the place before – especially a drop-dead gorgeous polar. Agenda Item One – wildcat attitude adjustment. Time for rough and tumble Chita – the wildcatter's dream *(and nightmare)* - to make her stand.

I strode over to the maitre-d' using my haute couture, long-legged strut and asked him in a loud, clear growl to take us to the room I'd reserved for our dinner. Bearyl sauntered over behind me. I hadn't realized till that moment that she was still wearing the sidearm she carried for protecting Belinda. Gulping once or twice, the host querulously asked the bear if she would leave her artillery in the cloak room.

Bearyl made a big show of making up her mind and then, with a shrug that looked like she was about to draw the pistol, she turned. Then, slowly rocking her head from side to side and glaring at each open mouthed member as she passed, she dropped the weapon at the cloakroom desk with a "clunk" and ambled back to join us. It is a well known zoological fact that most feral cats lack sweat glands. The maitre d' seemed to have found a few he didn't know he had. If Bearnice was the singer of the pair, Bearyl was definitely the actress.

We were a few minutes early, but when we opened the door to the dining room, three wildcats were already sitting around the table. *(I expected seven.)* I gave them my Premium Cheetah Scowl complete with half closed eyes. Then, without saying a word, I moved to the head of the table. Bearyl stood at the other end and the three little kittens sat in between, looking first at me and then at the totally unexpected bear.

"Gentlecats," I growled, "good evening. Welcome! I am Ms. Catherine Catt and this is my associate Ms. Bearyl Blanc. It's still a little early, so while we're waiting for our other colleagues to make an appearance; I suggest we all have a drink. Waiter, I assume you stock White Lightning. What'll you have, Bearyl?"

"The same." *(I doubt Bearyl had ever tasted White Lightning but what the hell, she has the constitution of a bear.)*

The waiter, also a wildcat, looked a bit shocked but said, "Aye ma'am. We have White Lightning - 180 proof – imported from Oklahoma. Don't get much call fer it, y'ken."

"Good, save yourself some walking and leave the bottle when you come back. Please see what these gentlecats will have."

One of the cats already had a drink that he'd brought in from the bar. The other two ordered single malt scotch – small batch. We began introductions. Cathcart, Gordon and McRae – the first two were independents; McRae represented the UK North Sea subsidiary of one of the conglomerates. It was really the indies I was concerned about. Any sell-out action by the big guys would get so tied up in anti-trust legal and regulatory nonsense; it would be a long while before they could even start negotiating. But the small timers could sell out in a shot. Perfect score for the evening would be total agreement by everyone not to budge. Passing score would be: hold on to the independents.

While the waiter was taking orders, three more cats ambled in. MacDowell, MacDonald and MacDuff. They all knew each other. I was the only "outsider" cat and as far as conversation went, Bearyl and I were being treated as such. We were waiting on Pringle – the last of the independents. From the phone conversation we had, he was a tough customer and a condescending antifeminist. He's going to be fun.

The waiter came back with the drinks, left the bottle of White Lightning and asked if he could begin serving dinner. I told him to wait another five minutes and we'd start.

Twenty after! Still no Pringle! The hell with him! I signaled to the waiter and suggested that everyone take their seats. The seat next to Bearyl was left empty. She looked at me and grinned. I grinned back. "Why don't we eat before discussing business? I think this session will go easier on a full stomach."

Just then one of the fullest stomachs I had ever seen came thumping through the door. To say he was a fat cat is to grossly understate. This guy was obese plus. He took off his Tam O'Shanter and tossed it on the table. He galumphed down next to Bearyl without giving her a glance, looked around the table, nodded at everyone but me and asked the waiter for a double single malt scotch. Then he looked at Bearyl and me and said in an almost unintelligible burr. "What's that yer drinkin'? Is that some of that Rooshian vodka?" He turned to Bearyl and asked "Are you one of those Roooshian polars, too?"

"TOO!" Bells went off in my head. This jerk just told me a lot of what I wanted to know. They'd been talking to another polar bear. Bearyl looked up at me and then at him and said, "No, I'm from Unst by way of Canada."

I said "We're drinking 180 proof White Lightning. It's all the oil crews drink back in Oklahoma."

Bearyl, who had been toying with her bowl but not drinking *(she had to fly us back tonight)* pushed it toward him and said, "Here, I haven't touched it yet. Give it a try while you wait for your scotch."

He sniffed at it and raised it up in his paws. Meanwhile, I very ostentatiously polished off my drink in front of the assembly. He stuck his tongue in the bowl, lapped cautiously and went into one of the most theatrical coughing fits I had ever seen. Grins spread on the faces of the other cats. Bearyl pounded him on the back. If he wasn't so damn fat she probably would have broken him in two. He hastily put down the bowl, wiped the tears out of his eyes and gave a sort of snort-growl. I meanwhile purred and poured myself another bowl of the rocket fuel. *(Which I would not touch. I had to stay sober to pull this off. I think I had made my point.)*

McRae broke the ice and said, "So you're from Oklahoma?"

I'd never been near Oklahoma but I knew enough about the oil fields there and lied my way through the rest. "I'm from everywhere," I replied. *(First true thing I'd said so far.)* This salmon is excellent."

"Bearyl is here as the representative of Bearoness Belinda Béarnaise Bruin (nee Black.) The Bearoness is very much concerned about this whole thing. I'm a close friend of hers, and when I brought the situation to her attention, she offered all her resources to assist. But as you'll hear a bit later, there's another reason she's concerned."

Slurps and munches as the meal progressed. We were lapping our coffee when Pringle, having recovered his mountainous aplomb, looked at me and said, "I'll nae pass up a good meal, *(that's obvious)* but I dinna see the point to the rest of this evenin.' Now, what's a wee lassie like you who's some kind of furrin' cat and who got her oil rig from a senile ol' lecher going to tell us perfessionals, hmmm?" An oily smile *(sorry, but it was oily)* crossed his ugly puss. *(sorry again)*

I wanted to rip the bastard apart but wonder of wonders, I controlled myself. Bearyl had tensed up at the other end of the table and the other cats started examining the ceiling, walls or their coffee bowls.

"Pringle," I snarled, "I may not be a *felis silvestris* but we cheetahs have a world–wide reputation for being fast, tough and this is important…smart. If you knew Kitt Kirkpatrick at all, you would have known him for a fine gentlecat without a lecherous bone in his well preserved body." I stared him down. First, at the oversized puddle of fur that once was his body and then at his stupid head. The message went right over it.

"Now, I have some information to share with you and it seems *(I glanced at Pringle)* you have something more to tell me."

"Whaddya mean "more?" he snarled. "We've told yer nothing so far!'

"True perhaps, if you don't count your meetings with a Russian Polar Bear."

"Who's been telling yer that?" *(He's an even bigger dope than I thought.)* He looked around the table angrily. The cats stared back at him.

Before I could reply, Cathcart scowled at him and said, "You did, you twit, when you asked Ms. Bearyl here if she was a Rooshian polar bear,TOO. How many Rooshian polar bears have you met lately? It's true, Ms Catt. We've had some early negotiations with a bear who claims to represent petropol, the Rooshian oil monopoly. We haven't seen him in the last few days though. At least, I haven't." He looked around the table at the others. Everyone shook their head negative.

"What did this guy look like? And please don't tell me – 'You've seen one polar bear, you've seen them all.' "

"Naw," said MacLeod, "He was different. I've seen those polar show bears from Bearmoral Castle. Bonnie! Verra, verra bonnie! This ursine had a sort of pushed in nose and he wore a jacket that should have been a flag on a racecourse. Never gave his name."

He didn't need to. That was Alistair.

"The last time we met with him, he had a younger bear with him, dressed like a 1920's gangster, with a moustache. Never seen a polar bear with a moustache before. It may be big in Rooshia."

Roary!!!

I looked down at Bearyl. She kept her face motionless but her eyes were doing backflips. We'd hit pay dirt. My turn to impart some intelligence. Speaking of intelligence or lack thereof, Pringle had sat through this entire interchange with his mouth shut. I shall have to inform the media.

"We know those two. You won't be seeing your friend in the checkered jacket again. He's dead!"

Pringle's mouth gaped open. *(The silence couldn't last.)* Chirps, snarls and growls around the table. I obviously had their attention. "He and the B movie slicker are both from Bearmoral Castle. His name is Alistair Bruin and he fell six stories into a moat and is no more. *(I didn't bother describing how he had been transformed into his lifeless state or his subsequent, taxidermically enhanced pelt.)* The younger guy is called Roary."

"Now, here's what you should know. All of these attacks on your rigs have originated from the castle....WITHOUT THE BEARONESS' KNOWLEDGE. That is one of the reasons Bearyl is here. To assure you that we're on the case. In fact, a world renowned detective, Octavius Bear, is here with his team, at the Bearoness' request, assisting Shetland Yard and the government in tracking down this gang and stopping the mayhem."

"And what has this smart-boots bear found, eh?" Pringle, who else.

"A phony Environmental Ministry Patrol boat tucked away in a cavern near the castle. All of your rigs have been visited by "environmental inspectors' in the past six weeks. In each case, shortly afterward, something nasty happened. An explosion, a mysterious fire, damaged drill bits, poisoned food. Each one on delayed activation. Timed to surface well after the 'inspectors' had left. Same with the sabotaged boats and helicopters. None of the government investigators had even thought of the possibility of a counterfeit inspection team. Neither did any of your rig managers. Neither did you, Pringle!"

"Now," I continued, "we're closing in on the masterminds behind this. *(a hopeful white lie)* Alistair and Roary were front bears. This took more cunning and planning than they're capable of. You've confirmed what we wanted to know. What we don't want you to do is sell out to petropol. This will be over very shortly. In fact, as far as you're concerned, it may well be over now. If the Russians get their claws on those rigs, all that revenue flows east and there won't be a wildcat left on any of those sites. I met with those poor cats. Most of them haven't got a penny left. I paid my riggers to tide them over. You might consider doing the same thing." I stared around the table as did Bearyl. Coughs, affirmative nods. Pringle, on the other hand, hadn't understood or ignored every word I had said.

"Wait a minute!" said MacDonald. "What about the disappearin' rigs and the blackouts. No inspector boat was involved in them incidents."

My long experience of lying with the most sincere confidence came galloping to the rescue. I didn't have the damndest idea what was causing all that stuff. So, I waved a paw and said, "We've got that one, too. Electronic jamming by the same bunch."

Little did I know that, probably for the first time in my life, when I thought I was lying, I was actually close to telling the truth. So I lied a little more for good measure.

"So, please stay loose. This will be cleared up completely in the next several days. We're talking to the government now, asking them to lift the ban on reopening the rigs. You should be able to go back into operation shortly. If any of you are too financially strapped to start up again, the Bearoness has offered to provide seed money to tide you over. All very confidential, of course." *(None of them would admit in front of the others that they were on the rocks. For all I knew, this meal may have been the best one a couple of the indies had had in the past few weeks. Pringle could live off his fat for an eon.)*

I turned to Bearyl and nodded. "If there are no further questions, Ms. Blanc and I want to get back to Unst this evening. I have your numbers and will be keeping you informed. Thank you for coming." I couldn't resist one last Premium Cheetah Stare in Pringle's direction.

When we got outside the building, I heard a thumping noise behind me. The sound of two ursine paws clapping in appreciation. "Brava, Brava!" she said.

I modestly bowed. We both laughed and headed off for the airport.

Chapter Twenty Five
Meanwhile, Back at Bearmoral with Maury

In this chapter, we'll let you cliff-hang.
We'll uncover a polar bear gang.
But we won't clear the stage
Till the very last page
Then our story goes out with a bang!

We didn't have time for a pre-dinner drink, much to my chagrin. The meal was already in progress when we trickled in. The "family" was all assembled. Aunt Albearta was holding forth on some earth shattering trivia; Roary was lapping up a cocktail while Bruinhilde was trying unsuccessfully to keep her napkin from sliding off her satin dress. Ethelbeart was in his usual semi-stupor and Ursula....where was Ursula?

Off in a corner, Madame Honoria Heifer was noisily ingesting a large bowl of soup and mooing musically to Bearbi. A match made in heaven. The two divas were no doubt one-upping each other with terribly sophisticated stories from the arts. The heifer was probably trying to get herself a substantial mention in the upcoming articles on the debut of Lepi and Bearnice

I noticed that Lepi and Bearnice were not with her. They may have decided to eat with the staff just to get away from the divine bovine. Octavius and Bel moved up to the head table, much to Albearta's annoyance while Howard, Condo, the wolves and I started toward a nice empty table in the back. Chita and Bearyl, as you know, were down in Abeardeen. Wonder how that was going!

I almost walked past Dougal without recognizing him. Waistcoat, striped pants, hatless, but still with the keys at his waist. Polished shoes that looked like they pinched. Of course, no pipe. That must be killing him along with the shoes.

"Dougal, mon, I hardly know ye." My best Scottish burr is a miserable failure.

The dog smiled at me and said, "Guid evenin' Mister Maury, I'm glad yer cuid join us fer dinner. 'Tis my maiden voyage, so ta speak. I hope ye enjoy the meal. Mrs. McRadish has done a bonnie job. Sort of a memorial ta Hamish, ye ken."

"This is quite a job you have - managing this whole complex. Tell me, how many staff members are there?"

"Weell, there are four maids, two cooks, Harold, four groundsmen who are also the pipers…."

"Oh, yes, the pipers. I must confess I wasn't sorry that the Bearoness suspended the piping while the investigation is going on."

" 'Tis an acquired taste, the bagpipe, but wouldna have done any good to start up again. All four of them have gone off without givin' notice."

"What??"

"I guess they felt insulted that they could nae play any longer. They're a sensitive lot, those terriers."

Light bulb!!! Superintendent Wardlaw and his sergeant were just coming into the dining room. I waved them over. Octavius looked up from the table quizzically but didn't budge. Belinda was talking to one of the maids.

"Superintendent, I think we just found out who those animals were who left so quickly today. I think we may also have identified the phony inspectors. They're all terriers, Dougal?"

"Oh aye! Terriers make the best pipers."

"So were the so-called inspectors, according to Fergus."

Wardlaw turned to the sergeant and said. "Get up to their rooms right now and search them top to bottom."

As the police dog left, Octavius rose from his seat and joined us. I explained my theory to him. We were beginning to attract attention. Albearta seemed annoyed that her monologue was being interrupted by those ridiculous Americans. Our team looked over from their table but Octavius waved them down. Bel rose and joined us. That really ticked off Albearta.

Suddenly, Ursula burst into the room, rumbled up to Belinda and shouted, "Vere is my Alistair? He is not in the library vere he belongs. Vot has happened to him? *(The Teutonic accent was getting thicker by the shout.)*

The Bearoness took her aside and from the horrified shrieks and "achs" was obviously telling her about Alistair's strange elevator ride. Ursula was livid.

"Booo? A sign that said - Booo? Vot is this Booo?"

"We don't know, madam." said the Superintendent. "We are in the act of investigating now. Sir Alistair's, er, remains are intact and unharmed and will be returned to their pedestal when we have completed our examinations."

"A disgrace, a disgrace! A Scottish nobleman to be treated so!"

While this North Sea storm was in progress, the sergeant returned to the dining room. "Empty, sir. Clean as a bone. Except fer this. We found it behind a bed." He handed Nigel a uniform cap. An Environmental Inspector's cap!

"Good work, sergeant. I want an immediate alarm sent out for these individuals. Impersonating officers of the crown. Interference with regulated commerce. arson, wanton destruction, and possible murder! Mr. Dougal will give you their names and particulars. We believe they left by helicopter today. No markings that could be seen. Is that correct, Senhor Condor?"

Condo nodded and said in perfect imitation of the collie's voice. "That is correct, Superintendent, they outflew me, heading south but I got a good look at the ship. It was silver but any ID numbers were painted over."

By now, the dining room was fidgin fain. *(Look it up!)* Ignoring Octavius' signal to cool it, the wolves had joined us and the condor had risen from his seat while he was addressing the Superintendent. Howard stayed at the table but was keeping a close eye on "the family" who oddly, were not stirring even though they were obviously interested. Honoria and Bearbi seemed oblivious to the entire proceedings. Strange for Bearbi.

In the middle of all this, Octavius' cell phone rang. The bear was annoyed *(what else?)*

"Bear here! Yes! Yes! Who! The two of them? Very Interesting! Well done...Chita! er, thanks! We'll take it from here."

He turned to the wolves and said, "Grab Roary!"

The Colonel was on the polar's neck in a flash and the Frau was standing in front of him as he tried to get up, her teeth menacing and her growl scaring everyone in sight. Bruinhilde screamed, "Дедушка,спасаться бегством!" and jumped up from her chair. I later learned she had told Ethelbeart to run like hell. There was a sudden transformation and the

208

doddering old sot became very swift and agile as they bounded for the library. Albearta fainted. Belinda grabbed Ursula and sat on her.

Octavius, Howard, Condo and I ran after the two bears with Nigel and his sergeant in the lead. Ethelbeart and Bruinhilde ran over to the paneled wall, and tearing off the tapestry, she pressed a remote control unit she had in her paw. Nothing! We circled the two of them. Howard said, "I don't think it's going to work for you. I changed the code."

"You'll be thorry! All of you!" she screamed. Ethelbeart pulled out a revolver and aiming at the light switches, shot the room into darkness. Thumping and thudding. Someone grabbed me. I think it was the sergeant. When he realized that polar bears are not two feet tall, he let go. Octavius shouted, "Give it up, Ethelbeart or whoever you are."

"Commissar Boris Bearents, you interfering dolt!' he shouted as he shot in the direction of Octavius' voice.

From the other side of the room, Octavius said, "You're surrounded. Killing more of us will only make things worse!"

"We don't know who killed Alistair or that stupid retainer" screamed Bruinhilde from a totally different direction. "We have killed no one, no one!"

"How about those wildcats that died on the oil rigs?"

"Well, no one important!' said the commissar, firing at Octavius' new location and moving as he did.

"There are too many of us, Boris." said Nigel.

The bear fired across the room at the Superintendent's voice.

Suddenly from behind him, Nigel said, "I think this sedative dart will help you change your mind, commissar."

Boris yelped and from the sound of it he toppled, Nigel had given him the elephant dose. Now where the hell was Bruinhilde?

A sudden burst of light as the library door opened and Bruinhilde tried to run for it. She was hit squarely in the face with a six foot billboard and before she could get up, Octavius, Condo and the sergeant were on her. That's the second time the condor has knocked someone out with his wings. (cf. *The Case of the Spotted Band*)

We dragged the dazed but still struggling Bruinhilde back into the dining room. The wolves had Roary subdued. Bel was still sitting on Ursula. The sergeant called in the rest of the crime scene team and we soon had all five of them stretched out and bound in the hall outside the dining room. Albearta had awakened and fainted dead away again. Ethelbeart (Boris) was down for the count. Ursula was screaming that she knew nothing about anything. Bruinhilde kept cursing alternately in Russian and in English. The lisp was real.

We all looked at Roary who stared back defiantly. "Leave my mother and grandmother out of this. They had no part in anything. As for me, I'm not saying a word until I see my solicitor. You're going to have to work to prove anything, you incompetents."

"Oh, we will, Roary or whatever your name is. There are several rig owners who can identify you as the negotiators for petropol and by the time we have taken apart that storage deck downstairs and gone over the boat, we'll have enough to tie at least you, your sister, your dead father and whoever Boris really is, to this whole thing." Octavius snarled.

Often, that tirade was enough to make a criminal break down on the spot. Give Roary credit. He didn't even wince.

Nigel came back into the room. "One of our Black Maria Helicopters is on the way to take these five into custody." He walked over to Belinda. "Do you really think the old lady had anything to do with this?"

"I don't know and I don't care. I just want the old sow out of here. She may not even be related to me. I don't think any of them are. My husband, Byron, was involved in a few shady deals, as I've discovered, and these people were here when we married. For all I know, they had something on him and decided to take advantage of it or he may have been up to his neck in it himself. He was a wheeler dealer and a lot of his money came from no apparent source. I feel a little itchy about staying in this place, myself."

Roary, who was listening to the conversation, broke out into gales of laughter but said nothing. I suspect his ride back on the chopper was going to be a little rougher than usual.

Bearbi, by this time, had fully immersed herself in the proceedings. Somehow she had gotten hold of Clarence who was photographing everything in sight until the Superintendent put a stop to it. "Oh, Belinda! What excitement! This weekend has been one long adventure series. How simply wonderful!!"

Honoria stood off in a corner being operatically horrified. I fully expected her to join Albearta in the swoon-of-the-month club.

Lepi and Bearnice had made an appearance along with the entire domestic staff. Bearnice relieved Bel in sitting on Ursula. Mrs. McRadish was none too gently applying smelling salts to Albearta. The scene was beginning to look like one of those Grade B farces but somebody had forgotten the punch line.

Suddenly, the front door opened and in stepped Bearyl and Chita. "Hi," she said, "Did I miss anything???"

Chapter Twenty Six
Bearmoral-the Morning After

Is the mystery all figured out?
Have the villains been all put to rout?
It's not easy to know
But if you think it's so,
I believe there's some room here for doubt!

Chita took one look at the police cohort and decided to make herself scarce. Mumbling something about helicopter rides making her sick, *(probably true, especially when aided by a healthy snort of White Lightning)* she told Belinda, Octavius and the Superintendent that Bearyl could fill them in on their meeting with the rig owners. She'd be in her room resting.

Bearyl reported on the dinner, leaving out some of the Pringle tweaking. When she got to the part about the cats being approached by two Rooshian polars, one in a checkered jacket and the other with a moustache, Superintendent Wardlaw turned to his sergeant and told him to get the names of the wildcats from Bearyl and then call them to appear tomorrow afternoon at Abeardeen Police Headquarters to review an identification lineup. "Better get the stuffed carcass of Sir Alistair down from the roof and bring it along with these five. He'll have to appear, too."

This set Ursula off on another round of cursing and swearing at the barbarity of the Englischers. Frau Schuylkill shut her up by letting loose a stream of Switzerdeutsch profanity that probably would have curled my ears if I had the slightest idea what she was saying. Ursula and Bruinhilde both stared at the wolf in shock.

Needless to say, dinner was something of a disaster or more to the point, nonexistent. After explaining and re-explaining the night's events to the uninvolved onlookers, *(there had been a few)* and watching the hustling off of the culprits to Abeardeen, we began to settle down a bit. Nigel had called the military and the oil commission as well as his own people and laid out the story. They were coming up tomorrow to inspect that storage deck. It occurred to me that with all our bluster, none of us had actually been inside the deck except

212

Howard, who had just opened and closed the door of the mega-lift on that floor. We might all be in for a few surprises.

Colonel Where came over to Octavius and asked, "When we go down to Abeardeen for the government inspection of the Ursa Major tomorrow, do you still want us to bring back the particle accelerator? After all, this affair seems to be all sewed up."

The Great Bear mused for a moment and said, "Bring it along and any other weapons you can tote, without seeming too obvious. Those four terriers are still on the loose and we don't know whether this group was the whole gang or just the tip of the iceberg." With that, he yawned, scratched and rolled over in a narcoleptic sleep.

It was too much work to move him and he'd come around in his own sweet time. Bearbi, Honoria and the domestics stared at him in his recumbent state but said nothing. *(A first for Bearbi.)* Everyone else was in on the story of his "ailment" so we left him there snoozing peacefully. When Nigel returned from seeing off the police copter, I explained Octavius' condition. The collie, smiled, shook his head and said, "Maybe we all better get some sleep. A full day tomorrow."

*****

Next morning I arose once again to blissful silence. Here's hoping those pipers never come back. I doubt the Bearoness liked the idea in the first place. Obviously, they were a ruse concocted by Ethelbeart-Boris – and possibly Albearta – for staffing their assault on the rigs. The more I thought of it, the more amazed I became at the thought, patience, expense and conniving that went into the whole caper. Several years in preparation, at least. Octavius may be right. This might just be a single floe on the petropol icecap. More to come? Who knows? The things we do for oil.

Life was slowly returning to normal, whatever that means, as I came down for breakfast. Dougal was standing at the entrance to the dining room suitably decked out as a morning host.

"Well, Dougal,' I laughed, "last night's debut as a dining room maitre d' got off to an unusual start. Think you can keep things under control this time?"

He chuckled and said, "We had a bit of a time with hysterical serving sheep but Mrs. McRadish took them in hoof. Now that they've calmed down, they realize they have something to chatter about for at least a month. I think

213

they all go to Bingo in the village on their afternoons off so it'll be no time before the Battle of Bearmoral Castle is a local legend, suitably embellished, ya ken. I still dinna understand, though, why they killed the bear and the boar."

"That's something we all need to get to the bottom of. Hopefully, the police will get a confession out of one of them that explains why. It may just be that Alistair and Hamish were trying to extort money out of the gang to ensure their silence. Well, they're silent now."

As I entered the dining room, the two wolves were just getting up from the table. "Herr Maury, we're going down to Abeardeen for the customs inspection of the Ursa Major. Would you care to join us?'

"And end up being arrested for attempted smuggling, if they find anything. No thanks, Frau Schuylkill. I'm going to hang around here and see what that storage deck contains. We meerkats are a curious species."

The colonel grinned. "Yes, you are rather strange. Don't worry! They won't find anything on the ship. Octavius wants us to bring back the accelerator gun. There's something rolling around in his brain but I'm not sure what."

"He doesn't like those four phony inspectors being loose. You never know what they might try. Although, if I were in their shoes, I'd be well on my way to Argentina by now."

"Assuming they ever got paid," said the Colonel.

"Interesting thought, Colonel" I said, "if they haven't been paid and they don't know that Boris et al. have been arrested, they might come sneaking back. Good catch! You might mention that to Octavius and the Superintendent."

"They've probably figured it out already. We're gonna be late for inspection if we don't leave right now."

"OK, *I'll* mention it to them. Good luck with the bureaucrats!"

He ran off to join Frau Schuylkill who had the rotors of the helicopter idling.

Octavius came trundling into the room accompanied by the Bearoness. Evidently, he had awoken some time during the night and made his way to his bedroom – I think. I waited until Nigel arrived and then went over and joined the three of them. No sign of Chita. Honoria and Bearbi were at it again, dropping names and playing *Can You Top This?* with stories of "culchah" and "susseyety." Otto was polishing off a platter of shellfish. Bearyl, Bearnice,

Howard, Condo and Lepi hadn't arrived yet and of course, the "family" was dining as guests of the Crown. I'm sure the wires were being burned up with transmissions of protest about false arrest to the "Rooshian" and German consulates. Good luck, Boris! You too, Albearta.

After I sat down, I mentioned the Colonel's idea about the terrorist terriers coming back to be paid off, if they hadn't already heard of the arrests. Belinda said something about killing them on the spot with her bear paws. Nigel winked and said, "Were ready for them! I'm off to Abeardeen." Octavius said nothing.

Chapter Twenty Seven
Dyce Airport - Abeardeen

As I'm sure all our readers have heard
Ursa Major's a wonderful bird.
Like a huge wingéd whale
With a six story tail!
Though its size makes it almost absurd.

After lifting off from the parking lot and sweeping out over the ocean, Luft- Kapitan Frau Ilse Schuylkill fine-tuned the helicopter's collective settings, adjusted the autopilot for Dyce, called into Air Traffic Control and looking over at Colonel Where, growled into her headset, "Well, Wyatt, what do you think of this muddle? Is it all over? Are the attacks on the rigs finished? Did the Bearents Bears kill off Albeart and Hamish or is that a completely different kettle of herrings?"

The Colonel adjusted his mike and said, "I can't figure out any motives for the killings except Hamish got too close to what was going on. But Albeart is a puzzle. I thought he was one of them, unless he decided he could do better by reporting the whole thing to the authorities. But what did he stand to gain from that?"

"Well," said the Frau, "from what Bearnice and Bearyl told me, Albeart didn't seem to be the sharpest claw on the paw. All he was able to talk about was deals and euros, euros and deals. It wouldn't surprise me if he outsmarted himself by threatening to blackmail them. That old booze-bear Ethelbeart turned out to be a surprise. Commissar Boris. Ach! He must have a dossier a foot thick."

"What about the females?" snarled the Colonel. "Bruinhilde was certainly in the act and I can't believe Ursula is really that upset about Albeart now that the jig is up. I wonder what the Bearoness is going to do with stuffed Albeart?" He chuckled. "The old aunt may be just what she claims but the Bearoness is delighted to get her out of the place, anyway. Talk about a dysfunctional family, if they were a family at all. By the time they sort out all the international accusations, suits and countersuits, they'll all be doddering. Of course, if the police can't blame one or both of the castle murders on them, there's still some sleuthing to be done. Speaking of sleuths, what do you think is going on in Octavius' head?"

"I have been with Herr Bear for many years now, and I have never been so bold as to suppose I knew what he was thinking, much less what he was going to do. You were the one who came up with the idea of the piper terriers coming back to be paid off. I don't think either Maury or Herr Octavius had considered that. Maybe one of them is a killer or all of them. One dog couldn't push a polar bear off a roof but they all could. I'm sure the Great Bear's mind is working overtime. I don't think he's satisfied with the way things turned out. He's got more to do and so do we."

"So why does he want to risk mixing it up with the local authorities by taking the wraps off the particle accelerator and bringing it up to the castle. He also wants some unobtrusive side arms. Oh, and maybe a field artillery piece or two, just for the hell of it. You and I may spend the rest of this journey in a Scottish dungeon."

The she-wolf smiled *(which was just as scary as her snarl.)* "You mean we can't outwit a horse and a couple of border collies? You're not getting old, are you, Wyatt? Or has all that alternate universe travel affected your taste for adventure?"

The Colonel swung at her with a map case. "No, but I'd like to get back to following that full time. This Shetlands folderol is all well and good but the Multiverse Project should be our top priority. Even Howard's annoyed that he had to come traipsing over here. But I guess now that they're married, the Bearoness is Octavius' number one concern. You know, though, I'm not sure I buy into that electronic GPS interference stuff as the full explanation for the wandering oil platforms. That shouldn't have affected the appearing and disappearing blips on the radars, and there's supposed to be a couple of eye witness reports, as well, of the rigs fading in and out."

"Wyatt, you're beginning to see teleportation in everything that happens. Before the Scottish military tries to confiscate everything, L.Condor gave the equipment a good going over. He's pretty convinced they used the GPS displacement and radar interference to create all the illusions. Not the fires and boat destruction, of course. That condor is a technical whiz. If he thinks they could have simulated the whole affair with electronics, I'm willing to give him my vote."

"Maybe!!"

The Frau called into Abeardeen Air Traffic Control again, reporting location, destination and estimated arrival time. She also asked them to inform Colonel McNeigh that they were on their way in for the military and customs inspection of the Ursa Major.

She then took another check of the horizon, looking for any wandering aircraft that may have been entering their space. Clear. The chopper's radar was picking up nothing but open sea. "I don't get this Dame Bearbi! I know the Bearoness is a show business queen but she certainly has peculiar friends. How does Bearbi know Chita, too? She certainly gets around."

"It's all one big alcohol fueled network, Ilse! Your idea of being in the fast lane is flying at Mach 2 in the Strike Eagle at 80,000 feet. Their idea of the fast lane is parties and fashion shows and gossip and parties and drinks and parties...."

"All right, I get it! But I'm surprised Chita has any stomach for such a ditzy dope."

"She is a bit tough to take. Almost as bad as that moooosical cow!"

They both howled and the Frau snorted.

"I hope she knows something about singing. Otherwise she's a total loss. I'm glad Bearnice and Lepi have to put up with her. I'd have made steaks out of her by now."

"Don't be too sure about either of them. They're only going to put up with her nonsense because of the Bearoness. After the recital you may find the cow floating in Loch Ness in pieces. I suppose we'll be going to the recital. I'll have to get my formal uniform out of the C-5A's stowage. I haven't the slightest idea why I brought it except we were going to a Scottish castle. I don't suppose the local inspectors will see anything wrong in my taking it off the plane. How about you? Do you have anything fancy to wear to the opera?"

"I didn't but Chita and the Bearoness said they would fix me up with something. Just as long as Dame Bearbi doesn't have a paw in it. Her outfits give me nightmares. I don't carry formal clothes around. In fact, I don't have any real dress-up regalia. I'm not a clothes horse like a certain wolf I know." Another swing of the map case. Another miss.

"Speaking of fouled up GPS and radar, time to check ours again."

They reported in to ATC. They still had half an hour to Dyce-Abeardeen. Between checking their progress, the surrounding airspace and the chopper's fuel reserve, neither of them could carry on a continuous conversation for very long.

"We'd better do a little planning and rehearsing on how we're going to deal with the authorities," said the Frau.

"OK, we want to get the particle beam projector, the portable side looking radar, several side arms and my clothes off the plane. We can hide the disassembled ray gun's power, aiming and firing units by including them in the radar containers. I can put the barrel in the sheath with my ceremonial sword. Anything else?"

"No, that's all I had listed when we did our pre-flight checkoff. But first, we want them to clear the aircraft for flight in this area. We're going to have to catalog and explain the unarmed weaponry mounted on the plane and demonstrate that no missiles or ammunition are stowed aboard. Most important, we're going to have to keep them from finding out that the Ursa Major has sophisticated stealth capability. They'd never let an invisible aircraft wander around their airspace. We'll just have to make up some story to explain the activation system, if they stumble across it."

The colonel snorted, "They'll probably just give the whole craft a cursory going over. One or two sniffs here and there. After all, we are on their side. As for finding the stealth functions, I can't imagine they have anyone on their inspection team who's familiar with a C-5A, especially our C-5A."

"Famous last words!" snarled the Frau.

They approached Dyce-Abeardeen! One more whirling locust homing in on the swarm. The airport was super busy now that the Scottish rigs were being cleared for restart. The wildcats had wasted no time in getting crews assembled and transported out to the platforms. As each structure was cleared to go on stream *(this time by bona-fide government inspectors)* the cats went into high speed reaction mode, setting up power, checking out pumps and drills, testing the pipelines and getting ready to send their black liquid treasure on its way to the refineries, and much needed euros on the way into their pockets.

In the midst of all the madly rushing air and ground traffic, the Ursa Major sat regally unconcerned like a Leviathan surrounded by frenzied guppies.

Off to the side, in sparkling blue and white, was Bearoness Bruin's hangar sheltering the Aquabear SST, several choppers, a Twin Otter and of course, the shops and maintenance center. Belinda's air force almost rivaled The Great Bear's. *(No missile silo, however.)* Between the two of them, they could probably have produced several epic air extravaganzas. Dogfights over the Shetlands!!! If the thought ever crossed the Bearoness' show-struck mind, the camera crews would have been on the set before she finished explaining what she wanted. Life in the hyper lane!

As Frau Schuylkill settled the Bearmoral chopper onto an open space between the hangar and the C-5A, the Colonel looked out of the bubble and gave a restrained howl. There standing next to the Ursa Major at close attention was Colonel McNeigh, Royal Army, Commandant of the Greater Abeardeen Security Force and a group of twelve *(count them, twelve)* uniformed members of the Security Force, Customs, Immigration, Airport Police and in their midst Superintendent Nigel Wardlaw of Shetland Yard. He had just beaten them down in a faster police copter.

"Ach!" snarled the she-wolf, "a cursory going over, ja??? There's enough of them there to tear the aircraft down to its rivets. Well, Wyatt, let's get to it. Whatever else we wolves are, we certainly know how to be charming!"

The colonel cocked an ear and decided to pass on making any comments. Ilse did not seem to be in much of a wisecracking mood. *(But then, she seldom was.)*

As the rotors wound down, they got out of the bubble and strode formally over to the waiting array. Greetings, salutes! "Colonel? Colonel! Colonel! Luft Kapitan! Superintendent! Inspector! Inspector! Inspector!

McNeigh turned and swished his tail. "I would like to introduce you to Wing Commander Stewart, Royal Air Force Retired."

A mature red fox, dark eyes set to "full military piercing," ears at total alert, nose thrust forward at a perfect $90°$ angle to the ground and dressed in immaculate RAF blue-greys stepped forward and saluted. The wolves saluted back with a bit less precision. They were trying to figure out who this guy was.

"Delighted to meet both of you and, forgive me, even more delighted to get reacquainted with the Galaxy."

Revelation! It didn't take telepathy between the wolves to figure out that the colonel was eating his words. *("As for finding the stealth functions, I can't imagine they have anyone on their inspection team who's familiar with a C-5A, especially our C-5A." Oh sure, Wyatt. Any other predictions you'd care to make?)*

The Frau recovered first. "You have worked with the C-5A, Herr Kommander?"

"Yes indeed, pilot in command during the Interspecies War. Hauling weapons and troops all over Asia. The RAF scrapped all of ours. Too expensive to fly and maintain in peacetime. Never thought I'd see another one; much less right here in Abeardeen where I now live. What extraordinary luck!"

"Yes, what luck!" chimed the two wolves as they mentally catalogued all the special modifications that had been made to the Ursa Major, selecting which ones they didn't want the Wing Commander to see. Nothing for it with the armaments! The missile racks on the wings gave that away. The nose cannons and special plexiglass turrets midships weren't standard issue either. But the Scots already knew the C-5A could be made combat ready, if necessary. The wolves just had to show that as of the moment, it was not in a state of readiness and could not be brought to that state during its visit to Dyce. The one thing they needed to "pass over" was the stealth system. If anything was going to get the plane impounded, that was it. Try explaining that they could fly this lumbering giant invisibly in Scottish airspace. Not likely!

The horse reared his head. "Well, let's get to it, shall we. If you would be kind enough to open the cargo bay doors, our customs crew would like access to the entire hold. I don't suppose you are bringing in any contraband but we would like to see for ourselves. I wonder, Luft-Kapitan, since you are pilot in command, if you would accompany the wing commander to the cockpit and if you, colonel, would come with me and the inspectors."

"Of course, Herr Oberst. We are at your disposal. I believe you will find several kegs of mead locked in the passenger compartment intended for enroute consumption. Herr Octavius is a noted connoisseur of honey wine. Of, course, none of it will be taken off the aircraft during its stay here. In fact, you may tell the customs officers that he intends to bring a substantial supply of your local product back with him when he leaves the Shetlands."

"Pardon me for asking, Luft-Kapitan, but how did a German national end up in the employ of the famous American Octavius Bear?"

The wolf's hair stood on end for a brief second and then, with a snarl/smile, she said, "I can understand your error, Herr Oberst, but I am not German. I am Swiss. I served in the Swiss Guard Air Force during the Inter-Species War. Of, course, I suppose it is as difficult for you to distinguish between a German and Switzerdeutsch accent as it is for me to tell a Scottish brogue from an Irish one. Herr Bear and I met in Switzerland while he was recovering from several wounds he incurred while chasing an infamous criminal. I nursed him back to health, we became friends and I have been on his staff for many years in a variety of capacities, including Chief Pilot."

McNeigh nodded his head vigorously and then looked fore and aft at the airplane. "Ah, Colonel Where has opened the cargo doors. Gentlebeasts, please let us proceed."

As the hinged nose pivoted upward and the huge aft cargo doors opened wide, the inspection team split into two groups. The horse stood aside as the customs inspectors filed up the ramps into the cavernous hold. A huge, unoccupied warehouse or as it has sometimes been described, a flying eight lane bowling alley! Large as the aircraft looks from the outside, it's when you step inside its fuselage that you get a true sense of the immensity of it. Especially now when, with the exception of the reconverted cargo container that Octavius used as an airborne seat and the oxygen masks, grappling gear, fire suppression equipment and other movable seats arranged around the perimeter, the C-5A was essentially empty.

The colonel drew their attention to two crates marked "auxiliary radar" and explained that, with the team's permission, they were going to take the portable side-looking radar back to Bearmoral and install it on one of the helicopters. He looked over at Superintendent Wardlaw and said, "We're not sure that everyone involved in the oil rig circus has been brought to book. We don't know what happened to the piper-terriers or whether there were other members of the gang. We want to mount surveillance on the air space and waters surrounding the castle. If they're coming back, that's the way they'll come. This radar should give us a good early warning on incoming shipping or low flying aircraft."

The collie nodded and said to McNeigh, "Makes sense to me. How about you, Colonel?"

"I agree, but for the sake of formality, will you open one of those containers, please. I'm sure there's radar equipment in there but we must follow procedures."

Wyatt hoped none of the inspectors were familiar with side-looking radar because packed along with the scopes, antennas and electronics were the deconstructed pieces of the portable particle beam accelerator. Only the barrel was left out and that was packed with the wolf's formal uniform which he told them he was bringing back to the castle to wear at the upcoming opera recital. Wardlaw had signed off on that as well.

They opened one of the custom padded packing cases revealing two scopes and several control consoles *(and one power supply and targeting unit for the ray gun.)* Heads nodded and McNeigh waved for them to close up the container. One of the customs inspectors said, "I don't suppose you have a secret weapon stored away in there, do you Colonel?" Loud Highland guffaws all around. Wyatt joined in the merriment.

Meanwhile, just to the rear of the uplifted nose, Frau Schuylkill and the Wing Commander had scrambled up the drop-down stairs and into the cockpit. The fox turned to the wolf.

"Out of curiosity, Luft-Kapitan, why does a private citizen like Doctor Bear use such an aircraft? Its operating costs must be enormous. There are smaller cargo planes."

The she wolf laughed, startling the fox. "Herr Kommander. Doctor Bear is enormous and everything about him including his homes and transportation must also be enormous. He can bearly fit into the Bearoness' SST. They had to alter the doors to accommodate him. Of course, you are correct. There are smaller aircraft that could easily have enough room for him. In fact, we have one; but the United States Government provided this plane and matching flight simulator to Herr Bear in thanks for an especially meritorious but top secret service he performed for his country. It is expensive to run but he is pleased with it for several reasons, not the least being how he came to obtain it. He can afford it."

"We live in different worlds." *(Given the wolf's involvement in the Multiverse Project, she laughed to herself at how accurate that statement really was.)*

"Yes, Kommander, living and working with Herr Bear is very unique experience. Now, what would you like to inspect?"

"Actually, what I would love to do is fly this bus but since that is out of the question *(You bet it is, Mein Herr!)* let me sit here in the left seat for a moment and see what I remember. Then I would like you to show me that the weapons systems are in stand down mode. Yes, this is a somewhat newer model than I flew and I'm sure you have made performance modifications. The fuel, power management and surface controls look roughly the same. The navigation gear, radios and autopilot are all updated. Now, here is something I don't recognize at all."

He reached over and ran his paws over a set of four blue levers, accidentally pushing one of them. A series of green lights went on beneath the lever. "Oh, I say, I am terribly sorry. Didn't mean to do that! First lesson: keep your paws off the controls unless you know what you're doing."

The wolf reached over and swiftly returned the lever to its neutral position. "Ach, no problem, Herr Kommander! No harm done."

The fox looked at the levers more closely. "What function do they provide?"

(Think fast, Ilse, think fast!) "That is a stabilization system for low level, slow speed flight. It senses the terrain, altitude and wind speed and makes adjustments during an approach. It's very useful in the desert with the shifting sands and crosswinds."

What he had momentarily activated was the first stage of the stealth system. The wolf didn't dare look outside. She hoped all of the inspectors were still in the cargo hold.

"Well, that would have been a jolly good thing to have during the war. No one believed how skittish this airplane could be on approach, especially lightly loaded. All that wing out there."

They both laughed *(for different reasons.)* The Frau risked looking out the windscreen. No one was jumping up and down and pointing at the Galaxy. No alarms going off. No ground control vehicles rushing to the site. She would get her breath back in a few seconds.

"Well," said the fox, "let's go back and look at the weapons systems and then I'll get out of here before I do something else clumsy."

"Not at all, Kommander. Just aft of the navigation station is the weapons center. Most of these were not standard issue on the conventional military models but this one was enhanced by the US government and pretty much left in that condition when they turned it over to Herr Octavius. You can see the missile targeting, firing and tracking systems, all inactive. There are no projectiles in the hold or in any of the launch mechanisms. For the moment, this is a bird of peace."

"For the moment?"

"It has been used once or twice in anger. Anger, I should say, that was sanctioned by the government. It has also been on international assignment for the United Species." *(She didn't mention blowing a couple of hot air balloons up in Las Vegas to thwart a homicidal genius duck.)*

"Well, Luft-Kapitan, I am finished here. I see nothing to justify continuing the quarantine. Let's see if my colleagues agree with me. Thank you for the opportunity to renew acquaintances with a part of my past."

"The pleasure was all mine. Perhaps one day on another trip, we may be able to satisfy your desire to fly with us. She is a beautiful ship for all her size. Not all good things come in small packages."

As they were clambering down the pawholds, they saw the war horse and his minions, accompanied by the Superintendent, standing casually under the wing. Wyatt looked relaxed.

The horse looked at the fox who had raised his opposable thumb and said, "Well, I am pleased to release this aircraft back to you. While you may, observing all traffic restrictions, fly it in the immediate area, I suspect you will think several times before consuming all that fuel to do what a helicopter can do."

"Absolutely!" said Wyatt. "In fact, it is our plan to load up the Bearoness' heavy duty copter with the radar and several other items including my formal clothes and fly back to Bearmoral. Thank you, gentlebeasts." He looked at Ilse and winked. She did not wink back.

As the inspection team moved away, Wyatt walked over to the Frau and said, 'What's the matter?"

"That dummkopf fox accidentally activated the stealth systems. Only for a second or two. I got it back to neutral immediately but I almost lost my breakfast. Luckily, I hadn't had any this morning."

"Well nothing seems to have happened. Let's load up the other chopper. The inspectors looked in the radar container but couldn't distinguish the ray gun controls from the amplifiers and duplexers. Looks like we got away with it."

"Just barely," said the Frau. She looked up. Superintendent Wardlaw was walking back toward them. "Uh, oh! Hello again, Nigel! Did you forget something?"

"Not really! I was going to beg a ride up to the castle with you but that would leave me dependent on the Bearoness to get back down again. I changed my mind while I was walking over but I thought I'd tell you something really funny. It shows how spooked all of these airport folks have become since those Russian Bears started pulling off all their electronic tricks with the GPS, the radars and the power. Colonel McNeigh got a call from one of the controllers in the tower, swearing that while we were in it, the plane disappeared for a few seconds. That is the very last straw." He broke out in hysterical laughter, unusual for the deadly serious collie.

"Amazing the tricks the mind can play," said Frau Schuylkill and they too broke out laughing.

Chapter Twenty Eight
On the Way to the Prince of Whales

Should a meerkat voyage out on the sea?
That just doesn't seem prudent to me!
But what can you do
When the Bear says to you:
"Get a move on! You're sailing with me!"

Octavius snarfed up his hearty Scottish breakfast, rose, looked over at Otto and me and asked, "Ready for a boat ride?"

I had almost forgotten our planned trip into the mists of the North Sea. Otto said, "I'll check and make sure Harold is ready." Sizing up Octavius, he said, "I guess we'd better use the big whaler." He zapped off.

Octavius guffawed, leaving all of us wondering what was going on in that ursine head. Smiling, *(an infrequent occurrence)* he led me out of the dining room, through the hallways, over the moat, down to the beach and out on the floating dock where Harold and Otto were waiting with the 40 foot whaler at the ready. It took the three of us plus a lot of flailing and near capsizing to get Octavius into the boat. I thought Otto might have tried to use his telekinetic powers but I think he was afraid to try them out on the Great Bear. After rolling about on the deck several times, Octavius finally righted himself and asked Harold, "How far is it to the seriously deep water?"

Another puzzle! The three of us had been sure we were going out to one of the oil rigs, perhaps Chita's. Didn't seem that way!

Harold looked out to the east and said. "The shelf under the North Sea falls off pretty sharply about three miles out. There are some places so deep, they've never been measured."

"Excellent!" shouted the Bear. "That's exactly what I want!"

I hadn't noticed till then that he had been toting a very large sea bag. He trundled over to it and began to lift out a mass of electrical cables, his oversized laptop and several yellow boxes that looked like they were water sealed. Spreading the cables, he began to hook them up to the laptop and to the boxes.

"Might I enquire as to what you are doing? Are we going to trawl for undersea wildlife?"

He looked up from his sorting and plugging, grinned and said, "In a manner of speaking, yes! I realize I am asking a lot of you, Maury, and of both of you otters but just be patient until Harold gets us to the briny deep."

Otto and I knew better than to try to pry open the Octavian Cone of Silence and Harold was too busy navigating and steering to have much time for questions. Thus it went for about an hour. Bouncing on a mildly choppy sea and becoming reacquainted with my breakfast several times, that barf bag attachment for my tail made more and more sense. I'll have to look into it. Octavius went on plugging and unplugging, testing and re-testing. Among his instruments, I recognized an oversized UUI PeaPod universal language translator. Otto, oblivious to all of the Bear's mysterious machinations had tossed himself off the boat several times and rode on the bow wave and then bobbed around in our wake. To Octavius' annoyance, Harold had to stop once or twice to pick him up.

"Otto, stay on board. You never know who's swimming around out here! You're holding us up. "

Finally, Harold looked up from the helm, craned his head over the bathometer and said, "It's over three miles deep here, Mr. Bear!"

"Wonderful, Harold, slow down and then keep station and you two help me set up this gear."

"What is this stuff, Octavius?"

"What you are about to toss over the side, Otto, is a high powered sound emitter along with a hydrophone for picking up undersea noises. They are both connected to my laptop which is programmed to create and send out very loud echolocation clicks to summon sperm whales. That in turn is connected to a conference size UUI Pea Pod universal translator."

Now, I slept through most of my school classes on zoology and faunapology but I did know that sperm whales are just about the largest living mammals on earth, second only to their blue cousins.

"You are planning to call up a sperm whale?"

"Not just any whale, Maury. The Prince of Whales! You no doubt saw his portrait hanging in the Lion and Unicorn."

"Yeah and from what I remember, he is big. A lot bigger than you - which is saying quite a lot." Octavius usually is the biggest beast among the various crowds we run in. An occasional hippo, giraffe or rhinoceros might come in with more weight, height or mass but generally, The Great Bear is The GREAT Bear.

"Yes," said the Bear, adopting his most professorial tone. "The sperm whale is the largest toothed whale, with adult males measuring up to 67 ft long and weighing up to 63 tons. They also have the largest brain of any known animal on earth. The blue whale is somewhat larger but they have no teeth and their brains are relatively smaller. The Prince of Whales, as you might expect, exceeds these proportions. Nobody has actually measured him but from our previous meetings, I would estimate he is close to 75 feet long and weighs at least 80 tons."

"Previous meetings? You know this guy?"

"Not as well as I would like, but as you have already seen, the logistics involved in settling down for an afternoon chat with him can be rather formidable. By the way, all of you, do NOT refer to this boat as a whaler while he is present. It's a touchy subject. He is true royalty but not in the least condescending or abrupt. In fact, he is quite charming, highly intelligent, an excellent thinker and commentator and I'm sure, quite attractive to the female members of his species."

"And just like that, we're going to summon him up from the deep. How do you know he is here?"

"Yesterday, I chatted with several dolphins who are part of his entourage. They said he winters here in the North Sea. With this echolocation gear, I will send out a message of clicks requesting an audience. The sound is quite loud and can be heard for hundreds of miles. Otto and Harold, don't get too close to the loudspeaker if you're in the water and of course, be very careful of approaching him at close range. By the way, don't speak to him until he has spoken first."

"I wouldn't think of it, Octavius. I'm careful about approaching or speaking to you."

The bear laughed, a substantial noise in itself. Harold stood at the helm, wondering how fast he could get the boat out of the vicinity if Octavius' scheme didn't quite work out. Of course, he mentioned nothing of this to the bear. A 9 foot bear or a 75 foot whale! After a certain point, size no longer matters to a 3 foot otter. With the bear, you could run but you can't hide and with the whale you can swim…but not for long.

"Alright," said Octavius, "let's get this rig over the side and the show on the road." *(This in the middle of a sea that is over three miles deep. Similes and metaphors are not Octavius' strong suit.)*

Firmly anchoring the laptop and language converter on the deck we paid out the cables attached to the underwater speakers and the hydrophone. When they had reached their limit, Octavius hit a key on the computer and a rush of bubbles and waves erupted next to the boat. We were "clicking." Sperm whale "clicking" is used by them for communication, hunting, and navigation – sort of a combined sonar and undersea conversation medium coupled with a fast food ordering system. Many whales sing. I found out that sperms don't. They click. Their voice and hearing apparatus is contained in their jaws and the sounds they produce are nerve-rackingly loud. More like "booms" than "clicks."

Otto's tours of duty in the Nevada casinos came to the surface. *(pun intended)* "What are the odds of us reaching him and of him coming to us, Octavius?"

"Wait and see, Otto!" Octavius was being his inscrutable self. I wondered if two otters and a meerkat could push him over the side. Maybe Otto could teleport him over. Nah, there'd be repercussions. So we sat and waited and waited and waited. The language converter repeated the clicks we were transmitting.

"Mr. Bear," said Harold, "What are you saying to him?"

"Just reminding him of an evening he spent off the coast of Kodiak Island a few years ago and inviting him up for a chin wag. Granted, he has quite a chin to wag."

Suddenly a small school of dolphins broke the water and swam around the boat. One, no doubt the spokesman of the group, started chattering at Octavius. The bear raised his paws, signaling "wait a minute," turned to the Pea Pod and computer, flipped a few switches, turned back to the dolphin and said, "Go ahead" in dolphin squeak. The bottle nose braced his flippers along the side of the boat while the others circled behind him.

"His Highness asked us to tell you he is feeding at the moment but will be along shortly. He says he thinks he remembers you. He doesn't know very many bears *(live ones, that is.)*

"Please tell His Royal Highness that I await his pleasure and look forward to renewing our acquaintance."

The dolphin nodded his head and blew out a spray from his nose that splattered on the deck *(not sure that was meaningful, playful or just getting ready for a long dive.)* He turned, seemingly rotating on his tail, leapt into a ring formed by his fellows and disappeared. Octavius reset the systems to whale conversation.

I couldn't resist. "This guy really does the royalty thing up brown, doesn't he?"

"Well," said the Bear, "Remember where you are. Monarchies are an integral part of the UK character. His father, the King, is reaching his 85th birthday and has turned over most of the royal privileges and duties to his son who I estimate to be about thirty. Whales can be very long-lived. Because he has now taken on the mantle of sovereignty, I expected he would be staying closer to home here in the North Sea. When I last met him, he was something of a play whale, travelling the world, attending all sorts of events and no doubt chasing his share of females. I assume he has grown more serious, now."

"Excuse me, Octavius, this is all very interesting and I look forward to meeting my first whale who I guess is the First Whale but why <u>are</u> we here? I can't imagine you are simply socializing in the middle of all the mess we're in."

"Absolutely not, Otto, this is hardly a social call. Just be patient!"

Suddenly a geyser of air and water blasted out of the sea. It was close enough to drench us as we stood on the deck of the boat. A squared off mountain of dark grey skin raised itself slowly above the waves, followed by the largest jaw it has ever been my fortune *(good or otherwise)* to see. A relatively small eye set back and above the jaw and just forward of a flipper stared at us intently. I looked up and saw a dorsal fin emerge near the stern of the boat and much further out a gigantic fluke smacked the surface of the water. Yes, this was a big animal. A very big animal. I tried only semi-successfully to keep my knees from knocking. I looked at Harold and Otto. Their jaws were at full drop.

The whale clicked loudly and the translator roared, "Your pardon for the drenching. I sneezed. I think I'm getting allergic to squid. Ah, yes, now that I see you I remember you quite well, Doctor Bear. Kodiak Island, was it not? On one of my goodwill trips. Visited Canada and decided I'd see what this Alaska place was all about. Lovely scenery, grand ice floes, wonderful diving and fish, fish, fish. I seem to remember you were part of a local welcoming committee. I also seem to remember that you were one of the few in that mixed contingent who made any sense. Welcome to the North Sea of which I am Prince Regent."

Octavius bowed his head just a bit and replied, "Thank you, Your Highness. I am privileged and delighted to see you again. May I present my associates, first: Mr. Harold Otter who is in the employ of Bearoness Belinda Bruin at Bearmoral Castle."

"Ah, yes The Bearoness. Never met her snout to snout but I have heard much about her, all quite favorable. Pity about her husband's accident. Do you think she'll re-mate?"

Octavius is usually as smooth as they come in one on one conversation. *(He only disappoints when he is making a formal speech.)* All three of us were watching his face and listening to what he might say.

"I think it is in the realm of possibility, sir. She is a most attractive sow."

"Well, let's hope some lucky polar sweeps her off her paws. Not good to have the nobility, even dubious nobility, *(the eye winked)* without issue to continue the line."

This time Octavius sneezed or unleashed something closely approximating one.

The Prince chortled *(setting off a sonic boom)* "God bless you, Doctor Bear! There must be something going around. I hope you're not allergic to whales. And who are these two worthies?"

The Great Bear recovered and pointing to me, said, "Your Highness, may I introduce Mr. Mauritius Meerkat, formerly of South Africa and the isle of Mauritius, now an American. He is my trusted assistant and confidant."

The whale squinted at me and said, "I don't think I have ever met a meerkat before, Mr. Mauritius. In what way are you related to the feline species?"

Oh boy, here we go again. The Unicorn Conversation! "I am not a feline, Your Highness. The name is an unfortunate misstatement brought about by some Dutch naturalist who was visiting Africa. I think he was a near-sighted mole." I almost launched off into my relationship to a mongoose but decided that once around that track was enough for one trip to Scotland.

Octavius interposed. "Finally, this young otter, a North American River Otter is an associate of Mr. Meerkat and myself. His name is Hairy Otter but he is popularly known as Otto the Magnificent, a stage name. He is a performer with a few rather remarkable abilities. How he got them we need not discuss. I'm not sure how much longer you wish to stay on the surface, sir, but it does bring me to my reason for seeking an audience."

"I may sound once or twice during our visit but I shall return immediately. By the way, I think we can dispense with the royal formalities. *(I thought I heard a squeak from one of the dolphins who had been swimming close by.)* That was my equerry, Sir Flipsalot. He's a stickler for the proprieties. I am not. Please call me Bertie and I shall call you what I believe I called you in Alaska – Tavi. And gentlebeasts, will Harold, Mauritius and Otto do?"

"Please call me Maury….er Bertie!"

The whale laughed again, almost swamping the boat. "Now what has occasioned your visit, Tavi? Have you come to beg a boon? (Another chortle!)

"In a manner of speaking, yes, Bertie. We have come across what appears to be an unusual phenomenon and we could use your assistance and that of your pod in trying to understand it."

"Ho, ho," boomed the Prince, "conundrums. Always enjoy conundrums. Tell me!"

The Bear proceeded to describe the "movable" oil platforms and tossed in a few of our other experiences from Project Multiverse to further season the stew. He also told about the Russians interfering with the GPS signals. This, he admitted, might be the entire problem solved but there still remain a few eyewitness reports of the rigs flickering in and out of sight. He would like any input the prince could offer and perhaps a check on some of the rigs' underwater conditions by a few members of his entourage.

The Whale clicked a bellowing "HMMMMM!" that made Octavius' "Hmmmms" sound amateurish. "Well, Tavi, I am of two minds about those oil rigs to begin with. As the symbolic leader of the British Isles, I am pleased that we are using these resources to better the lives of our citizens. On the other flipper, these platforms can represent serious threats to our oceanic ecology, especially if, as you say, they have developed the ability to get up and take walks. I will say one thing, though. Excuse me! I feel the urge to sound. I shall return shortly."

With a resounding smack from his fluke and a rush of water surrounding his submerging body, the Whale dove straight down into the 3 mile depth leaving us and a few of his dolphin "court" to await his return. His departure had rocked the whale boat dramatically and for a moment it looked like we were going to have to call upon the dolphins to help stabilize the craft. We switched the translator to its "dolphin" setting and looked out at the cavorting bottle nose who had first approached us before the Prince's arrival.

"How deep does he go when he does that?" I asked

"It depends," came the squeaky return. "He'll probably only go a few thousand fathoms before coming up again. I don't think he took in as much air as he might have wanted to. By the way, all of us could understand the click exchange between His Highness and yourselves so we are aware of your story and your request. That translator device of yours is quite competent. Ever consider producing one exclusively for undersea life?"

Octavius raised one of his vestigial eyebrows and said, "No, but I'd be delighted to have our labs work on a prototype and present it to the Court for testing and comment. A gift in return for your assistance! We would no doubt require the services of a clever and fluent multilingual cetacean to assist us in its design and development. Do you know anyone who fits that description, sir? Perhaps you, yourself? May I know your name?"

"My name is Marlin. I am the Prince's Chief Scientist, Magician and part time Jester. His Highness uses several different jesters to keep him entertained, according to his moods. I supply the more sophisticated forms of slapstick!"

"Marlin?" yelped Otto, "But you're a…"

"…dolphin, I know. Confusing isn't it? I think my mother was addle pated." He pushed away from the boat balancing on his fluke and skittered backwards for about 15 feet. Then he leapt into the air twisting as he went and to end the maneuver, back flipped into the ocean.

Bells went off in my head. Theatrical Agent Maury, ever alert for new show biz opportunities! This guy would be a natural for the new Interspecies Aquabear Review. The polars, Belinda, Otto and Marlin! Boffo! *(Whatever that means!)* All this plus working with UUI to develop the underwater translator. Maybe we'd finally find out what those Humpbacks and Blue Whales are singing about. His Highness could probably use the device to negotiate with orcas and sharks. Talk about win-win! I looked at Octavius and he winked back. He got the picture. Marlin swam back to the boat and balanced with the upper half of his body out of the water.

"We'll speak about the project with the Prince as soon as he returns," said the Bear. "In addition to working with us on the prototype translator, you could, if you wished, entertain with the Aquabear Review in the pool at Bearmoral Castle. We could also fly you back to the US in a tank secured in the hold of our C-5A cargo plane. You could work there with our scientists and engineers on the underwater translation device. We have a large Olympic salt water pool and we also have the Ohio River for you to swim in."

Otto jumped up and down, smacking the deck with his tail. "Otto and Marlin, what a team!"

The dolphin stared at him and asked, "Otto and Marlin or Marlin and Otto? Who gets top billing?"

Uh oh! This sounds like a job for Super Agent Maury but before I could get into the discussion, the Prince had resurfaced, surrounded by several members of his retinue including the ever present equerry, Sir Flipsalot. His entrances and departures were, not to put too fine a point on it, dramatic and aquatic. Water, water everywhere, mostly on our deck and all over me. Octavius was dampened, the otters didn't care but I almost drowned. Being small may have its advantages but not in this case.

"That was a shorter dive than I intended but I did want to get back to our discussion," boomed the whale. "While below, I remembered several recent instances when I felt I was momentarily in a different ocean. We cetaceans have a very keen sense of location and surroundings. On the way up, I quizzed my staff, especially my equerry with his finely tuned sense of time, place and propriety. They have shared my sensations. Very well, Tavi! We will investigate your rigs for you as well as observing any repeat occurrences of the shifting seas. Do you honestly believe we may be transiting between alternate worlds? Could we be living in a…North Sea Triangle?"

"Bertie, I don't know. An accumulation of evidence is pointing us toward that conclusion but it's much too soon to make any definitive statements. If indeed there are other universes, we must certainly examine the *overall* implications for this world. Incidentally, these world shift phenomena seem to occur mostly to animals while they are asleep. It is my understanding that you do not sleep in the conventional sense."

"True! Cetaceans do not breathe automatically as you other mammals do. We must do so deliberately. If I was totally unconscious underwater, I would drown. Even on the surface, I have to consciously breathe. But we whales are compartmentalized. One part of us sleeps while the other remains awake."

"That would make you and your court excellent observers and reporters of the universe shifts, if and when they occur. Asleep and awake at the same time."

"Well, as a sovereign-to-be and current Regent, I cannot ignore any phenomenon that may threaten or enhance the lives of my people. You and I must open a clear information channel."

"Indeed, sir, and as one step in that direction, I have a proposal to put before you."

He then recited chapter and verse the idea of developing with royal assistance, an underwater version of the PeaPod and the suggestion that Marlin be appointed to work with us. He promised the device would be presented to the Prince and if successful, manufactured in bulk for his underwater subjects. He also suggested that Marlin serve as a liaison on the Multiverse Project. Finally he slipped in the secondary role for Marlin as a member of the Aquabear Review."

Thankfully, the Prince was in a good mood. "I guess by letting Marlin join you, temporarily, mind, I'll be expanding my own contacts and information sources. Alright, Marlin, but keep this in perspective. Research and science first, jester second."

Spontaneously, Otto flipped from the deck in a series of somersaults as Marlin did the same in the ocean. They both swam around in circles and then to the amazement of the Prince and his courtiers, Otto zapped back onto the deck.

"Does he do that often?" asked the Prince.

"Often enough, Your Highness! *(back to formality as we were taking our leave)* We will leave the details of mutual communication to Marlin to arrange. We in turn will communicate with him through my aide, Maury and our friendly otter, Otto the Magnificent. *(I bowed and Otto blushed.)* We expect to be here in Scotland for at least another week. But we have several ongoing projects at Bearmoral that will require return visits, so I shall be shuttling back and forth in the future. I thank you for your assistance. It was delightful to see you again." *(slight bow)*

"I enjoyed it, Doctor Bear and I am looking forward to continuing a fruitful relationship. You there, Helm! Perhaps you should move your boat off a ways before I break for the depths. I gather I create quite a splash. He looked at sodden me and winked.

Chapter Twenty Nine
Back at Bearmoral

We returned with our whale of a tale
About seeing His Highness the Whale.
Meeting royalty's great!
But I'm forced to relate
I got soaked from my head to my tail.

When we came back from our whaling expedition, we rounded up Belinda, the Colonel and Frau Schuylkill who had just returned from the inspection of the Ursa Major in Abeardeen. We would have waited for Chita, the twins and our Geek Team, Howard and Condo, to show up but Octavius wanted to tell his story before Superintendent Wardlaw made an appearance. He didn't want to get all tied up with Shetland Yard and government protocol questions. After all, commoners didn't just show up at the Prince's watery doorstep. On the other hand, Octavius Bear wasn't just another commoner.

We started to tell them about our meeting with the Prince of Whales. Belinda seemed a little taken aback until Octavius said, "We weren't sure since you are a member of the nobility, if we would have to go through all sorts of formalities. This way, we unsophisticated Americans *(Harold excepted)* could just plead bad manners if there was any kind of a flap. Besides, I knew him from a rather riotous visit he made to Alaska several years ago. He does send you his kindest regards."

This seemed to mollify the Bearoness. Needless to say the Frau, a great respecter of crowned heads, nobility and aristocracy was impressed all to hell with our gaining a royal audience so easily.

Octavius went through all the agreements we had reached with the Prince and his Court about checking out the rigs and any other oceanic drifts and shifts they might uncover. Wyatt became very interested when he heard the Prince himself might have experienced a few world changes. Then we got to Marlin. Belinda's show biz genes came to the surface immediately when he mentioned the dolphin's entertainment skills. The idea of UUI developing an underwater translator for the Prince would certainly be a feather in her noble tiara. Octavius asked the Colonel and Frau to arrange for the construction of a portable water tank for the interior of the C-5A before we left Scotland. Marlin could travel in it whenever and wherever he was needed.

"The dolphin will join us in a few days. I want him to fly back with you to the UUI labs. We'll also have to work out some way of moving him short distances between the tank and other bodies of salt water."

Otto chimed in. "No problem with that, Octavius. If I can move a cheetah or polar bear, I can certainly move a dolphin."

Octavius smiled. "That talent of yours is becoming more useful by the day, Otto. Thanks." Belinda patted the otter on the head. I thought he would fall over in ecstasy.

Then the wolves related their adventure with the Galaxy. They reported the safe arrival of the particle beam projector and then somewhat sheepishly, Frau Schuylkill mentioned the brief episode with the stealth system and the report from the tower of a disappearing airplane. Fortunately, it was written off by the inspection team and the Superintendent as being residual nerves after all the other incidents at the airport.

Octavius snorted, "That was lucky but I am not a believer in luck. On our return, Frau Schuylkill, see to it that those levers have new innocuous labeling and a locking function. Nothing complex! We want to be able to invoke that system at a moment's notice. I assume we will be very careful in allowing pilots into that cockpit in the future. Especially ex C-5A pilots."

We decided to go down and examine the castle's storage deck before the arrival of the authorities so we could sound like we knew what the hell we were talking about when they showed up. Meanwhile Nigel had already arrived close on the heels (rotors) of the Frau and Wyatt after the Abeardeen inspection.

Belinda said, "I've decided to reconvert this place back into a resort. I want it to be a pleasant castle and right now it's anything but. Octavius has said he would join me in financing it. We're going to call it Polar Paradise. Families of polar bears and other chill-loving species can come and winter here and watch the ice form. We'll have all sorts of things for kits and cubs. We're also going to have plenty of warm facilities for animals like you, Maury. And a theater and aquashow pool. The Aquabears Swim Again!!! I'm going to set aside a suite of residence apartments for myself and my friends and we're going to start up that genetic institute we were talking about using Imperius Drake's materials. I'm sure he'd be soooo pleased to know that something he's done was being turned to good."

We all laughed at that. Nigel asked about the current whereabouts of the duck and we told him we weren't sure but we believed he was dead. But then, we've believed that before.

Chita, Bearyl, Bearnice and Lepi showed up together. Chita had been avoiding Wardlaw and the others were avoiding Honoria and Bearbi. This had all the makings of a door-slamming farce.

Finally, we were about to give up on Howard and Condo when the two of them poked their heads into the room and waved us out to meet with them. Belinda, Nigel, Octavius and I joined them out in the hall.

Nigel said to the bird, "Senhor Condor, I want to congratulate you on your wonderful mimicry of other animal's voices. You had those villains totally confused in the dark, imitating Octavius and me from different sides of the room. Boris thought he was aiming straight ahead at me when I caught him from behind with the stun dart. And then Bruinhilde walked right into your wing. She'll be bruised for days."

In a perfect imitation of Boris (aka Ethelbeart), Condo said. "Denk you, Soooperintendent, but I think the prize for deception should go to Boris. I was amazed how he carried off the disguise of a doddering old sot. I wonder if Albearta knew."

"Who cares," said the Bearoness, obviously severely ticked off at all of them. "Whether they're convicted or not, none of them is setting paw back here again – ever! I wonder, Senhor Condor, as a gift to your hostess, if you wouldn't mind not using that voice around here anymore.'

"In fact, Condo," I said, "isn't it time you settled on a voice of your own?"

"You are absolutely right, Senhor Maury" replied a deep, romantic Latin voice. "I am going to do voice-overs for Telenovelas when I get back to Brazil."

I wasn't sure whether he was kidding or not. For someone who looks like a creature of doom, he has a hell of a sense of humor. *(Another possible client? Steady Maury!)* We walked into the library and Howard opened the paneled wall. The Bearoness picked up the tapestry from the floor - A Polar bear all rigged out in kilts and a sword standing over a dying dragon. "Another one of Byron's phony ancestors. I think this will go out with the trash,"

The lift car came and we entered for the relatively short ride to the storage deck below the garage. "This elevator is going to be revamped. I can see it being used for bringing scenery and large displays into the convention ballroom."

"What convention ballroom?" I asked her.

"The one Octavius and I are going to construct down here on this storage deck. We have plenty of other storage room all over the castle and this place is ideal for a business show or convention." Ever the show biz mind. I could learn much from this bear.

We were standing in a high-ceilinged, open space that ran the length and breadth of the castle, broken up only by support columns. Howard had found the lights, and in the dim glow of the low wattage bulbs *(the frugal Scots, ya ken!)* we could make out boxes stacked to the ceiling and an area of cubicles and divider walls. Cots and wall lockers spoke of a staff larger than the four terriers. There was a kitchenette and what looked like an open privy against one of the walls. A small assault force had been living here. No longer!

Soft flashes of blinking lights and the occasional sound of a power source kicking on and off directed us beyond the dividers to an impressive array of computers, radar screens, radios and a couple of devices I couldn't identify. A smile formed on the condor's beak. *(I know, it's tough to imagine. Take my word for it.)* Howard literally ran toward the gear and shouted, "This is it. The command center of Operation Oil Slick," he giggled.

It was! Christmas had come early for the condor and porcupine. Toys, toys and more toys. They literally ran and hopped and jumped around the equipment. We all knew that as soon as the UK military took one look at this, the whole place would be cordoned off and then all the gear would be confiscated and shipped off to somewhere. "Here's the culprit," said Condo in his machismo voice. "This is the unit they used to foul up the GPS reference signals. Quite intricate. There must be a large antenna array camouflaged on the roof. Did any of you spot it? I didn't."

Blank stares. Then a beep on the Bearoness' pager. Dougal! "M'lady, there are some gentlebeasts from the government here to see you."

"Thank you, Dougal. Superintendent, would you like to accompany me upstairs to meet the members of officialdom." She grinned at Octavius, Howard, Condo and me. "Let's give the boys a little more time to play."

Chapter Thirty
The Edinbeargh Opera

'Twas the musical feast of the years!
A delight to my noise-ridden ears!
Yes, my heart still rejoices!
Such sparkling voices!
I broke down in a torrent of tears.

We stayed at Bearmoral a few days longer than our allotted 'fortnit' in order to witness the musical sensation of the decade – Bearnice and Lepi in Recital. They had been down in Edinbeargh for the past two days, getting familiar with the Opera House. That had the wonderful side effect of getting the 'moo-sical' Honoria Heifer out of the castle. It also had the unfortunate effect of Bearbi being without a chat-mate and she pounced on me, the theatrical agent.

"Mr. Meerkat – Maury dahling – we must absolutely do something with you."

"Dame Bearbara, I tremble to think what you could possibly mean."

She laughed *(a combination giggle, snort and roar – bizarre)* "Oh, you dear little animal, such a sense of humor. Why, I mean an article, of course! Chita told me your history along with that gorgeous Octavius. Your early days in the Kalahari. Your conversion from crime to crime fighting. Your adventures against Imperius Drake and other demonic dastards. Oh yes, you are definitely *Sow* material. '

This sow was as transparent as her fur. She was hoping to use me and my vanity to rope Octavius into a joint story from which I would then conveniently disappear. Oh, lady! It takes one to know one and I haven't forgotten anything my mob taught me about the con business. However, if I am going to make it as an agent, I need media contacts and unpalatable as she may be, Dame Bearbi was a *contact*. Soon, Chita would be, too. Now, she's a contact I could get used to.

Promising to get together with her shortly, *(with my tail crossed behind my back)* I bade the fair Bearbi farewell. Now, let me get you up to speed on a few other things.

When the police and military had left, after promising to return to empty the storage deck of all of petropol's pernicious pile, *(I'm sorry. It's something in the Scottish air.)* Chita started reappearing, usually in her black catsuit. Those of you who are familiar with our last adventure *(The Case of the Spotted Band)* know that Chita stole and sold Imperius Drake's genetic research notes and serum to Belinda for a significant sum. Chita decided to invest that significant sum back into the castle renovation and the new joint genetics venture. So now, Bel had two of the most unlikely partners you could imagine – Octavius and Chita. This should be fun.

As I mentioned, the wolves had returned earlier from Abeardeen and the inspection of the Ursa Major with only a slight tremor of trouble. They also returned with the particle accelerator. For those of you who are unfamiliar with this device, it is, in the words of Doctor Howard Watt, "an endoatmospheric charged particle beam weapon."

Now that we've cleared that up! OK, OK, it is not a laser although it looks like one; in terms of its power – it can exceed the punch of a lightning strike; in range and precision - it can lock onto and disintegrate a target three inches across at distances of thousands of feet and ignore all other intervening and interfering obstacles. For all of its flexibility and its destructiveness, it is amazingly light and simple to operate. It's too big for me but the wolves can handle it easily.

To quote Octavius whose lab at UUI developed the device, "It was not intended as a weapon. It was intended to be used wherever precise excitation of protons and electrons could be of benefit – mining, construction, demolition, excavation. Imagine its use in faunapology to meticulously unearth long lost tombs of great animal rulers. It can be used to stop landslides and even avalanches. It can cut through the polar ice caps. It can intercept meteors and asteroids. It is an instrument for good."

Unfortunately, while the device has many beneficial uses the fact remains: it can be an engine of destruction. Something we definitely want to keep out of the wrong hands. Imperius Drake had a stolen prototype and almost destroyed Las Vegas with it. He and it are now gone. *(I hope.)*

It still isn't clear to me why Octavius wanted to take the risk of bringing the gun to Scotland and possibly having it confiscated or what he intends to use it for while we're here. Maybe nothing! The Great Bear can be so deep that sometimes, I'm not sure he understands himself. But, hey, he pays the bills.

Anyway, tonight's the night. The concert of the century! We are going down after breakfast to Edinbeargh in two heavy duty helicopters. Belinda has reserved several suites and a small ballroom for us at the Bearbizon Hotel – "located for our guests' convenience just steps away from the Opera, Symphony and other Scottish cultural delights." There will be a reception beforehand at the Opera House and a party after the performance back at the hotel. The press has been invited and the recital will be taped for later TV broadcast. The Opera trustees, management and a large number of glitterati will also be there. I'll be taking notes all night when I'm not schmoozing. Talent agent Maury on the job!

After Dougal and the (D,H,M,P)ollies carefully stowed our formal clothes in the cargo bays of the choppers, we assembled at the helipad. The wolves were piloting the first craft with Octavius, Belinda, Otto and me. Bearyl was at the controls of the second copter with Chita, Bearbi, Clarence, Howard and Condo. Careful weight distribution. The flights would require one or more refueling stops and even so, would be operating close to the helicopters' operational range. So a little care was called for. I usually consider my small size to be a disadvantage, but this time it got me out of a flight from hell with Bearbi.

I sat in the vibrating seat trying to concoct in my mind a conversation between L. Condor and Dame Bearbara da Savile-Row in the other chopper. What a hoot that would be, especially if he feeds her voice back to her. Actually, there was not much chance of any real conversation. The noise from the rotors drowned out just about everything. This, of course, wouldn't stop Bearbi from chattering away non-stop. Chita was probably crawling up the wall. She hates helicopters and she'll no doubt, be in a great mood when she gets to Edinbeargh. But Lepi was her band mate down in Rio and they sang a lot together. So, support the team!! I wonder if she is jealous of Bearnice.

Thwock, thwock, thwock, thump. Hours later, those triumphant tones proclaimed the successful and final reunion of aircraft and ground! Edinbeargh! There were a couple of limos waiting for us as well as a fancy utility lorry for the Great Bear. Otto and I went with him while the Bearoness took command of the parade from the airport to the hotel. The Bearbizon is an old but grande dame, dripping with understated elegance. The incoming mixture of species may have thrown the desk staff off for a moment but as soon as the Bearoness came through the door, the manager and assorted minions were out in full force. We all got the TREATMENT! Not bad for a humble Meerkat. Otto fluctuated between giggles and gapes.

About an hour later, Frau Schuylkill, Wyatt, Howard and I were all battling to get a bow tie and formal shirt around Octavius' substantial girth. Otto was standing by, looking elegantly formal, holding Octavius' jacket if we could ever get it on him. I had never seen the Frau in evening dress. She was beautiful to begin with but tonight she was a total knockout complete with diamond jewelry *(probably borrowed from Belinda)* and a blood red ruby around her neck. Wyatt was in his dress uniform as a Colonel (ret.) of the US Armed Forces. He wore a military cape which I suspect concealed a weapon. The Frau was carrying a slightly oversize purse. Well, "semper paratus." By comparison, Howard and I were looking positively dowdy in our run-of-the-mill tuxedos. Getting a porcupine in a tuxedo jacket is no mean feat, either.

Finally with a roar of irritation on the part of the Bear and composite sighs of relief by everyone else in the room, Octavius was dressed. After the tussle with His Bearship, we, the "dressing crew" reassembled, adjusted our own clothing and were good to go.

Just as we arrived at the lobby, *(Octavius and I had to take the freight elevator [goods lift??])* another lift door opened and out stepped an older and younger version of every ursine's Dreambear. Belinda and Bearyl. I can see the pictures now after the recital. Lepi surrounded by three glorious polar creatures and not looking too bad himself. He may turn out to be the new teenager's *(and older matron's)* heartthrob. His exotic fur and luxuriant tail coupled with his inscrutable Oriental face get him stares wherever he goes. And he can sing, too. Wait till they discover he has a hard rock repertoire, as well. I now have an agreement to represent him and Bearnice. Wow, three sensational clients! Maybe four, if I can persuade Marlin. And perhaps Condo! The Great Bear may frown on my expanding enterprise. Choices, choices!

The Bearoness led the procession across the street to the Opera House, stopping traffic in every sense of the word. Waiting for us in the lobby and looking very elegant was Superintendent Nigel Wardlaw and a lovely collie I took to be his mate. "Good evening, Bearoness, thank you so much for the invitations. Lassie and I are delighted to join you and your party. It should be quite a night."

Sounds of clinking champagne bowls echoed in the Green Room as Belinda entered to the applause of the guests. Sounds of munching, lapping and sloshing resumed along with conversations punctuated by growls, oinks, baaas, an occasional woof and feline purrs and yowls.

Speaking of felines, I have been remiss. Chita had joined us in the lobby of the hotel for the grand march and was covered in a black formfitting something that showed her great legs off to perfection. Around her neck was the ever present diamond collar but this time she wore a matching garter on one of her legs. She was not pleased to see the Superintendent among the guests. Gapes and murmurs as she slinked in.

The wolves were also a subject of some interest. They, in turn, kept sweeping the room with their intense stares, looking for anyone or anything that might create the slightest threat. There was also a fair sized contingent of Edinbeargh's Finest patrolling the halls and public spots.

L. Condor was being chatted up by several members of the Opera Board. Gales of laughter as he would change his voice to match that of the last speaker. I'm not sure Edinbeargh society had ever seen such a collection of exotic fauna. Suddenly, all conversations stopped, jaws dropped and the exotic index went through the roof. Bearbi had arrived! *(Trailed of course, by Clarence, who no doubt, would be taking pictures all evening.)*

How to describe Dame Bearbara's outfit? "Shall I compare thee to a summer's day?" Not exactly!!! Perhaps an explosion in a paint factory. She was covered with veils of wildly different colors that fluttered and trailed behind and around her as she sauntered into the room. Her face below the eyes was covered with a transparent mask outlined by some kind of sparkling jewelry. Each leg was circled by gold and silver slave bracelets.

Belinda looked at her and said, "Let me guess! Of, course, Salome and her Seven Veils. Very operatic!"

"Do you think so, dahling? It's just something I threw together for the occasion."

"That's obvious!" grumbled The Great Bear, always the master of subtle nuance.

"One does try to match the event and this will indeed, be a festive one. We will be recording the entire evening, and Clarence will be taking an immense number of pictures of the performers and the sparkling audience. What a spread this will make in our magazines. Before this evening is over, we may have the sensation of the year." She came out with that weird giggle again.

I needed fortification. The Bearoness thinks of everything. There twinkling at me on the drinks table was a crystal bottle filled with fermented coconut milk, VSOP. Several of the older members of the crowd asked The Bearoness about her dear grandaunt and uncle. It seems they had been occasional patrons of the arts, paid for, no doubt, by Belinda. She artfully sidestepped the absence *(permanent, we hope)* of Ethelbeart and Albearta. No one mentioned Alistair, Bruinhilde, Ursula or Roary. Octavius, Otto and the wolves were deep in conversation, occasionally glancing over at the Superintendent and then scanning the room. They were expecting something. I walked over with my bowl of coconut milk, smiled at Octavius and said, "What's up, Doc?"

"Just ensuring no one and nothing dangerous happens. I hate crowds. The Superintendent has several members of Edinbeargh's Protective Squad on alert in the audience. I hope they like recitals."

"Do you really think anyone would make an attempt on the life of the Bearoness *(Or someone else, including me)* in a crowd like this? Too many things could go wrong."

"May I remind you of a maniac duck who made an attempt in front of a thousand animals in Las Vegas? Crowds provide cover, Maury. Plus, if we have any villains at all to deal with, they probably don't think in the same orderly fashion that you or I do. Unpredictability is their primary Modus Operandi."

I was grateful to be admitted to the Prestigious Order of Orderly Thinkers. The chimes rang, summoning us to our seats. We wound our way up the narrow, gilded stairway to the second level. Octavius had several near misses with wall sconces and had to squeeze his way around a curve in the passageway. The chairs in the Royal Enclosure looked only marginally capable of supporting his bulk. Who knows, there might be an unexpected addition to the program during the evening. <u>The Fall of Octavius</u>. I said a prayer that he would stay awake.

As Chairbear of the Opera Board and a titled *(however specious)* member of society, Belinda occupied the center box high over the stalls. She had also reserved the two boxes flanking hers, for our party. As we settled into our seats, *(plush)* I opened the program and read down the list of the pieces *(plush)* to be performed:

Welcome to The Royal Edinbeargh Opera

The Debut Recital of Ms. Bearnice Blanc and Mr. 猫 Leperello

Orchestra under the Direction of Sir Ian Bearbarolli

PROGRAMME

Duet: My Heart is in the Highlands *by Robeart Bruce*
Solo: Drinking Song from the Tails of Beijing *by 猫 Leperello*
Duet: Lacrymosa from Requiem *by Hector Bearlioz*
Solo: Elise's Fur *by Ludwig von Bearthoven*

Interval

Duet: Selections from "Kits" *by Andrew Laird Webear*
Solo: Love Songs from the Motion Picture 7.6 *by Federico Feline*
Solo: Stouthearted Cats *by Siegfried Rombearg*
Duet: Death Scene from Romeo and Juliet *by Charles Gooneybird*
Duet: Bonnie Annie Laurie *Traditional*

**The Edinbeargh Opera extends its
sincere thanks to the following benefactors who
made this evening's performance possible**

**The Prince of Whales' Trust
The Bruin Foundation
Universal Ursine Industries
Friends of the Opera**

*This concert is being televised for future broadcast. Only pre-authorized,
professional photographers may take pictures during the performance.*

Please turn off all cell phones and pagers during the concert

The Artists are represented by the Meerkat Global Talent Agency

The house lights dimmed, as they say, and to a smattering of polite applause, Madame Honoria Heifer came out from behind the curtain, getting tangled as she emerged. She stabilized herself and lowed. "Gooood evening, everyone! I am sure I need noooo introduction to yooou patrons of the arts but for the television audience let me say that I am Madame Honoooria Heifer, Vocal Virtuoso and Advisor to the Stars of Opera. Tonight, it is my extreme pleasure to introduce my latest protégées *(huh???)* at this, their first joint performance on Scottish soil…or any other soil, for that matter." She snorted at her little joke which was received by the audience in dead silence.

"Mr. Leperello comes tooo us from the mysterious east. He is a Himalayan Snow Leopard and a marvelous specimen of his breed. He has performed with The People's Opera in Beijing and has even written some operatic works of his own, one of which you will hear this evening. As yoooou will also hear, both of our artists also perform music of the common folk." Minor sniff of disapproval. She meant popular music but she wasn't going to say it.

"Ms. Bearnice Blanc is a close associate of our beloved Chairbear, Bearoness Belinda Béarnaise Broooin (nee Black). She is a highly accomplished singer who has appeared for several seasons with the Northern Lights Opera Company in Canada. It has been a pleasure assisting these twoooo extraordinary performers in their climb tooo stardom. And now, I shall retire toooo the wings and allow them to demonstrate their impressive talent and skills. Ladies and Gentlebeasts, Ms. Blanc and Mr. Leperello."

Fanfare, and onstage strode Bearnice and Lepi, both looking like a million bucks. *(or a million does, if you prefer)* Bearnice was radiant in an all white ensemble and diamonds that matched and reflected her fur. Lepi wore a short formal jacket which did nothing to hide his magnificent pelt and spectacular tail. They could have just stood there and they'd have captured the audience. The orchestra played the opening notes and the two of them launched their song and their careers.

During the interval, which arrived on a wave of massive applause, it was apparent that our two budding artistes were a smash, collectively and separately. I could feel my managerial whiskers quivering and I rushed backstage to see them. Honoria tried to block my way but I just skittered between her legs. Almost toppling her. Better luck next time.

I found Lepi gargling with some sort of concoction that smelled pretty strong. I hoped it wasn't alcoholic. "You guys are a smash!' I yelped. First time I ever saw him smile. These inscrutable Orientals! Probably just as well. His teeth were quite imposing.

"Are we really OK?" he asked.

"OK? Scots audiences are not noted for their enthusiasm and you two have brought the house down. From what I can see from the program, there won't be a dry eye in the place when you get finished with those love songs and traditional Scottish ballads. Who put the program together? Honoria?"

"Are you kidding?" he said. "That program is pure Belinda. She has an eye and ear for show business that is absolutely faultless. I almost choked when the heifer took all the credit in her introduction."

Bearnice emerged from the dressing room. She had changed into a Scottish blue and white costume. Probably Belinda again. She hugged me. Bear hugs can be harmful to meerkats but, hey, I didn't care. I kissed her on her cute black nose and said, "You two are a sensation! Go get 'em in the second half." I skittered back, trying once again to topple the cow *(a popular sport back in the U.S.A.)* but she had braced herself. Oh well!

As predicted, the second half was even better than the first. The two of them had warmed up to each other and the music and now had the audience eating out of their paws. I had returned to the box. Every now and again, I would see Clarence and his omnipresent cameras, stealthily moving from one vantage point to another. I turned and noticed that Frau Schuylkill was watching him very carefully. But then, the Frau watched everyone very carefully. Likewise the colonel. I suddenly realized that Condo was no longer in his seat. I looked up and saw him inconspicuously perched in the dark atop one of the light bars.

Belinda and Bearyl were completely mesmerized by the performance. Octavius seemed nervous and was fidgeting. Either that or he was at his wit's end with the formal shirt. Otto kept disappearing and reappearing. At one point I was sure he was sitting in the orchestra pit behind a bass violinist. Howard was listening intently but his eyes were on the colonel. I was positive the wolf had the particle accelerator under his arm keeping it away from the not very watchful eye of the Superintendent who was being very attentive to his beautiful companion.

With the plaintive final notes of *Bonnie Annie Laurie* echoing through the hushed auditorium, a sigh was released by the entire audience as they leapt to their feet for a standing ovation. Belinda was applauding loudly *(I swore I heard her whistle)* and standing in the front of the box, dangerously close to the railing. Thank goodness, Bearyl had a paw on her leg. Suddenly, Frau Schuylkill shouted, "Wyatt, Clarence has a gun!"

She disappeared and reappeared in a box on the other side of the hall where Clarence was aiming a weapon at Belinda. He fired and missed. Wyatt didn't. The particle accelerator converted Clarence's gun and a good part of his paw back to their atomic elements. As soon as he had fired, the colonel zapped over to help the Frau. Otto joined them. All three of them wrestled Clarence to the floor and he shouted, "Mother, help!!!"

Bearbi, who was watching this while leaning precariously over the edge of her own box, started to scramble for the exit but several of her veils caught on a decorative gargoyle under the rail and she toppled over backwards. She fell screaming, over the side to the floor of the center aisle of the stalls, just missing several members of the standing audience. She bounced off the top of a seat with a cracking sound and hit the floor. She was face up, dazed or unconscious. Condo flew down from his perch and using his wings as shrouds, kept the crowd from her as the police made their way down the aisle.

We abandoned our boxes and raced below. I looked on stage at the two performers. Simultaneously overjoyed and horrified, they stood fastened in place under the spotlights. A night to remember but not the way we had planned. The police were emptying the auditorium with efficiency and dispatch. Superintendent Wardlaw was lying next to Bearbi when Octavius, Belinda and I arrived. "She's still breathing," he said.

Her eyes fluttered open and she murmured, "Clarence, my son, is he alright?"

The policeman said, "He's wounded but alive."

Belinda spoke, "Bearbi? What? Why?"

"Oh, Belinda, isn't it just too delicious? Dying on the floor of an opera house! I would have preferred the stage, of course. *(pause)* Did you know that Byron was mine before you and your show-bear glamour came along? Clarence is our offspring. Byron's and mine. At least he gave me something he never gave you. *(coughs)* You got everything and I got Clarence. He's a sweet boy – a little slow but he'll do anything for his mother."

"Including kill?" asked Octavius.

I looked at Octavius, "How did you know and why didn't you tell me?"

"I didn't know. The wolves, the condor and I agreed that this might be a great opportunity for someone to eliminate Bel, especially if there are more oil conspirators waiting to retake the castle. We were just watching everyone. Clarence just caught the Frau's attention at the right time.

Dame Bearbara drifted off for a few moments. The police doctor was on his way as was an ambulance. She opened her eyes again and said, "Well, at least I'll get some satisfaction before I die, watching the reaction on your movie star face. The whole time you were married, I kept coming back to Byron. I came by boat and used that wretched cargo lift to get up to his rooms. You never knew but then you weren't home that much. I pleaded with him to divorce you and accept the two of us as his rightful heirs. He laughed at me and gave me a deed to the castle as a consolation prize. It was only good after both he and you were dead."

She had another fit of coughing and moaning. The doctor had arrived but the Superintendent held him back for a moment. She kept her eyes closed but continued to speak. "So I killed Byron – that is, Clarence and I. We set off the avalanche. Clarence is good with explosives as you found out on the road into Unst."

The Superintendent said loudly, "Dame Da Savile-Row, I must warn you that anything you say is being recorded by one of my officers and can be used against you in a court of law."

She laughed, "Are you going to prosecute a corpse? Shut up, Inspector or whatever you are. Clarence and I planned it all out. First, we had to get rid of that so-called family of yours, Belinda. We wanted the place to ourselves with no strings attached. We thought we'd get things started by killing Alistair, the lecherous creep, and scaring them off with mysterious nonsense about the lift doors and corpses that said "Boo!" (She laughed and choked with pain) Little did we know what "the family" was really up to. We should have just let them self-destruct. Then Hamish very politely told me that he had seen us dragging Alistair's body off the elevator and shoving him over the side. We had caught

Alistair on his way back from an afternoon of drinking and slugged him – hard. Hamish wanted money or he would go the police. Hamish was silenced."

"We thought we could kill you off tonight in all this crowd, and blame it on some mysterious other gang members tied up in that oil rig stuff. At least that's the way we were going to report it in the press. Those damn animals from America screwed that up well and truly. Anyway, be gentle with Clarence. He's not a bad boy."

"Oh Bearbi," said Belinda. "If you had told me, we could have worked something out, at least before you killed Byron. My husband seems to have been quite a swine. By the way, he gave those deeds out to every female he ever had an affair with. I've been presented with four so far. They're all invalid fakes."

The doctor was examining Bearbi during the latter part of her confession. He looked up and said, "Well, we'll have to move her to hospital. Stand back, please. I want to inject her with a strong sedative."

Bel said, "Doctor, is that necessary? Can't you let her die here in peace?"

"Die? She'll nae die. Least not from this. Plenty of broken bones and bruises but this sow has a lot of life left in her."

Bearbi opened her eyes briefly before losing consciousness. "Oh shit," she murmured.

Epilogue

Now, you've probably noticed a trend
Since these pages are nearing their end.
You're assuming it's true
That this story is through.
I'm afraid you're mistaken, my friend!

After a much dampened but still festive celebration for the new vocal sensations, we left the next morning on our return trip to Bearmoral. What an evening! The media couldn't make up their minds what to put on the front page. It took us a couple of days to decompress back at the castle.

The contractors had already started to arrive. With the departure *(hasty but complete)* of the "family," Belinda speeded up the timetable to turn the castle back into the resort the first Bearon had in mind. ***Polar Paradise*** would become the playground destination of choice for the northern ursine and other chill-seeking population. Chita, leveraging her partner position, insisted on installing several spas and saunas. That sounded good to me, too. The carousel was taken down from the parapet and was being assembled near the beach. The Bearoness had been quite adamant about it being fully restored. The castle's theatre was being taken out of mothballs and the pool was being refurbished to do double duty as a show venue. Some of the electric signage was salvaged and new electric and electronic glitz went on order. Much of the Scots décor was being preserved but updated with a "now" look. The moat was being totally cleaned out, refilled with circulating water, and the local seals and otters were hired to perform in it several times a day *(weather permitting.)* In fact, the new resort boded well for the economy and more jobs throughout the Shetlands.

Plans were apaw for year-round entertainment, including, of course, the Aquabears with Otto and Marlin, Otto by himself, Marlin by himself, Bearnice and Lepi and a visiting troupe of the Edinbeargh Opera *(sans Madame Honoria Heifer).* Bearyl was making plans for a theatre troupe. Chita offered to organize a rock group from her London contacts. *(The Spotted Band II? Starring Guess Who! Careful of the cops, Chita!)* She also agreed to set up a publicity and advertising campaign in the Da Savile Row publications. My talent agency work was flourishing, and I had to be careful I didn't rock the boat with

Octavius. Truth be told, while I enjoy show biz, my heart is still among the ne'er-do-wells. From time to time, I wondered if Imperius Drake was really dead.

We are also developing an annex of the Lion and Unicorn pub inside the castle. The idea is not just to sell drinks to the guests. We want to promote the real thing down in Unst village. Statues and pictures of the two worthy hosts, flags, drums, copies of the opening issue of Purr and the matching issue of Sow will be on display. And there will be mead, mead and more mead. *(Octavius' contribution.)* The pub's sweet little Dandie Dinmont barmaid had been promoted to manager of the castle's "lounge" and she was busy barking orders at everyone in sight. A tour jitney would run guests back and forth to the original watering spot *(a thrill ride in itself.)* Of course, the two proprietors were a major tourist attraction in their own right, complete with crowns and battles.

Doctor Vark would be coming to the castle on the next Belinda-Octavius shuttle to begin setting up the Highlands Genetics Lab based in part on a sanitized version of Imperius Drake's research. Hopefully, by that time, Otto will have received a clean bill of health while still retaining his amazing powers for use onstage. *(Once a theatrical agent, always a theatrical agent.)*

Chita had left for London, where she anticipated a few interesting rounds with the magazine staffs before they settled down to the idea of a feline publisher. It would take a while for the da Savile Row legacy to fade out. The odds on Bearbi or Clarence ever making a reappearance were small indeed. Hoo boy! She is one nasty and deceptive ursine. As for the petropol perps, it would be some time before all the charges, extraditions from the Bearents Sea and court trials could be worked out but there were plenty of criminals to go around.

The wildcat oil rigs were slowly getting back on stream and Fergus and the "lads' were back at it again. The phony environmental boat that had lain hidden inside the cavern was taken out, claimed by the UK North Sea Oil Commission as captured salvage, repainted and pressed into duty to replace one of the two boats that had been sunk by the raiders.

The "authorities" had come and dismantled the communications room including the GPS jamming system. That one was classified as a weapon and taken for comprehensive government testing and isolation. I wonder what they would have done if they had known about our particle accelerator or aircraft stealth system.

Marlin had arrived at Unst with his baggage and some inconclusive preliminary reports from the Court of the Prince of Whales. They detected some unusual oceanic shifts but nothing seemed to be amiss with the oil rigs they had examined. More to come! His travel tank was being built and installed in the C-5A down in Abeardeen. He decided to swim down there to join Frau Schuylkill, the Colonel, Howard, Otto and L. Condor on their return trip to Cincinnati with the ray gun and a lot of other gear. It will be interesting to see him in action at the mansion and UUI. A magician, wizard, scientist, jester and swimming phenomenon! Oh yeah, Marlin will fit right in.

Octavius, who seemed even more moody than usual, had wanted to hold off leaving for a few more days but a major flap at UUI made him decide to leave today. Bearyl and Bearnice are taking the two of us back in the Flying Aquabear after a helicopter run to Abeardeen Airport *(which was no longer bothered by electronic gremlins.)* After he undergoes more tests with the geneticists at UUI, Otto will return with them on the SST to Bearmoral, oops, Polar Paradise and pick up on his show biz career.

"Any idea where Octavius is?" I asked Bearyl.

"He's on his way down. Dougal and Harold are helping him with his bags."

"I said goodbye to Lepi. Of course, I'll be in pretty close contact with my three *(four? five?)* terrific clients. Where is the Bearoness? I can't leave without bidding her farewell."

"I'm afraid she's not available.'"

"Why not?"

"She's gone into hibernation," Bearyl said.

"Who are you kidding? Polar bears don't hibernate."

"Females do when they're expecting," she said, smiling.

"Expecting what??"

"Oh, Maury, you twit!!"

*****

Out on the North Sea, a heavy duty helicopter transferring a replacement crew of wildcats to Chita's oil rig, *The Hot Spot*, maneuvered into a direct vector for the platform's helipad. On the platform, the incoming flight went unnoticed except by the operations manager and the two cats charged with guiding and tying down the chopper after it landed. Suddenly, the aircraft literally disappeared into thin air.

On board the chopper, the pilot and co-pilot were amazed as the rig winked out in a "now-you-see-it-now-you-don't" exercise, leaving a tranquil stretch of sea where a million tons of concrete, steel and oil stood a moment ago.

"What's going on?" This simultaneously from the chopper crew and the wildcats on the platform's helipad. "It just disappeared."

Alarms went off aboard the rig as they dispatched a search team to look for the helicopter. But where to look? No one saw it crash. It just vanished. No radio contact. No radar blip. No wreckage floating on the water. No survivors bobbing in the waves. Nada!

In the cockpit of the chopper, similar consternation. Open sea where a 300 foot structure loomed a moment ago and nothing showing on any of the avionics. The pilot pulled away from his touchdown approach, moved out and hovered while executing a 360 degree pivot, surveying the seascape. Empty!

"Let's go back in for a closer look," he said. The shocked co-pilot simply shook his head and then continued to rub his eyes, check his instruments and call on the radio. Nothing on the scopes. Static on the air. They banked back toward the position where they had last seen the rig. Just as they approached the presumed location of the missing helipad, the platform reappeared only feet away from the whirling rotors. Executing a sharp fall away turn, the pilot averted by seconds, a catastrophic collision with a gantry.

Down on the deck, a crew of terrified wildcats watched as the chopper appeared, restabilized itself and then cautiously approached the pad. Over the radios, two semi-panicked voices, pilot and rig manager, now back in communication, shouted simultaneously, "You idiots!!! Where the hell did you go?"

End of The Case of Scotch
Volume Three of
The Case Books of Octavius Bear

Also from MX Publishing

MX Publishing is the world's largest specialist Sherlock Holmes publisher, with over a hundred titles and fifty authors creating the latest in Sherlock Holmes fiction and non-fiction.

From traditional short stories and novels to travel guides and quiz books, MX Publishing cater for all Holmes fans.

The collection includes leading titles such as *Benedict Cumberbatch In Transition* and *The Norwood Author* which won the 2011 Howlett Award (Sherlock Holmes Book of the Year).

MX Publishing also has one of the largest communities of Holmes fans on Facebook with regular contributions from dozens of authors.

www.mxpublishing.com

Lightning Source UK Ltd.
Milton Keynes UK
UKOW07f0404151115

262723UK00001B/4/P

9 781780 928388